Fire Horses

Mark Liam Piggott

Legend Press

Independent Book Publisher

Legend Press Ltd
13a Northwold Road, London, N16 7HL
info@legendpress.co.uk
www.legendpress.co.uk

British Library Cataloguing in Publication Data available.

ISBN 978-1-9065580-1-7

Set in Times
Printed by J. H. Haynes and Co. Ltd., Sparkford.

Cover designed by Gudrun Jobst
www.yellowoftheegg.co.uk

Legend Press
Independent Book Publisher

Many thanks to my wife and children, for their patience; to my extended family (especially nan and granddad) for their love; to my friends, for their belief; to Tom and Emma at Legend, for their courage; and last but not least, to John Russell and Linda Milnes, for everything.

'The past is a great darkness, and filled with echoes.'
Margaret Atwood, *The Handmaid's Tale*

*'Your heart beats you
Late at night'*
New Order, *Procession*

Procession
Words & Music by Stephen Paul David Morris, Peter Hook,
Bernard Sumner & Gillian Lesley Gilbert

2007

Does this twelfth Spanish bell toll for me?

As I crush a final grape under my tongue, the catholic chimes end their metronomic march and segue into freeform; firecrackers zip and dart between the feet of dancing celebrants like electric snakes. The ancient walls surrounding the village square absorb the cheers of gaudy revellers like bread dipped in wine, centuries of raucous gaiety soaked into stone.

Cool salt air from the Med throws clouds of fiery sparks like starlight condensed over the bubbling mass below me. Galaxies, compacted into one glorious instant, blistering out backwards to ashes, blackness, the promise of regeneration.

Dense thuds hammer my diaphragm and as my wife takes my hand to lead me down the steps I remember other celebrations in other, colder, distant places. My watch says it's a minute after twelve and I feel like I'm surfing on the crest of time. I made it.

As I chew on the empty grape sac a young woman appears through the jostling, jabbering crowd: late-teens, North European, wearing a mustard safari suit. For some reason this excites me, energizes my imagination. This stranger from Northern climes latches onto my mulberry eyes as though she can smell something in me that I'm trying to suppress: *fee-fi-fo-fum*. Shoving past Alona as if she doesn't exist, she pushes a flyer at me. One of my hands holds Alona's sweaty palm, the other the bottle. Releasing Alona I frown at the stranger, only half-seeing her face, illuminated by explosions and youth. I address her in English.

"What's this?"

But the crowd has already swallowed her whole, so looking for clues I glance down at the garishly-coloured piece of paper. It's illustrated by a rudimentary cartoon depicting a scowling John-bulldog licking something astringent from a leaf, a dock leaf, or maybe a nettle:

> Bulldog Billys English beer
> English food Spanish weather!!

Now I recognise the address, one of the alleyways connecting the square and the harbour, next to that Andalucian deli that sells port and spiced *chorizo*. Wiping sweat from my skinbare scalp I mentally vow that I'll never visit Billy Bulldog. I don't need to be near strangers like me, like the person I used to be.

People embrace like old foes. Alona laughs up into my face, teeth white. I lower my head and she shouts in my ear, warm breath and *Cava*-spittle, "You look so serious... are you happy?"

"Only when you touch me," I scream at her in Spanish. Screwing up the flyer I drop it into the sparky gutter and reach for her hand again, wet with cider, cold with love. Her eye-light is miraculous, skin effulgent. Above her orange hair *ano nuevo* fireworks spark and glow, their embers falling in the square and onto the dark water beyond the new houses where my boat rises and falls with the tide. The shallow breathing of the dying Med.

There are cracks in the night's shell and through the cracks someone is detonating mini-explosions. I wonder if the shapes of the stars are crawling across my face like luminous spiders, exploding and cascading in my watery eyes.

Fireworks expose the Spain of my lazier dreams – bulls' eyes flash red, bullet holes from antediluvian disputes thrown against the walls like ink spots. The empty nests of storks flare out from the tall steeples like shards, and all the people seem momentarily to shine: faces look up, awestruck, expressions frozen like dull-coloured masks or plasticine figurines.

Brassy Latin songs crank from loudspeakers and drown out the explosions, which also light up billboards advertising mobiles, cigarettes and gleaming motors. For a moment I'm fenced, surrounded by a cordon of enormous bared teeth.

Unwillingly, automatically, I frame pictures, landscapes; over by the internet café a black horse escaped from a bank advert whinnies and rears in fright, golden light shining off its back so that it seems to burn a space through the fabric of night. The little peasant or IT consultant holding it on a rope laughs drunkenly at the fact it could carry him away in its equine frenzy.

I shiver. The safari-suited woman reminds me of someone I'm trying to forget. Spitting sour grape skin into the gutter I watch it vanish beneath dancing feet. The finale booms lower and closer, and I have a sudden vision: that the fireworks are endowed with a high tonnage of explosive, raining devastation and transforming all these happy families into a bloody mess of hell and brimstone.

Strange how I shiver. There's an unseasonable warmth on the new January air, and I try to remember how England felt at midnight in a short-sleeved shirt, try to recall the smells of London and hold them up against these smells of seafish and scales skimmed from bone, tastes of wine and lemon, this romantic sense of unity and belonging that for all I know no-one else can feel.

As I suck harsh port from the gravel bottle and hold Alona

close, I resolve never to return to England; I don't need its complexities, its repressive natures and self-obsessions. Nor does it apparently need me. It has enough troubles, and at least from here I can't add to them.

Alona at my side, I shake hands and swap ravishing kisses with neighbours we have never met. My alien tongue swaps pleasantries; I've made it a point to learn as little of the lingo as is practical, but somehow it keeps seeping into my vocabulary, like the sly nudge of absinthe.

All the happy families, the old and the young. This is why I rarely venture out after midnight in Spain: children. I don't allow myself to get too close. Six-year-olds order drinks in bars and wear adult clothes; they don't fight or get drunk but otherwise they're like stately midgets prancing on the *paseo*... maybe I should get out more. Or maybe not.

Alona knows my discomfort; she finally succumbs and we're just leaving the diluting bustle when a feeling of dread forces me to turn and glimpse a shadow of the past, trapped at the corner of my eye; some dark ghost, some spectral vision cooked up by a guilty consciousness and booze.

Nada.

In the six years I've been living in Spain, I've discovered three ways from the town to the cave: the long, winding drive that coils round the hill in gentle hoops; a tortuous climb up carved steps between monumental rocks; and the shore path, which passes beneath the overhanging cliffs and up by the cut. Too kaylied to drive, too tired to climb, I lead asthmatic, wheezy Alona along the winding path. She wobbles in her heels and clasps her handbag to her like a fresh heart. I still hold the bottle.

The lights end with the *paseo*, and after that you need a torch or memory. Where the path turns up inside the mountain I look back. From here infantilised rockets are lost against the dark mass of the hulking mountains like moths attacking battleships.

"I thought, for your birthday, we could do something different," pants Alona as she climbs behind. Alona: Spanish for *light*. I'm walking and drinking and don't feel compelled to answer. "There's a new bar near the water," persists Alona. "It opens *manana*. No – today, later. There is a big party there Saturday, I know. Let's do something different for once."

I swallow port; way beneath us the Med sizzles softly, foiled.

"Let's not."

"It would be good," replies Alona, patient as gods, ignoring my stubbornness. "You might make some contacts."

"*Why* might I?"

"English. Money. They have all the money now."

A bulldog. A nettle. I stop. Alona shoves past me. Hates coming second.

"Alona, this wouldn't be 'Bulldog Billys' by any chance?"

"You know it?"

"Oh, yes."

"Then you'll go?"

"No." I smile, surprised she should ask. I don't need contacts now. Midnight has come and gone without a final appeal. The money's mine. To celebrate this and to see out the season I've made my own plans: a night at the *Laguna* watching Saggy Maggie and her disappearing Christmas tree.

Alona tuts and stutters ahead up the rough track, muttering breathless curses in Catalan. Dawdling, I watch her disappear. After a few minutes a rectangular hole opens up in the fabric of the mountain; light pours out as if from some orderly volcano, then a plug falls across the entrance as she closes the door. By the time I get home she'll have gone pointedly to bed and I'll make sure the chickens are fed, the house secure against intruders. But there's no hurry now, no love to catch up on, so at the top of the steps I sit on a flat rock and listen to the ocean as I drain the remainder of the bottle of port.

Maybe it's time to tell her about the money winging its way from London, our changing fortunes. But maybe I want to surprise her, or maybe I feel insecure, or maybe I just don't want to give her any; does she need it?

What really hurts is her latest complaint, implied in her mention of contacts, that we have nothing, instead of this home in the hills, two cars and a boat. What else does she need? When we met she told me she hated money, that her family skinned the rich. I grow my own vegetables and catch my own fish, but now she wants more? When was *that* contract rewritten, or did I miss a clause?

Still the placid air feels warm, the spare countryside brittle and dry. No rain for weeks; cloudless skies punctured by ancient lights from beyond history, sparks of extinction. I read somewhere that the universe is expanding unsustainably, all the empty galaxies rushing away from each other at vastly accelerating rates, so that in ten billion years' time when all the suns have died all that remains there will be an endless waste of cold, blank nothingness. I find this information disappointing.

Almost as disappointing as Billys Bar, its apostrophe left behind with the old certainties at Gatwick or Prestwick. I find myself cursing my home nation, but you don't reach 39 without spotting some patterns. It's the same trap as always: this need, this requirement, to be outside, *beyond*. That way you can't take the blame, assume guilt by association. Why shouldn't I drink in a bar for expats? What am I then, some banished conquistador?

Hardly. If you were flying overhead, an omniscient eagle with X-ray eyes, what would you see perched upon this harsh precipice? A tall, lank man approaching middle age, dressed casually and with a stance that's anything but.

My bony, puzzled, clean-shaven face too-easily adopts a scornful, aloof expression; a minor scar lifts the left of my mouth slightly, adding to this apparent air of believed superiority. But I've always been shy in company, allergic to crowds – self-contained, solid within myself.

Though of course, being an eagle, the thing you would notice is my bald head: tanned, smooth, no telltale speckles, another tiny scar above the place where my fringe used to be. It's rare that I remember what others notice right away, though sometimes I curse the way sweat gets into my eyes.

Noises behind me on the path. I shiver in my thin shirt, conjuring *Baba-Yaga*. Finishing the bottle I stand, resolving to go to the bar the next morning. Not because the Northern girl reminds me of the one that I lost, but... just because. Alona doesn't need to know. She knows too much already; about life and its calamities, its surging undercurrents and mega-tsunamis, if not about mine.

As I approach the gate, subdued, subsumed by artifices, something echoes out of the frozen past and hits me on the back of the head. I wince and stagger, certain for a moment (and unsurprised) that I've been shot. But when I carefully place the bottle on the gatepost and hold a hand to my bare skull, it feels cold, not with blood but with frozen water. Looking down I see the inexplicable evidence glowing on the path – I've been hit by a snowball.

Disbelieving, I kneel and pinch cold ice between shaking fingers. Then I squint round at the empty hillside. Even *Baba-Yaga* doesn't throw snowballs, and I doubt the locals have the technique acquired in Northern climes. So either Tony's dead, and Hell's icebox needs chiselling, or he's alive and in Spain. Either way, everything has changed. Maybe that's a good thing. I've been coasting on the coast for too long, resting on hardy laurels. I clear my throat and yell.

"Is that you? Tony?"

Tawny, like an owl, that's how it comes out; my accent flies home to roost. Some bird flutters but there's no answer, not even an echo, and I feel solitary embarrassment, a touch of fear. Certain that Tony's watching I close the gate and walk through the dusty yard.

The door to the mouth of the cave has been petulantly locked; maybe I should have gone for the boulder after all, but some miracles are beyond even me.

Sighing irritably, I turn to look at the first light of dawn seeping in over the water. It would be good to sit drinking 2007 *Cava* and watch the new sun light up the mountains, but Alona is waiting to make up. I bang on the door with my elbow and after a respectable interval Alona's heels approach. It opens on her arrogant, proud face. I follow her arse indoors, the melting snowball still in my hand.

Tony can wait outside. With all the other ghosts.

PART I: FROM ANARCHY TO ECSTACY

1982

The moment I threw the snowball I knew I'd made a terrible mistake but it had left my hand by then, and no rewind or pause would ever be possible. In the fraction of time before impact, Tony, my implacable foe, was standing with his mates in the dirty evening snow. The glint from his glasses and that ridiculous moustache made him look older and more solid than those other flickering ghostly faces. He was laughing, part of the gang, whereas I was the outsider, up on the buttress, watching the cluster of punks, like a company of bedraggled parrots, waiting for their bus back to town. All except Tony, in his shiny new leather jacket and immaculately lined-up studs, band names stencilled with surgeons' precision and an *Exploited* t-shirt ironed by his mum.

Despite my schoolboy error I wished I'd remembered the new camera to capture Tony, laughing, the mucky snowball hovering above, describing a perfect arc; to freeze that frozen moment and all that had come before it, the hurts, the sleights, Tony and Julie laughing as they read a book about a bird, my father's proud expression as he handed me the parcel, everything motionless in this, the coldest moment in the coldest night in history, still illuminated in my brain 25 years later like an image exposed by lightning.

From this great distance I sometimes fancy that as that ball of ice hung there over Millmoor, I also glimpsed lightning flashes of the future: of Becky's tears and Sarah's giggles, the moons of Australia and the smells of India; and perhaps the magic snowball even covered the sun's eyes as Hermione kissed me on a Cornish beach. Other flashes too, other glimpses, which I will perhaps only fully decipher when my life follows the snowball's trajectory and becomes a cold white point.

According to Zeno of Elea, the snowball could never reach its target because it needed to halve the distance from me to Tony and then halve it again, *ad infinitum*. But, not understanding physics, the snowball began its descent, my camera-less hands already in pockets, teeth chattering, the night black and white, the street lights orange. Tony was still laughing, pretending to shove another plastic punk beneath the wheels of an old green bus that sprayed the queue, making them spin and turn their backs. All except Tony, whose reactions were slow and who took the full force of the gravity-snared snowball right in the mush.

Tony dropped to his knees, face in hands, and his little gang of townies spread out like cowboys under attack as they looked in every direction but up. I stared down, swallowing unease, unable to see Julie anywhere in this tragic tableaux I had painted. I then ducked back out of sight and ran.

That morning I had finally accepted Mum's card wasn't coming. I couldn't blame the postman, whose delays had made my present a week late; nor could I blame the weather, the fierce ice-storm from Siberia, causing birds to freeze mid-flight and icicles so thick in tunnels that the trains to places where weather doesn't kill were stopped.

There had been no school since New Year; the boilers and caretaker had broken down, perhaps forever. Usually I spent days like these on the rampage, setting traps and catching out the unwary, the ungripped, the uninsulated, but Dad's giro still hadn't arrived and he'd gone to find it. He looked forward to giro day like dogs look forward to walkies.

Terrified the governmental cheque might arrive in his absence to find nobody home he'd instructed me to kick my heels and wait. So I'd spent the day looking through the dirty ice window, watching evil mists conceal faraway fields where horses stood rooted to the spot like cardboard cut-outs, the drift of pylons linking arms, electricity between them. I dreamed once that they'd dammed the valley, and as I skated across the thin ice to the hillside opposite, where Julie waited, I looked down through the ice and townfolk tapped urgently on the glass.

The hill rose sharply behind Stone Nest's two tower blocks, Hughes Court and Plath Court, circling each other warily. Even from the 20th floor, rockface loomed above you. The other houses clustered around like disciples with their tin roofs and cement walls, in lines of four with their tiny gardens, the alley in the middle so you could still reach the outhouse.

Before they gave us toilets you would sit there at night and listen to strange rustlings, feel spiders crawl beneath your arse, as you sat helplessly with your trousers round your ankles and goosebumps drifting and stretching across your skin like the sleepy drift of clouds.

In the bathroom mirror I pushed my floppy green fringe up to inspect Stig's tattoo. I'd asked him to write 'NO FUTURE' but unable to spell either word he'd settled for initials. I had a feeling this might cause problems at some point. Thank God for hair. At fifteen I had a bony, sharp face, glaring eyes and skin as white as a goth. My punky mop gave me colour, character, and cover.

There was a tender knock on the door so I let the fringe fall, bounced down the stairs and flung it open on a vision of loveliness in a bright pink anorak; tall, gangly, huge bush of ginger, top teeth protruding, cheeks already pinking: Julie Coxon.

Though I'd known Julie since playschool, it was only when we'd discovered new feelings about ourselves rather than each other that we'd been out a couple of times. There were the usual adolescent fumblings: bus shelters and chips, fingers in dark places. The night of my birthday we'd been to see *Chariots of Fire*. When we left the cinema the whole town was buried white, and we had chased each other through the empty streets and tumbled in the snow.

I believed that I loved Julie and she had seemed keen on me, but after the pictures she didn't ring. I blamed Colin Welland more than the fact we didn't have a phone. Having assumed our brief affair was at an end, on opening the door I was surprised. Thinking back now, so was Julie. Her purple lips actually fell open; her Caspian green eyes searched the empty hall.

"Hi Joe, er – is your Dad in?"

"No!" I cried happily, "come in!"

Grabbing her by the arm, I pulled her inside like a trapdoor spider. Julie seemed a little confused; maybe *she* wasn't sure why she was there, either. I led her into the front room and she dropped her school bag with its equine *leitmotif*, and unzipped her coat. The world went very quiet as I watched her reveal her layers to the hiss of the gas.

First, her shoes, black and buckled. Dirty white socks over leopard-skin legwarmers. The crumpled grey pleats of her skirt. Her blouse had outgrown her navy jumper, and her collars stuck up like a pterodactyl's wings. Her school tie was loose at her throat, then dangled over the shelf of her already tremendous breasts. A deep-ginger Hair-Bear frizz almost covered her puffy red/green eyes – her goth mascara and sulking cheeks. Something wasn't quite right; it then struck me.

"What you doing in your uniform? Didn't you know school's still cancelled?"

"Yes, I – Mum would've killed me, you know what she's like – so I just pretend to go to school, keeps her happy… so, where's your Dad?"

"He had to go and find his giro. How did you know I was home alone?"

Julie shrugged; looking back, I think I can safely insert the word 'miserably'.

"Oh, just a feeling…"

Swiping a lemonade bottle of Dad's yellow homebrew from the fridge, I led Julie upstairs to my room, my forehead smarting from the tattoo. She sat on the bed looking nervous. I found a tape: the soothing melodies of GBH, Abrasive Wheels and Discharge. We swigged yeasty beer then Julie burped and looked at me.

"Have you got anything?"

I hadn't. The assistant in the chemist was female and I hadn't yet found the courage to go in, but Julie seemed in a hurry to lead me from the land of virgin snow to a warm new continent. A brainwave washed me back down to the kitchen where I found a pack of Monster Munch left over from Christmas. Wolfing munchies as I went up the stairs I waved the empty packet at Julie, who pulled off her tights and lay down.

That was my first time; my major memories are the hardcore soundtrack, and Julie tasting of yeast, and the fact the packet stung a tad. But she was wet and warm and it seemed an interesting place to be. Julie squeaked, the packet crinkled and I winced.

We arranged that I would pick her up that night and take her to the gig, and then Julie left, quiet, subdued, sliding down the hill on underheeled shoes. From the front porch I quarried my nose and watched her, still mystified, but less so than before.

Dusk clamped down around three; short days in those Yorkshire winters. The window was a black patch framed by unlucky decorations, but if you looked closely you could see that orange lights and stars made vortexes of shapes spiralling in the ether. An Ozzy Osborne poster looked down from over the mantelpiece. Dad worshipped Ozzy and over the festive period had bet a rash tenner on his untimely demise so we could mourn him in style.

A bike unrevved, a Yale scratched and the front door opened on my prodigious father, full of Landlords' Bitter, a grit-toothed smile from within his vast beard – a NUPE pirate. From his tatty leathers Dad pulled a hard parcel wrapped in *The Sun*. A page 3 girl wrapped around my present, nipples at right-angles to one another like a pixelated Picasso.

"Happy birthday lad. Sorry it's a bit late – had to get me giro over the counter in town. Anyway, hope you like it."

Smiling doubtfully I looked at the parcel, adorned with Dad's neat handwriting. Pulling inky breasts apart I looked down at a Polaroid camera still in its box. I swallowed, disbelieving, and looked at my father with embarrassment. He shrugged.

"I knew you always liked pictures. Who's that bloke in the *Mirror*?"

"Murdo McLeod. Thanks, Dad. Can I take one of you?"

He shrugged again. As I hid behind the lens (feeling safe, in charge, invisible) his frost-and-beer-flecked beard flushed pink. The glossy film rolled out and we waited. I half-hoped Dad would offer to take one of me but instead he pulled off his leathers and sat by the gas fire with his rolling board, the scarred album cover of some Seventies' concept band that still pops into my head when I smoke dope. I've never smoked much.

As a belated birthday tea, Dad stuck a candle in a Fray Bentos and we watched the news. An aeroplane had smashed into a bridge in Washington; foul play was suspected, which seemed implausible. The weather was to get even colder and Mark Thatcher was lost in the desert. I was jealous – I'd never been on holiday, never been on a plane and the warmest place I'd ever been before Julie was Skeggy. I looked up at the mantelpiece: one card. Wise Dad with his beard read my mind.

"I was reading about this experiment in a magazine the other day," he said, through the clouds of his creation. Dad subscribed to Yank mags as well as wank mags, yet knew little about physics or biology.

"They got these chimpanzee mums and their babies and put them in a metal oven, then turned up the heat. As it got hotter the mother tried to protect her baby, holding it away from the floor. But the temperature kept on rising, scorching her feet. In the end, do you know what she did? She put the baby on the glowing metal plate and stood on it. Every time they did this experiment, the same result. That's what happens, Joe. You think they're always going to be around, but it's all just circumstances. Once things get a bit too hot, or something better flashes its feathers, they're off. She's probably at Greenham Common with all them dykes and lesbos. So there you are, son – it's just you and me now. Smoke?"

To compensate for Mum's mysterious absence, Dad considered it his duty to let me down lightly, to ensure none of life's little surprises came as such, that my hopes would never aim too high and my dreams remained realistic. Maybe that's why I was so surprised then when he gave me some money that night to go to the gig. I was glad to go, despite the cold: Julie waited. As he pressed the fiver into my palm, he looked at me meaningfully.

"Don't come home before eleven."

"Thanks Dad!"

Grabbing my coat I ran to the door, already braced for its opening.

"And son, a word of advice." I looked back expectantly. "Never eat yellow snow."

It was the only advice he ever gave me. Even with two jumpers and my Dad's leathers, the wiry wind sanded my cheeks. There was a working phone booth at the corner where the road turned down into town, so I went in and dialled Julie's number and listened for the pips.

"Hello?" Her mother's gruff voice responded; I pushed the five into the slot.

"Hello Mrs Coxon, is your Julie in?"

"Out."

"Oh. Right. Any idea where?"

"Some prat from her school, she says."

My blood, already cold, started to ice.

"Tony Clegg?"

"That's him. Now fuck off – I'm watching *Bergerac*."

The phone went dead. Mad as a box of frogs. But even so, there was little doubt that Julie was out with the new boy – after all I had seen them together, reading that book. Why else would she be out in this weather? All I had to do now was work out what to do about it.

Skidding down the one-in-three road to town, I contemplated revenge in all its forms and shades: hot, cold, sweet, mean, funny and fatal. One of Tony's strong points was cross-country running, in which we ran through subzero sludge while the teachers drank vodka-laced soup. The route traversed farmyards, where we hurdled over rabid sheep, apoplectic farmers waving sawn-offs. Was there some way I could sabotage a stile so when Clegg hurdled it the stile collapsed, and he fell in the slurry, some of it even getting it in his mouth?

Impractical: the slurry had frozen and I didn't have a saw.

If I waited till spring there was Sports Day. Clegg was pretty handy at the 100 metres, too. Perhaps there was some way in which I could sabotage his shorts so, as he ran in front of a packed school, they fell to his knees and he'd have a maggot no bird would want, no matter how it wriggled?

But what if he didn't have a maggot? The sneaky side views I'd studiously avoided in the showers suggested a rather alarming girth. Worse, he had hair, whereas I remained resolutely bald down below, despite the mop on my bonce. The girls would love him even more, and chase him *Benny Hill*-style over the horizon.

In the event I settled on something more practical, yet effective.

The cuckoo steps led between two rough walls of drystone, crisp grasses shooting from cracks, sprinkled with hard frost and new snow. Beyond the wall to my right a sheer drop to the town, terraced streets, Lowry-sketched chimneys that never bled smoke, hardware shops and desperate pubs that refused to install Space Invaders because they might frighten the dogs.

The wall to my left rose sheer, holding back the Pennines – halfway up, on a shoulder, Stone Nest. This was my moorland perch, blasted by three seasons. Spring rains scooped from the Irish Sea, carrying radioactive infections; autumn winds from Saddleworth Moor, bearing the neutrons of murdered children; and from Siberia winter blizzards, honking geese and misery. Ducking through a hole in the wall, I slipped down onto the cobbled lane that led to the canal.

It's for the benefit of our sanity that there is such a thing as selective memory; for if we remembered each divided moment our brains would boil over and our hard-drives crash. So as I skid onto the canal path, panting, cold, I don't see the well-kept lock, the pretty barges, the sheep dog's wagging tail; I have too many other worries to take in the goodness that modestly stands back from my fields of perception.

Why would a young boy notice tended gardens, civic pride? I'm angry, dislike school, cold, and feel my first budding love is under threat. I am not to know that the tears it will end in will enrich my understanding.

The path led me away from the silence and the shadows, the crystalline drips and drops, the sulphurous shadows of spirits on the glass canal. The Ripper stalked towns like these with his claw hammer, his furies busting through fog so thick you could trampoline between villages. From what I'd seen on the blue-grey flicker of the fizzing TV, the Ripper looked like everyone in town, especially the men; what if they'd got the wrong hairy-arsed nut-job?

Monsters are soon replaced; we need them so. Dad had plucked from the skip one of Mum's books about Russian myths, the most terrifying of which was *Baba-Yaga*: an ancient crone in a hut that moved on four chicken legs, screeching as she pursued her prey through the woods. If *Baba-Yaga* was crashing towards me, I'd lead where she couldn't follow.

Tentative, heart racing, I stepped from the dusted path onto ice that had clogged up the canal for weeks, cracking the pretty barges and starving the fish, making life harder for ducks and impossible for fishermen, but easy for light-stepping boys. Skating in brogues on the thin silver sliver between those satanic hills and haunted woods, those sad neglected towns linked by a road, a railway and the slash of ice chipped from its heart, as if the earth's core had frozen under and glaciers seeped through like arctic lava.

In the distance I heard a dog's muffled bark; snowflakes wrapped around branches, thick as potato skins, filling the earth with silence. The valley projected an air of tranquillity, of smugness, but this appearance was false. Beneath covered roofs lay blanketed feeling, emotions smouldered as red as dwindling embers.

The houses were built for it; at least the town houses were, the terraces, their slight-angled roofs retaining insulation. The new houses up top were different, tin roofs at steep angles so snow slipped off when weighty, that familiar thump as it crumped in the garden, making creatures of strange shapes that blocked the view south.

As I stooped to gather snow from a frozen wave, the only sound was the rub of my hood on my ears. My inner core felt colder than the snow I gathered in numbing fingers; my heart felt encased in a glove of ice. Gloves served no purpose, I had long since learned – when making snowballs they became wet, burning separated fingers. Digits need each other's warmth inside coat pockets.

My aching fingers moulded the snow, exerting pressure until it became quite round. If you kept on rolling, and the snow drained all your body warmth, would it become a perfect crystal ball? Perhaps I could see my future. I held it up to the orange streetlight, but could see nothing, so I kept on rolling until I held a smooth, transparent diamond.

Perhaps people are made this way too. Maybe constant cajoling pressures from unwanted fingers can turn even a child, soft and warm and pure, into something hard and cold; so hard it hurts.

Furious, impotent, unable to express, I threw the snowball and watched it explode into a tree like a falling star. Then I stepped from the ice, thinking about monsters that lurked beneath Europa's sixty-mile oceans, half-hoping the ice would break and I would be submerged, a tragic teen sealed in amber. But it didn't happen, so I climbed the buttress, the resurrected snowball hurting my fingers like a hot comet, and waited.

1983

Millmoor's streets were stacked in steps so they towered like tenements rushing to escape the valley. Some of the houses were built into the rock like Spanish gypsy dwellings, their back walls carving into cold earth, windows facing south. The mill cottages were being sandblasted, soot and muck removed with high-velocity hoses, but the money had dried up so half the houses were cream while the others dripped dirt.

Beyond the canal, nestled on the shoulder of the hillside opposite, lay the nest of terraces where Julie had once lived, sunken and shrivelled beneath an enormity of rock. Those streets never felt sunlight, not directly, she had told me; they retained the cold, drew it in upon itself, layer-upon-layer, cumulative ice. Grasses in the pavements withered and died, flowers forgot to bloom, cats slunk away to warmer climes.

Sometimes when I'd gone home she told me she'd watch enviously from her tiny bedroom as sunlight spread across the fields and the woods of the hills where I lived, imagining my skin warm in the sunshine.

"What are you thinking about?"

Julie's hands over my eyes, warm but hard fingers, big farmer's hands that covered mine easily, made me feel safe. Her mother had left her stepdad and taken her back to the farmhouse beyond Stone Nest where she'd lived as a girl. Each frosty morning we waited at the same battered bus stop for school; in the end, it was easier to talk than say nothing.

24

She'd never been with Tony, she explained, she just walked through the nights that last year to escape her stepdad. I forgave her. To prove it, I turned and kissed her projecting upper lip and felt her hand slide down my bare chest to my balls.

Safe. Dad working, a lock on my bedroom door, Debbie Harry watching in black PVC. I kissed Julie again, her tongue beckoning me in. Julie in her off-white bra and knickers damp with my come, shivering with a summer cold. A stone rapped the window; we both jumped.

"Shit!"

Julie's hand in my Y-fronts; cold, but worth it.

"Leave it."

"Can't. It might be Stig. He'd just break in."

Julie sighed and pushed herself away by the pelvic bone to rub in my loss.

"I don't know why you hang about with that Stig. He's a nutter."

"He's alright. Anyway – he's giving me driving lessons."

Julie ravelled up her tights; a hand floated to the surface like a netted squid.

"You wouldn't catch *me* on a motorbike with him."

"How about on the back of me?"

Julie shrugged, pink, a slight smile. It was worth it. That's what I kept telling myself as I left her there in my bed so she didn't need to go home. Worth it, to be holding onto the back of this lunatic, rocketing down through the bends of the town road and out through Millmoor like it didn't exist. Stig was shouting instructions I couldn't hear through the muffled helmet; I closed my eyes, stomach in mouth, heart bursting, sphincter fit to crush walnuts, as he joined the motorway and did wheelies in the outside lane. You could be in London in two hours, he'd told me as I mounted for the first time. My thighs held him like a prim lover; I felt naked, eviscerated, invisible.

On the way home, night circling like many crows, Stig broke another promise. There's a long tunnel under the railway/road/canal bridge, two semi-circles like sleepy eyes of brick. I sensed what he was going to do and shouted a muffled protest but to no avail; twisting on his accelerator he leaned right, shooting through the oncoming tunnel. A vortex of brickwork to all sides, sucking us further in. A lorry approaching, headlights blinding, horn blaring; it wasn't my past that flashed before my eyes, it was my future. But then Stig skidded, leaned left, the lorry became anecdotal and we were out the other side and safe.

As we skidded to a halt on the rough banking before my crescent, I leapt off and, unbuttoning my chinstrap, slapped him softly on the helmet.

"Jesus Stig! You fucking *nutter*!"

Stig removed his helmet. His green Mohican had flopped, the shaved areas slowly reforesting, and he grinned crookedly from his heavy, stupid face. His legs were scrawny like a chicken and his voice was curiously high and thin, although few people pointed this out.

Once he'd taken me fishing and caught a frog. He'd inserted a straw into its backside and blew, the frog's eyes bulging, throat quivering, until it had exploded amphibious gore all over the spring-washed rocks. Sometimes he sucked.

"Don't hit *me*, soft lad. Waste of time. Drop your kex."

"What?"

"Drop your kex. And your smalls. I need to check something."

"Stig, stop larking about."

"I'm not. Drop them."

I looked round; it was dark, kids all inside watching *Dukes of Hazzard*, mums in kitchens, dads in attics, sheds and allotments, and from behind our new front door the heavy metals: Deep Purples, Black Sabbaths, Led Zeppelins.

Shrugging, I unbuckled my belt, dropped my trousers and then, at an eyebrow-arch from Stig, my undies too. He frowned as he looked down into the warm hammock between my ankles.

"You'll pass."

I pulled my pants up, alarmed.

"What?"

"I might be off away for a couple of weeks. I need someone I can rely on. If you'd had skiddies no chance, but you're clean. I can rely on you."

Stig produced a key.

"Here's the padlock to the caravan. From tomorrow, if I go away it's your responsibility. Anything happens to it, you'll wish we'd hit that lorry."

Stig went back to court next day (something dismal involving an airgun and his ferrets), and I found myself praying for his incarceration so that Julie and I could be together somewhere warm. She wouldn't stay over when Dad was around, and we could hardly go to her house.

Like foxes at night we'd leave our respective houses while my father and her mother slept, and we'd prowl the rainy streets, smashing windows, breaking into shops, sitting beside babbling rivers where ducks slept in the tough grass, setting fire to derelict factories for the warmth and the sirens, fucking behind torn-up mills as oildrums exploded and timbers snapped.

Stig got a month for contempt and on hearing the sad news I led Julie down the track to the caravan. It had no heating and no illumination, other than stolen traffic lights, but it was secure and private, set back from a rough lane in the middle of Millmoor woods.

When I opened the door and we entered, she coughed a little at the smell and I rushed about hiding Stig's porn and makeshift weapons. But then I lay my coat on the bed and pulled out a bottle of Thunderbird and some johnnies, and I don't think any woman has ever looked at me with such love as Julie at that moment.

I wanted to volunteer to go to the chip shop but I was a little scared. So instead we held on tight, jumping when the owls called, fucking as if passion could keep out the wolves. Afterwards, shivering, night tapping the cracked windows, we whispered our lives to each other. Why we whispered I don't know; the nearest human being was miles off.

Julie found my family history hilarious – *Where was my Mum? Why was my Dad? Why was he what?* I asked her. Julie kissed my nipple, my stomach. – *Just tell me. Just tell me, ignore me and I'll do this.*

My life story was pieced together like a haphazard jigsaw designed by drunken children, which is what Mum and Dad were, really – pissed kids, not bad ones. Mother Mary arrived in London from smalltown Australia to start a revolution. As she put it, "if I'd wanted peace and quiet, I'd have stayed in Kalgoorlie with me fishing rod."

Mum was over six foot and solid of build – all that outback meat and milk. She looked like class but her father was a Ukrainian miner down Kalgoorlie way, her mother an antidepressant addict from a stiflingly genteel home who ran away with a stockman, whatever *that* was, and Mother Mary became a Communist in order to annoy her redneck neighbours – but especially her father.

A tall, broad, beautiful teenager in battered leathers, leather tassels fringing her curves, Mum took the tube from Heathrow looking for Mick Jagger. Walking through the city with her kitbag, frazzled by the size and noise of London, she saw a street sign: 'King's Road'. It wasn't until too late that Mary discovered she wasn't in Chelsea after all; the word 'Cross' had been partly concealed by a Labour Party flyer.

Mum thought she was in Mecca and went looking for trouble; she soon found it. In a squat in Camden she met Charlie, a biker from Manchester on a mission to buy cheap smack. Jet-lagged Mary formed the impression he was a rock star and Charlie didn't demur. Her motto was 'if it moves, fuck it. If you can't fuck it, eat it. And if you can't eat it, break it'. To poor innocent Charlie she'd eventually do all three. I was conceived about the time the election results came through – a famous victory for Harold Wilson and his pipe.

According to Mum, they fled North on his bike and I was born on the hard shoulder of the M1. But all this comes with a health warning, fragments of my mother's memory filtered through her addictions, my angst and Dad's general befuddlement – he'd insisted I'd been born in the toilet of some Camden underground club and we'd only gone to Yorkshire when I was five.

"That tasted nice," said Julie. I passed the last of the Thunderbird.

The last time I had seen Mum was in a leafswept Manchester park. I was twelve. We'd been to Granddads' funeral, which had put Mum and Dad in a mood for some reason. To cheer themselves up, they were fighting. They fought as they fucked: noisily, passionately and with scant regard for bystanders. When Mum drank she was the life and soul and heartbeat; when she was sober as a cunt (as she put it) – she was like a bear with Munchausen's-by-Proxy.

After the funeral they filled a hired van with Granddad's worthless tat and we were driving back out of Manchester when Dad admitted he'd voted Labour in the General Election. Mum always voted Tory to hasten in the revolution. The camel's back was broken. Mary said she needed to take a leak so we stopped at some park; she hopped out and that was that: *byee*.

"Lucky you," said Julie, meaningfully, pushing me down to the ginger frizz between her legs. I took a deep breath and waited to be trumped.

Millmoor and Brigden shared a deep valley, a spinal chord of road, railway and canal. School was situated in the no-man's land where the terrible twins collided in a tangle of semis, derelict mills, bracken-fields and scrapyards, palaces of rust. In lessons they taught you that the valley was important, that it had changed the world. Maybe it had but, apart from the new estates and the comp, the area had barely changed in a hundred years.

Only thirty-years-old and still a 'modern', the school was being carelessly dismantled; asbestos had been found behind blackboards, in janitor's cupboards and on school dinners, and the site was now a cluster of concrete boxes, yellow workmen's huts, unlit braziers. The playing field out front was half-swallowed by rubble and concrete mixers, and the science block had defied physics and disappeared.

From where we were being taught, in some quarantined annexe next to the lay-by, the main block looked set to collapse in on itself: the upper floors were missing, windows black and empty.

An empty caravan, a willing girl. Under the circumstances I considered it a criminal waste of spirit to force thirty or forty teenagers into a prefab and speak to them about facts no one could agree on. Putting my head down, I stretched my legs back under the rickety chair. My foot touched Julie's and I began to leak in my pants. Then she moved her legs away and I flushed into my forearms as if rejected.

At the back, some of the nutters were playing paper space invaders with pen and paper. I looked out of the window at the fields and houses, the playing field tenderised by a million studs, the sewage works beyond a fat sludge pie. Raindrops wrote love songs on the plastic glass. Above the hill opposite, a thundercloud descended like poison gas; a gaggle of jetlagged geese flew in star formation.

Even though the light was fading and rain spread across the valley, I felt this overwhelming urge to run to the moors and conduct lightning. Instead I sat very still, attempting to balance on the back two legs of my chair.

"So," said the teacher, Melville, middle-aged, thirty-something, pasty-skinned, with receding hair and a tea-drenched suit. "If we look in our exercise books at the two pictures, what do we see?"

I saw two pictures, one a Western street scene, the other China or Japan. The caption beneath said: '*Look at these two pictures. Do all the people in the top picture look alike? What about all the people in the bottom picture?*'

Melville's breath was second-best bitter and he had a pipe in his pocket that he occasionally pointed at his captives like a myopic Eric Bristow. No one had the will to answer. On the blackboard was an old column of four-digit numbers:

1314
1491
1066
1967

Mentally I chalked an extra line at the bottom. No, scrub that – at the top. The year I was born. History bored me as much as geography; why couldn't they teach you the future? History, geography, it was all the same – all maths, numbers underlined.

Woozy with fatigue I nodded, dreamed of *Baba-Yaga*, resurfaced. Tony Clegg was looking out of the window. I was looking *at* the window, the way the cheap plastic framed the brutalist hills, the clouds and slate roofs.

"Noone, Clegg, see me," said Melville at the bell. Everyone charged, even Julie. She'd be waiting somewhere cold and we'd go somewhere warm. That was how it worked. Tony and I looked at each other in confusion. We'd never even spoken, let alone plotted mayhem.

"Now," said Melville, "I know you two are staying on in the sixth, and you're both doing social sciences I believe? So I want you to do something together. A project."

"What sort of project, sir?" asked Clegg politely. I hated him for it.

"I'll leave that to your discretion," said Melville.

Outside, confused, we regarded each other balefully. We had a week to hand in a proposal to Melville. This would form the basis of our assignment for the first year of sixth-form. I had no idea who Clegg was; all I knew was that I didn't like him, and by the look of his squint he hadn't yet forgiven me. I decided it was probably worth starting afresh.

"Listen," I said, in a rush, "if we've got to work together fine. I don't know you; I don't know what you're into; nor you me. But we may as well make the best of it, so first off I'd just like to say I'm sorry I threw that snowball."

Tony stared at me, unreadably, just a slight tension in his neck muscles.

"Oh," I sighed. "You didn't know, did you?"

"Wait here," breathed Julie. Her coat receded into moorland darkness and I waited, in some empty lane, wind whispering, nearby dogs gruffing. I hoped the dogs weren't too angry. Farm dogs scared me. The moors scared me. I didn't belong up here, never had. Why had Mum brought me here and then run away again? What was wrong with *cities*?

A few minutes passed, and I wondered if Julie had been caught in the act of rescue. But then I heard footsteps, too many footsteps, an army of ghostly Romans. I tried to melt into the drystone walls, but Julie had bionic eyes; as she approached, pulling something large on a rope, she had a stupid grin on her pale face, illuminated by the moon.

After her grandfather had died, Julie's mum pulled her back to the moors, but being unsound she couldn't even run a car, let alone a working farm, and the animals were suffering. The week before a cartful of sheep had had to be put down after getting some complex disease. As we lay in the caravan one night, as she began to kiss down towards my belly button, Julie had asked if we could go on a mission of mercy to rescue her favourite, Brownie. I'd thought she meant a dog. *Yes*, I'd said quietly. *I will, yes.*

"This is Brownie," smiled Julie, at least having the decency to look embarrassed.

"Julie," I pointed out stupidly, "it's a horse."

"I know!" giggled Julie. "I'm a farmer remember?"

"Julie – we can't take him. Where the hell would we put him? It's crazy!"

"He could live with us at the caravan! He could stay outside and we'd feed him. We could train him to pull us to London like gypsies!"

"Julie, they need shelter, food, fucking – horseshoes… I'm sorry. There's no way."

She started to cry, plead, beg, promise, threaten, but to no avail. Stig was due for release, and I could imagine what he'd make of a horse in the caravan.

Feeling bad, but not entirely sure I should, I watched as Julie led the horse back to his stable. A patch of yellow light opened up in the farmhouse silhouette, but it didn't flash again. Julie's Morse code: one flash = no. Fine. I had work to do. Whistling, terrified, I walked back down the lane and into the woods.

1984

Dragged kicking and screaming from some confused yet compellingly erotic dream, I became aware that something wet and cold was dripping onto my face; a cold, slimy taste on my lips. I fought hard to lock my lids closed, to lock in my dream, but then I heard the melodious sounds of Chaos UK's *4 Minute Warning* as Stig straddled me and slapped my face.

As I levered my eyes open, I understood he was dribbling cold mushroom tea onto me, but there was no way to free myself from the ancient sleeping bag. My brain was still operating in some alternate universe of softness and light; I groaned, groggy and sore, my cheeks stinging and wet.

"Leave off you dozy wazzock!"

"Get out of bed then you spaz!"

"What for?"

Reluctantly bidding *adieux* to my harem, I squinted and shivered.

"I need you to do me a favour," said Stig, sitting on my legs and rolling his second or third spliff of the day on an Augustus Pablo album sleeve. That green Mohican still flopped over his polar blue eyes; he wore ragged denim shorts and an old string vest that showed off his heavy metal tattoos and biceps, his underarms smelling of superannuated stilton.

"What sort of favour?"

He squinted to trap smoke beneath his lids.

"I need you to collect some payments for me. I'm back

inside tomorrow and I don't know how long for."

"I can't, I have to finish me project."

"Not on the coach, soft lad – just round town. Here."

"What do I have to do exactly?"

As Stig explained, I took the spliff and inhaled harsh homegrown weed, neat, then coughed up my diaphragm. Why do people always laugh when you cough? Stig grinned malevolently, tired and wired. He never slept – too much speed, too many nightmares – which made him a somewhat unpredictable flatmate. Since he had come out of prison Julie had hardly been to the caravan; she said he scared her. I suspected she was still sore because I wouldn't rescue her horse.

Stig passed over the bottle of tea and I took a deep draught. The song ended with the sound of an explosion. There was silence then, apart from rain on the windows, branches scratching the caravan's back. Perhaps because he'd been adopted so many times, Stig had become surprisingly protective towards me, treating me as a younger brother, with all the attendant misery that implies.

"When I get out this time, we can do the rounds together. Beats sitting on your hairy arse and moping round town from March while September. Nothing going on round here lad. You snooze, you lose."

I shrugged, squinting smoke from my eyelids. "You sleep, you dream. Anyway – I'm still at school."

"Aye, and a right waste of fucking time that is. I should know – it's a mug's game, lad. They talk to you like you're shit on their shoe. You'll get your exams then be on a YTS down the pit, if you're lucky."

"It's not so bad in the sixth-form; they talk to you properly there. Anyroad – there *are* no pits round Millmoor."

"Don't be a cabbage all your life lad; you need to see the real world."

My head buzzed with mushrooms and dope, and Stig's mentalist eyes were burning my soul. Stig Doyle: free marketeer. He looked around the tiny caravan as if eavesdroppers may be lurking within its sixty square foot of ash, beer cans, soiled sheets and *Razzles*.

Having delivered a series of tortuous, complex instructions I had already forgotten, Stig revved off on his scrambler, a bike that enabled him to visit his regulars without using the roads. After he'd gone, I pulled out my project: a shoebox of photographs I'd been taking over the previous months and which Tony at least seemed happy with.

Unable to focus, I lay down and watched branches scrape the windows. My head hurt with cider, my belly ached and there was nothing to drink except the cold mushroom tea. There was a cider bottle full of the stuff so I took a deep swig, winced at the slimy taste, then took some more and jogged into the lounge to accelerate the poison.

It started to rain; drops thudded on the rooftop like ingots. The caravan was expanding in all directions, each tin room as massive as a cathedral. My project, suggested by my desperate art teacher, seemed suddenly ludicrous: photographs of Millmoor, Julie, Stig arsing around, six months of work – Christ knows how much I'd spent on film and developing.

Impatiently, I stuffed the project back into the box, vowing that from then on art and autobiography would always remain separate.

After locking the caravan with a rusty padlock, I pedalled my Grifter through the woods. Still having some Polaroid film left, I stopped in the quiet lane and looked around at the trees heaving and whispering beneath the onslaught of rain. Up in the sky were magic mushroom clouds. Tufts sieved down through the branches, washing up pure against trees and my shins.

In the first year of the sixth-form we were reading about the great philosophers. As I snapped, a gorse bush transformed itself into Nietzsche. I wondered if this should be my project: philosophers as foliage. A sycamore reminded me of Kierkegaard and an ancient oak became Schopenhauer. There were no banyan trees in Millmoor woods however, so Jung was conspicuous by his absence.

Feeling nauseous, I suddenly stopped dead in the middle of the wood. Spinning, faster and faster, trees sneaking up from behind, nobody for miles. An odd thought came to me, a strand of some philosophy of my own perhaps, or maybe just some deluded teen crap on mushrooms:

Here I am.

Stig's ruse had been simple, if fairly original. He signed on in about twenty different towns and cities across the country, using a variety of names and borrowed tax numbers. He'd go and sign on, moving from one to another, often doing two or three cities in a day, and at the same time he'd cash the giro from his last visit, safeguarded by his biker contacts.

On a Harley it was easy – he could do Leeds, Bradford and Manchester in a day, and be home that night in time to interrupt my nights of love and cider with Julie. But I didn't have a bike, I had National Express. So it was I who had spent a long, hard winter on dirty coaches, seeing nothing but coach stations, dreary bedsits, mental squats – the backside of England. I saw the Hulme crescents, the Sheffield flats, Toxteth and Handsworth, all ready to implode in exciting ways that Millmoor wasn't. On my second or third grand tour, I had the idea of taking my camera to record what I was seeing for our project.

Tony seemed pleased with my artistic and physical departure, but then he didn't have to come with me, sleeping on buses, dealing with dealers, walking round slums with hundreds of pounds in my pocket – which was not even mine as most of it had to go into some dodgy bank account for Stig to pay off a debt.

As I travelled across England that year, I realised what I had at home. There were no riots in Millmoor; nothing exciting ever seemed to happen but, when I got home, stopping off at Dad's to raid the fridge (much to his irritation), the woods closing off the outside world, with Julie waiting in the caravan to continue my tuition, I couldn't understand why anyone would ever want to leave. And that was pretty much how I felt spinning there, drugged up to my eyeballs on mushrooms and love.

And then I spoke to Tony.

The caravan had been home for a year. As I approached, it seemed pathetic, so small and battered by the seasons, bricks for wheels so it could never be moved. There was no sign of Stig's scrambler, so he was off somewhere I didn't like to consider, but his beloved Harley was safe under tarpaulin, away from visitors' eyes.

Inside I grabbed my sports bag of clothes, Stig's spare helmet and key, and a bottle of the tea. Then I went outside, locked the door, elbowed a hole in the window over the denim-stuffed sink big enough to reach in and touch the curtain with the flame of my lighter. The material was slow to catch, all those layers of mucus and damp, but soon thick black smoke billowed from cracking windows; red and orange tongues rolled across the roof.

The bike was in danger from the flames so I flipped off the wet tarp. The machine shone like flaming mercury. Knowing Stig could return at anytime, I sat on the bike swigging tea, appreciating the soft leather between my legs. Remembering hazy instructions from Stig's nightmare lessons, I put the bike into neutral and turned the key: the engine growled. Twisting the handle sent the bike spurting forwards and I fell off.

Luckily the bike was OK so I tried again, while the caravan popped and I stewed. Realising too late I'd left all my photographs inside, not to mention my camera, I made a half-arsed attempt to subdue the flames using my helmet and the rain. As the fire intensified I fancied I could see various scenarios from my past being played out in flames: leaving London, Mum vanishing, Julie's puffy cheeks billowing as I came. All gone. Time to take government advice and get on someone else's bike.

The lane levelled out at the top of the hill at the corner of Stone Nest, and I could see the small estate that had once been home. Except it had never really felt like home – because we had owned ours. It didn't seem so bad now, at least the houses were warm. Through the visor of my helmet I looked at all the little properties, old and new, my tiny primary school, smoke rising into the sooty sky. The streetlight at the corner of Natal Street and Brigden Road had been broken again by kids with time, stones and not much else. My house was almost indistinguishable, no blue plaque; the same old corporation blues and broken slates, but with its different front door ours was separate, irreplaceable.

As I approached, conspicuously slow on the great machine, I peeked down the alley to see if Dad's own old bike was resting against the shed. It wasn't. Smiling, I felt for my key, hungry. Since moving out I'd been back quite a bit, to attend parties and to give Dad advice, but mainly to steal his food. If I was lucky there'd be what Mum used to call a "happy fridge": full of food and nickable booze. Recently the fridge had been suffering a prolonged bout of severe depression. In fact, once it fell over and the plug came out of the wall.

Groans cascaded down the scruffy carpet stairs and I held my breath. A woman's sigh: had Mum come home at last?

Forgetting my hunger I tiptoed upstairs; the strangely familiar sounds were from Dad's room.

As quietly and slowly as I could manage I pushed opened the door. Julie was on all fours on the bed, pleated skirt up over her hips, tie dangling between her womanly breasts, mucky socks to her knees. Dad was behind her, kex down to his ankles, banging hard with an amazed expression on his beard. Neither noticed me and I crept away.

In the living room I found Dad's savings in their usual place behind the Tetley teapot on the mantelpiece. Eight fives: I'd got lucky for once. There was no time to pack; from upstairs the squeaking springs got faster, like Zebedee in an echo factory. My stomach cramped; finding a tabloid on the sofa (*'Go back to work!' says Maggie*) I squatted on the front doorstep.

The bike usually had a full tank, but just in case it hadn't, I chugged along a level section in neutral. In a grey field, a cow attempted to mount a bull. Through the railings a horse trotted jerkily alongside me like that film by Eadweard Muybridge. Flicking into gear I twisted the accelerator and the horse vanished.

Up on the tops the wind stretched the clouds bare and thin. At the highest point of the road out of town, I squeezed hard on the brakes and skidded across the road onto a ridge. Shivering, I took off my helmet and looked at the far horizon. With the helmet came the first clumps of hair; I laughed, threw them to the bracken. Short-sighted Tony had thought Julie was fucking Stig. Or did he? No matter, he couldn't see this.

The view from the ridge was like the cover of one of Dad's sci-fi mags; one of those rare milky days when the moon was as bright as the sun behind the pregnant clouds. Water columns breezed across the plain, chasing silver grass, ruffling like rabbit fur. Hard pillars of steel, circular and ponderous, one after another, spinning wheels of light. Naked air, transparent glass, airbrushing the sky clean turquoise; shadows of sunlight, fire-flares of crimson, burning the moorland to iced tinder.

A storm brewed. I felt vulnerable and exposed, shivering in my thin jacket in the coruscating wind. Revving up the bike, I stood up in my seat as I flashed across the hilltop road. The speedo tapped a hundred; if I hit a bump I'd bullet into some new dimension. The horizon expanded, the rain hurt my forehead, and the tyres began to slip and slide beneath me. As if unafraid, the roar of wind in my ears, I raised my middle finger to the darkening sky.

2007

So hard it hurts. Alona's tight backside rubs back against my groin in her halfsleep and through my boxers and her cotton panties I feel her cheeks relax, pushing back and wriggling teasingly from side-to-side. I'm angry with her, with this childlike pretence of sleep, when through my sealed eyelids I know the New Year sun is already halfway across the floor. And anyway, she never sleeps late – peasant stock, generations up with the birds.

Ungluing my lids I see her face in the dressing-table mirror opposite the bed, prettier in reflection, Catalan brown eyes half-closed beneath her hedgy orange hair, that little smile: what's she thinking?

We have a morning kissing problem; sensing each other's restless forms, falling out of our dreams, we move in and our bodies entangle, but my breath always stinks (wine, garlic, fear) and I have to decide whether to go to brush my teeth (and maybe try and piss upright) and then slip back into bed, by which time she's awake too, or just to flip her onto her stomach so we needn't touch lips and tongues.

Unable to face me, she pretends to corpse as if that's what I want: death warmed up. Yet somehow my hand has crept beneath her t-shirt and her breast is warm and rolling beneath my palm, her nipple as hard as the walls we chipped away to create this space, silent and high above the ocean.

In consciousness she never wants me because I won't make

her belly large, won't fuck her buck-naked even mid-month, and she crosses herself and crosses off matches on the wall of this cohabitation, this cell of loneliness where the window reflects bare sky and cloud, and at night only the night and stars. Since the Winter Solstice the morning light has begun creeping again, and I'm convinced that it's not global warming we're facing; the world is spiralling into the sun as I burrow into her from behind, pulling down her panties and my boxers and stroking between her legs for Alona to let me in.

The mirror presents me with its usual dismal vistas: my baldness, the blank tattoo, the small scar on the top right of my lip (that remote smile). Closing my eyes, I think about the mystery woman in the safari suit: younger than Alona and only a little prettier, essentially more alluring because of her unknowns, her different skin suffused with Northern cold.

The face I can't watch as it changes attitude, so sharp it could open letters, and her nose vanishes when you look at her straight, but her eyes are possibly even more beautiful than Hermione's: enormous, dark brown, endless, capable of transmitting every emotion. When she tosses her hair and rolls her eyes you understand everything – and if you don't, you pretend you do.

Alona's English carries a strong accent that gives way to Catalan at every excuse I provide; her moods are short and hot, and she possesses not an ounce of pretence. I like the way she wears short black dresses and long red heels to do the flamenco, hands on hips like my trophy, but not the way she dances like a spider enveloping flies in silk; I like the way she smokes a pipe, but not the fact she spits in gutters.

More than maybe anything, I like the way my pale semen splashes across her dark skin as I pull out and straddle her and obligingly she pushes her breasts together with her hands; she has her eyes wide open and watches as I ejaculate onto her breasts, some jerking onto her neck and a smear on her cheek.

What takes my breath away is how little I enjoy it.

Hiding her disappointment well, Alona pulls me down into the mess I have created and I shiver at the clammy sensation. She pushes my head down to her breasts.

"Lick them clean."

But I pull back, practically leaping from the bed and wiping myself on a towel. Alona glares at me then curls up in a ball. I take a cold shower and the water brings the hard-on back but I know I'll feel stronger if I don't wank, so I pull on a damp robe and pad to the kitchen where Alona has already opened the door to let in the morning air and the clockwork chickens that crap on the table and lay rotten eggs. The smells of old food and animal dung have become so familiar it's surprising that I notice them. I touch the kettle: hot. So she lied; she was awake from the start.

The cave is just a flesh wound in the mountain flanks, the frontage a squared limpet of precarious wood and glass, a porch like an airlock leading into the room that acts as both kitchen and what I still refer to as the 'front room'. The door to the left, next to the cooker, leads to the tiny bathroom, windowless, standing room only. The door opposite leads to the bedroom where we try to sleep and don't conceive, just lie in our worlds watching suns drift by.

Sometimes when insomniac, I feel the world is a gigantic bowling ball and I'm crucified against it, my arms pinned to the ground by guilt, my eyelids torn off by some idealised Apache, feeling the world roll beneath me and watching the first light touch the horizon ahead. For many years this was the only way I could experience the sunrise, by sneaking up on it from behind.

Like roughly half those children raised on Fray Bentos and fish fingers, our kitchen is the centre of action: a great wooden table scored with blade-grooves, records sloping against angles, concealed lighting; this before I ran out of money. The exposed mountain wall is a honeycomb of holes I drilled myself, some containing wine, others empty shadows like giant bullet holes.

After 11th September I briefly developed an obsession with storing enough supplies to get through World War III. First I started to stockpile wine in preparation for H-bombs, fearing the effect of radiation on the grapes. Then I calculated that at the rate I drink, if I lived another forty years we were talking holes aplenty, enough to bring down this cold mountain on top of my head.

The floor is flatter than I'd like, rugs covering the tiles and raw stone in an attempt to make the place feel more homely. Because we've only cut through the thin edge of this mountain, we have views on two sides. The double window at the far end of the front room looks out over the Med and the sunrise, although sometimes (with age forty impending) I wish I could spin the island round so it faced the sunset.

Taking a bottle of Lucozade from the fridge, I slam the front and only door (no escape, no fire exits, just a long tombstone into the rocks beneath), with its *faux*-oak nameplate ('*Dunme'eadin*'), and walk out through the garden, ignoring clucking hens and somnambulist flies, and drive the old Renault van into town for breakfast.

Usually when we fight, I buy sesame rolls from the *Mercado*, Alona makes coffee and we break our moods against each other like sea-waves. But it feels different this time and I'm not quite sure why; perhaps the fact no words have been spoken, just her glare of contempt, the futility of all we haven't done and will probably never do – at least not together. Something has changed; not her, maybe not even me.

Parking in a side street near the square, I see someone's scrawled something in the muck on the back of the van:

'*Deseo que mi esposa fuera este asqueroso!*'

Unable to translate, I enjoy the sensation of walking with the weak sunshine warming my scalp. Remembering the historic snowball, I look warily at passers-by. After buying *churros con chocolate* from the kiosk, I stand in the middle of the village square and watch the ancient waiter from the *Mexicana* put out chairs and polish tables, stray dogs sniffing around for crumbs, a coach full of dead-eyed tourists growling through the narrow streets heading for one of the new resorts up the coast. As I suck chocolate off the warm pastry, the waiter looks up from his duties and raises a hand nonchalantly.

"*Feliz Nuevo Anos.*"

Waving half a *churro* back in greeting, I walk through the square to the cramped street where Billys Bar has positioned itself, as oblivious to its surroundings as it is to punctuation. The left side of this particular street is always in shadow, which I like as the sun hurts my eyes after drinking too much; most mornings I walk in the shade.

As I cross the street and approach the bar, licking sticky chocolate off my fingers, a crocodile of infants pass me on their way to church. An orderly train of humour and good manners, unlike the world I thought I'd finally left behind.

When I first arrived in Spain I didn't speak the lingo and sometimes found myself in expat bars. One night I was talking to this extremely reasonable salesman from Nuneaton and we were getting along famously. It turned out he'd moved over here the year before and I asked him why. The salesman grinned. "I'll show you."

Standing on his bar stool and cupping his hands to his mouth, he roared at the top of his voice, "Niggers!" A few people laughed, but most didn't flinch. The salesman sat down again and slapped me on the back. "*That's* why I moved here. You can't do that at home, can you?" Work aside, that was the last time I went to any bar with a union jack flag on the signage.

Billys Bar looks authentic enough from the outside: brown wood, glazed windows, and a swinging sign with the bulldog logo that they've somehow designed to creak. In fact it looks *too* authentic – like a real pub back home rather than a Spanish mock-up. Inside I expect the usual expat scene, all laminated menus and rogue apostrophes, but when I push open the carved old doors and step indoors I'm puzzled.

There's something odd about the place. Absent are the framed football shirts, photographs of strangers laughing, flyers and bad joke stickers; instead there are framed photographs, black and white, representing the past. A mounted policeman coshes a pregnant woman in a South Yorkshire field; a *Mirror* front page announces Hillsborough; *Standard* billboards speak of carnage on the Underground.

The bar has the look and feel of a shipwreck: a Spanish galleon fifty-foot under. Against the tide and the shoals, I paddle to the bar between chairs stacked over chairs in organic columns like conch fossils. The solitary Sky screen above the Formica counter is a confusion of squares, red buttons, digital tapewords that make little sense. The sound is down and I clear my throat in the cavernous silence.

"*Ola*? Hello? Anyone there?"

Sometimes I feel like I'm missing not only something but *everything* – the only one not in on the joke/session/party. I could be sitting in a bar, on a train, at the supermarket, and suddenly I get this uncanny feeling everyone's waiting for me to leave – not to make fun of me, but so they can get on with things without me.

For a moment I think I hear stirrings behind the bead curtain leading to the kitchen, but it seems I'm mistaken so, with a slight shiver, I leave the bar, buy bread and cheese and drive up the coast to the marina attached to the resort's showcase beach.

Hotels and apartment complexes dot the horizon, separated by canals in which fish swim among supermarket trolleys, and dusty roads are patrolled by cats. A thundercloud has slipped from the summit of Mont Eterno and settled over the beach;

parking up by the water I watch miniature tourists cross the iron bridges back to the hotels, carrying their sunbeds and inflatables like giant leaves. Even though it's lashing down now, that plane is buzzing around again, pulling its banner, its message I can't quite read; squinting, it seems to be saying 'todos le ama' but I can't be sure.

The rain looks settled so I dig for an anorak and hurry along the pontoon decking. My boat is a small twenty-footer but it has a covered cabin and is airtight, plus I know the thunderstorm will be over shortly. So after running checks on automatic, I ease the boat between the larger yachts and fishing boats, and leave the harbour, pointing north. Rain-beads wriggle across the window.

Round the point I turn into a small beach accessible only by sea, great rusty cliffs dotted with clumps of maquis rearing high behind. Stalling the engine, I drop the small anchor and step out onto the windy, oily deck.

Cliffs rise perpendicular to the inconsistent cloud, the rain sporadic. The water smells rancid, stale, broken. Alona will be feeding the animals and cursing me in her native language. The thought makes me smile; she's a city girl, a part-time secretary for a crooked lawyer and training to be a beautician, and only tolerates the chickens and pigs because she thinks she should love that way of life. Every chance she gets, she skips back over the Med to Barcelona, to shop with her friends and drink better coffee, and for all I know to fuck some Alphonso or Xavier from her secret past. A part of me wishes this were so. The cuckolded husband has never been a fantasy of mine, but then at least I wouldn't feel quite so guilty about what I'm not doing; not fucking her, wasting good seed on her unexpressing tits and depriving her of the one thing she crazily believes brings happiness.

Since being a kid on a moorland bike, I've loved the rain on my skin, but I'm still hungry so, diving below, I grab the cool-box and eat bread and cheese as I look out of the window at water falling upon water. As a new tourist I rode in a glass-bottomed boat and though the experience itself was somewhat disappointing – more Geordies than fish – I remember being fascinated by the way the surface of water divided above from below. It seemed to have a six-inch skin, like rubber, so absolutely defined as it wriggled slowly across the window separating blue from blue – another illusion.

Opening a bottle of cheap table wine I throw the cork overboard and watch to see if some bird or sea monster will take it. Nothing's biting today so I tilt the bottle to my lips. The snowball incident troubles me. So what if it was Tony, does it matter? Aren't we still friends, despite Hermione, despite Becky, despite Julie?

After the rain blows itself out, I head back to the marina, moor the boat and drive to town. The wine has clouded my judgement and at a roundabout I have to remind myself to steer to the right. My mobile sits in a jacket pocket, and I'd turn it on except I don't really need a succession of regressively irate voicemails yet; I need a drink.

After going into an internet café and making my purchase – the largest I've ever made, more than I paid for the cave and boat combined – I walk over to the new place. Despite its unusual décor Billys Bar is doing good business now, but I'm lucky enough to grab a stool up at the bar. I'm disappointed that the safari girl is nowhere to be seen, but the youngish barman seems friendly enough when I hail him.

"*Cerveza, por favour.*"

The barman sighs. "Jaysus, pint of what?"

"Stella. How could you tell I wasn't Spanish?"

"The way your lips move."

"What's an Irishman doing working in an English pub?"

"What's an English pub doing on a Spanish island?

Two euros."

I reach for my wallet when a huge hand covers my eyes and I hear that gravel-gargling voice of old.

"Strewth! This bloke's got no strides on!" I turn and there's Tony, older, wider, sporting a ridiculous clipped beard. Even at 15 he encouraged all sorts of growths, now they're taking over. He grins and winks as if we'd seen each other yesterday, under happier circumstances. "Didn't you used to be an artist? Let me get that."

"Must be fate. My stars this morning said I'd meet a tall, dark stranger. They don't get much stranger than you."

"Nor much balder than you." Tony produces a thick wallet; I see a young girl smile. "How long you been out here Joe? Mister Malteser head or what. Where's the tattoo?"

Tony well knows the 'NF' was removed years ago; though if you look closely you can still see the pink scar. I touch the top of my head, embarrassed, but Tony's eyes are still smiling through his posh new specs. The barman pours him a Yorkshire bitter without Tony asking and we clink glasses and race to the bottom. Tony finishes first; he burps, he laughs, I sigh, Tony shrugs. I wave a note at the barman, who waves back, a crazy little conversation in semaphore.

"So," I ask Tony, "what brings you to Mallorca?"

"I was watching UK Gold the other night. Someone was asking David Seaman if kids took the piss out of his hair when he was at school and he said no, he was the cock of the school. Took me back to those miserable days of flares, fizzbombs, and you –"

"I never *wore* flares, Tony. Your memory's playing tricks."

Tony puts his glasses in a case that he slides into his pocket; he squints. I shrug and point at our empty glasses. The barman pours. Alona can wait.

"It does that, doesn't it? So how are they? Tricks?"

"Mustn't grumble."

I appraise his apparel. Tony looks irritatingly cool in his Ralph Lauren and Chino's, an expensive-looking jacket and manicured haircut.

"Looks like you're doing well."

Tony doesn't return the compliment and I'm annoyed. *I'm* doing well: I have a tan and a boat and a woman. Remembering that smile, I nod in the general direction of Tony's pocket.

"Who's the girl?"

Tony looks confused.

"What?"

"In your wallet."

"Oh." He smiles proudly as he pulls out a pic and hands it over. "That's Millie. Our daughter."

The girl is four or five, blonde, laughing in a fairy outfit and is the image of her mother. I hand it back quickly.

"Congratulations." For some reason I'm angry. "Where *is* Hermione, anyway?"

Tony smiles and shrugs tactfully.

"She didn't want to come."

I look down into my pint.

"Because of me?"

"Millie, you know – school."

Tony's evasive but I feel sick inside and swallow cold beer. We find a quiet corner of the bar and sit with our drinks: Stella for me, bitter for him. The place is rocking, full of sunburnt yobs and white-socked couples, despite the fact the jukebox doesn't seem to have the usual Robbie Williams/Phil Collins loop; I'm surprised to hear the Band of Holy Joy. Tony takes out a pack of *Fortuna* and I shake my head with mock sorrow.

"You *still* smoke?"

"A bad habit I picked up from you." Tony smiles slowly. "There's quite a list."

My accent has become so slight that I've been taken for a Midlander, or one of a 'higher class'. Maybe it's because I left town so young, was forced to adapt to Southern situations, found it easier to communicate. Tony has retained more of a Yorkshire accent, but because he wanted to. I remember as kids he could drop whole paragraphs. I sip my lager while he looks around smiling inanely.

"Where did you get the snowball?" Tony looks at me in surprise and I see from his red eyes that he's older than he wants to be. I'm older than I ever expected to be. It seems he shares my ingratitude.

"*Snow*ball?"

"Last night. Correction – this morning. Very funny. Got the shock of my life."

Tony smiles through his cigarette.

"I just thought it would be funny. Not a bad shot was it? Nearly as good as you."

"I'm a bit out of practice these days. The snow ain't what it orta. In Mallorca."

"Is that why you came?"

I'm surprised by the question; Tony obviously doesn't know me as well as he thinks.

"No – I used to love the snow. The way it made everything stop." And other things start.

Tony stubs his fag out in the Tetley ashtray and blows smoke in my face. That's always been his little smoke signal to say, 'you're boring me'. I smile and wave it away like I always have, more irritated than I remember.

"So, how did you find me?"

"Wasn't hard. Aisha told me you'd moved to Mallorca so I just looked up the town with the most pubs."

I want to pursue the Hermione question but once more decide against it. Things obviously aren't going too well between them or she'd have come along. Then again, perhaps not. Tony finishes his pint and waves the glass.

"Another?"

I shrug, surprised he's asked. Alona can wait on her owna. The eclectic jukebox is playing *Buffalo* by Stump. On the wall opposite there's a framed newspaper cutting of Diana, the one with her legs showing through. Diana, my first love; as an early teen I'd stare into her eyes with a fervour only adolescence can brew as I squirted onto her newsprint blouse. Tony plonks down the two-tone pints and I try to make normal conversation. After all, we *are* almost forty. Time to grow up.

"You on holiday, then? Or what?"

"Does it matter?"

"Just wondered how long you'd be around. Where are you staying, a complex?"

"No. I drove out from Palma last night. I'm supposed to be staying upstairs here but apparently there's no door. Fucking builders. I'll find somewhere later."

Again I say nothing; Tony's angling at an invitation. We've been down that road a few times and it has always ended in tears, women's mostly. Alona wouldn't be impressed, coming home pissed with another *loco Ingesi*. The more I think about it, the more certain I am that she wouldn't like Tony *at all*.

"Come and stay with me."

He looks grateful.

"You sure? That'd be sound. You live alone?"

I laugh. "All alone with Alona."

"Is she fit?"

"Course."

We soon slip into old time routines, comfortable as socks. Tony seems satisfied and nods, sleepy with drink and facial hair. Smoke billows round his head and I see a cartoon caricature of Patrick Moore. I look into my glass to find my past. A Stones track I haven't heard for years comes on the jukebox: time is on our side.

"Did you ever wonder how many times you'll hear a song

again?" I waffle. "I was listening to *Low Life* the other day and wondered how many times I'll hear the sonic bass line of *Sunrise* before I drop. 41? 86?"

Perhaps the same goes for foods, places, and love.

"You should get out more, Joe, listen to something new."

"Like what?"

"It doesn't matter. It just needs to be new." Tony waves round the bar. Filling up nicely. "So what do you think?"

I've just spotted safari suit girl; she must be the late shift. Her breasts are enormous. She sees me and smiles unreadably. I nod quietly.

"Nice."

"Think it'll do well?"

"I dunno, there are tons of English pubs… but it's a bit different, I suppose. Why, what's it to you?"

Tony smiles as proudly – and as infuriatingly – as when he passed over the pic of his daughter.

"Because it's mine. I own it."

Dangerously woozy I drive along the coast beneath the perforated black then turn inland. We are silent in the car. It's been a long time, even though we know each other better than anyone else – except possibly Herm. There's something about Tony's silences, his sly smiles, that I don't like – as if he's holding back. If there's a rule to friendship, it's that you never hold back. But then, how many secrets have I kept from Tony over the years?

"I can't believe you live out here," slurs Tony. "I mean, it's a bit different to Holloway Road."

"Exactly."

"Where did you meet this Alana bird then? She Spanish?"

"Alona. Yes. In Barcelona in a bar. I was on the mainland doing some business. She was on her own in this long white dress. Showed off her brown skin. She had the whitest teeth."

"Tits?"

I'd forgotten how coarse Tony can be when he wants to wind you up. It doesn't suit him, yet still he persists. Turning off the *autopista*, I pull onto a rough track, taking it slowly in the darkness. If Tony could see what I know is there: the drop to the rocks, the way the wheels skid and the track crumbles.

What Tony doesn't know – the way Alona was so disinterested when I first said *Ola*.

At the track's end, I stop the car and dig out the flashlight. Tony squints at himself in the window.

"Where are we? What's this?"

"Home."

"Fuck me, you live in a *field*?"

"Close."

We get out. Tony pops down his lock and we slam the doors almost in unison.

"Mind where you step. There's a bit of a drop."

"Fuck, it's *dark*."

"You get used to it. Where'd your glasses go?"

"I wear contacts too."

"Thought so. You looked in agony in the bar."

If I was to suddenly hurl him over the clifftop, who'd know? Who'd care? Relenting, I flash the torch in Tony's general direction. He freezes, a few feet from the edge; the ray of light shines on his horrified face, his sore eyes.

"Jesus!"

"As I said – watch your step. Follow the light."

Tony doesn't need to know that I deliberately parked out on the rise instead of the orchard; I didn't want Alona to hear our approach. The darkest part of me wants to find her bent over the sink, some hairy-arsed footballer in her tail. Worrying.

Treading softly I lead the way along the edge, then down a small impression in the earth and through lemon trees to the door. Behind me I can hear Tony crashing about and mumbling in protest.

Inserting the puny key into the side of my mountain, I open the door quietly, expectantly, but the kitchen's empty: plates in the sink, empty bottles, the way I left it this morning. Tony comes in behind me, breathing heavily after the exertions on the clifftop; he bursts out laughing.

"You Neanderthal! I always knew it. Evolution in reverse."

Alona's handbag stands aloof on the table. I point to the sofa.

"Make yourself at home. I'll just see if Alona's awake."

Tony slumps, looking dog-tired. Getting him a bottle of beer from the fridge, I head to the bedroom so I don't have to watch him open it with his teeth. The door squeaks open into darkness. From memory I pace silently to the bed and hear Alona's even breathing. Good: we can talk in the morning, if we're still talking. A great start to the year: we've spoken about a dozen words. Maybe a vow of silence will help us through, a Trappist orbit of gesturing and fucking.

Squeezing the door closed I go to the fridge, rescue a cold bottle, open it on a convenient slab of rock beside the fridge, and join Tony on the couch. But Tony is snoring through his open mouth; I sigh impatiently and turn on the TV, turning down the sound on Middle Eastern miseries.

Maybe I was wrong, assuming Alona wouldn't like Tony. For some reason he's always attracted women, drawn them to him; whereas, if I'm honest, I tend to wear them down. Not that I'm jealous, because women aren't the only things he attracts. Wherever Tony turns up, you can be pretty sure trouble will be sniffing his crack and ready to mount. Then again, if it wasn't for Howard Jones, I might never have seen Tony after escaping from Millmoor. That bloke has a lot to answer for.

1985

In the Elephant's Head, the paddy barman took exception to my standing on the table and miming along to Howard Jones. He half-hustled, half-carried me out to Camden High Street. I landed in a mountain of crates containing rotting veg, scraps of leather and the redundant covers of bootleg cassettes. As I lifted my head to protest, my old duffel bag landed on my bald, shining pate.

I grinned. "Cheers mate!"

"Don't come back!" yelled the barman, lugubrious, grey-haired, slack-jawed, sideboards bristling. The door shut me out and I lay in the sun for a while, Camden shoppers giving me a wide berth. I tried to remember what dim flicker of memory Howard's Wembley warbling had stirred in me. Not possessing an elephant's memory, it slipped away as forgettable as his song.

There was a shop opposite the street market where the winos from Arlington House rested, so taking up my bag I pulled on my ratty woolly hat, wandered over and slumped next to Jock, who always had a joke and the loan of a drink.

"Noone, you cunt!" roared Jock. I grinned weakly, sore from all the falling I'd been doing recently.

"Got a drink Jock?"

"You cheeky wee bastard, always on the scrounge. Here."

Jock passed over his Merrydown and I took a swallow – pissy bottlemouth although bad form to mention germs. I passed it back and waited till his back was turned before wiping my lips. Cider kills me on an empty stomach and I decided to go for something clearer.

By the time I emerged from the besieged supermarket with vodka, Jock was rolling on the ground with Mad Mick, the knacker who came along now and then demanding rent. Once, in some park, I saw Mick stick an ice pick into someone's thigh, levering out a great pulp of flesh. Backing away quietly, I ran down the High Road towards the City.

I'd almost reached Mornington Crescent before realising I'd left my bag back in Camden. Mick would claim my radio and spare pants, and good for him. Now I remembered the arrangement from one of my infrequent phone calls to Yorkshire: Tony, a party. Julie?

As I walked, the sound of Live Aid from open windows was drowned out by a harsher noise from somewhere to the east. I knew this music, an angry and monotonous blast from my past. I staggered towards the source, sobering, swigging from the bottle, past shattered flats and over a canal bridge. Peering over the side I squinted into the mucky depths but couldn't see my reflection. As I leaned, the pressure from the rail pressed into my aching stomach and I puked with startling velocity into the water. Clear liquid puke scattered onto the glutinous surface and ducks closed in. I walked on.

The radio was all I had. The Harley had made it as far as the Midlands before running out of petrol. Dumping it on the hard shoulder I'd thumbed it to London. Some of the ripped backsides of London were dark cold places that even this midsummer sun couldn't dry out completely – beneath the bridges, in skips, behind builders' portakabins, the hunting grounds and the resting places of the ones like me: the Camden parasites.

Down a scruffy dead-end street, navigating from memory. I'd spent time round here as Stig's little helper. The Churchill on the corner was overflowing onto the patch of waste ground at the centre of a square. Hundreds of people filled the patch of mud, and others drifted in and out of the houses. Two rows of four-storey houses converged at the opposite corner, behind which a railway viaduct split the evening sky. The gable end of the house nearest the boozer was spray-painted into a mural, a wildly optimistic portrayal of the street, complete with flowers, people of all colours laughing, smiling, smoking dope, and with the bright clear message: '*Welcome to Villiers Terrace, N1. Fuck the filth.*' This was the place. Falling down on the grass, I put the vodka bottle to my lips and picked up a flyer.

The gig had been disorganised by some anarchist group as an alternative to Live Aid, money from which they insisted would be squandered by the Ethiopian government on good Scotch and bad policies. Proceeds of this event were going to victims of the Bangladesh tsunami. Despite the fact that some hardcore band were the only alternative to Bowie and U2, the cash raised at least allowed the organisers to sit outside the Churchill rather than swig their own homebrew indoors.

A stage full of punks, a huge unlit bonfire and a double-decker bus dominated the wasteland. The bus was covered in graffiti, metal spikes welded to its roof and clouds of narcotic smoke drifting from metal-latticed windows.

Usually when I had come for Stig's giro it was quiet, but tonight the commune resembled a scene from *Mad Max*. There were freaks of all persuasions, bits of cars, fireworks and the clash of music: The Sugarhill Gang, Edith Piaf, Sisters of Mercy. Some closet reactionary had plugged an old TV into two barn-sized amps, and noise from the competition over Wembley way echoed round the streets. The Churchill looked inviting and I counted my coppers; not even enough for a pint, let alone the kebab I'd been promising my belly for months.

I walked over to the house at the corner of the two rows, from which partygoers emerged and disappeared in waves. Pausing outside number six, I looked upwards. Like the rest of the street, it was a crumbling four-storey relic. A couple of goths of indeterminate gender were snogging on bare stairs; in the front room a half-hearted fight was drawing to an unsatisfactory conclusion. In the kitchen, I squeezed between sweating pill-poppers and grabbed a can of lager. No food; fucked again.

Hovering above the goths at the top of the stairs, a black cat watched me fiercely, its belly full of kittens. When I blinked in submission it blinked back and sloped off. To ease the hunger I sucked the can dry. Dimly I became aware that someone was watching me from the front door and I looked up. Tony was there with a frown on his moustachioed face. I jerked my head and he came downstairs, following me into the chaotic living room around which punks, dreads and bikers lit flare-like spliffs, smashed bottles for hot-knives, snorted and spiked. I stuck to someone else's beer. The few remaining patches of floral wallpaper were nailed in place with Class War posters, Bobby Sands' quotes and items of furniture retrieved from skips. Tony looked disgusted, as if the decor was my fault, my life. In fact, I *aspired* to this; this looked great.

"Thanks," I said, "for coming."

"S'alright. It's on my rounds anyway."

"Stig's got you doing his thing then?"

"Just for a while, till I start uni. Pay's not great but you get to see the country."

"Yeah. I remember."

"Look Joe, I'm really sorry about what happened. I really thought Julie was shagging Stig."

I gave him an admonitory stare, still suspicious.

"Strange. I mean, me Dad's twenty years older and twice

the width for a start."

"It was dark, man. Me eyesight's been crap since I stopped wearing glasses. It was Stig's caravan. The light was off, he had a biker's jacket on. What can I say? How'd I know your dad would be there?"

"So you weren't just clearing the way for you and Julie?"

"You're joking, aren't you? Why would I want your dad's sloppy seconds? Anyway, after you left town Stig had nowhere to live so he moved in with Julie. She's expecting his babs now."

It was just over a year since we'd worked on our project (the one, I realised guiltily, I'd destroyed), and yet Tony seemed a lot older, careworn, hammered by the streets and the coach stops. Despite this he looked at me with an expression I didn't like: concern, even pity. I realised he hadn't seen me since my hair fell out, but I couldn't be arsed to explain. Let him think I was a skinhead. Noticing his beer was empty, I winked in what I hoped was a streetwise fashion and disappeared to the kitchen.

Stoned goths, popper-sniffing trendies: too easy. Filling a carrier bag with cans, crisps and an unopened bottle of tequila that I found behind a mod, I went back to the front room. The B52s came on the old turntable. I leaned back against some ivory-effect mantelpiece rescued from a skip, candles all along it like some altar to the Jim Morrison poster watching from above. The smell of joss sticks, drugs and dogs. I felt at home here.

"Does Julie ever... mention me?" I asked, hopefully. Tony shrugged, shook his head.

"What, after what *you* did?"

"What?"

"You killed her horse, man."

Sickness filled my stomach.

"What?"

"Stig said he'd look after it. I think he had plans for it to tow the caravan. Couldn't leave it outside in the rain so he put it in his room."

I opened the tequila and took a deep swig. Outside, flashes and bangs like the world was on fire. We swapped stories, brave boys in a harsh world. By the time the fireworks had all gone, Tony was almost asleep as he held up the mantelpiece. Over by the door to the hall, two women were talking intently, looking angry, sad and happy all at the same time. The smaller one had streetwise, Eden blue eyes, a pallid face and short black hair; she wore black tights and a mini-dress, pixie boots and a cap. The other one was taller, well-built, her weird messy blonde curls clashing with her lemon dungarees. She looked out of place: a vicar's daughter. The posh one held a bottle of white wine, the chippy one a joint, and both were drinking from white plastic cups that they held delicately like picked flowers. Finally the taller one put her arms around the small one and kissed her forehead; they both giggled.

"I've seen them two before," nodded Tony. "I came to collect a giro here once and found them in bed together."

"Are you sure? You have a knack of getting things... mixed up."

Tony looked at me sharply.

"And whose fault's that?"

"Yours," I shrugged, "for being so fucking vain."

Tony was about to reply and I was ready for an argument when, to my astonishment, the two women charged towards us, a look of alarm on their faces. Inexplicably, the shorter, dark-haired girl threw her wine over me, then the statuesque blonde did likewise. I wiped my face blearily and glared at the two women.

"What the *fuck* –?"

"You were on fire," said the short one.

"Like a Guy," said the posh one.

I felt the back of my shirt and dragged it round. A charred hole had burned right through it from the candles on the mantelpiece, yet I hadn't felt a thing. The two girls started laughing; so did Tony. I was shaken, thinking about horses, bum-grafts, the fact it was my only t-shirt and it would be cold on the streets later.

"I'm on fire too," said Tony. The two women started to move away. I didn't blame them.

"Wait!" I said. "Thank you."

"Anytime... you're on fire," The shorter girl spoke in a spiky London accent.

The taller one spoke differently, plums in her peculiarly small mouth, full of reproach. "Who *are* you, anyway? You don't live here."

"I'm Joe." I smiled as normally as I could manage under the circumstances. The tiny one with fierce eyes of bedevilment pinked. Out of the window there was a roar as the bonfire flared; flames lashed her cheek.

"Hermione."

The name sounded super in a London accent: 'Her, meow, knee', as in pussycat. Tony cleared his throat.

"Tony."

The vicar's daughter reached out a hand.

"Rebec- Becky." Warm, strong. Rather incongruously we all shook hands.

"So where are you girls from?" asked Tony.

"London," said Hermione.

"Brighton," said Becky.

"Wow!" said Tony. "Do you know Sussex? I start there in September!"

Becky squealed. "Me too!"

Hermione and myself looked at each other, left out. She lit a fag, then the two women looked down at their empty plastic cups.

"Another drink?" said Tony, as politely as he could muster.

"There isn't any left," said Becky, her accent transmogrifying into something more in keeping with the times. "We brought loads, but some bastard nicked it all. And me last one went over you."

"I've got some Tequila," I said proudly, producing the bottle from the bag like a rabbit. Hermione and Becky regarded me with open mouths; Hermione looked cross. One of her cheeks twitched. I knew then that I would love her.

"You tosser! You nicked our booze! Cost me a week's giro for all that!"

I backed away uneasily, holding the bottle to my chest.

"Here, hang on, I bought this with me own brass."

"Oh?" Hermione looked scornful. "Where from?"

"The offie, where else?"

"You can't buy it in England, you thieving bastard! I bought it on the ferry from Ireland."

"Ah," I sighed, gloomily, holding out the bottle. Taking it, Hermione appeared to be about to say something unkind. Suddenly a madman bellowed in my ear, "Noone! Where's me bike, you thieving cunt?"

Stig grabbed me by the neck and slammed my head against the wall; my legs kicked over the record player to general boos. His fingers tightened and my feet were dangling; I choked, knowing I was about to die, mortified with embarrassment. Hermione and Becky screamed and Tony put a hand on Stig's arm.

"Come on man, leave him alone."

Stig stared slowly at Tony.

"Get your hand off me fucking arm."

Tony kept it there so Stig reached out with his right hand and lifted him off the ground too. Tony's feet and my feet dangling, Stig strangling, cursing, panting in my face; his sharpened teeth, the smell of dog food. My fingers made no impression and I was going purple.

Becky began to scream louder. "Leave them alone you fucking wanker!"

Stig turned and looked into Becky's face, smiled, then spat in her mouth. Becky dropped to the ground and began to retch. Stig turned back to me, his eyes cold like abandoned planets. Becky's empty bottle was sat on the mantelpiece within reach and I began to grope. Suddenly Stig relaxed his grip and I crumpled to the floor, gasping. He was writhing on his side holding his crotch.

Hermione hissed down on him, "You've got twenty seconds to get out of my house or I'll call my friend over there." She nodded across the room at a huge Rastafarian in a rollneck sweater talking to a thin white girl. "Don't even think about it; he's got a hatchet. I once saw him chop up a bloke just for looking at him funny."

Stig thought about this, then painfully stood and left the room, huddled over like a Chelsea Pensioner. Hermione hugged Becky, who was green. I rubbed my throat ruefully, while looking at Tony enquiringly. He shrugged, eyes down. I looked at Hermione with admiration.

"What did you *do* to him?"

Shyly she held out a huge mobile phone, its aerial like a unicorn spike, and this time everyone laughed, even Becky who'd taken the bottle of tequila and swigged it neat to get rid of the taste. For some reason I was still looking at Hermione, and when she caught my eye in this new way I glimpsed the ferocity of her spirit: un-succumbed. The Rasta guy came over and smiled at Hermione and Becky.

"Well hello girls! You look *ravishing* darlings!"

He made Larry Grayson sound like James Cagney. I laughed and cracked open a bottle of Clandew I'd found in a psychobilly's arms. Smiling, glowing, sure that something was occurring and ready to see what happened next, we clinked plastic cups like pauper cavaliers. I caught Tony's eye again. Had Stig tricked him too, or had they both tricked me?

Somebody screamed.

"The bus! It's on fire!"

Through my fug of fiery dreams, Stig was banging a bottle against my head. Wincing, I opened my eyes, then put a shaking hand to my fevered brow. It wasn't drums, it was a migraine. Slowly, I sat up and faced the worst hangover I'd ever had. I then recalled that Hermione had taught us a way of doing tequila slammers, using speed for salt and Clandew for lemonade. I was drenched with pissy sweat, my mouth tasted like tea and coffee in the same cup, and my stomach growled and bubbled. My larynx was so bruised I could barely swallow, and the back of my head was tenderised. Despite my condition, I snorted a laugh.

It was a grey dawn morning and I was perched on the very edge of a bed in an unfamiliar bedroom. Rugs and heavy metal posters covered the walls. Hermione lay next to me, mouth open, hair askance, Becky next to her, a rough blanket over their fully clothed bodies. Tony, who had either fallen out of the bed or been pushed, was lying on the floor on Becky's side; the bed was shallow, two old mattresses welded by mildew. Tony's arm was pushed up under the blanket and over Becky. I suspected he was feigning sleep – his mouth was open and he was snoring. Dying for a pee and a drink I lay back down, wondering if I'd held Hermione at all. She was close to me and sleepily opened her eyes as I peered in. I could see myself in her eyes and wondered if she could see herself in mine. She frowned as if trying to recognise me and something hurt.

"Hi," I whispered, conscious of my awful breath.

"Hello."

"Thanks for letting us stay."

Something changed in her eyes and she relaxed.

"Any time."

"Stig's a monster, isn't he? How do you know him?"

"I don't. Becky met him at Glastonbury. I said he was a tosser. He scares Daithi."

"Your boyfriend?"

Damned alarm in my voice. Hermione smiled. "No. Me little brother."

Scared by the sensation of relief that flooded through me, I changed the subject.

"He burnt the bus out, didn't he? Aren't you worried he'll come back? I mean – when we're gone?"

Hermione smiled at something private. "Not particularly. Anyway, I heard he nicked your mate's coach ticket back to Yorkshire."

Tony leapt to his feet and rushed to the window. I knew it – he'd been listening all along.

"Oh, shit! How am I going to get home? Me Mum'll kill me!"

Tony rushed out of the room, slamming the door. I smiled at Hermione; she smiled back. I shivered and without a word she gave me one of her dirty old t-shirts, which I put on; my protector, my guiding light in this great darkness. Then she rolled over and hugged Becky for warmth.

My head pounded louder than ever and I felt sick. I was dying for a piss, starving hungry, and my mouth was so dry it was impossible to swallow. I was also broke, stranded and in love, so like a faithful dog I lay down on the floor beneath Hermione's side of the bed and went back to sleep. For the first time in months sleep didn't terrify me; nor did waking.

1986

Strobes knifed through dry ice; the raw powder made the beats faster, people prettier, colours brighter. White lines from my nose down over my lips, an electric walrus, poisonous booze trumped by dope and acid, speed and coke, filling my abhorrent vacuum with joy, energy, lust for life. I'd never heard music like it, a hard bass like hardcore punk but expressing love instead of rage, snatching all the vicious memories from my mind and grinding them under iron heels as my trainers twisted and I danced on wings of air.

- Empty pockets –

Shaking my head clean I passed the nasal spray to a black girl in a white dress who hugged me close, her full lips in my ear, laughing, her breasts full and hanging like water balloons, nipples like plums against my chest; then I was hugging everyone on the dance floor and the gaudy painted cars hanging from the ceiling suddenly made sense, the roller-coaster whooshing round the warehouse walls vital, and the music didn't just change everything; it was everything.

- Empty stomach –

I pulled out the tiny bottle of poppers and took another shot; the rush with the drug cocktail was almost too much for this world, enough to make me want to step off onto another place, off a 73 Routemaster onto a speeding street. My body filled the space and the smoke, and sweat poured off me like nitrogen. Another rush of amyl, another, and then the heavy-breasted girl was looking concerned and took the bottle off me. She pointed to my head and mouthed something I couldn't understand, so I shrugged and grinned happily, no bones of contention in my body. Time stood still and I danced.

- Empty heart -

Sweating cobs, feeling my headskin again, my throat-bone hammered by the bass drum, time got its breath and I plummeted to earth in the metal cube used for a toilet, and suddenly I didn't feel so good. The rollercoaster had carried me over pinnacles and down the other side; there was fever in my bones and repellent magnets chased metal filings round my veins. My lungs were scorched and lacerated, criss-crossed by hot knives, and my eyes ached from the smoke, fatigue and the sweat eyebrows were meant to cover. Calf-cramps attacked like robot rats and so in a toilet cubicle I pulled myself into a ball, moaning with pain, praying for someone to carry me home.

When the worst of the cramps had passed, I left the cubical cubicle and went to a wash-basin, twisting a tap. Stale air. I cursed. The organisers turned off the water to make you pay for the bottled stuff. They also charged a fiver to throw your coat behind a skip, to get you hot and thirsty with dancing. So much for unity; so much for love. And so much for the strobic girl – she left with some hoodies with razor eyes.

There were lines of ugliness like a gecko's sockets around my cracked eyeballs. Steam seeped from atop my head, ghostly wraiths of smoke weaving from my pores like spirits escaping, like being dispossessed. My nostrils stung from the talc in the nasal spray. When I inspected this stranger more closely in the cracked mirror, I saw there was a bump on the dome of my head where the vein stood out throbbing. Thank you, wherever you are, the lady in white.

Time to limp home, as soon as I could remember where I was, where home was. My coat was tied round my waist and drenched with stale sweat but I put it on. Pulling my baseball cap down over my eyes, I walked back through the cavernous room where the hardcore shook like crazies, and coarse paintings violated the walls, ragged banners proclaimed 'Mutoid Waste'. I felt wasted, dead, fucked up, burnt, legs like plasticine, like Morph; reminding myself to take heart I wobbled down some stairs, carefully stepping between all the rubble and couples.

As I exited the warehouse, a chill wind caught me in its fingers; it pushed and pulled me down a shattered road. Dawn's merciless light shone on a barren landscape of dead factories and smashed flats, and I was bullied along a cobbled street beneath empty buildings, no idea of where on the earth I was. Then my memory flooded back, like a dam laboriously built and recently breached.

I'd met Tony off the Brighton train and gone on an after-midnighter at the Bell in King's Cross Road. I then recalled that wasn't last night but the night before. We'd got into a fight with some Bemerton boys at a Scala all-nighter and at some point collapsed in the bushes in the middle of Highbury Corner roundabout.

We'd woken crawling with slugs and the shakes, and Tony had gone back to uni to sleep so I'd headed for the dawn chorus offie, drank Tennants till The Cock opened, drank on borrowed money till they closed at three, then met Pedo Pete in the Café Club on Upper Street for some speed to help me through.

Pedo Pete had mentioned the warehouse party which was, I then realised, somewhere between Camden and King's Cross. And here I was, running on empty, no food for thirty-six hours, ears ringing with acid rock noise like a Brighton seashell, t-shirt drenched, jeans ripped and clinging, feet sore. Insanely I threw my only coat into a skip and stiff Chernobyl breezes pecked at me like goose bites.

Finally, a road sign: King's Cross Road, the *'Cross'* removed by vampires. It wasn't far to Villiers, but I couldn't make it without sustenance so I patted my pockets and pulled out loads of change. My heart lifted until I saw all the cash machine receipts and more spectral memories came back, of demonic letters and monstrous phone calls, and losing a torturous labouring job, and not existing for angelic Hermione; all the things which the binge had purged were resurrected like zombies, snapping at my bleeding heels.

The wind blew me into a familiar shop where I bought a can of Tennants Super. Because of the unseemly hour, I was instructed by the one-legged Sri Lankan to put it under my coat, like I was still a Millmoor scamp. Outside in the alley I clicked, swallowed and gasped, doubling over as the cold hit my empty stomach. Sweat stung my eyes so I sat in a doorway and took some deep breaths.

Since Tony and Becky had gone to college, something more terrible even than loneliness nagged: ambition. Not that I had anything particular in mind, but something told me it was time for a change. Before heading off to uni, Tony had warned that I'd end up pensionless, living on some vast trailer park selling drugs to kids; sometimes that seemed relatively tempting.

The road to Villiers stretched out like rubber, and my rubber legs wanted to stop, but the wind pushed and pulled, harried and howled, and a sane inner voice told me if I stopped now, here, I'd never get there, or anywhere.

The patch of land in the square formed by Villiers and Geasey Street was covered by scorched earth and glass, and the two rows of houses looked about to collapse – but there was nowhere else to go. That same inner voice told me there was only one reason I went there at all; I slapped it down.

Pushing the door of number six, in that special way, quietly jumped it off its latch. The lights had gone out so I stumbled over rubble to the kitchen, where cold wind leaked through the broken window, sucking out the smell of dog food and over-cultured milk. Once I'd been cooking something vegetarian and the Parmesan wouldn't come out of its plastic tub quickly enough, so I'd looked inside to find it full of writhing maggots.

Crawling upstairs, clumping (as Hermione said) like on a pogo stick with a Doc Marten on the end, splinters from bare wood shredding my damp jeans, into a wrecked bathroom where I groped for the seat, I pulled down my trousers and sat for a wee as it was safer than standing. I read the sign I'd nicked off the building site: '*Danger! Spraying In Progress*'.

Being alternative, the house didn't believe in the established order of things so, as in a billion similar squats citywide, the living room was at the top of the building, the bookshelves were on sideways and there was no TV. Like some yokel after a bailing accident, I dragged myself up another floor, my designated bedroom stinking of tenements and tenants, spunk and smoke. For some reason Pedo Pete was in my bed and for some other reason he had company. Very reassuringly, an adult – never asked about the nickname. On up the bare stairs, rough wood on my hands, and into the front room where the sofa had transformed itself into a four-poster bed with silk sheets on, which I collapsed into in the nick of time.

It wasn't supposed to be like this. It was supposed to be me and streetwise Hermione in a mixed doubles v swotty Tony and snobby Becky, but fates and governments had somehow conspired against us. Since moving into the squat, the bonfire of passion (involving the hormones of four lonesome teens) had somehow failed to ignite; bashfulness, drink, work, and other pressing issues like who was cooking the veggie ratatouille, who was bricking up the smashed window, who was looking after Daithi, seemed to take precedence.

Then Becky and Tony started at Sussex, and Hermione and

I found ourselves living together for much of the time like a married couple, uxorious and yet chaste. Daithi was a great kid but took up a lot of Hermione's time and most of her giro. Sometimes I wondered aloud why her mum back in Dublin couldn't help out a bit, to which Herm never responded.

On Tony's 19th birthday something had happened; or rather, something didn't. There was a party at the squat (or what was left of it – most of it had been gutted in the fire). Tony and Hermione had fallen out about something – vegetarianism perhaps, or the IRA – and Tony stormed off. Snatching up my present I knocked on the forehead of James Connolly painted on Herm's door.

"Fuck off and die!"

"It's me. Joe."

"Ditto. Same sentiment."

With some trepidation I pushed opened the door. Hermione was lying face down on her bed in a green velvet dress that shone under the subdued lights. She looked up into my eyes and I cursed my luck, my looks.

Hermione O'Hare is the most beautiful woman I have ever met. She always cut her black hair short, pixie-like – Audrey Hepburn, except her huge eyes are light blue, and flash with emotion at the least provocation. Her face was always milky pale, unless enraged – as she often seemed to be in my company.

Herm was a little confused about politics. Coming from Irish stock on both sides she was a Republican in the American sense, hating the dole and people who signed on, and people who moaned – people like me. She listened to black records, which for some reason I found frightening, and when she wasn't working or taking care of Daithi she danced.

Often Herm accentuated her cheeky gamine look with little hats and berets, which drove me quite crazy with lust, but at that time had taken to wearing leggings and monkey boots which didn't entirely suit her, so it pleased me to see her in a dress.

Luther Vandross emanated from the stereo. I felt sick with jealousy, to be in her ears. Wiping her eyes Herm sat up; gingerly I sat beside her, holding my coat over my frantic bulge.

"I brought someone to see you."

"If it's Tony – tell him to kill himself."

Reaching inside my coat I produced a ginger kitten, black eyes wide and pin-mouth bleating. It sat on Hermione's lap, where it kneaded her bare legs, pleased with itself. Despite herself, Hermione stroked the cat, which melted beneath her touch like syrup. I wasn't fooled; feeding time at the squat was irregular, but there were plenty of rats to torture and kill. Becky, who hated cats, called them carpet sharks. Hermione looked at me in astonishment, her eyes shining and her lips natural pink.

"Where did you *get* this thing?"

"Next door. Someone told me the cat at number eight had had a litter."

Hermione looked at the scratches on my hands. "Hmm. You sure it's weaned?"

"Weaned? What do you mean?"

The kitten hopped off the bed and sniffed the floor so I picked it up and held it out. Hermione took the kitten, held it to her chest and bowed her head.

"Thanks. What's it called?"

I hadn't got that far, but inspiration struck.

"I know, let's call it Stig."

Hermione smiled and kissed the kitten's furry head.

"Stig it is. May your days be sleepy and your nights full of carnage."

Apart from the night we'd met, this was my first time within the sanctity of Hermione's bedroom and as I looked round the room at the newly-stuck Marxist posters, Bobby Sands poems, feminist tomes and ethnic weaves, I felt old; it was all the same. It struck me again that we were both on her bed. Springy, two mattresses, an empty sandwich.

I went to stroke Stig, but Stig wasn't there and so instead I touched Hermione's leg beneath shimmering satin, hot and bare. Her eyes flashed like she hated me, then she hiccupped. I leaned forward, her lips, Bailey's on her tongue. Her arms began to encircle me, to close me in. Then Tony's voice from below, "Come quick! The space shuttle's exploded! It's on telly!"

Fate, Herm called it – fatal fate. Not meant to be. So instead of making each other happy for once we went to watch endless re-runs of the spaceship and seven dreaming explorers split into atoms on their way to the stars, strange little smoke-tendrils sprouting off in all directions like diverging aspects of love.

In this dream Stig was *Baba-Yaga*; his head filled the caravan, which chased me on horse's legs through a Siberian forest. It was late afternoon when I awoke, sweating and shaking, intestines like knotted sea-ropes, heart metronomic. Hermione was sitting in the big old armchair opposite the sofa watching me warily, a dirty pink dressing gown over her man's pyjamas, her feet skinny and white, smoking a fag, glittery eyes wincing with the smoke; beneath her short black bob her eyes were a tumult of scorn, doubt or fear.

There was an enormous blanket over me, which I fought to escape; as I pulled myself upright torrents of sweat poured down over my sheepish face, which I wiped with a dirty hand. My headache came into its own now, solid and throbbing like a heart, and my eyes were as clammed up as my throat.

Hermione spoke. "You're back then."

"It... looks like it."

"For now."

For some reason I didn't understand, I felt ashamed. To avoid her eyes I closed mine in a futile bid to escape, only for her voice to drift through my ears and get to work on my tender brain.

"What the fuck are you doing Joe?"

"What... do you mean?"

"I'm just sick of it! Dossing here, out of your brains on drugs, just because you've nowhere else to go. And me looking after a little boy! Do you know how scary it is for him when you're off your face and talking crap? Why don't you get a job and sort your life out? You aren't a kid any more; we all have to get by – do you think I enjoy cleaning posh houses to get through night school? Think I love the fact I've been lumbered with a kid who isn't even mine for the next ten years? I manage. Why the fuck can't you?"

I hid my sodden face in my hands but her voice was right inside me. The lump in my throat wasn't just thirst, but realisation. Quite apart from the fact I'd started signing on in Tony's name, I'd given up my room and let Pedo Pete have it for a few grams of speed. I'd never been able to fight back when in the wrong, and this was no exception. I felt like curling up into a ball, letting her kick the fuck out of me; anything was preferable to this bruising.

This was the downside of sharing a house with someone who you loved and who hated you with an equal passion. Uninvited, a vision materialised like a hologram on the rug: joking to Tony down the pub about how I didn't have to pay rent, just paid in kind.

"I'm sorry," I muttered, softly, after some indeterminate time. It had been quiet for a long time and I wondered if I'd dropped off, was in fact talking to myself; but Herm's voice drifted across from the chair.

"What for?"

"Everything."

"It's got nothing to do with me. If you want to fuck up your life, that's up to you. But don't come crawling back here to recover. I'm not a charity worker. I'm busy."

To my relief I heard her leave the room and, ignoring feeble internal requests for a piss, a drink and something to eat, I slept. When I awoke it was almost night and Stig was asleep on my back, purring. Apparently they think you're their Dad, the boss man. The room was in semi-darkness but I knew she was there. My insides ached; two days without food, stomach as shrivelled as a nut.

"Herm?"

"What."

"Have you been sitting here all this time?"

A muffled noise, then she cleared her throat. "No." Like a child accused.

"What time is it?"

"Time to get up. Here."

Something cold was passed into my palm.

"What is it?"

"Stella, what else?"

"Thanks."

Herm said nothing; I realised she was trying to save my life. I stood and left the room without looking in her direction, close to collapse, the can of beer in my hand. After pissing brown steam I clicked open the can under the cover of the flushing toilet and drank long and hard, then scooped warm water over my face. There was something wrong with London plumbing, the water never got cold. Tony called it flats' water (he still rhymed 'water' with 'batter') even though he'd never lived in a flat. That font of all knowledge, Becky, spouted received wisdoms: that the water in London has passed through the human body seven times. As I always asked her, but then where does it go?

By the time I returned to the front room it was flooded with night. I was starving, and thought about asking Herm to go and rattle some pans, but it didn't seem wise in the circumstances. For the first time it dawned on me Daithi was absent; this depressed me. Not that he was absent, but that I hadn't noticed.

When I sat on the sofa, the unusual silence of the squat took over. Since the conflagration it had been much quieter; I liked it.

"I was born in Dublin," said Hermione, "an only child, unusual there – complications at birth. The other kids teased me, but Mum and Dad loved me, so did Uncle Sean. We used to sit in the back room of the house, just off the North Circular, and they'd take it in turns to tell me stories, not from a book but from their heads, memories, who cares. Not that they couldn't read; Sean had a play on once. But they were poor, worked with their hands, and happy. There's no snobbery about that over there. Never used to be, a bricklayer was as good as a doctor only better.

"I loved my Dad. His stories always seemed the best, they made me laugh, and cry, and he could sing a song or two, especially with the drink. I'd sing too, do a little turn for the neighbours, they even recorded me on a tape. That was the fortnight before he died. Sean got him a job in the factory where he worked. The old bastard who owned the place never bothered with health and safety, just bribed the inspectors.

"One day a rusty gangplank gave way and Dad fell into a vat of molten steel. Sean saw him screaming and put his boot on him, pushed his head under. They came running to the door and Mum screamed; I cried. The problem was he'd had a pint at lunchtime, so we never got comp – all I got was me Dad's watch.

"Sean stopped drinking after that day, took the pledge, never even drank at the wake. He'd sit in the bar, not sure what else to do with his life, knocking back pints of orange in a go. He never married, too many years of the grog. I lost my hearing, some stupid infection, and never heard my own voice for another few years. I bet you're thinking I make up for it now. Anyway we came here, Mum had Daithi, then went home, and here I am."

There was another long silence as I tried to interpret her words; I couldn't.

"You said there was a tape."

"What?"

"A recording. Of you singing."

"Yes."

"Do you still have it?"

Herm went quiet. I sucked my beer and listened to the rain and the wind on the glass. Branches from the old tree scratched on the panes like beggars, memories of the caravan. Julie: the only woman I had ever fucked. It got lonely sometimes, lying alone.

"Course I do, but I'm not playing it."

"Why not?"

"It's too much, Dad's voice and stuff. Too personal."

"Do you ever listen to it?"

"Sometimes. But no-one else. Not since Dad died."

"Please play it for me Hermione."

"*Why?*"

"I don't know."

She left the room. I finished my can and was debating a trip to the offie, but that would mean borrowing money from Herm – probably not a good idea. She then came back and turned on the small lamp by the stereo. The light hurt, but as I squinted at her face I saw she'd been crying. She looked defiantly at me as she turned on the tape, switched off the lamp, sat beside me and we were in another world.

There was the sound of laughter, of Irish voices. Someone

was singing something bawdy, and was shushed by a woman with a soft voice. "Go on Hermione," said one of the men, "Sing us a song." "What shall I sing?" piped a little girl with a Dublin accent. "Your favourite, whatever ye want."

The girl began to sing, the sweetest sound I'd ever heard; strands of a beach in Clare, rain, vivid memories fading. The song ended; the mood remained. The men were silent, and so was I. I couldn't speak. There was nothing else to say. I pulled off my hat and sat in silence.

"Joe?" said Herm, a long time later. I still didn't trust my voice. "Joe? You gone to sleep?"

"No."

"Are you alright?"

I didn't answer and she came closer, inches away on the sofa. I struggled to fight back the tears and took some deep breaths.

"Didn't you like my song then?"

Then I began to cry and she joined in; her arms were around me and we were holding on hard. Her warmth shivered through her furry gown and I could smell her warm close skin. My eyes closed and I couldn't move; we were motionless as our hearts danced. We held each other for a long time in silence.

Cars passed, laughing voices from the pub, cats yowled in the night. The moon through the dirty old window skimmed by, sending shadows dancing round the room. An ill wind was blowing in from the Ukraine. I could feel her shaking and knew that tears were being squeezed from beneath her warm soft lids, and there was even a chance that some of them were for me. She smelled of the moon.

"We can't," she whispered in my ear.

"Yes – we can."

"We *can't*, Joe."

"Why not?"

"There's... someone else."

My heart stopped a moment; I was positive that afterwards it would never beat quite the same again; drained of colour, of energy, just a metronomic footstep to the grave.

"Tony."

"No – I mean – not yet, fuck I don't know… I think I love him, Joe. I'm not sure. I need to find out."

I closed my eyes. Water escaped through the lids.

"Why Tony? Of all the people in the fucking world, why Tony?"

"I don't know I don't know I don't know… because he isn't you? Because he's kind and clever and makes me laugh?"

"Because he's posh."

"Don't, Joe."

"Sorry. I don't know, Hermione. I don't know anything. Do you?"

"We'll find out."

Warming to the theme, quick to make amends for what she hadn't done.

"And get hurt," I suggested, to help her out, to make her feel that guilt she needed, to make her feel responsible for her non-actions.

"Probably. Because that's what happens, Joe."

"Don't I know it," I whispered softly, throat hurting. Hermione stood up and straightened her dressing gown. A glimpse of unbuttoned pyjama as if signalling her uncertainties. Ejecting the tape she leaned down and kissed me on the cheek; even now, her soft lips burn.

"I'll tell you what: if we're both single when we're forty, we'll get married."

I felt unable to respond to such cruelties, such cowardice. Hermione left the room, and left me behind; readjusting, negotiating solutions, making wild resolutions, determined to prove her wrong, and yet taking fresh account of time's harsh limit.

1987

The morning after the hurricane I wandered across London, photographing the carnage and enjoying the way my adopted city licked its wounds. The more I wandered, the more I wondered: why, how, who?

Then I took the train to Brighton, occasionally pointing my new camera to the window to record the storm damage, trying to capture each moment like a mosquito in onyx, or maybe seal it in amber. The train's motion played tricks, looking out at the shattered trees and torn-up fields as if each moment was frozen, then a sickening lurch as time caught up.

At the side of the track beyond Wivelsfield some youths waved, not in the approved Agutter fashion, then threw bricks and ran: *The Railway Children Part II*. I wondered when it had all changed, when children became youths, stopped waving hankies and started waving fingers, piling sleepers on rusting tracks.

As the train pulled into Brighton I looked through my viewfinder for the sea but all that I could see were houses and flats, barely visible through the raindots and dirty streaks. Odd how I could see my own reflection and yet, with a mental readjustment, see the world outside in the same physical space.

Upon disembarking I felt my legs march me to the barrier like a press-ganged pirate. Becky waited, motionless. She was wrapped in a long coat and scarf, blonde hair wild from the elements, autumn brown eyes shining with excitement; as tall as me, great hips, and an intoxicated smile. Despite her brazen promises neither Tony nor Hermione were there. A part of me wanted to turn round and get back on the train, but then Becky waved and I waved back; I was stranded. Up high in the girders, the one long hand of the station clock spun out of control.

"So," I said, imagining cheap student pubs, "what do you want to do?"

"I know – the pictures!" said Becky, excitedly. Inwardly, I cursed.

Mickey Rourke in *Rumblefish* was probably my all-time hero, but with the exception of the sticky blood scene, *Angel Heart* was something of a disappointment. From the cinema we walked down to the sea, but it was darkening to an empty grey and wind chopped the water into hard fragments. Neither of us had much to say, so we turned right and walked out past The Grand, where I insisted on snapping her against this historic backdrop, and then the ruined west pier where starlings nested and swooped like a burst pillow. Becky pleaded with me to let her take my photo and begged me to take off my hat. I refused on both counts.

"I wish you would," said Becky softly, reproachingly. "I like it."

"What, my head?"

"All of you silly! Shall we stop for a drink?"

There was a low, concrete pub that looked inviting in the rain. We went to peek through the windows but it was closed for the afternoon, stools arse-up on tables like hands raised in surrender.

"Probably just as well," I told Becky as we walked on. "I don't drink in pubs with car parks."

"Whyever not?"

"I just don't."

Pub car parks are where bad things happen, where people get hurt. I didn't bother attempting to explain this to Becky, she'd only have laughed – what did she know? A typical student, naïve cynic. Still, she had other attributes.

Becky's beauty was a little more obvious than Herm's: she was taller, bustier, with long blonde hair down to her cleavage, usually on view in a summery dress or indie LBD. When she forgot to act prole I could imagine her cycling to church in a floppy hat and floral smock, her basket overflowing with flowers and apples. But when she was sulky, or epilepsy took hold, she withdrew into herself and couldn't be reached for days.

Becky's parents lived in the grandest of all the Hove squares, a great white Georgian bay.

"It might look nice," said Becky, reading my thoughts, "but it's freezing in winter. Daddy blames central heating for keeping the oiks lazy." Her accent had changed somewhere on the walk. In London she sounded almost local, *circa-*Circle line; now she spoke like the enemy, knowing it attracted me. I shrugged.

"He might have a point."

Becky laughed uncertainly and looked at me for reassurance, so I turned and looked at the ocean, crouching malevolently beyond the white fence.

She rankled. "It took two hours to get to school. I had to get up at six, winter and summer."

"I had a paper round," I lied.

Becky sighed and turned the key; the hall had the air of a cathedral. Portraits covered the walls and marched up the polished stairs, looking down in judgment like a Puritan courtroom. Becky flicked a heavy switch that made a solid click and led the way into the living room, where she drew the curtains. Who she was hiding from: monsters of the deep?

Pulling a bottle-shaped carrier bag from under my long black coat I held it up like an Olympic torch.

"Birthday present."

"Oh! Thanks."

Becky pulled the bottle from the bag: *Thunderbird*, which I'd nipped out to buy during the film. She laughed, but when I acted puzzled she stopped. I flopped into an enormous leather sofa and yawned, still drunk enough from cans on the train.

"Where *is* everybody anyway?"

"Mother's at her golf club. You'll meet her later. Daddy's on business as usual. We never know when he'll be home. He comes and goes. So to speak."

The wind was picking up again, some aftertaste of the storm howling along the seafront, but despite what she'd said the house felt warm. I stretched lazily, feeling at home. It helped that I didn't care. At least, not yet. Becky was looking at me intently, and oddly I began to feel nervous. The silence was awful so I rewound the conversation and pressed play.

"Don't you get on?"

"Mother's alright – a complete alcoholic, of course, but good for shoes. Dad's never around. As I said. Might I take your coat?"

I shrugged, stood and removed my coat. Unravelling the green silk scarf I had bought her, Becky unbuttoned her long dark Mac and I realised she was wearing a dress. It had been dark in the cinema and at the squat she mainly wore those damn dungarees. The dress was cut short, and I could see the dark film of nylon covering her legs. Her breasts seemed larger. I stiffened and adjusted my position. Becky seemed not to notice; she looked at me so seriously, so desperately, that I felt guilty. I noticed for the first time she had a strange white pigment in her left eye, like the end of telly used to be. But then, it had been her idea: she'd invited me to Brighton, to celebrate her birthday with all of her friends.

"Can I get you a drink?"

"Got any lager?"

"Afraid not. Daddy says it's for Geordie dockers."

I laughed. "I like him more and more. Whatever you're having."

Becky left the room and I stood, adjusted my straining cock and pulled the curtain aside like an actor with stage-fright. The horizon had disappeared, leaving only a brooding sense of the darkening mass of water. Lights bobbed out at sea, shingle sucked and dragged. I heard Becky's heels tut-tut closer, felt her bust press softly against my back.

"You soon get bored with it. You can tire of anything if you see it every day."

When I turned and looked at her she passed me a glass of orange liquid and sat on the sofa. I sat next to her, sipping orange heavy with vodka. You could tell it was a good sofa just by sitting on it: didn't creak, didn't fart. We clinked glasses. Only then did I notice her arms – blisters, scars and cuts like hieroglyphic screams. Becky followed my gaze with her eyes.

"I don't do it anymore. It's all about control, power over one's actions."

"That's funny. Seems like the opposite."

"We aren't so different. Remember that night the shuttle exploded? You put your fist through the window. You're not so clever."

"Maybe I was just asserting control."

"Ha ha."

Not so different, after all. Becky was a mess, a decontrol freak. Despite her family, or because of it. So different to Hermione, chalk and cheese. I could never remember which signified what. The ocean surged behind me, its weight, mass and drowning fish. I looked at her legs, contemplating the discomfort, the submission implied. Yet Becky didn't seem like she was submitting to anything, least of all me. Time to soften my tones.

"So how's college?"

"You're mocking me again. You always do that. It's the curse of the English, Joe: anti-intellectualism."

"Anti-inte-what?"

"Ha ha. You should study. I don't know why you don't. What *are* you doing, anyway?"

"Living on me wits. Which is why I'm completely skint." Thinking I was joking Becky conceded a smile.

"Why did you go to school in London? Aren't there any decent ones round here?"

"Of course. I attended a boarding school on the Downs for a couple of years."

"So, what changed?"

"Long story. Anyway I'm glad I went to London. That's where I met Hermione."

"And me, of course."

"Oh, yes."

Becky's punctuation and stresses sounded odd; you couldn't quite tell when she was being serious. I looked around at the silent statues, the motionless paintings and the well-made furniture, and suddenly felt a tremendous rush of gratitude for who I was, a blurred if selective memory comprising mainly of bus shelters, glue bags, and windows of ice.

"What does your Dad do? Must be something special."

"Who says he does anything? Maybe mother brings in the bacon."

"And does she?"

"No." Becky smiled relentingly. "He was in the air force for a long time – we moved around. Then – now, he's something in the City. We'd go up to town every day on the train together. He'd never say a word, just bury his head in his crossword. I'd look out of the window avoiding their stares."

"Who's?"

"The other commuters. Something about a young girl in a gymslip. Can't understand it myself."

Remembering my father's amazed beard I said nothing.

"It wasn't just the men," continued Becky, laughing with memories, curling her hair in her fingers. "The women were worse. There was this one, right, starchy type, bossy, overweight, forties or fifties, always in a white blouse and black bra – why *do* they do that? – anyway she started looking at me all the time. Down her nose, her *pince-nez*. I began sitting with my legs open so she could see the damp patch in my panties. Her boobs were enormous."

I shifted position, cleared my throat with drink.

"Were they?"

"One morning I was day-dreaming and when I looked up she was staring at me. I pulled up my socks to my knees and she went all pink. After a bit she went to the loo and I followed her. When she came out I asked if there was any loo roll left and she said, not much. She had a hankie I could use. So we both went in. I pulled down my knickers and sat down on the seat. She unbuttoned her blouse and unclasped her bra. Her nipples were the size of fucking toffee apples, huge and brown. I could hardly get them in my mouth."

Her big wet lips, small mouth. I shifted position again. Becky's arm was touching mine; if she put her hand on my crotch that would be that.

"I just sort of suckled on one – until she came. It was *so* horny. Maggie Thatcher was like my all time crush. But after that I never saw her again."

"And where was your Dad during all this?"

Becky looked startled.

"What?"

"Your father. Where was he?"

Becky became evasive.

"He – wasn't there that day. But most days Dad got off at Blackfriars and I went to King's Cross to meet Hermione. She only had to walk from the Cally. Lucky bitch."

"I don't know if that's a word I'd use."

"Hmm. Bitch, or lucky?"

"Either. Neither."

"You look cross, Joe. Your scalp crinkles when you're cross and you wipe your nose aggressively. Sometimes you make me feel nervous. Maybe that's why I like you. Shall I give you the tour?"

I followed her backside through the maid-scrubbed kitchen and up the stairs, all polished banisters and silent carpets. I had to resist an incredible urge to get on all fours and bite her cheeks like a child on Halloween bobbing for apples.

"This is my room," said Becky, nonchalant as an estate agent now, opening a door. The room was empty of effects. A tight-made bed, no posters, no underwear on the floor – not an inviting place for love. I spotted a small framed photo on the bedside table and picked it up: Becky and Hermione in a tent, covered in mud and laughing.

"That was at Glastonbury," said Becky, putting down her drink. "The Smiths had just finished and we were on acid. We met your friend Stig. He didn't take that though. I did, with a timer."

I put down the photo sadly; I could never compete, with Hermione or the Smiths. Spotting a sliding angle of albums I knelt and leafed through them like a fastidious monkey: the Velvets, Dusty Springfield, some of Herm's stuff.

"I wanted to be in a band as a kid," I said over my shoulder at Becky reclining on the bed, looking sadly down at me, "but it would have had to be like totally original, unlike anything you'd ever heard. I read a story in this magazine about this kid who they locked up on his own from birth so he never hears music, just so they can get him to write something completely new. And he invents his own fugues and crescendos, an original masterpiece that no-one will ever hear."

Her inscrutable wall of silence. Becky stood and beckoned. I followed her into the room of her sister. Pinks, frills, a hairbrush on the dresser. I picked up a framed photo of a church wedding and narrowed my eyes. An older version of Becky, but not so pretty; her laughing husband, a fool, disbelieving his luck. Someone was missing.

"Where are you?"

"I didn't go." Becky leaned against the door as if desperate to leave. "I hated her boyfriend. He's a policeman, CID. DI Lawson. Ever noticed how all cops seem to have false names? Armstrong, Shitell... watch the news. He was always trying to touch me up. Even when I was twelve, in the kitchen at Christmas. The others snoozing on brandy. He said he liked my tights, lifted my dress."

"So you refused to go?"

"Sort of." Becky smiled and sat on the bed, running fingers through her hair. I could hear the ocean beyond the transient walls. "I was fifteen but he'd got me this hideous little girl dress, all pink like a cake. Probably his jerk-off fantasy. I went into mother's dressing room to get ready and was brushing my hair. I had just straightened the ribbons and suddenly wondered what I was doing. I mean, I hated them. Both of them. *All* of them. There were some scissors so I just sort of chopped off my hair."

I watched great blonde fronds fall like sycamore over my eyes, wriggled my nylon-covered toes in the silken strands.

"You should have seen their faces. Mum tried to put me in one of her wigs but it was too dark, looked silly. So Dad said I couldn't go. Pity really, I was chief bridesmaid."

The chopping of hair: refer to clichés. Like she'd read it in a book. I gathered I was supposed to offer some sort of sympathy and I did feel some, but it was only the diluted brand you offer someone with a skiing injury.

Becky led the way into a larger, grander bedroom, a well-fingered Jackie Collins on the bedside table. "This is mother's room," said Becky. "The bed's bigger. Harder." Without any warning she fell forward onto the bed and flipped over onto her back, giving me a strange look. I sipped at my drink as she raised her knees then opened her legs. I glimpsed her stocking tops, white flesh, a smooth crack where her panties were supposed to be.

"Do you know what Herm's doing now?" smirked Becky, pulling her lips apart. "Sucking Tony's cock."

I shook my head, looking at her cunt.

"No."

"Yes. She said his semen tastes of Stella. Don't be jealous Joe, don't be silly. Come here, kiss my fingers."

She held them out like Cleopatra; feeling unwilling I went to her and took them in my hand, kissed them softly.

"They've touched Herm's. Touch my lips." Becky puckered; I kissed her on the mouth: vodka and blood. "They've tasted her. We're the same, you and me," said Becky matter-of-factly. "Outsiders, not sure what we want, not wanted by the ones we reach out to. Let's do it; a mutual appreciation society."

Carefully I placed my glass on the thick carpet, lay on the bed and stuck my head up her dress. She was shaved smooth; my tongue traced her lips to her clit. She tasted clean and rich and, even as my heart wept, her affluence aroused me. I stuck my tongue deep, kissed her thighs, and even then I knew it was right to lick her anus, slide a finger inside. Becky held my head close, pulled off my hat and caressed my skin as she grunted.

"Mm, lovely... like an egg..."

An exhausted metaphor; I hated her for it. Unawares, Becky pulled me up to her breast, so I unbuttoned her dress and flipped her tits over her bra. Her nipples were hard but she pulled my face to hers and pulling me down by the ears licked her juices from my head. Then she pushed me onto my back and unlaced my shoes, yanked off my ancient trainers and socks, and licked at my dirty feet; I was embarrassed, but she seemed to savour me. When she unbuttoned my trousers I reached out to touch her breasts but she slapped my hand away.

"Fingers off, dirty boy."

She pulled at my waistband and my boxers came off with a flourish: a magician with a tablecloth, china wobbled but nothing shattered. To my dismay Becky grabbed my cock like a microphone and sang a few lines from a musical. Feeling stupid, I looked up at the ceiling and wondered how to break the news to Hermione – in passing? In great detail? Did I have time to whip out the camera? What if she never spoke to Becky again? It didn't matter; she'd realise her feelings for me now.

Becky pulled off my t-shirt and now I felt more than naked because she was fully clothed; I tried to pull at her dress but irritatingly she slapped me again.

"Dirty boy!"

Throwing her knee over, without preamble, Becky slid down onto my cock and I grunted. She was tight and wet: we fitted. Maybe she was right: we *were* two misfits, joined at the hips. She started to move and as she leaned forward her huge breasts brushed my face and I took a nipple into my mouth. Her buttocks pressed into my thighs and the fastenings of her suspenders hurt my flesh. It didn't matter. I came deep inside her. Becky stifled a shout and leapt off, trailing her breasts over my still-spurting cock then taking me into her mouth, sucking me dry, until I could take no more and squealed with laughter.

Becky laughed too and stuck her fingers in my mouth. I could taste my own cold spunk and turned away, which made her laugh harder. She held me close, nuzzling in my ear, making excruciating baby talk. An ancient Chinese proverb came to mind: *two wounded birds help each other make nest.*

My vodka orange had spilled onto the white carpet, but Becky said it wouldn't matter; nothing mattered. Leaving the bed sticky and tousled we went downstairs and were in the vast kitchen, replete with gleaming instruments I'd never seen before and spices I couldn't name, me drinking vodka and Becky making cheese omelette, when her mother came home: a loud, vivid woman in her late forties, well-dressed and overweight, cleavage and pearls on show.

"Becky! Darling! And who's this? That boy you mentioned this morning? A boy-*friend*?"

"Kind of," smiled Becky.

"Well my God! Maybe I *will* get to buy a new hat after all. And what's his name, this boy-friend?"

I stood and held out my hand with a smile, introducing myself. Mrs Noyes shook my hand with mock decorum and giggled. I hadn't washed my hands, it didn't seem right, and so the hand she took had just fingered her daughter. I liked the idea; I liked her. Becky put a plate of omelette and fresh bread down before me and I started to eat. Surprisingly good, real parmesan melting through the egg. Mrs Noyes put a hand on Becky's lacerated arm.

"Becky darling, your taste is improving! But darling, would you run and get me a drink? I think I'd better grill this young man."

Becky raised her eyebrows at me and walked down the hall. Mrs Noyes' face changed to one of solemnity.

"Be good to her, dear. She hasn't had much luck recently."

She pronounced '*luck*' as if it were some magic powder. Maybe it was. I dropped my eyes, hoping to get the right balance of seriousness, reassurance and attraction.

"I will."

Satisfied, she winked. Becky came back with the bottle of vodka and a jug of juice. Things passed pleasantly enough for a half-hour, then the door opened and in walked a tall, respectable chap in a suit, with small glasses and a Bobby Charlton scrapeover.

"Meeting cancelled, bloody hurricane still causing chaos, and good job too... who's this in my house, your lover? *Miaah*!" His laugh sounded like an exploding cormorant. Again I shook hands. Warm, wet, too tight a grip.

"I'm a friend of Becky's."

"Yes yes, only teasing dear boy – my name is Theophilus, but my friends all call me Theo. You may call me Mr Noyes, what – *miaah*!"

I smiled politely.

"Thought me wife had got herself a toyboy, and not before time. Been nagging her for years to enjoy herself a bit, but she only has eyes for me, don't you darling?"

Mrs Noyes smiled unreadably. I sipped my drink, uncomfortable in case Theo could read my mind. He seemed to like my discomfiture and leaned forward with a smile.

"Never did have good taste in men, our Becky. Just women!"

"Dad!" said Becky, colouring. Her mother interceded.

"Oh really, Theo, you're making our guest blush."

"No, I'm not!" chortled Theo, "I'm making Becky blush! Don't you listen to me, old boy. No-one else does. Dunno why I come home, sometimes. A stranger in me own house. So young feller-me-lad, what's your game? What line you in?"

"I'm an artist," I said; the first time I'd ever said it.

Theo roared. "Another one! That bloody University, should be teaching engineering and training doctors, not a load of spongers lying around quoting Shelley!"

"You're right," I nodded seriously. Becky looked from me to her father nervously.

"Joe doesn't *go* to the University, Dad. I know him from London."

"Ah! A Cockney. Wait till I check me wallet." Reassured, Theo frowned over his glasses at me.

"Never have children, Joe. Never get married. It's the end, you know. Of everything."

"Don't worry," I smiled, "I won't."

I caught Becky's eye, then stopped smiling.

"I don't know why you don't like them," I said to Becky in the cab, "I thought they were really nice."

"You don't know what you're talking about," said Becky tightly.

"As you said about the view, see something every day and you get tired of it. To me they seem decent enough. Pissheads, but decent."

The cab turned in past the Pavilion; one of the onion-domes had been smashed in like an egg by a toddler. Becky hadn't wanted to sleep under her parents' roof, so we were going back to the University. I wasn't crazy about the idea; the Level had been levelled by the wind, and it still didn't feel safe to be out. Along the Lewes Road a whole line of telephone boxes had been skittled over and slumped at strange angles, glass everywhere. Tony was in London (inside her, inside Hermione), and Becky's parents had a ton of booze. I was stiff again, but hardly grateful. I thought I heard a stifled sob.

"Fucking hell, here we go. I only said your parents were

alright. Is that a hangable offence now?"

"It's not that – well, not just that. Did you mean what you said, about getting married and kids?"

"Why, you proposing?"

"F.O.A.D."

Something else she'd borrowed from Hermione. After crawling through the confused traffic the cab pulled up outside the university gates and Becky got out. I went to get out too, but she pushed me back and gave the driver a tenner.

"Drop him at the station."

"Oh for fuck's sake Becky, I've missed the last train!"

"I thought you were used to the cold?"

When I started to argue, to my astonishment she leaned back inside and kissed me on the lips; the same thick lips that had touched Hermione's.

"We'll be okay," said Becky. "Thank you for my present. I'll see you in London soon."

And with that, Becky slapped the roof and the cab started back towards town with me inside, seething with conflict and reflecting on the pragmatism of love.

Becky wasn't Hermione, but she would do, for now; she was a sentence in my life, not a life sentence. I might even grow to love her, and she me. Yet, as I justified it to myself, and the cab hiked up Trafalgar Street to the station, a nagging whisper in my head was telling me something else. Becky had once said she was an incurable romantic; I had a dreadful feeling, deep down, that I might carry a cure.

2007

According to received wisdoms we aren't supposed to find other people's dreams interesting. This has never been the case in my case – listening to Becky's public nakedness, Tony's *vagina dentura* variations gave me hours of laughter – but just in case you share this view I'll preface all my dreams with the words, 'in this dream'. That way we'll all know where we are.

In this dream I hear a baby crying and search through the woods pursued by *Baba-Yaga*. Finally I come across the infant lying naked in a clearing. Behind me *Baba-Yaga* crashes through the undergrowth and I run forward and look into this baby's face, except of course it's Becky, and she smiles coldly and dribbles blood.

I wake to find Alona taking my cock into her mouth, slowly licking my glans as she gently pinches my balls with her long fingers, her long rusting hair trailing across my stomach and thighs, taking it deep into her throat. Outside I hear that tiny plane buzz its message. I relax and prepare to let go but then she stops and slides upward over my body with that smug smile women seem to wear afterwards. She's wearing the slippery turquoise slip with the white lace fringe; straddling me she pulls me into her, surprisingly moist as if she's made preparations while I slept, although I know she hasn't because she believes it to be wrong. Once I'd bought her a vibrator and without speaking she threw it into the sea.

Holding my wrists apart Alona impales herself upon me, groaning like an old ship, my arms spread wide in a mock crucifixion. It came as a relief when I reached my 34th birthday because then I knew for sure I wasn't Jesus. Alona's eyes are closed and I know what she wants and I'm tempted to fake an orgasm, but we're sober and she'll go to the bathroom to inspect herself and find no semen.

You don't get to forty without learning a thing or two about women. Men can hold in their urine but can't pee at will; women can pee to order but can't hold it in. There are many other differences, though none spring to mind. Oh yes: some feel it when you ejaculate inside them; others can't. Alona's one of the latter.

"Wait," I whisper, remembering Tony next door. Maybe his hearing makes up for his piss-poor eyesight; maybe he can feel vibrations in the mountain as the earth moves by some infinitesimal degree. "Condom…"

"I don't believe," whispers Alona, sighing, eyes rolling.

"Nor me – I mean – wait Alona wait…"

A part of me wants to surrender, to give her the only thing she wants. A child she can love. So tempting it is just to lie here, feeling her breath on my neck, her nipples through thin satin, her little squeals of pleasure and hate. But if I surrender now I might as well jump out of the window to those rocks below, where the water splinters and sunlit spray makes rainbows, and the wind frolics with the St John's Wort clinging to the drop. So I lie back and think of England, and willingly wilt inside her.

Alona pretends this isn't happening, makes herself move faster, as if by her motion she can resuscitate my ardour, make me forget. But I can never forget; in the wintry blizzards of booze, in the summer pastures of love, working, sleeping or feeding the chickens I will never forget. Now Alona's slapping me ineffectually, sobbing with rage, and I roll her over and stand looking down, cock limp, pathetic yet victorious.

"Alona, you *know* I won't."

"Fuck you, you slob! You pussy! Who's on the settee – your boyfriend? Your ass-lover? Like I want you around?"

I stand there naked, my face in my hands.

"I told you when we met that I didn't want kids. My feelings don't change just because you suddenly like the idea."

"Feelings? What feelings? Your cock is dead." Alona starts rattling off in Spanish, too fast for me to understand. I feel embarrassed, sure Tony can hear every word; what if he speaks the lingo? But then, he's heard it all before – and more. Pulling on my dressing gown I walk over to the window and look out at the ocean. It's smooth enough; maybe I'll take Tony for a ride. Alona's still arguing but it's one-way traffic. I sigh and wipe sweat from my head with a towel.

"Alona – you know I love you. Always."

"No," says Alona, sadness personified; her moods change as quickly and impressively as the mountain air. "You have so much love, you are so full of love, and yet it's all for you, yourself."

"*Cojones.*"

"Yeah, empty ones."

Shrugging, I pull fresh boxers over the source of her woes. Unless I'm covered in come I never shower after sex (even half-sex) because I like the smell of her, and when masturbating later I'll still be able to taste her. Alona watches me from the bed with a sneer I don't like.

Once I explained that love is a war of interdependence: two flesh magnets covered in spikes, yin and yang, locked in an embrace for all eternity like matter and anti-matter. She wasn't exactly cheered by the news.

My hangover seems to be a creeper; there's only one

course of action I can contemplate. Before yesterday I hadn't drunk in the daytime for years: bad influences from Northern climes, the snowball effects.

"Who is he, anyway?"

"Who?" I pull a black t-shirt over my head, knowing it's too young for me but frankly stumped for alternatives.

"Your English *friend*."

She stresses the nouns and pronouns in three different ways, all negative.

"His name's Tony. We're old mates."

"You never mentioned him before."

"There are lots of things I don't mention." I lift my foot to the stool by the dressing table and tie the lace of my trainer. With a jolt I realise in four days' time I'll be officially too old for sports shoes. What the hell am I supposed to do then?

"Is it you are ashamed to like the boys?"

"Alona – don't." I tie my other lace, noticing the laces are grey and crusty with salt from the sea. Maybe I'll just go on wearing trainers; go the whole hog: tracksuit and bling.

"Nothing to me. So what if you fuck boys. You should have moved to Morocco not Mallorca."

I sigh patiently then smile serenely, knowing it winds her up. Alona kisses her teeth. I reach for my jacket and pat the pockets for keys.

"Where you going?" The first hints of conciliation in her voice; her rages are quick and hot, like her sex, like the food she cooks when she can be bothered; like her.

"I thought I might take Tony fishing."

Alona thinks about this slowly, examining the statement for weaknesses like a monkey with a brazil nut, and seems to conclude this isn't necessarily a bad thing.

"You could get some *chanquetes* from the market and tonight I cook?"

"I'll have to see – they're getting expensive. Miguel almost got caught last time he went out."

"That's Miguel's problem. You pay, he takes the risk, we eat."

I lean in to kiss her vivid lips; her eyes are wide, mesmerising.

"We'll see."

"And get the van cleaned," Alona calls after me. "You see what they write on the back?"

"I did see it – what does it mean?"

Alona pauses, then smiles. "'*I wish my wife was this filthy*'."

She laughs, so do I. Opening the door to the front room I stalk slowly to the sofa, hoping to leap on him, but Tony has gone. No note, no bags; if Alona hadn't mentioned him I'd believe last night (my whole life) was a dream.

When I open the front door I see something's missing and I freeze in the clearing, blinking stupidly. The Renault: Tony's taken it. Then I remember I have the keys in my pocket, and recall the stupid drive to the clifftop. Climbing to the lip of the hollow earth I find the van.

There's a great dark cloud over Mont Eterno; I drive into town and park under a tree's shade in the square. It's warm for January and I start to sweat. The hangover's spreading through me, taking control: doubts, anxiety, depression. I look at my old-fashioned watch, almost ten. Time for a drink.

Billys Bar is already open so I go in and order an English breakfast and coffee, congratulating myself on being so sensible. I have a pint while I wait. The gloomy, submarine light of the pub is filtered by irregular beams of sunlight: light-sabres dissecting melancholy spaces. My pint sits on the windowsill; the chipped glass refracts the fractured light, anemones of light exploding within its shallow depths. A twentieth empty. Shards of yellow air cut through gloomy fabrics like splintered glass; dust rises slowly, enchanted stardust spreading magic.

Sunshine and Love comes on the jukebox; the girl behind the bar starts to move in time. Even safari-suitless she's pretty, late-teens or early-twenties, small breasts beneath a Happy Mondays t-shirt. I do a quick calculation; she'd have been about eight when the song came out. At the oldest. She has dark hair tied back in a ponytail, shining full lips, and her eyes are as brown as Becky's; sometimes she emerges from the strangest of places. The girl smiles professionally.

"You don't look like a tourist." She has a strong Geordie accent.

"Why's that?"

"Too tanned."

"Maybe someone dark got between the sheets a few generations back."

"I like dark men."

I smile back and if I had eyebrows they'd be arching suggestively. It's rare, to flirt; the bars I frequent are served by old men in white aprons, or wizened belladonnas in print dresses. It's also hard to flirt in a foreign language: cadences lost, intonations wasted. I nod at her breasts.

"I saw them once you know." The girl looks puzzled. "The Happy Mondays. Top band."

"I don't really know their stuff," she admits.

"You should. The reason Shaun Ryder never got a Knighthood – do you want to know who they hate most, the English establishment? More than the 'Krauts', the 'Paddies' or the 'Frogs'? Their own working class. Take Shaun Ryder and Tim Henman. Shaun grew up on some backwoods' estate, started a band on the dole, wrote songs that brought pleasure to millions, and made a fortune for the nation. Henman grew up with a tennis court in his bedroom, complete with umpire and line judges, never won anything, and he's a 'national treasure'."

The Geordie girl smiles uncertainly and I feel daft. The

song finishes, a bell rings. Geordie goes to the hatch and brings over my breakfast, cooked in some windowless galley by slaves. What was that one Tony told me, how many women to change a lightbulb? *Let the bitch cook in the dark.* Misogyny, get thee behind me. I think about staying, flirting, then go to sit in a booth. After this morning's let-down – voluntary or not – I have no wish to make small talk as I munch on a large Cumberland.

In the next booth a middle-aged couple murmur cosily; I assume they're Brits and I'm surprised when I glimpse the upside-down calligraphy of their newspaper and see all the Scandinavian spots above vowels like bullets sprayed by a soft-hearted revolutionary over the heads of the old.

My booth has a small window that looks out onto the street, and I'm not too surprised when Tony emerges from a food shop with some carrier bags and waves. Pretending to read *El Pais* I munch toast. Then waving casually at the girl, who waves back a little too enthusiastically for my Marxist leanings, Tony slips onto the bench opposite, his beard irritating me more than ever. The distribution of hair: so unjust.

"Sorry I didn't leave a note. I looked in your fridge and there was fuck all in there, so I thought I'd stock up."

I look at the pile of bags Tony plonks on the table. "You staying till Easter?"

"The state it's in upstairs, who knows? Anyway, you needn't worry – I can get a room in town."

I'm about to say there's no need, then remember Alona.

"Unless you have plans," I tell him, wiping egg off my plate with the last of the bread, "I thought we might go fishing."

Tony smiles and strokes his beard. "I have no plans. At least – none that can't wait."

Something Tony said yesterday still bothers me: "didn't you used to be an artist?"

I don't think I ever stopped being one, it's just sometimes I wish I wasn't. Everyone else seems to want to be different; I always wanted to be normal, to fit in. Then Dad bought me the camera and I found it thrilling, capturing these empty moments, painting with light. I wasn't just trying to record the moment, I was trying to freeze time.

The thing is, I was no David Bailey; I was allergic to chemicals, dark rooms and patience, so I mainly used cheap 35mm. It was always about ideas, and accents, imagination rather than ability. I was no Nan Goldin, either; I liked her, but always got the impression she wanted to be in that world I wanted to leave behind for palaces and chandeliers.

Anyway I decided to call myself an artist, despite the opprobrium. For a few years I dined out (cheaply) on that haphazard label. I even began entertaining notions of being a good one, with exhibitions and celeb friends. All I needed to do was to create something truly shocking, something that would get me noticed.

I knew it was all over when I saw Rick Gibson's earring upon which dangled a tiny, dry, human foetus. That's when I stopped being an artist and became a snapper, a salesman.

Tony disapproves, I know, that I sold myself short; he liked me being wild and arty because he could never get over the fact he went to university, not to study history or literature, but advertising. That's like loading INXS onto one's iPod, or reading the *Quaedian* – relatively harmless, but a complete waste of time.

But then, that's all we're doing; we just kid ourselves that it matters more to read Dostoevsky than watch *Casualty*, to travel abroad rather than close your eyes and imagine new worlds. Like so many other misguided youths I wanted to do something timeless, something that mattered; I don't wanna be a wannabe. It wasn't about having something to say; it was about making a statement, presenting my raging ego like a fresh heart. All artists, architects – all of us womb-less ones, at least – are essentially saying the same thing:

Here I am.

"You never told me you had a boat!" exclaims Tony excitedly.

"You never asked."

"Looks expensive, too. Where'd a scumbag like you get the money for a boat like this? And a house – sorry, *cave* – in the hills?"

"Rich relative."

Tony laughs. "Yeah, right. Seriously – what do you actually *do* out here?"

"Bit of fishing, private trips for tourists."

"I thought you hated tourists. You said you never go in English bars."

"I *do* hate them, but that's where the money is. Someone's got to cash in on our post-industrial riches, might as well be me."

"Don't forget our glorious empire."

"It wasn't mine, Tony."

"So – you take tourists out fishing and it buys you a cave? They must pay well, these Brits."

"It's the pound, Tony. Goes a long way."

While Tony poses out on the deck in tiny shorts and a cut-off t-shirt I manoeuvre the boat out of the marina and along the inner wall of the ancient harbour that still reminds me of the last place I saw both Tony and Herm, that Cornish village. Tony ducks beneath the window for a bottle of beer, and I notice gleefully that he's finally receding.

The open sea's choppier than I'd expected, and I look again at the dark cloud over the mountain. Sometimes they sit there for days, as if impaled on the spike; other days they slide evilly down, ruining holidays and my wine budget.

On reaching the small bay in its horseshoe of cliff I turn off the engine and dive below, re-emerging with Tony's bags. I'm impressed; as well as a whole cooked lobster there are olives, local cheeses, and dark raw *chorizo*, plus three bottles of *Franja Roja*. Carefully I distribute the contents on the salty wooden deck.

"You should at least save the wine," says Tony half-heartedly, as if some better person is trying to climb out. "It's a sort of present for your wife."

"She's not my wife."

"Oh – I just assumed. Do you think you'll marry her one day?"

"I told her I have an allergy to precious metals."

Tony shrugs and I pass him the corkscrew; he opens the wine and pours the dark contents into two plastic cups. I rip open the lobster and taste its sweet meat. A bird launches itself off the cliffs above us and heads out to sea. We touch cups and drink. Tony winces.

"Jesus! Reminds me of that moonshine you and Stig used to brew."

"Don't knock it, Tony. It was good stuff."

Taking an army knife from my jacket pocket I cut some cheese: waxy, white, almost like Halloumi. The olives are bitter and unstoned. I spit mine into the ocean, wondering if a fish will eat them. In Australia a fisherman told me the crayfish were crazy for rabbit fur. How did that happen? Was there some fish down there with a penchant for Alona's Rabbit?

I speak. "You haven't said much about Millie."

Tony shrugs, looks out on the sea.

"What do you want to know?"

"I mean, were you at the birth? Is she like Hermione or you? Is she clever, at school, what?"

"I missed the birth," says Tony. "She came two days early. Hermione was working right up to the due date. I told her: give it up, take a rest, but you know Hermione."

I let that pass.

"Anyway, on May Day she was trying to get into the building down Threadneedle Street and all these fucking anti-whatever types start jostling her, giving her shit. So she slaps this Swampy type in the mush and goes inside, but the stress set her off. She dropped two hours later, in Bart's. My phone was flat so I missed it."

Tony squints unseeingly into the water as he chews on a lobster claw and looks for fish. The wind picks up and he shivers, rubs his arms. Not afraid for me to see him weak. Friendship. Tony's theory is nicked from *Childhood's End*: that we're all joined underwater.

"This thing *does* have life jackets, doesn't it?"

"One," I lie.

"Fuck mine."

Tony looks nervous; the swell's picking up and olives are rolling round the deck. Seeing his doubts I feel a vague pang.

"Only kidding – there are two."

"That's useful. One for you, one for a friend."

I let the word hang between us then dissolve into the sea air. The wind drops and I feel a wave of sunheat on my bare head. Tony stands again and peers out at the horizon, hand over his eyes like some model from an old Burtons' catalogue.

"How long would it take to get to Ibiza from here?"

"About eight hours, on a good day. Why?"

"Remember we were supposed to go there once? Maybe we should go now, you know. For old time's sake."

"Memory lane's a cul-de-sac."

"I read about this theory at college," says Tony, squatting again and slicing some cheese, "that all moments in time exist at the same moment; it's like a train track, except you can only move in one direction. But it's kind of comforting, isn't it? Knowing that even as we sit here eating cheese and talking crap, all those other moments are with us as well."

"Sounds like *Wallace and Gromit* – the wrong trousers. I've got a better one: 'History is a nightmare from which I am trying to awake'."

"Who said that?"

"Your wife said it once."

Tony swigs wine, staying calm.

"Why did you stay with Becky, Joe?"

"Because I loved her."

"But you loved – *love* – Hermione."

"No," I sigh, as if he's been twisting the corkscrew into me and releasing a pressure that's been building over decades. Tony shrugs, looks at the horizon and drinks some more, while I try to read his mind. Then I try *not* to – who knows what evils lurk therein. Draining my cup I toss it over the side; a gull swoops and pecks at it before flying away. Tony strokes his beard thoughtfully.

"So if you don't love Herm – why not marry Alona? She seems cool, you seem happy; what's the problem here? You scared of marriage, or something?"

"Of course I'm not scared of marriage. Don't you remember? I'm a widower."

Tony frowns, confused.

"A *what*?"

"You forgotten, Tony? Here, of all places? I was married to Becky."

"It wasn't a *real* wedding though, was it Joe?"

It doesn't seem like Tony's being deliberately provocative, but I still give him a harsh glare.

"Wasn't it?"

"It was a fucking charade. We were all loved up. None of

us really knew what we were doing."

"And we do now?"

"Maybe not."

"She's left you, hasn't she Tone?"

"Maybe I left her."

"Did you?"

"Kind of."

"Oh, fuck. Who was it? Anyone I know?"

"You tell me."

There's a storm gliding in from the sea; waves start to chop the boat and I get a fine spray in my face. The same surf in which I made love to Becky, and where even now my semen and her eggs wash against the coast like polluted foam. Tony gets sea sick, I now remember, so gnawing on the remnants of the ancient lobster I turn the boat back towards the harbour.

PART II: THE ARCHWAY AND THE ANGEL

1988

To my surprise I sold some hurricane pics to a news magazine and to my astonishment they asked for more. If the money wasn't quite good enough to give up signing on, it was enough to purchase a new camera. Herm went back to her flat in Amwell Street with Daithi and I was living with Becky at the squat.

Becky had left Sussex under a cloud but wouldn't divulge; and I didn't pry. When he wasn't at Sussex, Tony was staying with Herm most of the time and for a while I thought things might actually work out. After all, Becky and I had something very close to love, something better than love: need.

When Tony suggested celebrating his graduation from Sussex, we agreed to take a holiday together, the four of us plus Daithi, who was by now a fairly cherubic four-year-old with blond curls and freckled cheeks. We were supposed to be going to Ibiza to catch that wave but Tony got his airports mixed up. So it was as the ecstasy took a grip we found ourselves weaving round the narrow roads of Mallorca's downbeat twin Majorca.

At the hotel Herm and Tony went one way, Becky and I the other; despite the drug inside me I was sulking as Becky threw open the shutters.

"Oh my God," said Becky quietly.

"What?" I walked up behind her, dreading what I might find. We'd been deluged with horror stories ever since telling friends we were destined for Ibiza. As for Majorca, I had no idea what to expect as I'd thought it was in Portugal. But when I saw the view I went quiet.

The orange sun was heaving itself dripping from a motionless lake. There were black mountains far away over the water, enchanted shadows etched into the horizon, and a precarious fishing boat plop-plopped from right to left, its wake a bare scratch that gravity skimmed smooth. To our left palm trees and beach bars stretched from the beach to a small fishing port. The air was cool with a hint of hot days to come, and birds sang softly in the dense undergrowth of the steep slope to our right.

Becky was leaning on the balcony and I put my arm around her. She leaned her head on my shoulder and we watched the night slide away, souls mixing like honey. I kissed her gently, and she held on tight, stroking me, giggling. The early air was formidably bright, as if some other source of light apart from the weak old sun was infecting the sky. Three vapour trails bringing other dreamers bisected each other so that a triangle formed. There were two plastic chairs on the balcony and we sat drinking vodka and orange, kissing and whispering giggles. I remembered the camera and shot some pics till Becky superimposed herself upon me.

I knew I should sleep, but I didn't want to miss a moment of this. The air was heating up now, the sun had gained new confidence with height, and the colours of the mountains changed by the moment. I saw a silver sliver of road wind its way round a mountain like spidersilk and knew that it led somewhere good.

Leaning over I whispered in Becky's ear, "Marry me."

Becky's eyes widened and I was sure she'd refuse; then she burst out laughing.

"Yes, lets! When?"

"When would you like?"

"Now, Joe," said Becky with a sad smile, "right now."

We made silly plans, then, Becky's arms about me, I slept.

We were woken from tumultuous dreams by the sound of knocking on the glass. I grimaced as I opened my eyes; the sun was a demon of heat, I had a hammering headache and a bursting bladder and my scalp was throbbing sunburn warnings.

Becky was asleep, her funny little mouth open like a baby's, and Daithi was banging on the glass, grinning excitedly. I stood up, peeked over the balcony, and nearly threw up; it was a long way down to the car park. When I tried to slide open the door it wouldn't budge. Daithi pressed his bogey-stuffed nose against the glass.

"Daithi, open the door."

"I'm not touching it!" said Daithi.

"Very funny, let us in now."

"I'm not touching it!" repeated Daithi, grinning as he held up his innocent hands. I tugged on the door handle again impatiently, but the door wouldn't budge. Daithi stepped back a few yards, as if to prove his non-complicity in the matter. I wiped my roasting forehead with my hand and shook Becky awake: she groaned and squinted her eyes against the harsh light.

"Becky, we fell asleep. Daithi's got in to our room somehow, and locked us out. Wake up."

"Oh, Jesus – my *head*."

Impatiently I rattled the door again to make it change its mind. Daithi looked bored now and I beckoned him over.

"Daithi, where's the key? I'm cross now."

Daithi's lower lip protruded and his eyes watered.

"I haven't *done* nothing! Honest!"

"I know Daithi, very funny, just let us in and we'll forget all about it."

Daithi burst out crying.

"There wasn't a key! Wasn't me, I was asleep! It's your fault for going to sleep outside!"

Muttering under my breath I inspected the door more closely. In the glass I could see our bed, and my own eyes.

"Jesus. He's right, it isn't a key, some sort of latch thing."

"Well, get him to open it then."

Eyes blurring in the bright heat I attempted to turn the latch, without success. Becky was getting flustered and I started to laugh, so she turned on me with rosy cheeks.

"It's not fucking funny! I need to use the bathroom. What are we going to do?"

Shrugging I looked at the silver road, a tiny metal beetle sliding up it.

"Wait till Tony and Hermione wake up. They'll sort it."

"I can't wait that long! I'm busting!"

Again I turned to Daithi. "Daithi! Try it again! Otherwise we'll be stuck out here all week."

Daithi tried again, but the small metal knob needed stronger fingers. Throwing up his arms he retreated to the bed where he flopped face-first, crying. I sighed unwillingly; ecstasy escaped me.

Having Becky in a bad mood wasn't helping – I was dying for a piss myself. And a drink. Something was dawning on me, some new memory, but each time I reached out it slipped playfully away. Looking over the balcony I craned my neck to each side. On my right, there was nothing but steep earth and battered olive trees down to the coast road and up to the sky. On the left there was a narrow partition between our balcony and that of Tony and Hermione. I turned to Becky.

"I'm going round."

"You *are* fucking joking?"

"It's easy! It's only one step." I peeked over the edge again. "There's even a foothold," I added doubtfully.

"Joe, you are *not* going to kill yourself on the very first day!"

The connotations of her words made us pause, then laugh. I craned my neck round the partition, but could only hear Tony snoring. Becky hugged me goodbye as if I was off to the Harrods' sale and I threw a leg over the concrete wall. I remembered hanging off Stig's mum's Hughes Court balcony as a kid. I'd always been told you should never look down, so I did, for the hell of it. The car park was a huge drop, its white markings like alien warnings, inviolable hardness abstract as death. So easy to straighten my fingers and fly.

Shaking the urge I hopped over onto Hermione's balcony like a cheap Romeo in nylon shorts. Though the curtains were closed the door was ajar, letting in the breeze. I peeked through the waving curtains into the darkened room. Tony lay on his back, Herm between his legs, her tiny tight arse pointing at me. Seemingly unsurprised to see me Tony waved and smiled. I wasn't sure what to do so I watched as she sucked him. Tony started to point to her arse, raised his eyebrows and mouthed something. I looked again, her tiny behind, naked and pink. Tony looked like he was about to laugh but he was coming so I backed out onto the balcony and made some noise. When I re-entered they were asleep, a coy sheet over the two of them, Herm's mouth closed so not to spill Tony's seed.

By the evening we were slaughtered again. The beach bar we were in was packed with toasted yobs, and apparently Daithi wasn't happy, offering the occasional hint such as prolonged bouts of weeping, shouting, and falling on the floor. I knew how he felt; my scalp was sunburnt and tender as hell. The more drunk we became, the more Daithi's antics became amusing. The booze was cheap and the general mood so light that Tony was even allowed to make jokes about it all being 'Balearics'.

"I'm hungry," complained Daithi.

The restaurant was in a small cove away from the main drag, fishing boats within spitting distance of our quayside table. Yellow lights swayed merrily above the thatched canopy and a light wind eased away the last of the day's heat to make it fresh and clean for the morning.

Becky took my hand; for a second I'd been somewhere else. Closing my eyes I gently tasted her olive oil fingers, then kissed my way up her bare brown arm like a cartoon French skunk to her taramasalata mouth. Tony and Hermione stopped arguing about vegetarianism for a moment and whistled, and even Daithi went "woooh." We hadn't really shown our affections before; Herm looked wryly amused as she lit a fag.

"Leave it out!"

"Pass the bucket!"

A waiter brought Tony's lobster, sat on the plastic bottom of its bucket with a gloomy aspect, as was its right. Tony was winding Hermione up, smacking his lips and saying "*mmm!*", and Herm fell for it as usual. Becky looked offput and took another look at the menu.

"Maybe I'll go for the fish," she said faintly.

"Coward," replied Tony.

"No I'm not! I just don't know if I'd like lobster. It doesn't look like it's got much meat on its bones."

"Lobsters don't have bones," I reminded her, "they're crustaceans."

"I don't know where the hell you get these useless bits of information, Joe. Didn't you say you left school at fourteen?"

I looked uneasily at Tony, who smiled knowingly.

"Fourteen-ish."

"Following a torrid affair with your geography teacher."

Tony laughed. "Really, Joe? I didn't know you and Melville were so close."

"Oh fuck off," I said through gritted teeth. "Are we having this lobster or what?"

"Well, I am," said Tony, "Can't wait to sink me teeth into the bastard."

"Might be better if they cook it first," I suggested, "bit hard on the teeth old boy."

"Do you know how they cook it?" said Hermione, lighting a fag and looking witheringly from under her cap. Tony shrugged. Hermione told him. Tony seemed crestfallen.

"You're kidding."

He looked into the bucket where the lobster waited patiently, only its claws making any movement. "Poor little bastard. Fights all its life on the floor of the sea then we come along and boil it alive."

"That's life, I suppose," said Hermione. She looked at Daithi, who looked tearful again, and tried to change the subject. "Would you like chips, Daithi?"

He shrugged miserably; I swigged San Miguel, warm and flat; Tony looked green; Becky looked out to sea with that infuriating wan-ness; Hermione stubbed out her fag impatiently. "Well, I'm having calamari and salad, what're you all having?"

I looked round at the other tables, which were mostly empty. The three aproned waiters at the kitchen door smoked and joked. "Not many here, are there? Where's all the fucking waiters?"

"Language, Timothy," reproached Tony, looking at Daithi. He leaned over. "Know what we should do, Daithi?" Daithi shrugged. "We should liberate the lobster. Why don't we just chuck it back into the sea and run for it?" Daithi giggled.

Tony looked at me. "What do you say?" I smiled. He

looked at Hermione, who nodded seriously, and at Becky, who lit a fag and shrugged. She didn't believe him, even when he looked round for the waiters and picked up the bucket.

"Ready?" said Tony. I picked up Daithi, Herm grabbed his pushchair handles. Tony tipped the bucket into the sea and we ran, shouts behind us fading beneath our laughter.

We'd arranged to meet at dawn on a deserted beach beyond the last of the hotels. I sat in silence with Tony and smoked a spliff like a condemned man as we watched Becky and Herm carry Daithi across the pebbles like a mini pope. He was asleep, Becky's coat over his knees. Soon he'd wake and the madness would begin again. The ecstasy was wearing off and I felt cold and fatigued and bewilderingly alone. If this was the comedown, I'd stick to beer.

The sun scolded me from the horizon but Becky looked good in the long white sheet she wore as a dress, damp patches of sand at her breasts and bush, a local flower in her long hair. I was still in my luminous shorts and sweaty club t-shirt and felt over-dressed.

"Before we begin," said Tony, Master of Ceremonies, "I'd like to say a few words. Joe, you are my best friend; Becky, you are Hermione's. I love Hermione as Becky loves Joe. We all love Daithi and we all love life. So let us celebrate this union, and pray as one that England sack Bobby fucking Robson any day now. Cheers."

Tony raised his bottle of San Miguel and drank, then passed it round. The beer was warm and I wanted coke, but I smiled, a little replenished, ready for what might lie ahead. We let the now-awake Daithi take a pic of the four of us; I put my hand over my face, watching the sun and the way it greened the palm leaves. Then Tony slapped my back like a Great War Corporal sending someone over the top.

"It's time."

We stripped to our underwear in the liquescent light and made our way to the ocean's edge. An old lady on her way to a cleaning job watched from the edge of the beach, mop in hand like a centurion. Out we waded until the freezing water was waist deep, or in Daithi's case up to his shoulders.

Priestess Hermione spoke. "We have gathered here this morning as witnesses to the joining of Becky Noyes and Joe Noone in unholy matrimony. Let any fishes who object please break the surface." The waves lapped gently, but nothing emerged. "Becky, do you have words of love for Joe?"

Becky turned to me and she did look beautiful: her healthy skin and wet breasts, her love for the man she hoped I might become.

"I do."

"Speak."

Becky looked into my eyes and I tried not to laugh; hers narrowed warningly. "Joe, I need you more than I need my giro, and that's saying something. Never leave me, never hurt me, and if you stop loving me I'll cut off your balls."

Herm turned to me.

"Joe, do you have words of love for Becky?"

I looked fiercely into Hermione's eyes, where humour seemed to play ring-a-roses with some other emotions.

"I do."

"Speak."

Reluctantly I turned in the swirling water and looked at Becky, just about remembering the words I'd composed on a fag packet in the club.

"Becky, you are more beautiful than the first flower that bloomed. My love for you is purer than the silence that fills the star-lit cosmos. There is a star in the sky I named after you and it will always be yours."

That last part was true; it had cost me a week's wages for

the certificate. To their credit, nobody laughed.

"It is done," said Hermione, sprinkling icy water over us. "You are one. We shall leave you now, and the only witness to your love shall be the watching lobster. See you back on earth."

Her cold legs unsteady on the stones Herm waded ashore, followed by Tony with Daithi, who waved gaily. I looked after them, after Hermione, who was holding Tony's hand. A pang, a fleeting moment to reflect on the bizarre party we'd found. The three took their clothes and left the beach without looking back; the cleaning lady moved on and we were alone.

Becky shrugged off her sheet. We kissed softly and were rippling shadows in the water. Currents ushered us toward the shore. We lay in the hissing surf and made shivery love; stars exploded and moons fell apart, and I filled her with oceans and down came the sky.

1989

It seemed after returning from Majorca that we might make it, at least through the honeymoon period, those heady early days of living together when you brush your teeth at the same time and giggle. But with the slowdown in the country's fortunes the magazine stopped commissioning photographs, and were taking everything on spec. Becky said she could help me; her father was something in something and he could make me famous. But nothing happened.

Because Herm wanted Daithi to live in a place with a backyard, we swapped; Becky and I moved into Herm's old place off Amwell Street, a red brick square of five or six storeys that had been full of squatters and addicts until the ILEA brought in teachers and the place went downhill fast. Becky hated it even more than I did.

By now I was back on the sites, a camera in my jacket so I could tell myself it was all for research. As money ran tight, so did our lust. Somehow I'd trapped myself into living with a woman I wasn't certain I could love, walled myself in with Elizabeth Bathory.

Our passion was less about biology, or chemistry, than physics. We mixed like water and electricity. Becky couldn't cook and I couldn't clean but that didn't matter because we were usually pissed and the bed was the only place our war declared a ceasefire, a dirty great football pitch between the twin trenches of misunderstanding, the sheets flags of surrender.

Quite apart from her naïve views on politics, Becky had some odd ways about her. In the sack she often liked to pretend she was dead. I thought this was lazy, but didn't really care because I was all energy then, and when she 'corpsed' she allowed me to ejaculate onto her chilled marble face, onto her rosy cheeks and full red lips, and the fact she was dressed in a white sheet and was motionless really didn't matter.

The trouble was I hated condoms and she hated the pill, and she grew tired of wiping my seed from her face, and then one night in the Fountain she told me she was pregnant. I wasn't sure I was ready, whether we could make it work. And so we flushed the baby away. And, if all of our past ordeals had somehow brought us morbidly closer together, confirmation of a harsh-lit world, the abortion tore us slowly apart; we weren't just products of that world, but producers.

Two weeks later, a freezing November morning. I'd offered to work, despite the fact it was a Saturday, but I was already regretting it. I'd been on a bender with Tony and this hangover was exceptional. I was trying to eat breakfast and listening to Radio One (all my brain could cope with) when Becky emerged from the bedroom, an ancient dressing gown over her pyjamas. When I made her a cup of tea she pulled a face.

"What's up?"

"This tea, ugh!"

"What's wrong with the tea?"

"It's the wrong strength."

"What, it's too weak?"

"No…"

"Too strong?"

"Noooo…."

I sensed it was going to be one of those mornings.

Realising she was on shaky ground Becky made herself some acceptable tea and sat opposite, watching me across the vast plateau of a chipped blue Formica table.

"Will you be home tonight?"

A hard one, this, after ten hours hard graft: home with deathly Becky watching *Birds of a Feather* in silence, or another night down the pub?

"Dunno."

Becky splayed her fingers and dragged them through her messy hair.

"We don't seem to spend much time together now. You're always out with your friends."

This wasn't strictly true: I didn't *have* any friends. Apart from Tony, who had a better offer most nights.

I deviated. "You could go out yourself, you know. Why don't you see Herm?"

Becky spun the radio tuner away from my music. The kitchen, I now saw, was composed entirely of shades of grey.

"She's always with *him*."

"Anyway, I like a few pints after work. What's wrong with that? I work my arse off seven-days-a-week, come home and you're sitting in your dressing gown watching fucking *Neighbours*."

Becky glared at me as I dipped my toast in my tea, knowing she hated the habit. I wondered idly if there was such a word as anti-uxorious. She was always nagging me about my drinking, mainly because she preferred dope and I hated that whole Hobnobs-'n'-hotknives lifestyle; it always felt like a rainy Tuesday afternoon and you didn't have any milk. I'd never hidden my thirst, my love of pubs, but Becky's view was when I was working I drank far too much and when I wasn't working I drank twice that.

The flat was quiet and the only noise was Brian Hayes droning righteously on LBC as I slurped my tea, belching chilli sauce, Becky's eyes burning holes in my scalp. My clothes were damp and stiff with sawdust and my bones felt the same.

Becky got defensive. "Do you know what your problem is?"

"I didn't know I had one."

"You never learn, Joe. No matter what you do, where you are – you *never fucking learn*. You're like... the man with the child in his eyes."

"Goo-goo. Ga-ga."

"Don't take the piss Joe, I'm being serious."

"What do you want me to say? What's to learn? You work you get money, you don't you don't. End of."

"You *know* I'm looking for work. It's not easy without a degree."

"So why did you leave Sussex? You never wash up, never cook a meal, never do *anything*. We never have *sex* –"

"I had an abortion *two weeks* ago!" blazed Becky.

I shrugged, swallowing soggy bread. I didn't even like dunked toast, but I wasn't telling *her* that.

"Well, whose fault was that?"

Becky gave me the sort of look mediaeval midwives gave Siamese twins. I went to the hall for my coat and left the flat, slamming the door.

As a wall fell in Berlin and Europe celebrated, in England the wall was going up. As I walked through the City to work I saw young suits talking into digital bricks, and my superego felt a part of this gleaming new age; I was helping to build up its wealth, or at least carry the chipboard.

Mostly, I carried chips. I hated these suits with their mobiles and wine bars, and wished I was back in Majorca, back in bed, anywhere but here, in a corrugated shithouse behind a skip in the docklands, vomiting black water into black water.

When I'd finished bringing up my tea-dunked toast I slumped on the open hole, not caring if my trousers were dampened by the incendiary urine of others. Some wag had scrawled on the metal sheet door:

'The English are a strange race, they call the Irish paddies but little do they know the Irish are their daddies.'

Taking the disposable camera from my anorak pocket I took a snap, hawked soggy bread onto the poem by way of critique and groaned. From the next cubicle a Cockney chortled.

"Sounds like someone had a good night."

I hadn't, as it happened; the thrusting, affluent Eighties had somehow passed me by. I don't believe I ever saw a woman in shoulder-pads from 1980-89, and the only time I even saw a Filofax was when someone won one on *Blockbusters*.

Work on the site was tough, monotonous, but not exactly back-breaking. Mostly I was carrying slabs of damaged chipboard from the top floors to the skip, pondering waste and growth, taking hurried snaps when I got the chance.

It never occurred to me that I might have been warmer and safer working in an office. I'd left school with no qualifications, very little idea of what office work entailed, and some instinct told me I'd be better off using my hands so that my brain could otherwise engage. Despite the snobbery attached, unskilled manual work always paid more than unskilled clerical work. Plus there was overtime, and the laughter seemed more heartfelt. Besides, I liked working outside, the smells and the feel of wind and rain.

It was the danger, that's what made me such a UCATT firebrand – the randomness, the helplessness in the mouth of fate. Two weeks before, a bloke had been hit by a scaffolding pole that speared down from the heavens and through his helmeted head like a cocktail stick jabbing a grape. I'd glimpsed his quivering legs through the sawdusted crowd, the angry mutterings, the gaffers surreptitiously glancing at watches and shaking hard helmets.

Putting on my rented hard hat and picking up the piece of chipboard I carried everywhere I walked across half-finished foundations like a cowardly trapeze act. On each side pipes and men stuck out of the cement. A cold wind was blowing off the Thames but sweat pricked my scalp. The paddies admired my energy, if not my somewhat contrary views on The Troubles: I'd suggested building a dividing fence through every street in Belfast, *a la Steptoe and Son*, right down to the swimming pools and public toilets.

A gang of men were at the entrance to the stairs, talking in low voices. Seeing me pass panting, the gaffer, O'Neill, growled, "Clegg, you seen the darkie?"

Remembering who I wasn't, I turned and glared into O'Neill's unsmiling eyes, boss-eyed and lonely of aspect after thirty years shovelling shit on the sites and byways of my ungodly country. The 'darkie' was Radio, as in Rental, a mixed-race kid from Dagenham or Plaistow, wider than the shithouse I'd recently exited. I shrugged, shifting the heavy slab of chipboard on my shoulder, my fingers sore inside thick purple work-gloves.

"Not for a while."

The cover-up instinct; for all I knew, Radio was reclining in a deckchair on the top floor, cocktail in hand, Kim Basinger between his meaty legs. I hoped so – he attracted more than his fair share of jokes, usually variations on the theme of lights being inexplicably extinguished and, should this event occur, Radio's radiant smile still being visible.

O'Neill scowled.

"Well if you see him tell him he's in the shite. Now fuck that chip in the skip."

There was a certain poetry in the line, especially in O'Neill's Athlone accent, and I hoped I'd remember it later.

One of the men pointed upwards. "There he is Pat."

Radio hung off a scaffold high above us, roaring into the darkness. O'Neill shook his head, cursing.

"Jesus. You! Monkey boy! Get down here a minute will you?"

"What's the problem?" I asked O'Neill, shifting my chip from shoulder to shoulder. I hated the man, but chatting beat working.

"The crane's fucked and they need the mixer on the sixth in a hurry."

"So?"

O'Neill looked at me as if I'd asked him to go to the pictures.

"So it's seven fucking hundred quid to hire one for the day. *Durr*!"

His cronies laughed. Radio emerged from the darkened stairwell with a grin on his face; his teeth didn't appear luminous. Some of the men cheered ironically, but Radio wasn't big on irony and took a bow. O'Neill slapped him matily on the back.

"Gunga Dinn – want to earn a few extra quid?"

"Dunno boss."

"Right." O'Neill took off his hard hat and passed it round the men. "Every minute we're not working we're all losing money here. I'll put a tenner in and anyone who matches me gets two hours overtime."

Economically this seemed a non-starter; some of the men muttered but most stuck in their notes. I would have done the same, except I was brassic. Though as I was only the lowest form of labourer O'Neill ignored me and slapped Radio's meaty back.

"Now then son. The men on sixth need this mixer here. If you can get it upstairs you get everything in this hat."

Radio looked at the mixer and shrugged, then hugged it between his vast arms to weigh it up. He nodded; cupping his mouth O'Neill shouted up the stairwell, "Clear the way! Man coming through!"

With a roar Radio lifted the mixer above his head, ran at the stairs, and disappeared. I listened to him charging up through the building, men cheering him on; O'Neill laughed and pocketed the money.

"I'll give the bunny a twenty, should keep him in bananas. The rest's for the kitty."

As the lift was broken I walked upstairs, cursing. I'd gone up four flights before realising the chip in my hands was for the skip, and threw it behind some coils of wire. As I approached the sixth I heard terrible screams and left the stairwell, stepping carefully across the chess patchwork of metal plates and holes full of wire, like snake nests, where the floor would eventually go. Over the far side a group of men gathered around the upturned mixer. Radio was rolling round on the floor, whining, blood everywhere.

Behind the men, London soared: towers of light, spotlights as if from a film. Because there were no walls on the site, just layer upon layer of floor, when the men parted to let me through Radio seemed to float on a cloud of lights. Recognising one of the sparkies I tapped his shoulder.

"What happened?"

"Jesus Christ." The bloke, a decent old cockney in his fifties, shook his head. "Radio comes running across the floor with that thing on his head, trips over a brick and goes flying. The mixer went down a hole and took his hand off."

He nodded, and I looked again at what I'd thought was someone's glove on the floor next to Radio. He'd never work again. Whipping out the camera I took some shots of his bloody stump, the grey limp hand, the rock-faced men and London as the backdrop, monstrous, growing, oblivious.

Already I was planning how I'd present this misery for the delectation of others, a blow-up of his severed hand superimposed over the main image so that it resembled some sort of grey/white protest: stop. But there was no stopping, the buildings just kept rising. I heard O'Neill behind me.

"What happened here? What's with monkey boy?"

Someone explained and O'Neill frowned, looking at his watch. After a moment's thought he emptied his pocket, put the contents into Radio's and slapped his back.

"Here's a few quid son, I'll give you a lift to the hospital. Someone grab the hand. Maybe they can do something."

Nobody moved so O'Neill picked up the limp hand and put it in his hat. I took another photo and seeing the flash O'Neill glared at me.

"What the fuck you doing?"

"Just getting a few pics."

"What are you, health and fucking safety? Give me the fucking camera, son, or by Jesus I'll throw you off the roof."

I backed away until my back was against a pallet of breezeblocks, O'Neill in my face, eyes wild and askew. Radio was still howling; O'Neill was holding the hat in his left hand and he grabbed the camera with his right. Taking off my cap and liking the cold air on my scalp I nutted him spot on the nose, which split, causing O'Neill to drop the hat and my camera on the harsh floor. Radio's hand spilled out onto the floor; grabbing the camera, I ran.

Pulling the soggy woolly hat down over my head I stalked through the rain, wondering if there was any way O'Neill could find out where I lived. When I'd walked into the dodgy agency I'd given Tony's name as usual, so *that* would be alright; the only thing that would be.

As I walked from the City towards Old Street, relishing the freedom of a rainy dark afternoon, I saw a man trapped in a phonebox, banging on the glass. I've never been one for confined spaces; whenever I feel trapped, I lash out.

Once, Becky described her bouts of epilepsy as like being pulled backwards down a very long tunnel, like Friern Barnet corridor, with all the people at the other end seeming very far away. When my anger comes on like that I know what she means. For some immeasurable period of time I become quite untouchable; then, whether I want to or not, I have to come back.

The humming in my head was fading; as I got near the flats I stopped to examine a discarded kebab in the gutter, congealed fat making pretty colours on the shiny street, quite beautiful in its way. Time for a photo. I pulled out the camera and cursed. It was smashed but luckily the film seemed intact. Slipping the roll in my pocket I threw the camera into the nearest skip.

1990

Just after midday I hurtled wild-eyed through Angel station as if hunted by the wolves of time, rather than a few portly and unmotivated ticket inspectors. I was late and broke; vaulting the barrier I fell down the spiral staircase to the platform. There was a smell of electric dust on the underground, rumblings and coughs and tension. Above the humming tracks and eyeless mice, an advert for life insurance with numbers underlined asked: '*What have you got to look forward to?*'

No-one was behind me so I slowed to a dawdle, slaloming between suits and cases. There was a sexless junkie up the far end of the platform in smackhead uniform: baseball cap, jeans. More afraid of any potential embarrassment than they were of the junkie, commuters split like the sea. They get a bad press, junkies, but egalitarians all: colour, class, sexuality, none matter. As I boarded the canister of light I realised that I wasn't even uninterested – I couldn't even rouse that level of feeling. London had deadened my nerve-ends.

At Euston, the northbound Northern Line splits: the Bank branch rattles towards Camden Town, dosserville, while the Charing X branch breaks for suburban-sounding Mornington Crescent. The line map above oblivious heads looks like a syringe: the Northern Line screws you up. Morden at the sharp end, Mill Hill East the answer to your dreams.

Hanging onto a leather strap like a martyred saint I raced northbound, still breathless from the chase. Then an apparition: the Charing X line tube came into view, all those disconnected faces like a machine full of ghosts. I wondered what I looked like, grey plaster dust from head to toe, hands rough, eyes bagged.

The escalator at Camden Town was broken so I climbed silver steps slowly, waiting for a rush of commuters to surge up behind me. There was no barrier, just as well as my jeans had ripped at the other end. Secreting myself within a knot of Japanese girls on a pilgrimage, taller than they were by a head, it was more than the ticket inspector's job's worth to challenge this wild-eyed scruff immersing himself in Orientalism.

Emerging from the guts a bitter wind blew city grit that stuck to the tears in my eyes. Sucked into the street at the World's End, the sweet whiff of diesel and dope, denim, *dim sum*. All the culture-tourists looking for salvation in poverty and cool. I had little time for them, with their anachronistic bondage and haircuts, their credit cards and *mothers*, but I was too rushed to trip them up, to scream in delicate ears.

Tony waited with news; why here, of all the boozers in all the boroughs? Could be worse: could be Archway. Through Camden market, bootleg-sellers glancing nervously and leather belts hanging like slaughtered snakes. It was raining harder now, drawing out the smells of shop garbage like salt draws blood from remnants of carpet; raindrops smashed like syringes. The new batch of pissheads from Arlington House sat outside the tatty supermarket opposite The Good Mixer: no Jock, no Mick, no Cider Mary.

Tony looked out of place in the Mixer, in his good suit, his well-cut hair, a tiny 'tache and his vodka glass before him next to the coffin-shaped tobacco tin he carried for effect.

Seeing me in my steelies, dust flying off me like fag

smoke, Tony stood. "My round."

When I shrugged Tony bought me a pint. I owed him over eight hundred pounds; the knowledge was an uncomfortable barrier between us – drinking conversations had to be carefully skated round the thorny issues of that and every other rainy day, until alcohol intervened and we adopted the Jungian approach to money.

Hoping to find stimulation, I looked around the pub. How many days and nights? Not just me but Tony, everyone in the place. Was there nothing else to do? Every society, every continent, had its place where citizens could gather to lose their minds. What about Atlantis, Lemuria? Did they have their escapes, or did their people have other, higher ideals?

Tony sat down; I jerked my head in query. "You flush then?"

"Mustn't grumble. Things are looking up."

"They're always fucking 'looking up' where you're concerned. You must get a cricked neck. What's it this time, trip over a Picasso?"

"Something like that," laughed Tony. "I got a new job!"

"Yes, so have I. So what?"

"Joe, I don't mean a labouring job. I mean a *real* job. I've been taken on at Shannons."

"*Who*?"

Tony clucked and sighed with mock exasperation; lighting a fag he blew smoke in my face.

"*Shannons*? Only the best advertising firm in the country?"

"*Advertising*? What for?"

"What do you mean, 'what for'? For money, Joe. Lots of it. New car, relocation…"

A part of me had refused to even register the fact that Tony had studied Advertising at uni for three years. Now he had a job with a *salary*; it was hard adjusting. I stopped looking at the tubby goth girl in fishnets and black mascara scowling my way.

"*Relocation*? Where to?"

"Manchester. Perfect. I can pop back to Mum's with my washing."

"What – you're leaving all this behind?"

I gestured round the pub and we both laughed, though in my case it was a struggle. Tony seemed to get all the breaks; meanwhile I was still living in a slum with Becky, who had left some temp job at the council because of what she called 'bullying'. I felt she was partly to blame – every day some bloke came round the offices taking requests for knock-off tellies and videos, and Becky had reported him.

Looking embarrassed, Tony took a parcel from a bag underneath the table, wrapped in gaudy foil, and passed it to me. I held it, weighed it, shook it, weighed up our friendship.

"What's this?"

"Open it and see."

Blushing deep, wondering if the goth girl was still watching, I ripped away the wrapper to reveal an expensive-looking camera. I looked up at Tony, who shrugged and smiled.

"Don't worry, I haven't turned sausage jockey. Me Mum gave it to me for getting the job, but I've already got one."

I inspected the camera more closely, and when I realised it was a top-range Nikon it became heavier, more fragile and difficult to hold. I put it down and pushed it across the pub table.

"I can't take it Tony."

Tony pushed it back; a small puddle of beer on the worktop smeared under the lights.

"Don't be a spaz Joe. You're a good photographer. I know your last one got knackered. This might help you get somewhere."

I hesitated. Since O'Neill had bust my old Kodak I'd found myself using a camcorder I'd looted at the poll tax riot and liked the extra dimensions it gave me, but this was a thing of beauty.

"All right," I sighed, as if assenting to do Tony a favour, "I'll take it. Would you like a drink?"

"Just a shandy for me. I'm driving."

"Wait till you get to Manchester, Tony – ask for a shandy there and you'll be garrotted. At least."

"It's changing Joe. Manchester's on the up. The North's moving on. Plus of course all that fresh air, green fields. Trees."

"Complacency. Incest. Small-mindedess."

"It's changed, man. There's a Javan restaurant in Brigden now. Good schools."

"What do you mean, 'good schools'?"

Tony sipped his pint; his eyes met mine over the glass. I wonder how many times I saw him like that, a horse with a crystal nosebag. I knew he had more to add and knew it would be along soon, so I said nothing, just looked out of the window. Over the road they were changing the *Standard* billboard, and when I read the new one I smiled and raised my glass.

"Goodbye."

"We haven't gone, yet. Two weeks till we –"

"Not you," I laughed, "I'm saying goodbye to Maggie."

Tony saw the billboard, grinned, raised his glass and clinked mine.

"Good riddance."

"New beginnings," I said, holding the camera tight. As I trained the lens through the dirty window, feeling untouchable, by chance I focused on a clown walking down the rainy street, mouth wilting, makeup melting, eyes sorrowful as his big floppy feet slapped in old puddles. Tony slapped my back.

"Come on. Let's make a night of it."

Tony rang the bell of the pool club. A camera swivelled and I felt x-rayed, then the buzzer sounded and we pushed the thick metal door and went upstairs. The pool club was run by a dodgy family and the clientele were mainly off the local estates, but it had lock-ins every night and you could usually get a table.

Three local lads in white shirts with lime green pinstripes, the uniform of the Marquess and Packington, were playing pool. I stomped past looking rough so they ignored me; but Tony was in a suit. In London they twat you for money, in Yorkshire they twat you for a laugh; I'm not sure which is worse. The bar man was Antipodean; absently I wondered why anyone would swap the beach for this. Then I remembered Mum. Tony winked and went to the bar, slamming his hand on the surface.

"Fresh brandy and horses!"

The barman emerged from some dark recess and lifted his head in unenthused query.

"Champagne!" laughed Tony. Without any discernible change in his expression, the barman went to the fridge and returned with a bottle of Moet. I noticed the three lads had stopped playing pool mid-match and were watching closely, hands on vertical sticks as Tony took a bulging wallet from his trousers and counted out some notes, then clutched the bottle and came over.

"So," said Tony, "my other news. Herm's preggers!"

I wanted to burn the world down. Suddenly the whispering, smoky pool club was a chasm of futility, lonely people knocking spheres into holes, wasting time in a timeless vacuum where you went to learn how to stop dreaming. I looked into my amber pint like it was a tunnel to Australia.

"That's great."

Tony snapped his fingers. "Shit, hang on – I forgot the glasses."

As he approached the bar, the tall, ginger youth said something I couldn't catch. Tony looked annoyed, but ignored him. The youths laughed. The barman's face as Tony asked for two flutes was a picture, but I'd still to work out how to use the camera. Tony came back with two wine glasses, shaking his head and the bottle as he sat down.

"Fucking pleb – you'd think I'd asked him how to travel through wormholes in time. Woah!"

The cork, released from the bottle, flew across the room and landed on the pool table. It was a relief in a way – so that was that. The lads walked over, raptors in shirts, and the tall ginger one held out the cork. He had the sort of face that told you his philosophical outlook wouldn't change an iota if UFOs landed on Islington Green.

"This yours, yuppie cunts?"

It was all I could do not to laugh out-loud; here I was wearing labouring rags, covered in concrete dust. Tony, on the other hand, looked the part in a new suit and shining shoes. He held out his hands in an appeasing gesture.

"Sorry, lads. Got carried away. Just got a new job and got a bit excited. Here, let me stand you a round."

"Go play with some sheep where you come from, you yuppie cunt."

"Look lads," I said, patience wearing thin, "he said he was sorry. Do you want a drink or what?"

I stood and started to walk towards the bar. The shortest of the three pushed me in the back.

"What are you slaphead, his rent boy?"

There was a dull ache spreading through me like sarin, a long dark corridor. I stopped dead and closed my eyes.

"What?"

"He's in his posh whistle and you look like a tramp. What, you suck his cock for a pint?"

I hit him quickly on the turn and caught him nicely on the jaw. The lad went over, but then I felt a shattering blow at the back of my head and dropped to my knees. Tony tried to intervene but was pushed backwards over a table. The tall ginger one had hit me with a pool cue and I heard a whistling noise in my cranium. A boot smashed into my face and I was flat on my back, my lip cut and bleeding, mouth filling with blood. The three kicked me all over my body and the lights began to fade. The ginger youth picked up a wine glass and toasted me, laughing.

Tony swung a bar stool and glass splashed everywhere, pretty colours turning in the lights. Ginger screamed, holding the broken glass against the exposed artery on his neck before dropping to his knees. Tony kept swinging and another dropped, and as the third turned to run Tony tripped him and stood over him, a blank look in his eyes. The youth held his arms up, silently pleading. As if deep in thought Tony stamped on his groin then, when the youth groaned and moved his hands, slammed the butt of the stool leg down into his face. Once, twice, three times, his face a frenzy, the boy's face mash and tommy sauce. When I looked round no-one was looking; some were leaving. The barman had disappeared.

Apart from the cut I didn't seem badly hurt; hauling myself to my feet I grabbed Tony by the arm, and pulled him out of the door and down the stairs. Outside in the cold we tried to hail a cab. One finally stopped in Penton Street, but when it saw the state of us it drove off; Tony shouted after it angrily. Holding each other aloft we walked home through quiet backstreets in painful silence.

"I don't know about you," said Tony, as we limped round to my place, "but the appeal of London is beginning to wane somewhat."

Tony made sure I could get upstairs then left to lie to Herm. In the flat I washed my face, turning the sink pink, then sneaked to the bedroom. The room was icy – Becky couldn't sleep with the central heating on because of the thermostat problem. She was curled up on the bed in her long jumper and white knickers, legs bare, toes pink.

Following the abortion we didn't have sex for weeks. Then, one evening I'd come home to find Becky washing up naked, apart from an apron. She played at ignoring me, even when I'd began tonguing her ear, dropping to my knees and licking her rectum. Grabbing the washing-up liquid I'd squirted it all on her backside and my cock, gasping at how cold it was; bending her over the sink I fucked her in the arse, our breath escaping in little spurts in the cold room, gasping again at how hot and tight and slippery her rectum was, already lubricated it turned out, my soapy cold hands holding her breasts, closing my eyes so I couldn't see her marigold-covered hands that I held down in the cold suds; when I came it felt like shooting a calf with a bolt gun, stars went off in my head.

After that we fucked in the kitchen, bathroom, park, car, that length of Victoria Line between Seven Sisters and Finsbury Park – anywhere except the bed. We had handjobs and footjobs and ear, nose and throat jobs, I came on her face and tits and clothing, she rubbed against my shin, my arm, my hips and the top of my head; she wore uniforms and lingerie and rubber, PVC, leather, once a pretend nurse's outfit that split halfway through. We tried boss/secretary, schoolgirl/teacher, maid/mistress, daddy/daughter, mother/son, footballer/linesman, fireman/cat; we tried everything, everywhere, except naked, in bed; cock in cunt, lips on lips, heart to heart; and so of course I began to fantasize about making love – the ultimate fetish.

Although I enjoyed dressing her up for sex, browsing through the nest of cobwebs in her lingerie drawer, really she looked her gamine best as she was that day. Draping my bloody jumper over a chair I lay behind her and traced her ear with my finger, then leaned and kissed the tender lobe. Becky turned her head and I kissed her newly black hair. Herm's colour. Undeterred I lay behind her, my groin against her buttocks, and slid a hand up inside her jumper, her stomach warm and smooth. But I realised she was sobbing so I curled up and pulled her closer. It was a time to whisper.

"What's the matter?"

"Hermione's leaving London."

"With Tony. I know. He gave me this."

Jumping up, still stiff, I produced the bag and showed her the camera. Becky shrugged, her eyes stained delicate crimsons, mascara by Sam Raimi.

"Oh my god Joe! What happened?"

"Nothing. Got jumped. Be fine."

"Jumped? Who by? Those lads from the market?"

"No. Some nutters; never seen them before. I'm fine."

To my annoyance Becky took my word for it and lay down with her back to me.

"What will I do without her Joe? She's all I've got."

"She's only in fucking Manchester Becky, you'll see her all the time. Anyway, Tony told me we can have the squat, so long as we look after Stig. That means we can leave this dump."

Becky clung to my arm excitedly. "Really? That's wicked! I hate it here Joe, hate it... I don't know anyone, they all stare at me, I've no-one to talk to... at least at the squat they don't judge you for signing on."

Becky went quiet as I stroked her neck. Her plunging depressions had been going on for months, and I felt she needed to get a job.

"No-one's judging you babe, I just – you know, it wasn't such a bad job was it? Paid well, easy?"

Becky said nothing; I kissed her ear to encourage her. "So why did you, babe? Leave I mean?"

"You want to know why I left? One winter afternoon, you know, dark outside, strip lighting sending you to sleep, I had to sort out all the old personnel files, the dead files. Some of the people really were dead; I'd look at their meaningless photos and read their death certificate, then came doctor's notes confirming their illness, then the odd sick day, then the confirmation of their appointment, and finally their optimistic application form, passport photo attached, smiling faces full of hope."

Still in the dark, I shrugged and tried to say what she wanted to hear. Man's puny computer, every time a woman speaks it chugs into gear: do I need to do anything, say anything, buy anything? No? Then *relax*... except I knew she would remain silent for months, aeons, unless I said something.

"You have to snap out of it," I said finally. "This – *malaise*, whatever it is. You can get a job. We'll have a new house to live in, room to breathe. I mean, I'll miss Tony too but it's not like they've gone to the moon."

"It's different with me and Hermione."

"How so?"

"You know why."

I pushed in close behind her, my crotch rubbing as if by accident against her warm backside.

"What, because you had a crush on her? So what?"

"It was more than a crush, Joe."

"Was it?"

A part of me wanted her to tell me, in intimate detail; another part wanted to block it all out, fearing the jealousy would destroy me.

"Maybe that's what you want with Tony; what you're doing to me now. You want his arse."

"Don't be so fucking – *stupid*."

"I don't mind. It might make you more interesting. I quite like the idea of two blokes. Sucking each other off as I watch. It would close the circle."

Angrily I scooped an arm under her and double-cupped her breasts: nipples like healing blisters, sensitive as lips. Becky was breathing hard, as hard as I was against her. She pushed backwards and I slid a hand down her panties. Warm, not quite wet, but getting there. I pulled out my cock; pre-come already sticky on her buttocks.

"Then I'd hold you down," murmured Becky, half to herself, "as he fucked you up the arse. I'd love to see that. You being penetrated like you penetrate me. Rough, impatient."

"You like that."

"Not so fast. Yes I'd like that, to see you with spunk dribbling out of your bum like it spills out of mine. Maybe that's why you fuck me like that, Joe – you're a little queer."

"No. It's so we don't get pregnant."

"I can hardly talk. Me and Hermione messed about when we were young. And later. Maybe I'll tell you about it one day. So I could hardly complain if you did the same. Dabbled."

Spitting on my hand I greased my cock, pushed against her sphincter. Becky groaned and adjusted and I pushed harder till I was lodged tight inside, her muscles pulsing. I could never last long when sober, but drunk it was harder to ejaculate, so we'd pound on the ratty bed, springs snapping and *poing*ing for the neighbours, and sometimes I fell asleep inside her; but now, sobered by my beating, tender to every touch and needing this acceptance, I could feel my balls tighten and I pumped harder.

"Give me a baby," pleaded Becky.

I didn't want to. I didn't like babies, never had – their shittiness, their single-mindedness, the assumptions they made about their rightful place in things. So far as I knew, Becky had always felt the same – or why have the abortion? Then again with a new flat, a new camera, and the end of Maggie, maybe having a kid wouldn't be so bad.

Becky pulled out my cock, rolled over to me and we kissed, and I could taste vodka on her lips. She yanked my trousers to my knees, then lowered herself onto me, like the first time on her mother's bed in Hove. Another age. As we fucked I saw us as others would in our dirty flat, ancient sheets, old johnnies under the bed, Becky's Dorothy Parker posters, books about the rippers of Yorkshire and London.

Becky sank lower on me, barely aroused, on a mission to catch my seed, and bowed her head as I gasped with shock and came deep inside what since the abortion had become a taboo zone. She bowed; her hair covered my head. After a few minutes cold spunk dribbled on my thighs.

"I think we'll be all right," whispered Becky.

"Yes," I panted, "so do I."

I wasn't quite sure if she meant it was the safe time of the month, or the best time to conceive. No point in asking; we'd find out soon enough. If Tony could have children, so could I. Her eggs, already complete, had been there at her birth, pre-ordained and waiting for someone like me to come along and alter her biology, to subvert DNA gene-spirals and inscribe some momentous new history. So I held Becky and listened as the struggle within her system began.

2007

According to her note in fickle Catalan, Alona has gone to the market in the Arab quarter of Palma, which means she'll be gone all day. I haven't been sober since New Year's Eve, and don't intend to start now. By the time I reach Billys Bar Tony's already merry, laughing with the Geordie bargirl and munching chips. I smack him on the back with *El Pais* and he jumps, then turns with a grin and belches in my face. The Geordie girl's wearing a sleeveless black t-shirt and blue jeans, depiction of a beach on the shirt, her breasts a forty-D, nipples beneath gently waving palm trees. For the second day running I nod at her breasts.

"Nice view."

"Glad you like it. Stella?"

"*Muy bien.*"

Geordie frowns and reaches for a glass; colouring slightly, I sit next to Tony at the bar, imagining the red lava of my blush spreading across my pate so I look like Mars. Only froth is pouring from the tap so, cig in mouth, Geordie goes to change the barrel. Tony smokes and I squint. Following the drifting smoke swirling upwards I notice for the first time an assorted collection of bras in various colours and styles stuck mirthlessly to the ceiling.

"I always went for women who smoke," says Tony. "It meant there was a chance they'd be dead before me."

I try to remember if Becky smoked: can't. On the polished

brown counter before me are (*left to right*): a small dish of cashew nuts, a Watney's beer mat and some matches with the bulldog's scowling face. I'd ask Tony to change the bar's name to the Lost Apostrophe, but he's touchy about his illiteracy so instead I chew a cashew nut while he raves.

"Has she got space hoppers or what?"

"Dead heat in the – whatever."

On the big screen above the bar they're showing a recording of a *La Liga* match: *aburrido*. I despise football, more so since I started getting mistaken for some Italian referee called Cholera or something. Cricket's my game – I love the statistics, the psychologies, the day after day of grinding boredom, the fact that Yanks can't comprehend a five-day match ending in a draw.

Tony's looking up rapt, as if listening to an address from an alien emperor. With his beard and expanding gut he seems to be turning into my father. I nick a chip and wipe some egg from his stained plate.

"Tackled," murmurs Tony, as in, *good tackle* – the 'goods' are silent. It takes me back to the swampy school playing fields, the rain, the temporality of our childhood woes. Maybe every moment, each memory, is being burned in realtime on some Saturn-sized CD-Rom, and in the moment of my expiration someone will press rewind and back I'll go, not in the moment, but watching it. Except you don't rewind CDs, you wipe and burn.

Geordie re-emerges and pulls the pint. I take a sip of the clear cold liquid then look at my watch: not yet ten. I'm excelling myself, my high resolutions. For years my definition of success was being able to afford a pint on signing-on day.

"I could get used to this," sighs Tony, "drinking all day, good football, good food." Nothing about the company. "Never thought it would be your cup of tea though – out here,

I mean. Always saw you as a bit like Ian Rush's wife."

"*Who?*"

"You know – when Rushie got transferred to Juventus, they interviewed his wife and she said, 'It's alright over here, but you can't fit the bread in the toaster'."

I laugh in a short, sharp burst. Geordie smiles and for a moment I see myself as she might: tall, healthy, browned and solvent. Maybe it's not so crazy after all. I've been drunk since New Year and her breasts look warm and soft and as smooth as my head. Me and my twin in a swimming pool, Telly Savalas with a cracked head – what was that joke again? Geordie catches me looking and doesn't seem to mind; I *must* be drunk. I look at the football. Tony's right: this isn't so bad, it's half-time.

"So," I say to Tony, "how is the old cunt?" Concern registers on his face. "England, I mean."

"The same as ever – worse," he replied. "I was at home over Christmas, having a can with Mum. I heard some cheering out the window so I looked out and there were these kids about twelve, thirteen. They'd caught these two cats and had sprayed paraffin over them, then set them alight and raced them up the street. I told Mum what was going on and she just went, 'boys will be boys' and opened another can. I wouldn't mind – but these were girls."

"That's nothing. I remember these lads up Stone Nest caught one of them wild horses on the tops, tied it to a car and then set the car alight. Said you never heard noises like it."

"Did you take a photograph?"

"I didn't have a camera then."

"Don't you do photographs anymore? You used to be pretty good. That's why I bought you the camera – remember? Remember when you won that competition in Manchester?"

"I didn't *win* Tony, I came *second*... The thing is, what I'm *trying* to say, is if we all lived in the inner city, there wouldn't *be* any of these problems... it's in the peripheries, the ring roads, the doodlers outside the margins where it all falls down. The outer estates are always worse. In the inner city you can escape. We should build a better world – of concrete."

"I travelled all over the UK," says Tony, in broad agreement. "Coventry, Aberdeen, Derry. They all looked the same: cleaner, more vibrant than the Eighties of course, but each exactly the same: Smiths, M&S, Waterstones. They reckon Britain's the most diverse place on earth; the most homogenous more like, the most hostile. Have you ever *been* to Aldershot?"

"The least tolerant. If you were to walk into 95% of the pubs in Britain, if you looked or sounded different in any way or said anything one degree outside the local paradigm, you'd be in trouble. That's smalltown Britain: the nicer the place, the worse the people. And as for the countryside... every time you walk along an English country road, it just seems to mock your mortality."

"You've changed, Joe. I mean – *paradigm*?"

"People change."

Tony injects a serious note into the conversation; I munch cashews.

"Has it changed you, then? Being here?"

I pause for thought. The more you drink the less room there is for thinking – the more your tongue over-hypes and makes up its own mind. My glass is empty.

"I mainly like Spain because it's *not England*. There's none of that can't-do crap here; you want to build a house, it gets built. Know what my favourite saying is? *Por que non*?"

Tony frowns and searches his memory banks. "'Why not'?"

"*Kind* of; it's untranslatable, that's the *point*... pint?"

"*Por que non?*"

I wave at Geordie, who's now been joined by another girl, even younger, prettier, unquestionably out of my league. It's a good thing, maybe the only good thing about maturity – you know your limits, your outer ring roads.

The match is over. *Sky News* is on. I close my eyes. Tony nudges me in the ribs, knocking out my breath.

"Don't look now, but it's your bird."

Feeling nauseous, guilty, angry, I swivel as if moulded to my bar stool and peek through the low window at the sunlit street. Alona's marching towards the bar but then seems to change her mind and veers off at a tangent into the baker's. I whistle low under my breath. I don't need a scene: not here, not anywhere. People stare enough without the raised voices. Becky used to scream in the street and I'd run away. Alona hasn't resorted to that yet, but it's to be expected. Every night I go home and she's asleep, and in the morning she rages, my head throbs and I wonder if this is a new thing – a re-negotiation, a repositioning – a temporary blip or the beginning of the end. Typical Tony: the minute he turns up my women get weird. Maybe I change too.

"Looks like you got away with it," he says, laughing.

"I never get away with anything."

Tony says nothing, and the words sit in a low cloud between us like a cloud between two mountain peaks. Emotions are waging war inside me; time to go. The boat's relatively safe. If Alona sees the boat's out of harbour she'll have to assume I'm working, and won't try to reach me; the mobile never works round the headland.

I look out at the sky, boiling brown with storms. Probably another day before it really breaks; I'll risk it. Better than sitting here watching old football with the sound down. Tony's stance seems to disagree; his mouth hangs open as he chews on a chip, watery eyes full of wonder. On the counter

I open my paper to the results but Tony doesn't looks down. I sigh.

"Got any plans today?"

"Nope. You?"

"I have to take the boat out for an hour or two." I speak loudly, so Geordie can hear.

Tony shrugs. "Cool."

"You want to come?"

"I don't think so. Not today. Looks a bit rough. Not a big boat, is it?"

I'm heartbroken, but I'll cope. Slapping Tony again I smile at Geordie and exit the bar. Walking past an open window towards the car park I hear piano music and look in to see a young ballerina execute what looks like a perfect pirouette in the sunlight. As I walk to the van I look for Alona, but she's disappeared; dissolved, probably, in the vapours of her dissatisfaction. Footsteps behind. I half-expect Alona to fall on me in a flurry of blows, but the voice is English.

"You forgot your hat."

Surprised, I touch my scalp as I turn. I never forget anything, least of all my hat. Geordie holds it out with a strange smile on her bulbous lips. She's squinting in the sun and I wonder if the reflection is from my head. Reaching out I take the cap from her outstretched hand and smile.

"Thanks."

Geordie seems awkward now and turns to go. The beer in my system makes me reckless: I no longer want to wallow alone out on the ocean.

"Don't suppose you'd like a trip in my boat?"

I've never used this tacky line before but then, since I've had a boat, I've always been with Alona. I flush, knowing I'll never go into the bar again.

"I mean – you've probably got work to do. I know what a bastard Tony is."

Then Geordie smiles.

"I'd love to."

I've long held this theory that if you really, really want a woman to fall for you, you should get all your friends to slag you off behind your back. Thanks, Tony.

There's only one cloud in the sky. It looks a lot like Bruce Forsyth. The plane buzzes in the distance again and now I'm convinced its message is '*todos le odia*'. Maybe it's Alona, knowing what I'm doing. What *am* I doing? Geordie lies on a wet towel beneath the cliffs, her whirlpool of a navel puckering.

Flipping her over, with my index finger I brush the damp sand gently from her thighs to reveal sunburnt flesh. Geordie doesn't moan; she sighs. I lean over and kiss her ear and she smiles, pretending to sleep. I kiss her pink buttock and sand sticks to my lips. The beach is silent and the cliffs too high for anyone to look down on our transitory love, if it's even that. If not, what matter? Alona will leave me like they all have and time runs short.

I kiss Geordie's inner thigh and pull the bikini aside. I want to kiss her arse, delve with my tongue inside her, taste all of her smells, but she begins to giggle and wriggle and flips onto her back, pulling me up and kissing my sandy mouth. She grimaces, turns away and spits. "Yuck."

"It's only sand."

"It was nearly something else. I'm not into that."

"What *are* you into?"

Geordie pulls me closer and feels for my cock through my shorts. No-one, apart from Alona, has touched me in a Millennium. Geordie squeezes hard; I make a little pained noise and she licks my ear, whispers. "Well, I'm a big fan of romance."

"I can do romance." I roll between her legs and she pulls

down my shorts and pants. She's wet. I can't wait; I push into her and stop, wanting to freeze the moment.

"'Course you can," grunts Geordie, eyes closed, head weaving from side-to-side. "Big, big romantic you are. Don't even know me name, do you?"

I kiss her, softly, push in and withdraw completely, sliding my glans across her slippery clit, wincing as her nails rake my backside.

"Course I do. It's Geordie."

She rakes harder, drawing blood; I yell.

"Fucking hell, alright! What *is* your name?"

She giggles, kissing me softly.

"I'm glad you asked. It's Sarah."

I stop pushing, hover above her.

"Ha ha."

She acts all puzzled.

"What?"

"Is this a fucking joke?"

I feel her begin to clench. For a moment I believe I might be able to keep pushing, kissing, touching, to ride the moment, to wake from history; but then I shrink dramatically inside her and roll off. Geordie looks shocked, ambivalent, and avoiding her eyes I pull up my shorts with as much dignity as I can muster, put on my t-shirt and sandals, and wade out to the boat. Sarah shouts something behind me, but I don't hear her; then the engine kicks in and I pull up anchor and point the boat out to sea, praying to Mr Dawkins that I'll find an iceberg.

1991

Late August: cloudy day, fresh breeze. After taking a few photos and filming some street scenes with Tony's camera I walked up from King's Cross to the Terrace to find it empty. The note was in Becky's handwriting and simply said, '*Dropping. Gone to Whitty.*' Grabbing the video camera I'd liberated the year before, I caught a cab to the hospital.

19.08.91 UNTITLED.
SCENE 43. INT.
A HOSPITAL WARD – DAY.

A hospital bed. **BECKY** lies on it, legs wide, screaming silently, sweating. A small black lump appears between her legs. Blood flows outward. An uneven split tears to her anus. The **REGISTRAR**'s scissors snip round her vagina. The **BABY**'s head appears. **MIDWIVES I & II** cluster. Her wild terrified eyes open. **BECKY** screams wordlessly, holding out her hand to the camera, wanting, needing, to hold that holding hand. The **BABY**, perfectly formed, wet and helpless, is extracted from her vagina. Purple and screaming, the **BABY** is put to her breast. **BECKY** closes her eyes. **MIDWIFE II** mops **BECKY**'s brow. A hospital bed.

While the midwives wiped white goo off the outraged baby (giant brown eyes, scrawny limbs that had bent over backward)

I held Becky's hand waiting for her usual tricky questions. She was quiet now, dozy, so I stroked her cheek.

"She's perfect. I'm glad I was here."

Becky smiled sadly, spoke softly. "No. You weren't."

Mother and daughter were home within a day, and we called her Sarah after no-one we knew. Sarah couldn't take to her mother's milk and Becky seemed to sleep all the time, so I soon became accustomed to the double rasp of nappy tabs, the smell of sterilising fluid, the hollow thud of plastic bottles. Sometimes, as I held her in the night time, Sarah's mouth would grope down from my throat searching for a nipple, her own little bottle substitute, until finally I let her suckle the emptiness from my chest as we watched the sleeping Becky, my resentment surpassed only by Sarah's.

Occasionally, as if awakening from a trance, or death, Becky would rise, her eyes light up eagerly, and she would snatch the child to her; but it seemed she did it too hard and still she couldn't feed Sarah herself, so after a while the child would cry with hunger and I would prise Becky's fingers away and take Sarah back.

Sometimes I'd look up to find Becky staring as if we were intruders, and I nursed Sarah with the formula milk till she slept, then I would sleep. When I awoke with a start I'd look at Becky and she too would be asleep; delicately I'd lay Sarah down in her cot, switch off the light and climb carefully in, my arm snaking about Becky's slimline waist, but her back would be to me and always so cold, like a whale beached and crushed by its own weight.

Here is Becky's thermostat problem. Say you programme your central heating to stay at a constant seventy Fahrenheit. It warms up till it reaches the right temperature. But then what? It goes a billionth of a degree over and it stops; a billionth under and it starts. I told her, thermostats aren't that sensitive. Nor are you, she said.

The truth was, for all her beauty, Sarah wasn't magic. She couldn't perform the one thing we needed. To make our love for each other stick.

The quiet, even breathing from Sarah's cot woke me early, alert as I was for opportunity. Raising myself quietly on one sore elbow I looked down on my wife in the dirty, curtain-strained light. Becky looked at her most beautiful when she slept: no trace of the anger, the angst, the unfulfilment, just her pale face, small mouth, thick blonde hair falling across her neck and the pillow. Reaching beneath her syrupy night-dress I touched Becky's nipple with shaking fingers. As it hardened I went down to explore and took it into my mouth. Through the thin mesh I could taste a little milk, warm and sweet – wasted.

When I licked her lobe Becky sighed, which seemed a good sign, so I stroked her belly and the frizzy hairs of her cunt and she seemed to respond; though I knew she was still sore down there so I moved up the bed and slid my cock between her lace-covered breasts. Her sieved, wasted titty milk coated my cock so I trailed it over her lips and cheek so she could see for herself it tasted fine.

"What the *fuck*! –"

Becky woke and glared at this thing in her face and began to struggle so I rolled off and fell on the floor. She was screeching and I found my trousers (my cock still hard, still pleading), feeling undignified (to say the least); Becky threw a trainer at me; ducking I stood on an upturned plug and hopped from the room (Sarah beginning to bawl), down the rickety stairs. I hopped into Amwell Street, hard-bitten by frost, little pools of broken glass at regular intervals all the way to the main road.

It was all Tony's fault. When he started his new job and gave his national insurance number to payroll, the computer had apparently flashed red lights, steam had shot out and it had a breakdown. I'd been signing on in his name for so long, I'd forgotten how to sign my own name. So I had no more excuses, there was only one thing for it – I had to find a job. And if not mine, someone else's.

Out of work and keen to provide, I trudged streets that became meaner each day. In a recession, you find people's eyes grow harder, faces more set, courses resolute. I ducked and weaved the pavements like some demented slalom racer, between job centre, employment agency and building site, but to no avail; it had taken a while but O'Neill had spread the word well and I became accustomed to the sight of yellow helmets shaking from side-to-side, humourless smiles, jerking thumbs.

The more I walked the more wretched I felt, as if my legs were being ground to stumps on the bitter concrete. Passers-by seemed less inclined to step aside. It seemed the older I got and the harder I looked, the more beat-up I felt inside; snipers sniffed out my weaknesses, my phobias and fetishes, my allergies and addictions and, above all, my fear – what if I met the pool club boys?

My paranoia grew. As I crossed a side street between two waiting cars I was convinced the one behind me would slip off the clutch, crushing my legs beyond repair. Waiting at Britannia Junction for the lights to change I expected to be pushed to oblivion beneath the trucks that hurtled past. Sat atop a bus in the dark I was sure some brick would at any moment hurtle through the window, blinding me forever.

Nearly every day I rode buses, mainly the 43 from Angel to Archway, and back again. The Archway was mostly grim and poor, the Angel mostly trendy and bright. Sometimes I used the camcorder, other times Tony's camera and, in theory, the two projects were distinct; the photos had no particular theme but my film had a working title: *Rule 43*.

Peering through a lens from the bus' top deck I recorded

black bin liners clogging the branches of the dismal trees of Holloway Road like skewered crows. An old man I recognised as being Irish sat on a mangled bench with his can of Tennants, and I realised I was filming an endangered species: the Fifties' émigré, rubble-dust streaking his grey hair, rollie on his lips, one of the abused generation who had found austere post-war London preferable to the auld sod but who were already dying out, to be replaced by thousands of smart young chaps and chapesses clutching doctorates in IT.

When a screeching crocodile of teenagers embarked at Jones Brothers, I braced myself for their antics, their nudging and giggling and piss-water bombs; I hid my camera like porn beneath my coat. But after a few minutes in my solitary haze I noticed something, or the absence of something, and looked up to see a grassland of hands dancing through the air as if sculpting light, a party of deaf children signing a cacophony of invisible words I would never hear.

While I insisted to Becky I was looking for work, mainly I was looking for pictures. She wanted me to flog the camera from Tony, but even when we were scraping the bottom of the formula milk tin I refused. Things would turn my way; they always did when you were right down. I just needed a break.

Enclosed in a congratulatory card to celebrate Sarah's birth, Tony had enclosed a cutting from the local Manchester arty-farty magazine, *de Quinceys*:

Do you live in Manchester?
Are you an artist?

Whether you're a cartoonist, sculptor, musician or photographer we want to see your work. Manchester is Britain's brightest city, and we want to celebrate that fact by holding an exhibition of its brightest new stars!

To enter, you had to prove you lived in the city, so Tony agreed to let me use his address (some flash place in Chorlton).

Now all I had to do was get some decent shots.

In some ways the camera was a hindrance; each time I pulled it from my coat pocket I felt stupid, a dreamer, playing at being someone special instead of a lowlife dosser who could barely feed his child. I found myself drawn to people and places that shared my angst, my misrepresentation – buttoned-up pensioners waiting for a bus with the 40-storey might of Peregrine House on their shoulder, aimless wanderers who took buses from nowhere to nowhere, each with their own seat as if unwilling to be contaminated by human contact.

All I wanted was to go home, to hold Sarah. Yet it seemed I returned later each night, freshly humiliated by the shrinking bags of groceries.

At one time I had bought home Parmesan, yoghurt, a tub of salt that lasted forever; the bag dwindled to a meagre tin of beans, a loaf of bread, a pint of milk. I began pondering on fantastic schemes: selling the council flat, becoming a rent boy, mugging Chelsea pensioners. Too poor to drink I dreamt of Becky's titty-milk and hid my erections on the 43 (the meaning of life plus one), unable to move, watching the world rolling by and feeling old and shrunken inside, as if my summer had passed without being aware of any spring.

Becky slept like Sarah didn't. When she'd got herself pregnant I'd vowed to be the best father in human history; but by the time Sarah's blackened cord dropped off her navel and she'd stopped shitting meconium I'd rewritten the vow somewhat, lowered my ambitions a tad; my vow then was not to be the worst father of all time. It wasn't an easy promise to keep.

Becky had always been close to her sister but when her mum and dad split, she'd taken her father's side and that was that. Sometimes she'd go and meet him somewhere, taking baby Sarah, and return with money and guilt – at least until he claimed to have been cleared out by BCCI, after which she got *nada*.

Since leaving Sussex University, Becky had hardly had contact with her mother and by the time she fell pregnant with Sarah they'd lost touch completely. I couldn't understand how it had happened; but then nor could Becky understand my relationship with my Dad. Since walking in on him with Julie I'd never been in touch. Now, all these years on, I wondered what had really happened that afternoon; what if she'd made all the moves, as she had with me?

As a boy I'd found Father's behaviour baffling but less so now; maybe we just want to fuck ourselves backwards through time. Sometimes I found myself wondering what might have happened with Julie, if circumstances hadn't got in our way. In his latest letter, Tony had mixed news: Herm had had another miscarriage, and Stig at home was dead. He had no more details; I didn't want any.

In the end I wrote to Dad at our old address, but the new owners just said they'd bought the place at auction; the previous owner had lost it due to 'negative equity'. Dad's mum and dad were dead, he had no other siblings, and I had no way to contact him. Something told me he'd left Millmoor; maybe he was even in London, looking for me and his grandchild. If that's what we were.

Apart from his selling out the working class, another of the accusations Mum threw at him was that he was some sort of inadequate, a Jaffa, unable to provide her with other sprogs. If this was the case, I reasoned, how could he have sired me? Maybe he hadn't. I was always on the lookout for other dads: that bookie from Cheadle, some unknown Croc Dundee from home, or Georgie Best.

Consider this: Mum hung round Chelsea, Mum hung round Manc, and she often boasted that she took a glass from that foaming champagne fountain – was she talking metaphorically? Plus: Dad despised United, being a true blue

("C-I-T-Y- City!!") Alright, I couldn't kick a ball, and my flowing locks would soon be gone, but then so would Mum.

I started to have other fantasies: what if she'd met Ian Brady some dark Mancunian night? I tried doing the maths, but that was never my strong point. Maths, and realism.

I thought I saw him once, my father; I was watching some interminable drivel where people send in their clippings of desolate families, teased animals, pocket catastrophes. In the background there was this tramp, bearded, weary, shuffling out of shot: Dad.

Becky let me hold her in the night-time, but whenever I pressed against her unambiguously she froze: 'corpsed' is perhaps the wrong word. She told me she felt fat and undesirable or, as she so delicately put it, "bloated as a drowned puppy". So I would wait till she slept then go to the bathroom and take a porn mag from its hiding place above the water tank. All that potential, all those composers and presidents flushed away.

The deadline for the competition was fast approaching, and I needed the money to get all those films developed. To do that, there was only one thing for it: I sold the camera, my nostrils filling with the acrid smell of burning bridges.

That night a part of me didn't want to go home, or even get off the bus. I had a travelcard and was happy to sit for hours, watching London frown. The female driver, when I said, "Thanks, love," remonstrated with me as if I'd said something terrible. I only wanted to be kind.

As if this wasn't bad enough I'd recently discovered, courtesy of David fucking Attenborough, that the lobster we'd liberated in Majorca had been of the freshwater variety; it would have died in agony the moment it was dropped into the salty depths. It seemed nothing and nobody wanted my goodness, no-one wanted me to do good.

As the bus crawled up Pentonville Road hill I saw a road-worker standing like a statue, a vat of hot tar emptied over him, white eyes blinking like a mime artist in a wind tunnel. The bus crept on, so I hopped off at the corner of Penton Street and went in the Belvedere. I had enough cash for one pint of Guinness, and sat looking at the flawless design, wanting to savour it more than I wanted to drink it. There's an Irish expression I learned on the sites: "I'm after having a pint." The pint has already been consumed; whether or not the pint is drunk is no longer a matter for debate.

I took two hours over my drink, then spent the last of my daily coppers on a *Standard* for the jobs. Some fat Czech had bounced off his yacht. Not feeling the event was of any real relevance to my life I walked as slowly as I could back to Villiers Terrace; dreading the moment I'd walk in to find Becky still in her nightie, Sarah screaming in her sodden nappy because I'd forgotten to get new ones, no clean bottles and a long night's rocking ahead.

Yet as I opened the front door and trudged up to the first floor I heard remarkable sounds: laughter, Sarah giggling, Becky cooing. The living room was clean, the baby coddled in clean pyjamas, and curry smells wafting from the kitchen. Becky had never been a cook; she just devoured.

As I hung up my coat on the nail driven into the wall, Becky gave me the kind of radiant smile I remembered from years before, when she first convinced me we could make something work. Without a word she held out a letter with a Manchester postmark and a *de Quinceys'* masthead:

'*Dear Mr Noone*

Congratulations!'

I'd won a prize, or a promise of a prize at least. Becky held me, and against my will I hardened; gently, firmly, she pushed me away.

1992

Since Grandad's funeral I'd never been back to Manchester, blaming the city in some odd way for swallowing my mother. My work was on display alongside the artwork of the other prize-winners at Bar Fresh, a galleria/display space made out of exposed piping and focaccia in some renovated district of warehouses and bistros.

Bar Fresh was part of a complex that also housed a cinema, screening exclusively foreign films, music studios and the usual vegan café. The gallery was too bright, warm and well-dressed – I was wearing a shirt and denim jacket, and sweat poured into my eyes.

My 'exhibition' seemed clichéd, and I was mortally embarrassed. They'd blown up the photos to poster-size, and because of the low-res I'd used before getting Tony's camera the images seemed too grainy. They obviously assumed the decision had been a deliberate one. Mostly the pics were dark, black and grey: picturesque urban decay, nothing original and I knew it.

Apart from the colourful Majorca set, which shone out and pointed to something more promising, plus that chance image of Radio screaming against a city backdrop, the only ones I liked were a roll I'd taken of office workers smoking outside, huddled in doorways like pinstripe fugitives. But they'd clumped them all together in a montage, reducing the impact I'd sought in their segregation, their repetition. When some local hack snapper half-heartedly attempted to get me to pose by my display (a sneer on his face) I refused.

"There are so many people!" gasped Becky, looking around with wide eyes. "I'm sure that's that – you know – that bloke off the telly."

"So what? He's only a *critic*."

The free wine wasn't worth the money. Becky's awe was irritating; you'd have thought she'd never seen a profiterole before. Or maybe the fizzy wine had gone to her head – she didn't get out much. She was overdressed in a tight red dress with long sleeves to hide her scars of self-harm. She'd hardly cut herself since we'd got together, so maybe I wasn't *all* bad. Or maybe it had been part of her adolescence.

Irritably I wiped my forehead. The train ride north had been stressful, due partly to Sarah's excitement as she relished her newfound mobility, and partly to Becky's selective deafness when that mobility encountered obstacles. We'd arrived at Manchester Piccadilly to be met by Tony, but not Hermione, who was 'working'. That had annoyed me intensely. I hadn't seen her in years, what the hell was she scared of?

Tony had gallantly taken a screeching Sarah off our hands so we were free to enjoy the prize-giving. Later, Sarah and babysitter willing, we planned to go to The Hacienda. I wasn't looking forward to seeing Tony and Herm's flat: posher than the squat, no doubt. But then Tony didn't have an exhibition. One to me.

"Joe, isn't it?" asked a pretty Asian woman in her twenties holding a glass of wine; when I nodded assent she held out her other hand and I shook it. "I'm Aisha, arts editor at *de Quinceys*. I wonder if I could ask you a few questions about your work?"

Perhaps unreasonably, I felt a trifle put out as I entertained an unformulated notion that art worked best when it was unexplained, in fact, that it was demeaned by meaning. But Aisha wore a short black dress, shiny heels and fishnets; her bob reminded me of Becky's pin-up girl Louise Brooks, and her face was an intelligent one that turned heads. Her friendly eyes were large and oyster grey and, essentially, she looked interested in what I had to say; outside of the job centre, this was a novelty. I felt Becky bristle and smiled. "Fire away."

"There seems to be a recurrent theme to your work, would you agree?"

Bus shelters. Building sites. Spanish waiters. What bloody themes?

"I don't know."

Apparently undeterred, Aisha moved on.

"What I mean is, if you take the series as a whole – people waiting for buses, drinking alone – they seem to be representing alienation. Would you say your background has given you a sense of this isolation?"

"Not really."

I sighed and wiped my eyes, shrugging and tugging at the collar Becky had made me wear. I wanted to expand, I really did, Aisha's eyes were still encouraging, but in her reflection I saw Becky looking at me as if I was joking. What the hell was she doing here, anyway?

"You grew up in a small town in Yorkshire. Have you ever been back to take photographs of your working-class roots?"

"Not really. Too dark."

Too bright in here; the people at least. Too bright and shiny for me.

"This picture here – *Dilution*." Aisha pointed at an image I'd taken from the upstairs back seat of a 43, a fortuitous moment when every seat was occupied by one person, all looking forwards except for one old man who had turned back to look at me, his quizzical features smudged by the wrong sort of exposure. "It seems to me a hopeful image –

we're all alone, but humanity is never far away. Almost Yungian. Would that be right?"

"I dunno. I just like riding around on buses."

To her immense credit, Aisha tried a final time.

"The overall title of your work – *Pixelation*. Can I ask what it means?"

Shrugging I pulled a denim sleeve across my eyes. Rough. Behind her I could hear braying laughter; in my fragile, self-doubting state it seemed bolstered by a lifetime's security.

"I just like it. I mean, pixilated means pissed and everything seems to be getting digitised, down to binary numbers... I don't want to say more than that, really."

"Well, thank you, Joe. You've been very helpful." Flushing red, Aisha drifted off. Becky turned on me angrily. "You could have made an effort! She was genuinely interested and you were really rude!"

"I don't think I was. Was I?"

"Joe, you were awful." Becky looked close to tears; she hated being shown up. I emptied my wine glass.

"Maybe I should go talk to her."

"Maybe you should. Why are you acting so arrogantly?"

"I didn't think I was."

"Arrogant, and fucking rude. You aren't *that* special. In fact I heard *someone* say you're only here because you lived on an estate."

Tension in my stomach, a sinking feeling; if they found out about the whole right-to-buy thing they'd probably throw me out.

"Who said that? That fucking hack?"

"I don't know, but I heard someone say it. So don't be so cocky. Maybe you aren't as clever as you think."

Before I could think of a retort the ceremony began. Lights dimmed and a small stage lit up. I grabbed another glass of wine and affected a bored expression, seething. Becky clung to my arm with a tight grip, as if to stop me from running. To my disgust my heart pounded and stomach hurt. Aisha was on the stage and got a small round of applause. I would have joined in but there was nowhere to put my drink so, gently, I stamped my foot.

"Ladies and gentlemen, *artists*, thanks so much for coming today. I think we've all been overwhelmed by the sheer quality of the artwork on show. Manchester has always been Britain's most creative city, and this exhibition proves it." I looked around at the smug faces for signs of dissent but they concealed their doubts well.

"All the artists on display here are winners, and it's almost impossible to choose between them, but that's what we must do. So, to the prize-giving. In third place, for her beautiful display that injects traditional weft knitting with a new, urgent riff, it's Melissa Sands for *Material Girl*."

As some white girl with dreads took the stage and shook hands with Aisha, I realised I hadn't bothered to look at any of the other exhibits; too late now.

"And in second place, for his stunning representations of the inner city, it's Joe Noone, for *Pixelated*!"

Everyone looked round, smiling politely. Becky started clapping. Aisha squinted through the darkness. Shrugging off Becky's arm I walked back to what I'd laughably called my 'exhibition', ripped down a few pictures, then stormed out, pursued by unhappy noises.

Manchester's panel beaten sky pressed down as I stomped, swarms of doubt buzzing in my head, afraid and lonely like a cloud, but not pristine, white and fluffy – dense, electric, yet empty. The city's Victorian grandeur and tattered facades meant nothing to me; relics of a bygone age. I was only vaguely aware of the emptiness of these streets, allowing their gravity to deflect and guide me south.

Then I was on a bleak road with great cold buildings beside and over it, traffic lights hanging from girders, like I imagined America. It felt like I imagined America, too: hot, humid and impersonal. As the train had drawn into Manchester, I'd looked out over my father's city for the first time in over a decade. Odd, how the houses were separated from the roads by great green shoulders, like buffers to protect drivers from car-jackers.

Dirty orange Fingerland buses crawled along Oxford Road like metal Clementines. I passed the Royal College of Music with its northern shoe-horn, beneath Mancunian Way, the university, where no-one I knew had ever been, would ever go, past the park where my mother had vanished one winter morning.

There were people with rosettes and clipboards outside the schools, and I realised that again I hadn't been able to vote; there always seemed some obstacle to prevent my participation. Spotting some waste ground I crossed it, towards some vaguely familiar flats. Some were the shape of colossal horseshoes; others just boxes, linked by concrete and graffiti. They weren't derelict; people, not artists' impressions, still lived here.

The emergence of the sun from behind a cloud seemed almost ironic. Not remembering much of the estate I was stunned by its scale; it was almost grand. I even felt a moment's regret at its coming demise. Soon it would be reduced to the status of modern myth, a bad memory in the minds of former residents. The people who designed this place had the arrogance of murderers. This was the opposite of architecture: Le Corbusier's nightmare made concrete.

As I walked through this devastated place I felt watched, and threatened, especially when I shot a few seconds on the camcorder. Then I remembered my walkman and my spirits were lifted by the sounds of Bizarre Inc, Moby, and SL2.

Eventually I reached what appeared to be some kind of shopping centre, except you couldn't see what was sold within any of the shops as all the windows were covered by steel. I went into an off-licence, and there was just a small metal hatch through which I asked the suspicious-looking Asian man for a can of Tennant's Super.

In the middle of the precinct I joined a few tramps slumped on a cluster of aerosol-decorated benches with their badges of blue. Furiously I raised my can to the setting sun, purples and reds melting into the blood behind my eyes. Sucking hard on the bitter treacle I waited for the numbness I sought and sat with my head down so as to avoid what was all around me; if I couldn't see them, they couldn't see me.

Dad was born in one of the flats overlooking the precinct, but I had no idea which one so I looked down at the dirty ground through blurred eyes. This wasn't the place for tears, to reminisce; I had to get out of there, had to walk, before I became a victim of my own past in the fading light. From my pocket I took the piece of paper Tony had slipped me: Dad's address in Millmoor. Why should he get the last word?

Draining the can I stuck it on a low wall, then went back into the offie for a bottle of champagne, which took a while to appear: confusion all-round. Swigging on the bottle (a months' worth of the good nappies) I drifted back out through the flats. I took a bus back into town, looking for Herm but not seeing her, not even knowing if I'd recognise her any longer, so different from my fantasies she had become, to a dark gothic cathedral where the trains headed east into the rising dusk.

Without thinking, as if pre-programmed to fuck up, I boarded a train and headed out through Manchester's streets and blocks and mills, blazing lights scattered among bracken-fields in the night rain, out into the satanic hills of my youth, cowering beneath as they towered above, awesome and cold and immovable.

In the reflection I found my eyes: I was terrified, rigid with self-pity and drink, and couldn't stop myself when my feet forced me to rise as the train slowed, stepping onto a ghostly platform and walking through the empty ticket barrier at Millmoor.

Then I was in the cold night and windy rain, scared by the rustling leaves in the trees, remembering *Baba-Yaga*. Walking on the mud beside the dead canal I smiled to myself, breathing that same foggy night air that had warmed my ears like the insides of Julie's soft, smooth thighs. We'd emerged from not watching *Chariots of Fire* at the cinema to find a blanket of snow over the town, luminous and benevolent. Sixteen and in love we'd skidded through empty streets; like children we'd thrown ineffectual snowballs until, by the canal, I'd caught her and dragged her tumbling into the snowy drifts.

It is a cause of some embarrassment to me that for many years after, exiled in London, I would portray my hometown as some dirty *noir* wise-cracking bitch, a Harlow Jean or a Mansfield Jayne, rather than what she really was: a neglected, but still pretty, fading actress who'd just missed the big parts but somehow hung onto her looks; someone who'd known greater things, been upstaged by greater people, but who still had enough to make you fall in love with her if the lights were right.

Partly it's due to fractured memory, selective feelings. For years all that I could recall of Millmoor was the night: the claustrophobia of the crowded town, the agoraphobia of the hilltop fields, the desolation of the browning moorland and the dereliction of the redundant factories where my sometimes father sometimes worked. The wind on my exposed skin, so cold it dried up my eyeballs, freezing snot to my face so it hung down like ambergris.

Only from this monstrous distance can I recall vividly the sun in the trees and the way the birds swooped over the valley, the sound of snowmelt water shining stones, the pretty village that Stone Nest had swallowed whole, the friendliness of the old gimmers with their harder lives and longer memories, their ancient moralities and tartan-fleeced boots.

I vomited stinging liquid into the black, sanguineous waters, wiped my mouth and sniffed the warm, wet air: so fresh and real. More memories: Dad, old friends and foes and fights, accidents, laughs and football in the empty streets.

My mouth tasted vile; I needed a drink. Plucking up courage I left the canal and limped into the town square, quiet like a minefield. It was always dark there, raining on my whole childhood. After visiting an offie – the same bloke behind the counter as years before, now grey – and a few minutes of panting up the still-familiar, yet astonishingly steep, hill tough on unpracticed London legs and lungs – I stopped, panting in surprise. Just one block, no longer two. Hughes Court had been demolished; Plath Court fingered the sky but cruel semis still dotted the moorland.

In one of his letters, Tony mentioned that he'd heard my dad now lived in one of the old terraces propping up the hill. I paused outside the door; it was late, but the lights were on. I took off my headphones and the sound of Utah Saints was replaced by Right Said Fred. I knocked on the door, quietly so as not to wake him. Big-sounding dogs barked.

The door opened and there stood Julie. I froze, and it crossed my mind that Tony was playing another trick on me. I was as shocked as Julie seemed to be. And she looked so much older – already there were lines beneath her bedraggled ginger fringe. She was only in her early-twenties, for fuck's sake; in her dressing gown and slippers she looked at least thirty. Each hand was holding the collar of a dog; both looked ravenous, snarling, paws skidding on the lino. I smiled nervously, but Julie spoke first.

"Fucking hell, look what cat dragged in." She looked me up and down like a frog regarding a Flymo. "What a state you're in Joe."

"Well, thanks a lot. I wasn't sure you'd remember me."

She snorted cynically. "How could I forget? Well, you'd best come in I suppose."

"I'm not – interrupting anything?"

"Do you think I'd ask you in if you were? Down Tyson!"

Pulling the dogs out of snapping range Julie opened the door wide and I pushed into the tiny living room. It was dirty, untidy, and smelled of shit. There were toys on the floor, scribble on the walls, dirty plates and scraps of food everywhere; rather like the squat, except on the mantelpiece above the hissing gas fire I saw silver foil and candles, the apparatus of escape. Locking the dogs in the kitchen Julie shivered and rubbed her covered arms.

"You'd best sit down I suppose."

Julie pushed me back hard onto a tatty sofa with sharp springs smelling of children. She sat in a big armchair opposite, nearer the gas fire. I was conscious of her legs: hirsute and blotched, but still a woman's legs. I smiled, but Julie didn't, just lit a fag and didn't offer me one.

"So," she said, her voice semiotic hoarseness. "What did you come back for?"

I sighed and picked a tortured Ninja Turtle off the floor.

"I dunno. I was just –"

"Passing?" She looked scornful, cynical, resigned. It wound me up.

"Alright. Look. I didn't come all this way to see you; I thought me Dad lived here."

"He does. Most of the time."

"What – you live together now?"

"Jealous?"

"Don't be fucking stupid Julie. Where is he? I haven't got all night."

"Alright, keep your hair on – oh, you can't, can you?"

I scowled, Julie laughed.

"He's up the school if you must know. Election."

"What's that got to do with *him*?"

"He's the schoolkeeper, Joe, someone has to lock up after the prats go home." I put my eyes down, too tired for a fight. "And no, Joe, we don't 'live' together. He took me in after Stig died. Nice of him really – two kids, lost me flat. He's a good bloke."

"And what does he get in return?"

"He works long hours; I look after his dogs. They won't let them in the school."

I looked around, sobriety looming, depressed by the claustrophobic little room. Next to the foil on the mantelpiece some unopened bills were propped against a stopped clock. When had it stopped, I wondered, maybe the day I left town? Above the fire there was a poster of a horse. I looked back at Julie, at this stranger. So different, still the same; she'd always loved horses.

"You've got kids, then?"

"Two boys. Billy and Adrian."

"How old are they now?"

"Two and three. Little bastards." She smiled, so that I wasn't sure if she meant it. "What about you?"

"A daughter. Sarah."

Sarah. Christ, what was I doing here? Who was looking after Sarah?

"Congratulations. Married?"

"Yes."

Julie's face seemed to convey sadness and pain. I sensed it was a face that others seldom saw, seeing above her head a vision of what she'd been like before drugs grabbed her attention: in the pub, one of the lads, drinking beer, swearing, getting fucked; then the crackhead, hoarse voice and leggings. This was still the Julie I knew, albeit briefly and with the blinkers of youth. She dabbed a tear away and laughed, embarrassed. I tried to look concerned; in my head I was taking pictures. Except they weren't to represent her life, they were to represent mine.

"Are you alright?"

"'Course, I'm just being silly. Do you want a cup of tea?"

"Alright."

Like all the old mill cottages that backed into the hillside, the place had a musty feel. She stood and walked the three paces to the minute kitchen, shooed the dogs from the door. I knew it would be dirty, could hear her clattering about in the sink for cups to rinse; a kettle was filled, there was the hiss of gas, the '*woof*!' of the flame, and she appeared in the doorway, clutching her dressing gown about her. All that was missing were the rollers. I smiled; her eyes narrowed in suspicion. "What's so funny?"

"Nothing. I was just remembering. I was walking by the canal tonight."

"A long time ago, eh?"

"Ten years."

"Seems longer." Julie frowned, bags under her field green eyes, IOUs of sleep.

"So – what happened with Stig? Tony didn't say much."

Julie's face drained. "He were pissed one night, scrambling on the moors. The silly bugger drove straight over the edge of the quarry. Funny thing were, they said he were alright for a bit, walked about for fifteen minutes laughing. Then he took off his helmet and dropped dead on the spot; his skull were cracked like an egg. This were before I dropped Adrian."

"I don't mean to speak ill, but I don't know what you saw

in Stig. He was a nutter."

"Well that's funny, he thought *you* were. He gives you bike lessons – you nick his bike. Lets you stay in his caravan – you burn it down. You fire horses, all alike –"

"Us what?"

"Fire horses. I'm into Chinky astrology at moment. You and Tony are the worst."

"Oh? Why's that?"

"Because you're fire horses, twice over. Conceived and born under the sign. You're the end of the world, you two."

"Oh, I don't know... I didn't think we were *that* bad."

"*Were*?"

To my horror, Julie looked like she was going to cry. I stood and held her shaking body awkwardly, letting her cry on my shoulder, stroking her head as she cried like the young girl she had been.

"Shhh, I'm here now."

"Not for long." It was muffled, but it still stung. She was right: not for long. I lifted her head up and looked into her wet eyes. So much pain was mirrored there; how much had I caused? She squeezed hard, like a sumo wrestler. "You'll fuck off back to poncey London again, leave me behind like last time."

"Do you blame me?"

"Don't bring it all up again Joe; it's fucking years past."

"But you live with him."

"We're friends, fuck sake. Friends. He took me in when I needed someone. Me own mum wouldn't have me in the house. He's a good man, your dad."

"He just likes little girls."

Julie looked at me angrily. "No, Joe, no. We *liked* each other. Age didn't come into it."

"So now you live together as friends, and you don't have sex?"

"Does it matter? Why does it fucking matter?"

"It matters to me."

She then burst into tears. I stroked her back through her gown, wondering what lay beneath.

Julie spoke into my shoulder. "Is she pretty, your wife? What's her name?"

"Becky. Not bad."

"Do you love her?"

I shrugged.

"Did you love me, ever?" A need to be told the only answer I could give.

"Of course I did."

And I did, at least some of the time – the times she wasn't there.

I bought out some cans and we drank. Julie was taking something to help her get off drugs: another drug. I remember sucking her bottle as she held me, and laughing, and rolling on the floor among the dogs. At some point Julie came downstairs in her old school uniform, buttons popping off the blouse, the skirt reaching mid-thigh; she lifted her pleats and showed me her panties and I clapped and cheered.

Dad never came home: maybe a recount. I woke in his bed, Julie snoring beside me, her school skirt hiked over her hips. Downstairs I found her two boys crying with cold and hunger; we watched *Thomas the Tank Engine* and I cut mould off bread to make them toast. Eventually Julie descended in her dressing gown, opened a tin of dog food and slopped it onto the floor. As I watched, my blood icing, stomach rising, the boys crawled on all fours to the plates, pushed the dogs out of the way and ate the cold meat, squealing with delight as if it were all a familiar and yet deadly serious game.

Mumbling some excuse I ran away. Again.

1993

The three of us – the Noones of North One – wrapped up against the chill spring wind and were about to set off for the park when the doorbell rang. Hopping down the darkened stairs to the now-derelict ground floor I opened the door on a pasty postie chewing gum, a glazed look in his eyes as he held up a parcel and pen.

"Sign here."

Frowning suspiciously I weighed the Jiffy bag in my hands. Oddly, it was addressed to Becky; it bore a Brigden postmark and an unfamiliar scrawl. I held it to my ear, but could hear nothing ticking so I signed for the parcel, closed the door and began ripping at the paper like a demented chicken-plucker.

The parcel contained my camcorder. Lifting it out carefully I shook my head in amazement: it even had the original tape in it, *Rule 43* written on the spine in Tipp-Ex. There was no note: why would Julie have sent it back now, a year later? Becky's voice from above made me jump.

"Are you ready, Joe? Sarah's getting stroppy."

Instinctively I put the camcorder out of sight behind a sack of cement.

"Coming."

Becky squinted down the dark stairs, unwarmed by a lightbulb for months. One unexpected benefit of the confabulation Stig had started was that most of those cyber-hippies, apocalypto-punks and other degenerates known by Tony's collective appellation as 'breeds' had moved on to pastures new. For much of the 80s and 90s the site was overlooked but rarely seen, except by a few junkies and homeless, the odd pro pushed from King's Cross and Euston to a damp mattress on one of the lower floors, abandoned by everyone except the rats and burglars with vertigo. I liked it here. More, it must be admitted, than it liked me.

There was a damp smell downstairs since the other squatters had moved out, and I usually carried the pram upstairs where it was warmer in a futile attempt to prevent the onset of rusting. The night before, however, I'd been tipsy pushing Sarah home from the daycentre and left the pram in the hallway, and now had to push past it to get upstairs. Sarah's little face peeped round our reinforced door; squealing with delight she ran into the living room, from which Becky emerged in a huff.

"Who was at the door?"

"Jehovah's Witnesses."

"Again?" Becky wound her scarf round her throat. "It's either them or the Liberals every morning. I'm not sure which is worse. Are you ready to go out?"

"I – can't. I need to work."

Becky's mood changed visibly.

"On a *Saturday*? You promised you'd come with us to the park."

I know, it's just – there's some editing I need to do. I haven't had much time lately, what with work and all. Feel like I'm neglecting stuff since the Manchester thing."

"You did come *second*."

"Exactly."

Becky wasn't happy; she grabbed up the bag of baby things and Sarah, and held her to me. I held Sarah under the armpits and lofted her high; she squealed and dribbled onto my face.

I kissed her on the forehead and she turned away, laughing. I handed her back to Becky, who snatched her harder than was necessary. Avoiding my eyes Becky walked down the stairs, Sarah looking back as I waved, her one-word question: "Twinkle?"

Since she could remember she'd loved me to sing twinkle twinkle, but there wasn't time.

"Daddy has to work," I smiled, waving. "Love you." Sarah turned away and her woollen hat bobbed down towards the front door.

By the time she was twenty months old Sarah was running marathons round the flat and had a vocabulary of around fifty words, some in approved dictionaries. Like all parents, we convinced ourselves that she was not only special, but gifted in some way yet to be discovered. If we could have afforded a piano she'd had rattled off a symphony; only the local drought of canvas and oils prevented her daubing some masterpiece rather than the crayon wall-scrawlings that gave the place its new improved identity.

Perhaps Sarah would be the artist I'd tried and failed to become; she was a pocket surrealist, and on the mornings you found a sardine in your slipper you were not surprised. Einstein's theory of relativity couldn't have explained the contents of her nappy; but to make up for it once I discovered her with an illustrated book of pirates trying to step into the picture.

The fact Sarah never slept was a good thing, for it meant I spent more time in her bed than I did with Becky, who only succumbed to sex once a month, at the heaviest point of her period, and it would be metronomic: eyes closed, her own lights out, too lazy even to corpse. Afterwards I'd wipe the blood from my cock, close my nostrils to the tangy odours and get a beer from my shelf of the fridge.

I could deal with the nappies, and the fatigue that permanently enveloped my senses, making the world a Ripper-haunted fog; what I couldn't take were the limitations imposed on my art. Becky kept quoting some critic about prams in halls, but I didn't believe it; Sarah wasn't keeping me from my work, Becky was, by getting a job. She'd found a great way out of love-making – she'd taken a job at some office or something, leaving me to cope with Sarah all day. Sarah being Sarah, a cute tomboy both cheeky and self-contained, I mostly coped; but sometimes my temper went and I'd snap. I never hit her but when I shouted she flinched, and I'd feel awful, especially when she ran from me as if afraid, running to a mother who wasn't there.

I'd already noticed the way friends changed when they became parents; they're still the same with you, but there appears this authoritarian aspect, this dominant streak, when addressing their kids; this look in the eye of protection and provision, this intolerance and reordering of priorities. Somehow, somewhere, I had acquired it too.

After running away from Julie's I'd gone to the town square where I'd once hit Tony with a snowball and rang Tony's flat. To my annoyance, Hermione had answered. Becky had gone back to London in tears. Herm's voice told me plenty; what she thought of me now. A part of me wanted to go hide on the moors, but I was scared of bumping into Dad now so instead I caught the train back to the city.

The front of the papers all showed John Major's grinning face, so I looked out of the window at the scarred brown fields: the borderlands. From Victoria I walked to Piccadilly for the London train, having dipped my Apex ticket in an early Guinness so the guard couldn't read the date. All the way home I slept, only waking once at Rugby, when I dreamed Julie was *Baba-Yaga*.

As you pull into Euston there are hundreds of brick arches alongside the track, erected for some utilitarian purpose like keeping the city from falling down, but I always imagined they were bricked-up tunnels to foreign countries, to the future and the past, to the iced-over oceans of Europa, to parallel universes and different dimensions, any one of which would have been preferable to going home if only Sarah hadn't been there.

Being brassic – and as a penance – I walked from Euston to the squat, feeling paranoid as I walked through Somerstown. London always felt foreign when I came home. I gave Becky some crap about needing to think and sleeping rough in St Peter's Square, and she gave me the silent treatment for a while, but Sarah giggled.

All-in-all I felt I'd got away lightly until I went to film Sarah in her bouncer and realised I'd left the camcorder at Julie's. I could hardly ring her now, so that was that; back to square one. Or so it had seemed.

After the front door slammed I gave Becky a safe few minutes to remember what she usually forgot, and when she didn't return I bounded back downstairs and fished the camcorder from its hiding place. Skipping back up I went into the front room, the warmest in the house, pushed old Stig off the comfy chair and inspected the camcorder. The battery was flat, but apart from that it appeared intact.

Locating the charger and plugging in the camera I went into the bathroom, dug out a hidden magazine of over-forties housewives, and ejaculated across the pixelated breasts of some scowling brunette and her dodgy headboard. Wiping my cock on the towel used for a bathmat I wrapped the page in a plastic bag and buried it in the kitchen bin, then went to my own little shelf in the fridge for a bottle of cider. Now I could edit in peace.

My film thus far comprised a dozen three-hour VHS cassettes that I was loath to throw away: they all just seemed too *important*. But I'd managed to do a highlights job, just under an hour, and hoped to end the film with Sarah's birth, which was on the tape Julie had, at last, returned. Sipping my can, relishing the unnatural silence of the house, I slipped in the newest tape and pressed search/rewind:

DISSOLVE TO:

A hospital bed. **MIDWIFE II** mops **BECKY**'s brow. **BECKY** opens her eyes. Purple and screaming, the **BABY** is pulled from her breast. The **BABY**, perfectly formed, wet and helpless, is pushed into her vagina. **BECKY** screams wordlessly, withdrawing her outstretched hand. Her wild terrified eyes close. **MIDWIVES I & II** move apart. The **BABY**'s head disappears. The **REGISTRAR**'s scissors heal the bleeding cuts round **BECKY**'s vagina. An uneven split from her anus to her vagina seals. Blood flows inward. The small black lump disappears. **BECKY** lies, legs wide, screaming, sweating. A hospital bed.

Pressing pause I leaned closer; Becky's breasts were heaving beneath the thin material. Trouble was, I couldn't concentrate; all I could think about was what to do with the camera itself. If Becky found it the whole business about my lost night up north would come up again.

All these conflicting thoughts were still preventing me working when I heard a muffled crump. I'd heard bombs before, and soon enough heard the first sirens. According to the radio, the explosion had been at Bishopsgate. Pulling on my coat, I grabbed the camera and a fresh tape and bounded down the stairs, almost tripping on one of Sarah's teddy bears and cursing her. Then I felt guilty. And then I remembered

Julie's kids, and didn't feel quite so bad.

The cops wouldn't let anyone near the City so I spent the afternoon in a morose tap room in Hoxton. Later that night, exhausted and drunk, I pushed open the door of number six and clicked the switch, remembering even as I did so that no light would appear. As usual I tutted at my own stupidity and groped my way upstairs. Oddly, there was no light there either, and no sound from the front room. That meant Becky was putting Sarah to bed, and there was no point in going into the child's room as she'd only get excited and that would irritate Becky even more.

The kitchen was dark and there were no warm smells from the oven. I put an ear to Sarah's door, half-expecting to hear Becky's deep breathing, but there was nothing so I went back into the front room and clicked on the standard lamp. The house was cold; the gas fire was out and the pram nowhere to be seen, yet Becky's favourite winter coat was draped over the sofa and Stig was asleep on it, covering it in feline fluff.

Shivering I clicked on the fire, then noticed the TV was on standby. Finding the remote control I clicked. For a few seconds it was hard to make out the image on the screen – a video stuck on *pause*. I pressed *play*.

09.04.92 UNTITLED.
SCENE 46. INT.
BEDROOM – NIGHT

Darkness. We see someone's breath billow like smoke in a small, pokey room. There are no curtains on the windows; we see fairylights sprinkled round the hillside, **JULIE**'s naked reflection.

JULIE
(WHISPERS)

Joe?

A grunt from under a duvet. A wall plastered with posters of dogs. **JULIE**'s hand lifts a duvet cover to reveal **JOE**'s sleeping face.

JULIE

(LAUGHING)

Welcome back to Millmoor, Joe. Hope I was worth it.

Blood cold, I pressed pause, rewind, play, rewind, in an attempt to make some sense of it all. In the distance, more sirens; I wanted them to go away, to go and find some fresh atrocity, but instead they came closer. I closed my eyes so that I couldn't see my own stupid, sleeping face. On the inside of my eyelids, Sarah smiled up at me as she was carried away down the stairs.

The knock on the door; the slow-mo float down the dark stairs. The two cops ascertained that I was indeed Joe Noone, husband of Becky Noyes-Noone, father of Sarah. Now I was sitting in an empty chair. The policewoman sat on the sofa opposite, on the wet patch where Becky sat to change Sarah's nappy. Behind her the other officer stood, looking uncomfortable, staring at some point on the wall. Already I was shaking, nausea rising.

"I'm afraid I have some bad news," said the policewoman, with her made-up name, professional standards of sadness in her voice. She had a small indentation on her cheek, a scar or reverse pimple. There did seem to be genuine tears in her eyes. "This afternoon, we were called to Camden Town station to deal with an incident."

Flashing lights in my head; I hugged myself with my arms, freezing, rocking, groaning. "According to witnesses, a woman holding a small child jumped down onto the platform; then she walked into the tunnel." The WPC struggled to control her breath. I closed my eyes, shakes, silent heaves; spikes, glass, extremes of both heat and cold. At one point I believe I may even have laughed, my chattering lips gummy blue.

"I'm afraid to say she was struck by a train shortly afterwards. Both the woman and child were killed. According to her identification, the woman lived at this –"

The animal growls and screams flashing from my gut blotted the rest out; I vomited onto my thrashing legs, and the shaking got worse, every synapse seeking new sources for fresh kinds of pain. As my convulsions increased they injected something in me. As darkness crept upstairs and warm delusory sensations took over I could hear Sarah laugh, and sing, and I looked for Becky but she was already fading, and in her place was this great slab of a tombstone upon which was inscribed one word:

Guilty.

"Wait here."

"Joe, I –"

"Wait here, Tony. I promise I won't do anything stupid."

We were sitting in Tony's car outside the squat a few nights later, drugs still raging through me. When Tony had arrived and promised to take care of me they let me leave hospital. The funeral had taken place without me. Hermione had attended, along with Becky's mother and sister; her father was incommunicado. Afterwards, Tony took me to the crematorium at Golders Green and looked away as I lay down on the ground.

Tony said he'd take me back to Manchester for a while – Herm had moved out – so I asked if we could go back to the squat for my things. Gathering my videotapes I put them all in a box, but the 13th was missing. After searching high and low I remembered and turned on the TV. Still frozen in time:

Julie's hand stroking my head. Ejecting the video I put it with the others, made a small pile in the middle of the floor and looked for a match. I lit one and held it to the pile, but it wouldn't catch so I blew it out.

I grabbed the camcorder, went into Sarah's room and filmed her cot, her mobiles, the crusty old nappy beneath the bed, then packed all the tapes in a cardboard box addressed to Aisha and went into the kitchen for the last of the cider.

Becky had written a three-letter note on the back of the star-naming certificate I'd given her in Mallorca and left it where she knew I'd find it: on my shelf in the fridge.

'*I [something] U.*'

The central letter or symbol is a rough circle with two string-ends, and I'll never be entirely sure whether it says I O U, or I♥ U. I still have the note, and take it out from time to time when melancholy with wine; but I still haven't figured out whether the manic squiggle is an O, as in *owe* or a rough-crafted heart, as in *love*.

1994

On a rainy Tuesday afternoon I found myself sitting on a picnic bench outside Filthy's with Tony. Now I remembered why: the phone call had finally arrived. My heart pounded and I felt for my wallet, drained my diluted pint. Pulling the hood of my coat over my eyes I watched some kid in a red uniform laboriously pedalling a Sainsbury's rickshaw containing two unenlightened feminists watching the Georgian wedding cakes of Amwell Street unfold.

Oblivious, deep in some tender thought, Tony sucked like a horsefly at his pint, hair sprouting from ears, nose and throat like some tropical disease, lycanthropy-lite – his lashes greying, the first vestiges of a beard proper. Following his split with Hermione he'd returned from Manchester and bought a flat in an old grey house at the scruffier end of St Paul's Road, its front doorstep framed with ornate plaster columns peeling as if from psoriasis.

Tony's career appeared to have stalled; but then I was on the DLA and living on his sofa. The job centre wouldn't even let me in the building now; every two weeks I turned up anyway, in need of routine, so they'd employed a belligerent guard to keep me out. Aisha had finished editing my film and was trying to flog it, unsuccessfully, which was why Tony thought we were sitting beneath a cloud.

"They're all turning into lesbians these days," I said, a delayed reaction staring after the receding heads of the rickshaw separatists and wishing I'd brought a camera. "I suppose that's what I'd do."

Tony shrugged and wiped rain off his nose, sniffing wetly.

"You always fancied lesbians."

"I wouldn't have let my daughter marry one, mind."

"They're easy to spot," said Tony.

"They drink pints and wear sensible shoes?"

"No," said Tony thoughtfully. "They just look happy."

It started to rain harder than ever and the coat Tony had bought me in the charity shop an hour before sprung a leak, so we moved inside to the snug warmth of the deserted tap room. Posters of Irish writers plastered the green walls, investing the place with an air of literacy. There were flyers for Sadler's Wells and literary evenings, a flickering telly hovered and the silence hissed like static.

In search of answers I peeked outside into the grey sleet of afternoon. A tramp I vaguely recognised caught my eye and raised a can of Tennants: *slante* to the man with the child in his eyes. A kindred spirit, it happened all the time. I guessed I should worry about this more than I did. Tony banged expansively on the sticky brown bar.

"Fresh brandy and horses!"

The barman was through the other bar and didn't hear him. I sat on the wet stool and sneezed, thinking about lesbians.

"I was holding a torch for you," I told a photo of some old capped Irishman on the wall regarding me solemnly, "but I dropped it down a mineshaft."

Looking out at the rain I sucked my pint, attempting to drown. A policeman entered to inform the clientele that due to a bomb scare in the vicinity everyone was asked to please remain on the premises until further notice; Tony and I clinked glasses joyfully.

A few minutes later we were sat by the window, looking out at the rain in silence. The gloom in the pub was the dark green of underwater; shafts of light from the surfaces were swallowed by the murk, even the clientele moved slowly like drowned pirates lashed to some forgotten wreck. Golden ponds draped across the metal table like doubloons, like clotted mirrors. There were men on the moon; the moon was under water.

When I leaned my forehead on the cold copper support, rain dribbled down to the bar. Time smudged like the old purple carpet that used to line the floor. Hours were lost, the sky darkened, alcohol began to coat my brain and eat away at all the layers of sophistication, culture and self-consciousness, centuries burnt out by booze, back through history to a world before laws, art and morality to the endless Kenyan plain.

Then I remembered why I had come, who I'd been waiting for. At the corner of my eye I could see him. The booze was kicking in harder to compensate for the emptiness in the pit of my stomach; memories sat on my soul like flat toads squatting on lilies. I just needed a way to include him, to draw him in.

"Fuck drugs," I said loudly, so he could hear, "all these chemical generation wankers going on about smack and e and coke and crack as if they're on the edge. I'm not on the edge, I'm at the *edge* of the edge. I've done them all and there's nothing like booze. Nothing in the world."

"Fucking right," nodded Tony, needing little encouragement. "All the greats were boozers. The best rockers, the best actors. It's the toughest drug there is. These teetotallitarians lecturing you on units… Bogart was right: they're all bastards."

"I couldn't agree more," said the well-spoken man next to Tony, elderly with a rumpled suit and cravat like a failed actor and long, thinning, swept-back greying hair, failing to keep the shine of his dome away from the light. A tad John

McCrirrick-ish – I've never trusted people who think you have to dress slightly wackily to be interesting. The man had small horn-rimmed glasses like the woodpecker in *Bagpuss*, giving him the air of an old schoolmaster before teachers were all drug-crazed social workers – when they used to *teach* something.

"Booze," said the man in an unholy Trinity accent, "has cost me my family, my job and very shortly my life. But I have no regrets. *Miaah!*"

An exploding cormorant.

"Best way mate," laughed Tony, drinking his pint. The man looked over his spectacles at me, sensing my mood.

"Ah, I see that we have an intellectual in our midst," he said, his breath smelling of cheese and pickle. Narrowing my eyes I lifted my head; whatever.

"What?"

"Tell me your name, young man?" He spoke with inherited authority; I had to answer.

"Joe."

"Joe." The man rolled the name around in his mouth. "*Hm*. Pleased to meet you, 'Joe'."

He held out a small hand; I took it. Hard ice. Something else I've never trusted, people who squeeze too hard. So many in every walk. Don't they get it?

"What's your name, mate?" laughed Tony, who looked like he was already getting there, or trying his damnedest to. The man raised his flashing eyes to the television set, where Jerry Springer's guests were stripping off to pixelated squares for a delightedly horrified audience.

"My name," said the man, waggling an admonishing finger, "is irrelevant. But I'll tell you anyway. My name is Theophilus Noyes." Not linking the surname, Tony laughed. I didn't. For some reason I seemed to excite the man's curiosity. Maybe he could sense my anger, maybe he could read my mind, intercept the calls.

"You've really been very kind, Joe. I know this has been difficult for all of us, but I simply couldn't allow –"

"No no no! I'd LIKE to tell him Mrs Noyes..."

In my brain I build a graffiti-covered brick wall with anarchy scrawled across it, a cuckoo in Midwich. Theo's pupils pierced through thick lenses; I watched bugs burn.

"Tell me something, young man," said Theophilus.

"Like what?"

"Oh, anything, anything at all. Whatever comes into your head."

"I'm an artist," I said.

There was a gloomy silence; Tony tried to break it with a laugh but the sound went bouncing, echoing, spinning down a deep dark hole. Wiping rainwater from my forehead and stinging eyes I looked into the foam.

"Married, chaps?" asked Theophilus, hastily moving on. "Settled down, I should say. I know how little time the younger generations have for such antiquities. *Hmm*?"

"No," said Tony, after a too-long moment adding an embarrassingly unnecessary, "not yet." As if. He once asked Hermione and she turned him down. Theophilus looked at me and I slowly shook my head. Theophilus was delighted and clapped his hands, thin and strong like termites.

"Oho! Three young chappies on the town, what a hoot, what a hoot! Confusing species, what? Have you ever wondered, why it is that women wear perfume and makeup?"

"Because they're ugly and they stink," I said wearily, bored but biding my time. Amazing, how frequently the currency of misogyny is employed to seal bonds between men.

"Miaah! You've heard it!" Theophilus's excited laugh; he noticed I hadn't smiled. "Well, how about this one then. Men shave their chins so their mothers keep loving them. Ladies shave their pudenda so their fathers keep loving

them. *Miaah!*"

"All right," I submitted, "all right. What do you call an Irishman who likes women more than he likes beer?"

For once Theophilus looked disconcerted, and shrugged, yellow eyes bulging. So, with some glee I said, "A queer."

Theophilus's face cracked. "My dear boy. Let me buy you another."

I shrugged. My hat slipped down over my eyes and I pushed it back to eyebrow level.

"Why?"

"Because I am a rich man – you appear to be of less fortunate means. Of course I may be wrong," Theophilus added hastily lest there be any offence. "For all I know you are the heir to Alan Sugar's fortune."

"Nah."

"Then please allow me, and let us see if the three of us can't clear up a few of the unpleasant conundrums of our time."

"Pint of Guinness please," said Tony seriously, unzipping his anorak to show he meant business. Tony had a fervent belief that drinking was a full-time job, especially now he'd lost his *actual* job, and he was burning with ambition. Theophilus looked at me; I detected a sparkle of humour beneath those severe eyebrows. Now I remembered why I was here, and almost felt sorry for him. Almost.

"Same," I said with a nonchalant shrug.

"Two pints of Guinness, my good man," said Theophilus to the hovering barman (a degenerate Pole in a Rolling Stones t-shirt), "and four double Absinthes."

"*Four?*" laughed Tony. "You were right about the booze, weren't you?"

"They aren't, of course, all for me," said Theophilus hastily, "only two. As my two new friends you must allow me the courtesy of extending a warm Irish welcome to you both."

"Irish, are you?" Tony grinned.

"Born in the wild west, my good man. And you, unless I am much mistaken –" Theophilus allowed himself the liberty of another look at me as he sniffed his nose and slid the sickly-coloured Absinthe along the treacle-bar – "*Fee-fi-fo-fum*, are very much Englishmen. Am I right?"

"Mm," I replied.

"Do not be so sad about it Joe, the English are a fine proud race."

"Bollocks."

Theophilus raised a teasing eyebrow at Tony as he regarded me with an open mouth.

"Oh dear dear dear! You mean to suggest your blood doesn't course with the fiery fuel of patriotism? You never stand for Her Majesty or the last night of the Proms? Does the mother of all Parliaments mean nothing to you?"

"I hate it. Hate it all. That's not England."

"That's not England…?" repeated Theophilus teasingly, as if to a sick child. "Then tell me boy, what is England?"

I paused, trying not to dwell on that word: 'boy.' Tony watched me apprehensively now, wondering why I was being so obstreperous; Theophilus was still wearing that annoying smirk. I swallowed the bitter green liquid in one gulp and took a sip of the new pint, ears throbbing with angry heat.

"Snobbery. Bradford tower blocks. Chips. Sexual repression. Shane Ritchie. America. Inwardness. Music. Fighting outside nightclubs. Fighting inside nightclubs. Student-bashing. Smugness. Cider with Rosy Glasses. Glue sniffers. *Oh, Doctor Beeching!* Football. Stephen Lawrence. Stubbornness. Pubs. 'Look at that queer playing with his kids!' Chips."

"Chips twice? Indeed indeed. Many of them nestled on your shoulder, covered in curry sauce, *hmm*? So bitter for one so young. But you know, many of those attributes may also be attached to other nations. Your England is not unique."

"It's not *my* England granddad – you can keep it. You know those white cliffs Dame Vera and our Gracie were always romanticising about? Know what they are? Mollusc waste. In short, a great big pile of shite."

"Pal, pal," said Tony, shaking the old man's shoulder and trying to inject a note of levity into an increasingly tense situation. For all his advanced years, Theophilus had a wiry build and a mean disposition under his cheery exterior; he looked the sort to carry a homemade knife of clay and glass, razor and metal. "Don't talk to Joe about England, he's in a bad mood."

"Very well," said Theophilus with a shrug. "I must confess to having certain days like that myself. But I have a suggestion to make, young man. If indeed your day is so awful, perhaps you should just take yourself off home. Sleep on it. Things will be so much better in the morning."

I considered this, or beating Theo to a pulp. I considered crying at the wonderful meaningless word: 'home'. Sighing, I swallowed some more liquid.

Theophilus cleared his throat. "Well, at least you've straightened your face. As reward I shall not only extend you another drink on this special day, I shall tell you the secret of women."

"This should be good," laughed Tony, forgetting. I doubted it, but I needed another drink.

"Women," announced Theophilus, one bony finger raised, "say one thing and want another. That is their basic secret. All you need to do is read between the lines and you shall emerge a victor in this, the oldest of wars."

"Give us an example," said Tony, grinning at me. I wished I could be as open and as happy as Tony. No wonder women loved him; the stupid cows were suckers for crap like that.

"For instance. There is a popular myth currently gaining

currency in the trendier quarters and the PC journals, that somehow women do not like to be hit." Theophilus stared sternly at me over the top of his horn-rims. "This is patently a nonsense. I shall give you fine chaps an example."

I was about to burst his bubble, to finish him off. Sarah waved as she floated down the stairs into the darkness. *Well if you wouldn't mind, Joe. But – be gentle, I know he's never been the most... responsible of fathers, but whatever Becky might have said he's no monster. His heart –* Sucking the Guinness, I shook my head quietly, but Theo didn't notice.

"A woman acquaintance of mine had a certain notoriety in our drinking circle for attacking her male suitors. You all know what harridans the creatures can be once they get their precious feathers up. She'd attack them with her claws, her teeth, aiming straight between the legs with her stilettos. Of course, most men were terrified of her. They couldn't even hit her back lest they find themselves dragged into court."

I looked round the bar, worn leather chairs and a fake fire; there was nobody there. I was no longer even sure that *I* was there. I wondered if people walking past in the rain, taking rides on rickshaws, could see anyone at all. Theophilus emptied his second Absinthe, turned the tumbler upside down and put coins on top. The barman brought three more over and, unaware, Theophilus death-rattled.

"Now. This woman, whose name escapes me, made the fatal mistake of arousing my interest. Big mistake. *Miaah!* Indeed indeed, big mistake on her part. Her woman's intuition was sadly unfocused when she picked me out of the crowd. *Miaah!* One afternoon we were in a public bar drinking with friends. We'd all had one or two too many, and the silly girl made the mistake of slapping my face. Big mistake big mistake. No?"

Tony laughed and looked my way; I hid inside my glass. Annoyed with me, Tony encouraged the old man, who seemed to be looking at me in a new way I didn't appreciate because I couldn't read it.

"So what did you do?"

"My dear man," said Theophilus, his face a mask of severity, "I picked the little thing up, put her over my knee, lifted her skirts and spanked her. Right there! *Miaah*! Goodness gracious, yes!"

Theo slapped his hand on his thigh with mirth; the reminiscence had brought a misty look to his eye.

Tony cleared his throat nervously. "What did *she* do?"

"Why, she went crazy! Attacked me with a bottle. I had to punch her on the nose." Theophilus reflected sadly. "Of course, things were never the same between us after that."

"What *did* you do," I asked, changing the subject, "for a living?"

"Mm?" For one moment, lost in his fantasies, Theophilus had clean forgotten our presence. "Futures, dear boy. In the City. Following a long, distinguished career in Her Majesty's air force."

"So first you bombed the world, then you fucked it up the arse."

"Aha. A communist. Hmm? It is pointless dwelling on a subject where there is complete incomprehension on both of our parts. Let us instead drink to the afternoon and the love of life."

"I'll drink to that," said Tony, relieved. He looked at me anxiously, as if to say 'don't fuck up a free drink' – that most heinous of crimes. I shrugged like a stroppy teenager, raised my glass of Absinthe, glowing like Kryptonite, and the three tumblers chinked together like metal slugs. Theophilus looked into me.

"Cheers," said Theo.

"*Salud*," said Tony.

"*Slante*," I said, downing mine in one. This was it.

"How about kids?" I asked Theophilus. The old man looked taken aback, but decided to make light of it.

"Why have a thirty-year-old when you can have two fifteen-year-olds? *Miaah*!"

"No. I mean – do you have any?"

Theophilus shrugged uncomfortably. "I have two beautiful daughters." He looked tetchy. "Why do you ask?"

"Seen them lately?"

"As I have already informed you young man, I have been overseas for some years. It is my primary mission once I have re-established myself in fine old London town to inform my daughters as to my wherea–"

Producing my wallet, I slid the photo of Becky and Sarah out and placed it beneath the old man's nose. Theo frowned for a second, then his eyes widened considerably beneath the thick glass lenses, a sparkle of excitement as he focused – Becky, in the park, holding a child who could only be her own blood. I pointed at each in turn.

"Your daughter. Your granddaughter." I paused, savouring the delight in Theo's face, the reunion prospects, the proud braggart of the public house. "Don't get your hopes up. They're both dead."

It was easy: Theo's ex gave me his pager number when he came back into the country. I never did find out where he'd gone. Prison? No, too easy. Patagonia? Maybe. Maybe he'd joined the Libdems. Anyway he was back a few hours and I paged him:

'Hi Dad it's Becky meet me in the Fountain – surprise!!'

I'm not proud of what I did; nor am I ashamed. In a way I was saying goodbye to Becky and her past, once and for all. Theo pushed her into that tunnel as much as I did; why shouldn't he share my pain?

I know now that it was a ludicrous fantasy. The guilt, and

Becky and Sarah, will never leave me. With Sarah, it's simple: I killed her. With Becky, more complicated: I pushed her over the edge. I know that now, knew it even as the WPC held me down in my shock and grief, but sometimes I still like to pretend it wasn't my fault.

I'll let you be my judge.

Leaving the pub, where Tony attempted to console the inconsolable, I bought a badge of blue from an offie, then walked back up Amwell Street just as the rickshaw man came freewheelin' down, looking for fares and trying to act nonchalantly.

Blankly I drifted along Pentonville Road to Baron Street, through Chapel Market onto Upper Street, which I hardly recognised any longer: the Fox had gone, and so had the Pied Bull. Even the portrait of that old bespoke tailor smiling kindly as he sewed trousers had been replaced by a shop selling irredeemable tat. Why does no-one *make* anything anymore?

Mixed with the drugs they still prescribed to make me feel better, the absinthe was making me delirious. Colours were coming back into my life, into my world-view, except too vividly to focus, to separate their subtleties. Further along Upper Street two little girls waited outside a shop. The smallest, about five, was in a wheelchair and laughing as she span around. The older one, who already had it all worked out, looked as sad as an ancient. A businessman flashed past on a unicycle; by the fire station doors a man leaned in towards a window and a woman leaned out like a death row scene, their hands separated by glass or adultery, or some other barrier to happiness.

Outside Islington Town Hall I began to howl, causing pedestrians to race for cover and pigeons to scatter. The Tennants Super was reacting to the cold onion bhaji I'd had for lunch, and I vomited into a bin outside a restaurant I'd never heard of, then lay down in a comfortable pile of vegetables, old news.

As I lay there, listening to the sounds of the streets, the pulse of this city that had nurtured and ravaged me – and seemed inclined to take me now anytime it wished – two men ate Italian rabbit and polenta in the restaurant and debated the future of our glorious nation. Now and then I'd catch one of them look up at me where I slumped, lying in the gutter, looking at the scars, and sometimes in whimsical and preposterous moments I fancy that I helped shape their plans for the future.

I knew, lying there watched over by these two men, that political ideology is both prison and prismatic: it refracts and it imprisons the truth. Maybe it was Presbyterian Brown, eyes averted from his beloved, doing that odd thing with his mouth as he nodded out of the window at the forlorn young man adrift on the pavement; utilitarian Brown, reflecting on the curse of booze, vowing then and there that he would do all in his power to get the drifters and the dreamers back into work.

And then Messer Blair, his socialist principles – like everything he said and did – warped out of any recognisable shape by his faith, as black holes corrupt light from a collapsing star. I sometimes like to think that when he saw me lying there, as he discussed carve-ups and careers and wolfed swan canapés, Tony resolved to do whatever it took to change this unacceptable face of the country he loved.

And sometimes I wonder if either of those bastards loved me, even just a little.

2007

"Are you awake?"

Alona's whisper behind me in the darkness, breath warm and present-tense on my naked shoulder. Her hand stroking the bumps on my spine as if she were blind, reading some sleepy romance.

"Yes."

My voice had cracked in the night, my throat sore with ancient tears.

"You have bad nightmares."

I know it; in this dream everyone on earth is lying in bed, eyes wide open even as I sleep. I open my eyes towards an invisible rough-hewn wall. The window is covered by thick felt: hermetically sealed, this side of the cave achieves almost total blackness so that, disorientated, I begin to imagine light. Alona's hand strokes me but still she snores softly, nurturing even in sleep. It isn't her fault; none of this is her fault. Why shouldn't she have children of her own? She'd be a great mother.

Last night we argued again ('argue': such a nondescript word for such revealing agonies; so like 'agree', so un-onomatopoeic), and I was drunk with both decades-old and hours-old guilt. Alona was prying like a pin in a clam, and I couldn't say anything that would make her feel better. What if I give her a child and then disappear? Would that be a good thing? I'm no longer sure.

Yesterday, in the bar with Tony, a cloud of smoke formed the face of Becky, and then Sarah, laughing as I wriggled my nose. These moments come upon me less frequently now, but always when I least need it. Sometimes I *do* need it: to see Sarah's face, her tiny fingers around mine, the way she gurgled with joy when I bounced her on my knee. When I consciously try to summon her she shies away, as she sometimes had from my open arms, running to her mother.

After her death something shorted deep inside me; sparks doused, lights dimmed. Like shadows at night, I could see the same shapes but the colours were faded and dull. All the sublime magic of youth had been knocked out of me; I was still wandering, but all the wonder had gone.

Every day I press rewind, or perhaps the word is re*wound*. Fresh wounds, layer upon layer. In my artificially vivid memory, Becky comes home to an empty house, no sterilised bottles, no nappies. As she tries to feed Sarah, screaming with winds both internal and citywide, Becky sits on the remote for the video and absently presses rewind then play. Watching silently (Sarah snuffling hungrily) as the camera wobbles through some derelict estate, me on a railway platform. The film stops and Becky and Sarah are nodding off together, when Becky hears a loud, clear voice. "Joe?" A grunt from under a duvet. A hand lifting the duvet to reveal my sleeping face: so familiar, so foreign.

Becky presses search/rewind and watches again. A small, cold room: the camerawoman's breath escapes like smoke. There are no curtains, and Becky sees fairylights sprinkled round the hillside, while at the same time in the same space a naked woman's reflection. Sarah sleeps; Becky presses search/rewind again. Again. Sarah sleeps, trusting.

Because I never saw their bodies I saw Sarah and Becky for years after, in women and pushchairs, in the laughter of toddlers. For a while I became convinced this was all some huge joke, some ultra-Beadle, the WPC a kiss-a-gram, and I would wake one dark morning to feel Sarah tickling my toes. At the inquest, they said when Becky hopped off that platform with her leaden, sleeping bundle the indicator said the next northbound train was due on platform 2. Maybe she thought she'd be safe? But as she walked into the black hole up it flashed:

CORRECTION: NEXT NORTHBOUND SERVICE PLATFORM 4.

Nobody stopped her; for years I raved and cursed and planned ways of tracking down these strangers who watched her walk into the tunnel with her bundle – a twenty-month bundle! Bigger than a midget, come on! But then, would *you*? Then I tried to convince myself that she didn't mean it, that she was making a *point*; except that at the inquest the tube driver in question (fifties, haggard, ruined) said that as his train lights shone in the face of this woman holding a sleeping child in her arms, and he frantically jumped on his brakes, she smiled sweetly, eyes full of hope.

Sometimes of course I dream that I'm the driver, rattling around the electric warrens beneath some inhuman city, knowing what's coming but unable to find the brake; knowing that all too soon my lights will shine upon two faces, alike and opposite, two sides of a spinning coin. And sometimes I dream that the baby-eating monster stalking the woods has my face.

I sleep late and when I wake Alona's made continental breakfast. I forgive her, and I'm trying to watch Negroponte's resignation speech and methane lakes on Titan when she comes in with the letter. Why is it the only time that she talks to me – after sitting in reverent silence through Latin American soaps all evening – is when the news comes on? She'll say something complicated that demands a complicated response, involving trips to the filing cabinet and the car, while over her shoulder I see news clips of burning cars, sinking ships, UFOs.

The letter bears a London postmark and feels expensive; you can tell by the paper, the very font mocking our hillbilly address. Alona's watching me with an expectant expression and I'm surprised to see her smile as if she knows what's inside. The envelope contains a solicitor's letter and advises me to check my bank statement.

"What is it?"

Like Chris Tarrant I show her the letter; she gets her fingers on it and I try to snap it away, but she's too fast. After reading the letter – a lot of legalese about appeals – Alona kisses my cheek. The impression burns with my guilt; she's kissing Judas.

"It's about time." She's being conciliatory; I can't bear it. "You deserve it."

"Do you think so?"

"Don't be stupid. Of course!"

"We'll be fine now."

Alona looks very pleased and shrugs, which works her gown loose and I glimpse the top of her breast over her nightie. She catches me looking and covers herself demurely.

"Does this mean you will give up the job?"

"Not sure yet." I sigh. Truth is I enjoy the boat, even if it rarely pays dividends. The thought of never heading out to sea (losing contact with the shore) depresses me. But then there's no reason why I can't keep the boat, or buy a bigger one. So long as Alona's happy I can do as I like. Now she can stop typing love letters for that old sleazebag lawyer and open the beauty parlour she's always wanted. I kiss her cheek and feel her tit against my forearm.

"Why don't you go into town," I tell her. "Treat yourself. Or rather – my treat. I'll cook us a meal to celebrate."

Alona rushes to get ready and I read the solicitor's letter again. Aisha had sued me for breach of contract, but the judge felt she was being unreasonable. She had taken far too long to make the deal and at the end of the day (the letter used those exact words), it was my story and my project and my art. Her chance to appeal expired on the last stroke of midnight, 31/12/06. I tasted a grape.

And anyway, I deserve this. Becky owes me. That's what the note says.

She owes me.

After Alona hurries out, brandishing credit cards with their newly raised bars, I sigh and flick the channels, bored with the shape of the screen, the box. Why can't someone design one that's circular, octopus-shaped? The satellite picks up several dozen channels from four countries, but there's nothing I want to watch, just the same regurgitated nonsense: a David Jason special, *A Touch of Frost* hot on the heels of *Open All Hours* sandwiching *Fools and Horses*.

Do you think David ever watches his life on UK Gold? With Sky Plus he can skip decades: one minute he's young and fresh-faced, virginal and innocent, in a tatty apron; then a wise-cracking wheeler-dealer ducking and diving, and relentlessly cheerful; now old, cynical, weary, investigating murder and rape against his own soul.

The disease of nostalgia has spread quicker by satellite. When people watch *Dad's Army* it isn't nostalgia for some ancient war; it's for a misplaced childhood watching *Dad's Army*. My nostalgia is for watching *Dad's Army* repeats in the eighties at the squat. Now I watch repeats of *TOTP2* just to remind myself of the halcyon daze of the early nineties, when Becky and Sarah were still alive – a decade, a century, a Millennium before.

When I hear the music of my youth, the overriding emotion

I feel isn't sadness, or regret, or happiness – it's vertigo. I'm rocketing away from those times, from the dark bedsit fumbles and giroday celebrations, spiky-haired girls with sweet lips and puffball skirts, the students and squatters and lefties and rollups, so long ago and vanishing like maps beneath my feet. If you're young, enjoy it all – the poverty, the insecurity, the longing – particularly the longing, because grown-up longings are different, slower, as permanent as life.

I've made no plans to meet Tony today, but not wanting to be alone with my blood money I pick up my mobile and ring him.

"Hello?"

"It's me." I'm vaguely annoyed that Tony hasn't programmed me into his phone. At the other end he stage-whispers conspiratorially as he walks.

"Joe, what the fuck were you playing at with Geordie? She had to wait hours for someone to pick her up off that beach! She's going mental here!"

"Are you in the bar now?"

"Yes, she's telling everyone you took her out to some island and just dumped her there!"

I sigh. Without wishing to appear pedantic, it *wasn't* an island and you *could* get a reception. Although come to think of it, I hadn't actually checked to see if she had a phone. But then, everyone does these days; it's another form of tax.

"I wouldn't come into the bar again Joe, you'll be lynched!"

Tony's obviously now outside; he's allowed a hint of amusement to tint his devil-may-care-but-I-don't voice.

"I don't intend to. Dodgy clientele. Look – are you still there?"

"Outside now. Geordie gave me a funny look when me phone went. She wanted your number but I said I didn't have it. I went in the back and deleted you just in case. She's after your *balls* mate."

"Well – she *was*. Meet me in the square in ten minutes and I'll take you somewhere more – Spanish."

Looks like today will be another day wasted. Still, there's always tomorrow; just as there are yesterdays. What was it Tony always used to say when we were spending our last pennies and it was a week to dole day?

"Worry about tomorrow the day after."

But then, that was a long time ago. The first thing I'll do is check the balance of my account.

The nameless restaurant is at the end of a dusty coast road, a cove on some remote headland, thin metal chairs stuck in pebbles a few feet from the water. You can sit and watch the gentle tides from beneath an old wicker shade that dapples your skin in speckled light; even my bonce looks good. I like it here because you can see across the bay to the mountains, and the wine's Moorish, but mainly because it's the only place in town that still sells *chanquetes*.

"Not bad," nods Tony, prescription sunglasses covering his eyes, squeezing lemon onto his steaming plate.

"Put some salad on your bread, then the fish, then the lemon and an olive. Nothing like it."

Tony does as he's told and nods in approval; juice glistens on his beard and I nearly gag. Never did understand beards. Pulling my cap down over my eyes I hail Alphonso, the owner, who smiles.

"*Vega Sicilia*." The waiter laughs and says something I can't quite catch before moving off. Tony raises an eyebrow above his glasses.

"What's this in aid of? Even in the *Caprabo* that stuff's not cheap."

"We're celebrating."

"Celebrating what?"

"You don't know?"

Tony shrugs and tucks in, and I watch him eat, nauseated; I suck on a few olives to help the wine down. A huge gull lands on the rail of the wooden veranda and stares at me with hard dinosaur eyes.

"I tell you," says Tony, laughing, "Geordie's out for blood. What the fuck were you playing at out there? Wouldn't she shag you or what?"

"I don't want to talk about it. Finished?"

Tony pushes his plate away and dabs at his beard with a napkin; my stomach churns, but he looks pleased.

"That was superb."

Superb; almost forty and he's finally shaken off the shame of his origins, a house with a name. Sipping the heavy wine I nod at his greasy plate.

"Enjoy it while you can. That was *chanquetes*. The more people eat, the less there is. In the end they'll become extinct because we love them so much."

"That's love, Joe. A dangerous game."

The water glitters and a delicate breeze sets wind chimes singing. Tony looks comfortable; I clear my throat.

"You still haven't told me what happened with Herm."

Tony shrugs, black glasses looking out to sea.

"There's someone else."

"You, or her?"

"Things have been rough for a while… in the end she just said we couldn't love each other anymore. Odd, the way she said it: *couldn't*. As if you have a choice."

"You don't think people choose who to love?"

"Fuck, too profound for me." The fish oil in his beard catches the sun, like he's feasted on rainbows. "How about Alona – do you love her? A lot? Or a little?"

"In Spain there are no words for *town*. Only *pueblo* and *ciudad*."

"And in Spain you started talking in metaphors – that don't work." I smile and nod his point. Just when it seems I might have underestimated Tony, his sense and sensibilities, he ploughs on like a runaway lorry into a bus queue. "Anyhow, you can't love her that much if you're trying to shag some Geordie."

"Her name is Sarah," I say quietly. Tony's eyebrows climb over his shades, oil glistens; I feel this sudden overwhelming urge to give him a shave.

"*What?*"

"Geordie. Sarah. That's her real name. I thought you'd have known that – I mean, you *own* the place."

Cogs must be whirring behind Tony's eyes. There are lines there; soon he will be as old as me. In the end he shrugs.

"I didn't – she never said. Anyway it's a common enough name, Joe."

"I know."

"You never – I mean, you don't talk about them, much. Becky. Sarah." Tony clears his throat and flushes pink, down to his beard, uncomfortable with the conversation but drawn to it. "Do you think – she meant to do it?"

My glass empties; picking up the bottle I pour. The gull has vanished. Tiny waves slip close. Once I fucked Becky in the surf of the Med.

"Of course."

Tony looks out over the sunset, as if someone's told him that's what you do.

"She were a fantasist," says Tony. "Never straight about anything. Remember that shit about the older woman on the train? All crap. She never went to school in London. Herm says she met Becky at Glastonbury."

"It hardly matters now, does it?"

Tony shrugs. Feeling sorry for him, I continue. "I sometimes wonder what her last thoughts were," Then I blurt out: "Was she thinking about me, or Sarah, or did she have the cure for cancer? That must be the loneliest moment: your final thoughts, knowing you'll never express them to another soul. All those million upon millions who die alone, all those useless thoughts…"

"Unless we live on."

I shrug; seagulls circle like they're listening for profundities. Then they wheel away. The waiter has disappeared but he knows we'll meet again. When the sun touches the water it will fizz and smoke. Tony blows his nose and inspects the napkin. I eat nuts as Tony sets out his little stall.

"I suppose I believe in momentum, do you know what I mean? Your emotions are too powerful, an energy in themselves. They can't just *dissolve*. I think afterwards your emotion keeps turning for a while, depending on who and what you are."

I finish my drink, stand.

"The worst, the loneliest death, is when nobody knows where you are and no-one misses you and as you die you realise no-one will ever know, and no-one will ever find you. And if they do – they won't care."

"Pint?"

"Happen."

"Billys?"

"Hardly. Let's go into town."

As we walk back to the car Tony elbows me in the ribs.

"Talking of God. Richard Dawkins goes up to the pearly gates and knocks. God says, 'who is it?' Richard Dawkins says, 'it's me, Richard Dawkins.'" Tony pauses. "'Hello? God?'"

A few months after breaking the news to Theophilus I went back to Archway. It was only a short walk through the cut and up some stairs (gasping, holding my sides) and I was on the iron bridge; as I walked to the centre, wrought iron defaced the horizon. In the middle I hiked myself up and over, standing on the ledge and admiring the view.

From up there during the day you can see to the edges of London, blurred in its sepia of poison mist like a *hazchem* haze, Bhopal-lite, but it was a surly evening, and coloured lights stretched to infinity like a huge model of space, except for all the ordered vertical lines of blocks of flats, offices and public buildings like astrological clusters of reason; places where things get *done*.

Closing my eyes, I released my fingers and gravity was pulling me when a hand grabbed my arm. I looked back, into the disturbing grey eyes of an old guy, fifty or sixty, scruffy, with a mass of curly hair, wild and as untameable as wire wool, an erratic mess of spikes and loops. I pulled at his grip, but not too hard. He averted his eyes and I followed his gaze across the city; sirens called.

"They sound a bit like bells, after a time," he said quietly, in an Irish accent. "The sirens. Do you know, it was about here Dick Whittington heard Bow Bells. Telling him to turn again."

He'd gone there for the same reason I had: to fall and to fade from view. But there was someone there first – they could hardly have jumped together, the papers would think it was some weird pact – so he'd convinced this other bloke to change his mind. After that, that was all he did, wait for people like me. He told me he always knew who'd jump, and I asked what about me. You know the answer to that one, he said.

And so I turned. For a while I thought he was my real dad. He died that winter: hypothermia.

Despite the fact I don't like *Vega Sicilia* I've drunk way too much, and several times the van skids on loose roads as we drive back along the darkening track to the highway. Tony's in chatty mode; I realise that just this once I don't mind.

"You'll never guess," says Tony. "I should have told you before. Julie's got a novel out!"

I almost veer into the ocean.

"*What*?"

"About her drug hell apparently. Aisha got her a six-figure deal. Apparently it's brilliant."

I'm struggling to comprehend the enormity of this news when something comes to me.

"Is it Pedigree, chum?"

Tony frowns.

"What?"

"How about prizes – did she Winalot?"

"Prizes? It's not even out, yet. Julie let me have a read of it."

"Did she? That was nice of her."

"Interesting actually. Apparently you never fucked her when you went back to Yorkshire."

I concentrate on driving, let Tony do the waffling. Bullshit, it's what he's paid for.

"According to her book you were so out of it, Julie put a duvet over you and left you to sleep it off. She was mad at you so she turned your own camera on you for once."

"Does Hermione know all this?"

"Yes," says Tony, "she knows. Wasn't too pleased with Julie, as I'm sure you can imagine."

"And does she still blame me?"

"How would I know?"

I'm too shocked to be angry; Julie's stupid trick sent Becky into that tunnel. But then I'm hardly blameless myself. Maybe I could sell my story to the *News of the World*. Then again, perhaps not. Too many secrets of my own. In any case, who cares about writers?

I look sideways at Tony, his long fingers gripping the door handle; the stupid Claddagh ring Herm always made him wear has disappeared.

As we pull up outside the house I look at my granddad's watch: almost six. I'm supposed to be cooking a meal, haven't even been shopping, forgot the *chanquetes*. There are no lights from within, and I shiver in the last of the sun. Tony waits outside in his world.

I know instantly she's gone – her clothes, her stupid ornaments, her toiletries. And, presumably, our credit cards. There's a note on the table I try to avoid; finally, reluctantly, I pick it up.

'Are you awake? Or do you sleep every day and all night long? I thought we were happy. I was best in my class at economics. My father was once mayor, and my mother quite like Franco. You never asked. I am going to be happy one day. I never told you this but my sister have histerectomia so one day I will have babies and I will own a salon. Once I went to Morocco and it rained the whole time and another time I was in a film. You never asked about me, my life; now you never will.

Remember what you told me, about the flesh magnets? I'm leaving before I start to believe you.

With love,

A.

PS thank you for not telling me about your daughter.'

PART III: BRITANNIA JUNCTION
1995

With our youthful dreams just about intact we boarded a Dum-Dum jumbo and flew out over Bengal bay and across the Burmese delta, me silently processing my mental pictures of India, Tony beside me apparently asleep. In his case, travel had narrowed the mind; for me it just reinforced those opinions I already owned.

Did you ever see that Hagar the Horrible cartoon? Hagar's polishing his armour, his adoring young son watching. Hagar says, "You know, son, when you grow up you'll find people are pretty much the same all over the world." His son says, "Really, Dad?" "Yup. That's why I got this nice shield…"

After Calcutta, Bangkok airport seemed like a glistening neon dream, and the cab ride into the city was an aircon shock streaking on smooth highways between office blocks and shanty towns, the night hot but not so humid nor as polluted as I'd feared, looking out through jetlagged eyes at the homeless crouched beneath billboards advertising choc-ices with Western lips, Dunkin' Donuts, KFC and the twin golden arches of MeccaDonalds, with its halal burgers and *baht*-deals.

By the time the cab reached Khao San Road the weariness had set in again, the same travel fatigue as in Delhi and Pushkar; banana pancakes, scarred Western white boys,

Trustafarians with dreads, short-sighted pedos on the pull, suburban chancers under the misapprehension that Easterners are stupid and don't know about money and they'd make a pile out of carpets, whiteboards outside cafes offering coach tickets to Chang Mai and slow boats to China, identical destinations on the *Rough Planet* itinerary, discreet street boys selling grass, ass and bang lassi, tie-dye Hampstead girls with their umbilical chords to daddy's purse-strings, mothers worrying and sending letters daily via *Poste Restante*, hustlers selling flea-bitten rooms above brothels and video bars, Australians rowdy with beer fighting Kiwis in the street over some issue of parochial pride; traders flogging t-shirts and UV-minus shades, postcards to your friends so they'd know how fine you are, how experienced, how *travelled*, East 17 blaring from every pub and Kodak and Xerox and all the other dollar badges, toned-down green fish curries and watered whisky. Then the room – aircon cool, and spread-eagled on twin beds beneath the swooping fan watching toxic smoke drifting up to be caught in its rotors, wondering lazily, as I snap away before drifting into sleep, how many others have seen similar views of Asia and thought they were the first.

I was going boldly where many others had been before because my Aisha-edited film, *The Archway and the Angel*, had come second in an Arts Council-sponsored competition. Although the prize was piffling I received a bursary from an artist's trust to research my next project. Immediately I bought two tickets round the world. There were too many memories in London, soaked into every wall and public house.

I didn't want to go alone, and Tony was between jobs and Herm-spells; besides, I was still on his sofa. I think he regretted coming the minute we arrived in India. I spent most of the time demanding to know who'd won first prize and why. My wife and daughter dead, and it was only worth second prize? How to win – murder everyone I'd ever met?

When Tony woke up we bought a bottle of Mekong and wandered the streets, where we were propositioned half-heartedly by beautiful girls with glossy hair and diminutive bodies who worked on stalls selling short-term clothes, porn postcards and *khao phat kai*. This part of the city was less seedy than King's Cross; compared to Calcutta, it was a doddle. In the name of research we went down Pat Pong Road.

It was better there, dangerous as a knife; there were blackboards outside clubs: '*girls pull string razor blade outa vagina!*' Inside bored-looking women shoved ping-pong balls up their cunts, before plopping them into pint glasses. It all seemed rather futile, desultory and dull. None of the dancers knew how to suck up a ball without touching so we grabbed a ball out of a glass and started kicking it about, and got ejected. Bangkok was too hot anyway, and the pollution accumulated over the days so that night we took the night train from Hualamphong.

Dawn found us in the sticky southern swamps, a rising red sun bleeding over everything like ketchup. On a rickety boat to Ko-Pha Ngan we sat on the stern and tried to smoke a spliff, but the waves kept breaking over our heads and made the Rizlas soggy. We soon bored of the beautiful people playing volleyball, the arseholes on water skis and other aquatic shite, and used old Triumph motorbikes to explore the interior. Tony started to grow a disastrous goatee; it took a real effort of will to even speak to him without trying to yank it off.

On the fourth morning we found what we'd been looking for since leaving Heathrow. Scrambling along a track over the mountain the jungle got wilder and the track disintegrated into a muddy rut. At one point a long, almost luminous, green snake crossed our paths; we gave it respect and right of way. Finally we rounded a bend and discovered the pool.

It was actually a lagoon, separated from the beach by a sandy sliver, the water surrounded by Yungian coconut trees, durian trees, jeruk, mangosteen and rambutan. In shorts and sandals we flopped the bikes over onto the soft sand, grabbed our clinking shoulder bags, climbed a large rock that overhung the deepest part of the pool and sat panting on its flat top.

Tiny dazzling fish soared through turquoise clouds, swooping and shoaling above the sandy floor. Birds called softly in strange accents and the sunlight splashed clean, light warmth over the clearing, the fragrant air a friendly skin touching mine. I wanted to cry but Tony would think I was being soft so I spat.

"Not bad."

"Seen worse."

"Not as good as Millmoor, is it?"

Tony mocked outrage. "Is it fuckers like."

"Be nice if it had a bar on a raft in the middle."

"Selling Stella."

"Full of topless barmaids."

"Ah well." Tony began to roll a joint of pure Laos grass. I just started laughing, could hardly speak.

"You know that Lennon song I used to sing on the sites? *'Nobody told me there'd be days like these?'* I always thought that was about the bad days, about all the shit. But I never knew – I mean, nobody told me that life could be this good."

Tony passed the spliff and I peered out through my viewfinder over the pool, palm fronds dipping like pickpockets, fruit splashing from branches like half-charlies, sunlight in every shade, in every nuance. Becky had once told me that when she was six, she saw an illustration in one of the encyclopaedias littering the house – the earth next to the sun to give an idea of scale. Becky had thought they were really as close as that; that at any moment one sunlick would incinerate the planet. Tony opened his bottle of Singha beer, took a suck and went "*aaah*!", as he always had. I looked at him curiously.

"Where were you?"

Tony narrowed his eyes, evasive.

"Eh?"

"The night before leaving London. When we were meant to be packing."

Tony scowled. "I went to see Hermione."

"And?"

"We sort of got back together."

I sucked my beer, warm from the ride.

"What do you mean, 'sort of'?"

"I mean we had sex and got on okay, and she said go with Joe and we'll see how we feel when you get back."

Tony spat a long way into the pool; tiny fish surrounded the floating green globule and closed in on it like a giant iris, a kaleidoscope of scales.

"And how do you 'feel'?"

"I love her, Joe. I'm going back."

"But I bought round the world tickets!"

"I can cash mine in. I don't want to go to Australia. I want to go home."

I could see no point in arguing, in many ways I was relieved. We said nothing; the sun was shifting and losing tone and it would soon be time to take the bikes back to the rental place, then spend another evening watching satellite football and drinking lousy beer. I realised I wanted to go home too; to London, to the pub, the murky purple carpets and the rain, to the evocative names: GEC Alsthom, Pirelli, Setanta, Ferodo; to Albanian babies, gypsy fag-sellers, snarled-up traffic and hoarse shouts in the night.

"Come back with me," said Tony, stabbing out his spliff. "Hermione says Aisha wants to be your agent."

"I know she does."

Hermione and Aisha had struck up a friendship in Manchester, and sometimes I had the uneasy feeling I'd only come second in the film-making competition because of this friendship. The thought of getting somewhere after all this time in the wilderness because of nepotism filled me with horror; almost as much as having an agent.

"So you and Herm are getting back together?"

"It won't be easy," admitted Tony. "It's like Becky's always there in the background. Hermione blames herself, you know."

I was shocked.

"*Why?*"

"You know Becky always had a thing for her. They dabbled once, but it wasn't Herm's thing. She was experimenting, and they sort of agreed that was all it was. I mean, Becky was fucking everyone then. You, me –"

I looked at him keenly.

"You fucked Becky?"

Tony blanched; his goatee quivered.

"Oh fuck Joe, I thought you knew, man! She didn't want to know me, mostly, but this one time, you were in London, we were in her rooms –"

"You *cunt*!"

I went for him and Tony, surprised, was pushed backwards; but he was still stronger than me and flipped me onto my own back, his fingers at my throat. He leaned in close, his nose close to mine, his goatee tickling, and for one awful moment I thought he was going to kiss me. To my relief he began to strangle me so I levered his fingers away and we punched and kicked each other on the flat rock beneath the baleful sun, fighting about musty rooms, dusty women, neither willing or able to administer the final blow. To paraphrase James Joyce, you can't fuck and you can't fight.

So finally we lay on our backs panting, watching the man in the moon, passing another spliff between the three of us and feeling our skins tighten and age. There was a cloud above us: it looked a lot like Descartes. I started laughing. Raising himself on one elbow, Tony squinted questioningly through the smoke.

"Today's the day I'm supposed to be in court: non-payment of council tax."

Tony started to laugh too, and drained the bottle. I took a deep drag of the spliff. Then, still laughing, we got to our feet, took a couple of steps back, ran forward with a roar and jumped from the rock into the pool.

Something else had occurred to me. Now Tony was out of the way, there was nothing to stop me finding my mother.

1996

It was still winter. Though the calendar said March, snow-clouds crept over the moors, burying heather and drystone walls beneath cumulating waves of aching bone-powder. There was something almost timeless about those wet shades of silver, musky tussocks and moss-filled pools. Sheep sprouted from the hillside like fossilised cauliflower, and the ancient stone-walled village clung defiant.

The tiny octagonal chapel – grey-corniced, gargoyle-haunted, a monument to piety – was designed by Wesley and, apart from a temporary incarnation as HQ of a coven of hippy white witches in the Seventies, it had provided solace for the village folk of Yorkshire ever since the stern hand of Methodism had guided the flock centuries before.

I looked out of the chapel window upon the desolate vistas of the moor tops. The wind had picked up, but the sound was drowned out by the congregation trilling *All Things Bright and Beautiful*. I've never liked hymns much but they might at least have chosen something rousing: *Lord of the Dance* perhaps, or something by Take That.

But this wasn't my day; it was my father's. His vast body lay on its back in the open coffin, the heart that killed him stilled. As a child I imagined that all the star-atoms that make up one's body stop vibrating with death: an ultimate stillness. Dad wasn't doing much, just waiting for the earth to fall, when he'd become a part of it all. Perhaps when you die you simply go back to a world before people.

As if through a lens I scanned the scratching choir, sweating and blinking in frilled collars and multiple-piercings. The Phoenix Singers were evangelised ex-addicts, earning them the unofficial moniker 'The Crackhead Chorus'. I scanned the row of aghast white faces for Julie, but she wasn't there. Pity; she would have looked good as an angel. So they must have split up; their love fallen down the generation gap.

The grey-haired, over-nervous vicar was halfway through his faltering join-the-dots eulogy when the great oak door opened, snow-powder scattered across the boards, and the wind blew out the candles. I looked round in admiration, quietly tapping the *EastEnders* drum roll on a pew; some entrance.

The woman was tall and broad, and wore black, complete with veil, heels and gloves. For a moment I was sure it was my father in drag, but when I checked the coffin he was still there. I half-expected this Forties' throwback to whip out a cigarette holder, but she made herself small and sat quietly at the back.

Things were looking up; I'd been hoping for some sympathy, some warm embraces, but I wasn't exactly tripping over single women. Millmoor appeared to have been taken over by lesbians and hippies, with their PLO fridge magnets and 4WDs plastered with Greenpeace stickers, opening wine bars, converting barns and antagonising locals. I resolved to introduce myself to the mystery woman at the Wake.

"Would anyone like to say anything?" asked the vicar, desperately, looking right at me. "How about you lad?"

A vision came to me: Dad, kex down, his astonished beard. I shook my head, smiling hardly.

After the service, six brave male volunteers were called forward to carry Dad to the grave. Unfortunately, six couldn't be found. In desperation, the vicar asked for six fit *adults* to do the job. Two women stepped forward, one of them the woman in black. One more was needed; sighing, I straightened my legs and walked to the front; the vicar frowned disapprovingly at the woolly hat I wouldn't remove.

The mystery woman took the front left corner, so I positioned myself behind her. As I helped carry the lead coffin across fossilised bracken, treading carefully lest I slip in frozen cowshit, my eyes were on the woman's arse beneath her tight skirt. My cock began to unfurl, and it was a good job I was in my big coat as there would be little I could do to disguise it.

There was something camp about carrying his coffin across the snowy tundra. At the grave we held the straps to lower him into the ground and I somehow resisted melodramatic urges: to spit, or to rant. When the earth fell on his coffin, in horse-thuds and cluster-bombs, I closed my eyes against the snowy wind that was provoking unwelcome tears as if by acupuncture.

Some poetess was buried nearby behind a tree (the spit of Mary Wollstonecraft), so I urinated onto the fresh flowers and snow covering her grave, remembering my father's only words of advice and vowing to disobey them. Then I thought better of it. Time to grow up.

Wiping my eyes and cursing the callous wind I walked through the graveyard and through hard bending trees to the village. Stone Nest had been expunged from history, replaced by tiny Barratt homes fit for zeros; only the old school remained. Like Julie I had attended primary school here, a tiny building where the children of farmers and thieves formed uneasy alliances against the teachers.

Dad's story had somehow ended where mine began, as a much-loved caretaker at the school. So the piss-up took place among views over the town and valley as seen by children of four and five – incongruous collages, idolatry flashes of humanity in felt and bracken. I didn't know anyone, so after a few bored minutes I took a glass of red wine over to the woman in black, who was staring impassively at a mediocre interpretation of a tractor.

"Thought you might like this."

She turned, then: "Thank you, Josef, but I don't drink."

After Stalin; Mum named me after someone more saintly, less plausible. An Australian accent. I looked into her sugar brown eyes. She seemed to shimmer like the ghost she had become, but it was only my eyes bleeding. Mother Mary shivered and shone. Mother. Mary. Save me.

"Oh, Josef," she sighed. "Whatever happened to your *hair*?"

Australia had disappointed me; not that it seemed to *care*. All anyone ever seemed to talk about was how large their country was; small conversations about big continents. Pedestrians waited for the lights to change before crossing the road. I found myself wishing Tony was here, to help me take the piss, instead of being at home with my Hermione.

Each desperate night in the hostel, in the depths of another cask of cheap wine, I trawled the small ads for women. One sounded perfect – slim, indie, kinky – until I read the last two words of the ad, pretty much unparalleled in their savagery:

'*No dreamers.*'

Maybe it was too soon to try again. In any case, I still loved Hermione, who presumably was making up for lost time with Tony and his goatee. I needed something to take my mind off the whole sex/love conundrum. When some earnest German in a city pub suggested I take a scuba trip north I agreed; I was bored, and my pics showed it.

Though I'd passed my test years before, the joys of motoring had always been wasted on me; but it was different here. I set out along the coast road north in an old rusting Ute. My over-zealous scuba instructor persuaded me to dive off a reef with a sheer two-thousand-metre drop at its ocean side, the closest I would ever come to flying.

Sometimes though, I just wanted to lie low, to crawl through the spinifex grass as I had rolled through Yorkshire hayfields, carving my name out for the gods: *fuck you all, though I can't see you I know you're there.* Except the spinifex grew tall and insects bit ineffably; my writhings left no trace, and I felt sheltered and naked in that great distance, both agoraphobic and claustrophobic like Millmoor.

Right up north, where the scrub ruled the roost and wild cats lurked within the ribcages of roadkill kangaroos, there were flowers like upturned ice lollies; perhaps it was the heat. I began to drive the two thousand k's back to Perth through harsh empty bush, passing strange little towns in the middle of all this nothingness, dominated by cathedral-sized pubs; the Australia I'd built from Mum's lurid diatribes.

Mum came from Kalgoorlie, not already pregnant apparently, and for all I knew that was where she'd returned, but I didn't particularly fancy another trek into the desert and my funds were low. I'd taken over a hundred rolls of film and had no way of developing them. Pulling into one of the country pubs for the night I went to buy a beer in the honky-tonk bar, all check-shirts and beef-hides. The barman, a log of a man, frowned at me.

"You from England?"

"Sorry. Yes."

"Driving a mustard Ute up north?"

"On my way back to Perth actually; why do you ask?"

"There was a message on Triple J, asking for a Joe Noone to ring England."

Triple J, the national radio station that played indie music. I didn't have a radio in the Ute because of the poor reception, and had driven to the northwest and back with a dodgy compilation tape. The barman pointed to a phone booth. Inside there was a jokey sign:

No Poms No Poofters. Boongs and Sheilas by admittance only

At least, I assumed it was a joke. A memory came to me: as a small child, watching Mum scoop cat shit from the tray into the toilet "to feed all the starving Abos." I hoped Hermione would answer the phone but it was Tony.

"Joe – I'm sorry man. Julie rang. Your dad died."

Finishing my beer I got in the Ute and drove through the night to Perth. As the sun came up and I sat in the departure lounge it struck me; I had gone to Oz looking for my mother, and ended up losing my father. Yet as the plane landed at Heathrow I wasn't thinking about either of them; only the fact that I was closer to Herm.

"I met a doctor," said Mary. I felt hot and wanted to take off my coat but didn't want wine spilling on tiny desks. Mary was self-contained, too smartly dressed to be a Marxist. Still pretty, still sparkling; her deep eyes, sharp chin, aloof manner both practical and somehow aristocratic. She looked rich, with that confident sheen of the self-made. It was dusk, and the whiteout glare through the window was dimming; in a few short hours the rain had come and massacred the snow.

"A good man. He took me away."

"You left us."

"Yes. I thought it best. Charlie was a bum. Loved all the girls. I never knew what love was, till Simon."

Mary put her glass of water on a low-down table, knocking her hat to the floor.

"Why have children with someone you don't love?"

"I *thought* I did love him – big dreams in sixties London. And we didn't have a choice. There was no abortion then, remember. Charlie was good to me – and you."

"I can't remember."

"We can't help our memories, even selective ones. I'm sorry I left you, Josef. I wrote."

"It's Joe. And no. You didn't."

"I did. But you moved. Couldn't find you, couldn't come back –"

"Where did you go?"

"Spain. I went to Spain. We have a little house near Valencia. Simon has a practice in a *pueblo*. Makes a lot of money. Come to Spain with me, you'll meet him."

Mentally, I scanned my pockets: twenty-seven pounds and twenty-six pence, half a National Express ticket and a can of Kestrel Super. "Maybe."

I looked up at the television, where for once the faces of smiling primary kids filled the news, then back at Mary, my mum. I remembered something that had jarred, caused confusion as I had sought to make connections.

"You don't drink?"

"No. I'm an alcoholic."

"Well, why not have a beer then?"

She didn't smile; I flushed, realising she was looking at me, what I had become. A mess. A waste. A *man*. Mary looked uneasy and I wondered why she'd come all the way from Spain; she didn't even *like* Dad. I drained my glass and looked around the room, looking for Julie, but she still wasn't there.

"Come to Spain, Joe," persisted Mary. "You'll like Simon. We can get to know each other. I'm not – pushing anything. I know it was wrong to leave. But Simon was a student then and I didn't want you eating out of a suitcase. You needed stability."

"You left me with Dad. Who was on the dole."

"Well yeah. I mean, I tried to help, buying the house –"

"What?"

"Charlie didn't tell you I bought the house? Simon took out a loan, that's why he was so skint. So at least you didn't have rent to worry about."

"Thanks, Mum."

It sounded harder than I'd meant; incredible, how minor inflections can change history. Mary looked sad, and for the first time in my life it dawned on me that bitterness wasn't the most gorgeous of traits. I finished my drink.

"How long you in town for? When're you leaving?"

"I have to catch the six o'clock train to the airport. Come with me, Joe."

"To Valencia."

"It's alright. Free oranges."

"I hate oranges. Anyway I need to get back to London."

Neither statement was true, as Mary probably knew, so she shrugged and took out a hankie and lippo. "Here's my address," she said. "And my number. Anytime, Joe. Just call and we'll buy you a flight. You'll like Simon. You'll like Spain."

I doubted it. But I folded the hankie and hid it somewhere safe. "Can I ask you a question?" Mary shrugged warily. "Who was my *real* dad?"

Mary looked scared.

"*What*?"

"My real father. Who was it? I have this memory of a bookie in Cheadle…"

To my utter surprise, because it seemed so against this tough cookie image I was already building up, Mary began to cry. Even more unexpectedly, I found myself joining in. Uncertainly I put an arm around her shoulder and tried to understand what she was saying through her sobs. Even when

I heard her properly I didn't quite understand, couldn't quite make the connection.

"It was Charlie, of course! *He* was your father."

Me and my imagination; me and my maths. Putting down my glass I closed my eyes.

"And who was my mother?"

Mary looked blank.

"*I* was. Am."

"No."

Mary shrugged and raised her eyebrows archly. I'd been rehearsing this speech for years, but now words wouldn't come. Mary sniffed and stopped crying.

"They always blame the mother, don't they? A lot of feminists blame Freud, but I don't – *I* blame his mum. For all the ills. Ibsen –"

Shaking with pain I put a finger across her lips and Mum stopped dead, eyes wide. I held her by the arms, wanting to tell her how I'd wanted to find her. To tell her she'd had a grandchild, and then also to tell her about Sarah's mangled corpse as I had told Theophilus. About sleeping beneath buildings, fighting for scraps, about being cold in the summertime; about how when she left I had changed, become something hard, something remote. I was hating my bitterness, knowing the good-news world hated it, wanting to tell this alien, who had materialised before me, about drink and drugs and bleak distractions, other absolutions. My only comfort on countless lost nights was that Charlie wasn't my father, that somewhere out there I'd find him; and now she'd even robbed me of *that* unhappy ending.

Unable to look at her or hold on any longer I looked out at the darkening moors, furies gathering slowly within me. I felt cheated; I felt robbed. Worst of all I couldn't say anything, couldn't hurt her, because I knew I'd need her now.

Mary was speaking but I wasn't listening, just watching

her lips move, staring above her head as rain-beads cracked against the glass like glass against glass, mourners laughing heartily as they drunk the free booze, children sneaking sausage rolls from trestle tables, lovers kissing forlornly behind black drapes, children on the TV screen smiling sweetly, mother talking to me or to herself while my friendless father lay there all alone in the lonely ground by the cluster of ash trees.

Alcohol whirling through my body, my tongue sweet with wine, Becky sleeping – no, dead and rotting, like Sarah, whose ashes blew from Golders Green crematorium to the stars. Wanting to tell my mother all about this interminable life, but instead turning and leaving the school and walking back to the grave beneath the trees, all the new snow stripped away by sharp angles of sleet, to that place in the soil where my father kept up his pitiless silence as his dead eyes mossed over and his memories dissolved; his past burnt out of existence, evaporating like a fading star into the ether of the chill Yorkshire night.

1997

It didn't feel like an auspicious evening when I decided to walk from my new flat in West London over to Tony and Hermione's to catch the election results. I'd just voted for the first (and, as it would turn out, the last) time – the first time I'd been able to, first time I actually lived where I said I did, in my own name. I'd reappeared; I felt reborn.

After much badgering, bluffing and blackmail, a housing association for soaks had got me a flat in the backside of Marylebone, but I hated it: too posh, all mink coats and ermine accents. I knew I was being silly, but after all those years of having a mouldy old pub across the road it didn't seem right to have a French restaurant with fat middle-aged women lunching outside all afternoon, magnums of champagne at their side as they talked about shopping.

In a vain attempt to get extra money out of the dole, I'd taken to throwing the contents of my commode out of the window, exasperating said diners to distraction. It was all a bit too much for the well-heeled neighbours, and only that morning the caretaker had stuffed a note through my letterbox:

'Mr Noone. May I remind you it is against your contract to hang washing out of the window. Furthermore you are causing offence. And Pierre has asked me to discover who is responsible for the outrage last Sunday. The Trust takes a very dim view. p.s. also your rent.'

Frankly I was sick of sitting around watching reruns of *Chico & the Man* on UK Gold; I needed to be back in Islington/Camden/Hackney, my Bemused Triangle, rooting and snuffling round bins like a pig looking for truffles. I didn't want to climb the ladder; I wanted to burn it down.

Perhaps I was suffering from class paeans; because Mum had married a doctor, Hermione said I was middle-class. At least, that was what *Tony* said; I hadn't laid eyes on Herm in years. I've always defined class as whether you were cannon fodder in wars, factory fodder in peacetime. Yet now it seems everyone who's middle-class wants to be working-class, and everyone who's working-class wants to be middle-class. During this particular election, the Georgian terraces of Barnsbury and other middle-class ghettos had red slogans plastered in their bay windows, while the double-glazed, triple-locked windows of Packington and Andover remained a Euro-sceptic blue.

Tony's definition was simple. "Both working-class and middle-class folk argue over the bill in restaurants, but the working-class are fighting to pay the bill, the middle-class are trying not to."

Not that I minded the new social status Hermione had conferred upon me; on the contrary, I quite liked the idea. Maybe it would help me to meet girls. So I toned down my accent, took the *Quaedian* and tried listening to Radio 4, kicking myself one afternoon when I caught myself watching *Family Fortunes*.

That day the first month's instalment of my business loan was due to be repaid. I'd taken one out to pay off all my credit cards, then spent it all on booze. I'd imbibed the myth, swallowed the advertiser's shit sandwich, that taking out a credit card to pay off the interest on another can continue indefinitely like some sort of musical chairs, music to the ears of the vultures circling my statements in red. I could almost see all the men in suits drain away to their banks, twenty-four hour Capital, scratching their baffled heads as they examined my account and the numbers didn't add up.

An anarchist – it tickled me to see it come back into fashion. For that's what capitalism is after all: a form of anarchy, albeit one starting on an unequal playing field, one painted on the side of an Afghanistan cliff. There's a photograph in the Tate I never tire of looking at, by Andreas Gursky of the Chicago stock exchange, thousands of traders in tribal colours. Capitalism equals loneliness; the meek shall inherit the mortgage.

Tony had sold his bachelor flat and was reunited with Hermione in the new complex they'd erected between Villiers Terrace and the viaduct. I'd been past on the train a few times, amazed how close the new apartments were to the track, close enough to glimpse all those terrible secrets: gerontophilia, infantilism, philately; but Hermione and Tony didn't appear to have any such skeletons, or cupboards for that matter. Maybe they'd left them behind at Villiers, now a boarded up block, like a film set or a paint ball range, due for dynamiting. As I walked past the sulky silhouette I stopped and bowed my head.

Hermione worked as something in local government, and Tony was still in PR: hence the posh door knocker. He answered with a preoccupied look on his face, which had filled out a bit since Thailand; a grizzled beard was spreading slowly across his cheeks like Ebola. He was obviously expecting me; he wore a dressing gown and slippers.

"Oh, hello. Forgot you were coming."

Wondering again how someone so tactless could make a living in PR, I pushed past him into the tiny hall and through to the empty front room.

"Where's Herm and Daithi?"

"Daithi's on the rampage with his mates. Herm's been commandeered at the polling station."

Tony led me into the lounge, with its miniature leather suite and drinks cabinet. You can find identical estates beside railway tracks all over England; they deck out the show flats with mini-furniture to make them look bigger. But the tasteful art-deco posters were framed, there were potted plants, and Hermione had left us belly-lining nibbles: olives stuffed with feta and pomienta.

I wasn't sure I liked this world, and was reassured when I sat down to discover that the settee was criss-crossed with scratches from Stig's claws, as if he'd been trying to send messages to some cat god. The second I sat down Stig rubbed my legs then hopped in my lap; his fur had gone grey and he had a limp, but his eyes were still alert and he started to hum.

Tony had eaten so I ate some *vol-au-vonts* as I watched various excited Dimblebys, my throat sore from drinking, an image in my head of rocks tumbling into an underground lake. He produced thick glass tumblers (the sort Becky had at home in Hove, the ones I'd always wanted) and we made inroads into my Netto whisky as we watched Peter Snow. As results started to top the balance Labour's way I raised my glass.

"Good riddance, Tory scum."

"I *almost* voted Tory," admitted Tony after a short silence. "I mean, look at Labour – how dismal can you get? Look at those *suits*… The Tories are the party of rock 'n' roll! Think about it, think about it: New Labour are the molly-coddlers, the nannies, the Tories are into kinky sex, drugs, shooting!"

Tony's greatest heroes are Alan Clark and Terry Thomas but, then, Tony's always been a little confused. I had a theory that the less sex you get, the more right wing you become; Tony was disproving that one. I sighed.

"Don't let Hermione hear you say that."

"Joe, she's changed, man. You haven't even *seen* her for ten years. You know I told you she's on the polling booth? She's working for the Tories."

"Blimey."

I was less surprised than I made out; Tony shrugged and drank, eyes sliding back to the screen like they used to slide over to women in bars. Snow over Britain in red, white and blue.

"She's a woman of property now, that's what happens."

"Women are always right wing," I guessed, stroking Stig's back. "Have to be, family values, nests. Right-wingers lie to others; lefties to themselves. Just like men and women. Men are dogs. Cats are individualists, capitalist, dogs loyal, pack-lovers. If a dog's owner dies that dog will howl and pine away at their side, eventually to die of loneliness and hunger. A cat will have your eyeballs out before you're cold."

"And which are you?"

I grinned and licked my lop-sided lip. "Miaow."

Stig vibrated on my lap like a sex toy, a Rabbit. When I lived with Becky he used to yowl to be put out on the dark stairs, but as soon as the door closed behind him he'd get scared and come in so he'd scratch and sharpen his claws on the door. But the moment I'd open the door, light would flood the stairwell and he'd be torn between coming back into the warmth and wanting to stay out, to explore with the light. I'm a bit like that with love.

Tony waved the bottle; I held out my tumbler. He poured, serious face and serious slur.

"So do you still believe in the pragmatism of love?"

I growled, "Woof. Woof."

"I wonder how many women you've said that to late at night. What you're really saying is follow your heart."

"If you have one."

Tony tried to look deep. "Do you?"

"Love is blind as I can see."

"Who said that, David Blunkett?"

When Portillo was dumped on his arse I brought out cigars coated with cannabis oil and insisted Tony play my record of the moment: Nina Simone's *Ain't Got No*. In this vibe I dropped my tumbler; it didn't break on the thick cream carpet but made a decent stain. Posh tumblers: pointless. We started drinking from the bottle.

"How's work these days?" asked Tony, wincing.

"Alright." I blushed.

Aisha had got me work filming commercials: kitchens, shampoo, washing powder – just to keep the money coming in while I completed my installation. Mostly I did semi-pornographic clips of steaming cuisine in this, the first age in the history of mankind in which we fear food.

"Aisha wants me to do an advert," I admitted to Tony at last.

"Really? What for?"

"Some new jeep. They want to lift part of my installation and use it in the ad – they say they'll give me a fucking fortune."

Tony shrugged. "So what's the problem?"

"I'm not like you, Tony – or Aisha for that matter. She says it's just selling a product; I say it's selling out. We had a terrible row."

"What, because of a fucking advert?"

"Well – not only that." I smiled bitterly. Aisha had been a good friend to me, during some of the worst periods of my life, but that was it. We'd been at a restaurant, celebrating the latest book by one of her celeb author hacks (a socialites' A-Z of London, all the way from Knightsbridge to Kensington) and discussing our fledgling deal but getting nowhere except drunk. By the time we got back to mine, I was paralytic and asked her to put on Becky's old night-dress.

I decided to change the subject – or at least divert it slightly in its course, like sitting on a meteor and turning on a hairdryer.

"I'm with Bill Hicks. Anyone in marketing is Satan's Little Helper. My installation isn't a commodity: it's a political statement."

Tony appeared uninterested; he looked at the screen, munching on tortilla chips.

"What's it called then, this film?"

"Installation."

"Whatever."

Tony did that teen thing with his fingers. Been hanging round with Daithi too long.

"You ever have driving lessons?"

He shook his head, still looking at the screen. The Dimblebys were orgasmic. "Nah."

"You should read the green cross code man, it's hilarious. It's got all sorts of useful advice, but my favourite is in a piece about level crossings. It says: '*always give way to trains*'. That's my title."

Tony shrugged, baffled. "Why?"

I tried to explain about fate, and some things being impossible to change, but Tony was more interested in slagging off women in general and Herm in particular, so when the bottle was empty I left.

As I walked down the alley back past Villiers Terrace, someone vaguely familiar came towards me. A woman, in her thirties, in a long Mac, her black hair long over sad blue eyes. Hermione. We stopped, a few yards apart in the narrow alley. It took her a moment to register who I was and she smiled uncertainly.

"Well well."

She drew closer, and her beauty made me rage against the universe.

"Hello Herm. You're looking good."

She did; she'd grown up. As an Irish teenager Hermione had been a culshy colleen, albeit a dazzling one, with her pale face, butter-knob nose, raven hair and luminous eyes; but hard work and new money had put colour in her cheeks and assertiveness in her standing, the way she stood. I reflected sadly that she'd been in London too long. It did that, the Smoke – gave you false confidence, fatal arrogance, but stole your time like a wallet. London mugged your youth.

Against all expectation Hermione seemed pleased to see me, and I shivered.

"How come you're back so soon?"

"There didn't seem any point hanging around. After the Portillo result I just wanted to get home."

I smiled to myself, wondering if it were possible to love a Tory.

"I'd better get inside," said Hermione. "We should meet up sometime."

"I'd like that."

Hermione hesitated, then kissed me on the cheek and was gone. I went back to Villiers Terrace and sat outside number six, listening to the sounds of the empty house that had been full of what I now realised was hope. Her drawings and crayon-marks would cover the walls, and had been covered in turn with newer, older writings.

Up in the sky was the star I had named for Becky; except I'd had a letter from the Royal Astronomical Society a few months before. It turns out it wasn't a star at all, but a galaxy. I couldn't decide if this meant my love had been magnified or diluted, to the power of a hundred billion. What it really meant was, it was all over. Time to find a new star.

2007

The Fire Horse possesses a menacing black gleam, shaded windows and bars that could write off a stegosaurus. An eco-goon with his recycled bike wouldn't have a hope. That's the thing with jeeps; once I heard on the radio a school-run defender explain why she had one, living in an area of Primrose Hill – not renowned for its mountains and dirt-tracks – and she said, "You're missing the point. If I have a crash, I'll win."

I don't know if *she* got the point: no-one wins in the end, death and taxes and all that malarkey. But at least you feel protected. Pressing the button on my key I hear a satisfying click: lights pulse, the alarm blips. Pulling on the handle I'm accompanied by a multitude of satisfying clicks and whirrs, as if the car is announcing itself: *here I am*.

Out of habit I open the left-hand door to find myself peering across a vast expanse of leather to the wheel at the other side; I must have ordered right-hand drive from habit, as if I browse 4WD catalogues online every day.

The jeep smells of new shoes and plastic; it takes a while to trek around the other side to the driver's side where I climb in panting. I've never seen the mountain track from this height before; my seat feels like it cares for me, wants to help. When I push in the unique ignition card and type the pin the car drives for me.

Others have remarked of the relationship between

Americans and their cars. They are said to feel safe, hermetically sealed, to become different animals once they slide into 'drive'. Yet (being European) I feel the opposite: every time I sit behind a wheel I feel afraid, vulnerable. Perversely, the larger the motor the worse the feeling. As I cruise down to town I'm certain that on arrival I'll be scraping little *ninas* and *ninos* off the wheels like so many brown berries.

Once I get the hang of things, learn to relax, I do feel above it all, untouchable, like an American; that is, until I drive into the underground car park and attempt to buy a ticket. When I lean across I can't reach, and have to get out, smiling apologetically at the driver behind. This is not Wood Green; he jovially waves.

When I emerge from the lift in the middle of the plaza, the late afternoon sun follows my movements, insistent and dazzling; I left my shades with Geordie on that deserted beach, and keep forgetting to buy new ones.

A gang of youths are sitting on benches in the square, shouting aphorisms and glaring at the old men and women who have failed in the tasks nature has left. At least half the people on the street are younger than me; this is my tipping point. The children are circling with the ferocity of sharks; you're in our world now, swim if you like and take your chances. This is our world, fluid like the seas, and there's nothing you can do except kick out and wait for the pressure-needles of our teeth.

Tony's sitting outside a café with a cold drink that looks teetotal. His beard straggles: ever more my father. His dark, fly-like glasses point my way; he nods vaguely as I sit and wave away the waiter. Last night, when I found Alona's note, I drove him to town without a word before going home to weep. He was probably slagging me off to Geordie in Billys all night trying to forget he's in love.

"Tonight," I tell him, "we don't get pissed – we hunt."

Presumably Tony blinks.

"Why can't we do both?"

"Booze and crossbows don't mix."

"Crossbows?" The burqa-strip of Tony's face that's visible seems worried. For all I know his eyes are laughing, or dying. "What are you, the Holloway Hemingway?"

"Don't worry – you'll enjoy it."

"There will be *some* booze though, won't there?"

"Maybe."

Tony leaves money and we walk towards the plaza. We're about to cross at the lights by the cinema ('*Helen Mirren en la Reina*') when they change: Tony nips across and looks back, laughing, as I wait for a lull. People always seem to do that, at least to me: maybe I'm just too slow for this world. Always grasping the wrong end of the shitty stick, somehow.

We descend to the cool dark car park and Tony looks round for my old car. With a smile I press the key-button; there's a hi-tech *blimp* and the Fire Horse lights up like a miniature city. Tony whistles; he's always taken a baffling pleasure in cars. Pulling up the ramp is like driving downhill – the jeep defies gravity. I point the car at the hills, the evening sun setting behind monolithic slabs.

"Let's pop back to the cave. I forgot something."

"Roses for Alona?"

"She won't be back."

"How can you be sure?"

I explain to Tony about Alona's baby cravings, my yin yang theory; Tony laughs.

"Moth/flame might be a more appropriate analogy."

"Apt word, that. Analogy: the study of arseholes."

Only now, after she's left, do I realise what I've lost, and though the pain is almost unbearable, its familiarity is also comforting. The longest I'd ever been out with anyone was

Becky – five years, six months, seven days. I've just realised I've been with Alona for over seven years. Yet it's as if I barely know her, hardly registered her significance until it was too late.

The cave seems emptier now, as if what was accumulating here is draining out through the wine-holes in the walls. Taking his shades off, Tony slumps on the sofa and watches the last of the Ashes on Sky; England wiped out 5-0 by Australia. I take the crossbow from a hole in the wall behind the photograph of Radio screaming in London. The back of Tony's head pokes up like a furry coconut; I aim, squinting like he does when his contacts go crusty.

"Tony."

Tony turns, bored, and I'm amused by the way his expression changes; his eyes widen, his complexion whitens, his beard seems to grey. One squeeze and his features could change even more dramatically. I laugh and point at the ceiling.

"You mad bastard! What the fuck you *doing* with that thing anyway?"

"Everyone has a weapon here, Tony. What did you expect to hunt with, catapults?"

"So let me get this right. You live in a cave – and hunt with a bow and arrow."

"And ride a Fire Horse."

Tony advances, hand out. "Can I hold it?"

Making sure the catch is on I shrug and hand over the weapon, an old Barnett I bought back from Valencia one summer. Tony weighs it in his hands, enjoying the way it balances, the way it's made. I let him cop a feel; no sense going shooting with a complete novice. Accidents happen. Eventually Tony puts it down on the table. Spinning it slightly so the arrow aims at the wall, I take two beers from the melancholy fridge. Without asking, as if he lives here, Tony grabs them by the neck, goes to the wall and flips lids. We clink bottles.

"Cheers."

"*Aclamaciones*."

Tony looks round the cave as if for the first time. But then he's only ever seen it when pissed.

"Some place you got here. Why did you say Alona left again?"

"She wanted kids – I didn't."

With the main lights on, the house looks bright and huge. I twist a dimmer; with the lights subdued it's hard to tell where the cave ends and the building begins. Now I look up at some old Moorish portrait Alona brought home excitedly and swallow. Tony sits at the table.

"Because of Sarah."

I shake my head, unable to form any words.

"You'd never have kids because of what happened?"

"Would *you*?"

"I don't know if I want *more* kids... They're hard Joe, so fucking hard. It's hard enough when they're in nappies –"

"Yeah, I remember."

"But when they're walking, talking, it's a whole new ball game. You just sit and watch your life flash by; one minute it's *what's the story morning glory*, the next it's *what's the story in Balamory*. Children cry for a reason; that reason is narcissism."

"Tony, is this your weird attempt to make me feel better?"

"I'm just being honest. No-one ever is, about parenthood. I know you'll never get over what happened, but I'm also saying it's made you idealise children. It's unhealthy."

I shake my head definitely. "No."

"Yes. I was the same, before Millie. Do you know how hard me and Herm tried for kids? Miscarriage after miscarriage, sometimes four, five months in?"

"Oh well, look on the bright side, you saved a fortune on contraception."

Tony looks disgusted and I know I've gone too far. It's the perverted imp in me, I just can't stop pushing. He goes to the fridge for another beer, then looks at me as he opens it.

"You know what you are? Living here like Herm's fucking Hermit, a bear with a sore bald head chasing people away? You're *sad*."

I take the bottle off him and he goes for another one. His tone is reasonable; so am I.

"I remember," I tell him, "before Thatcher, *sad* used to mean something else. Now it just means *loser*. See also: Billy No-mates; do-gooder." I swig my beer. "Know what I'd do, for that and all the other miseries of her revolutionary ardour? I'd hang the cunt for treason. Crimes against the state."

"The revolutionary prole with his four-wheel-drive. The Marxist marketeer."

"I'm hardly *rich*, Tony."

"You're not exactly living hand to mouth, either. Whatever happened to Joe Broke?"

"I got bored with him. Bored with all that. Anyway – it was *your* idea."

"What was?"

"Getting me into advertising."

"Maybe it was. Though I don't suppose I had any idea how whole-heartedly you'd sell out."

I laugh, but there's an edge. "Tony, I sold one advert. You've spent your *whole life* polishing turds."

"Don't knock it, Joe." Tony waves his bottle round the room before sticking it in his beard. "Look what it bought you. You never change, do you?"

"That's not true. I was ill, now I'm okay."

"Sounds like it."

"I just needed to – purge my system, that's all. Make it

pure. I got caught up in the filth and now I'm clean. I'm not proud, Tony. You're right: I sold my soul. Now I'd like to buy it back."

Tony smiles – *maturely*.

"If it's still for sale."

Before we leave I dig out the DVD the agency sent me and show Tony the advert, which at my insistence (and Theo's solicitor's suggestion) never got screened in the UK; in a few short years it'll be picked up by aliens with antennae for ears.

I've hardly ever seen a car advert that I understood. In every one there's some smarmy-arsed driver with that same weird, smug, one-sided smile, like they've had a stroke. If adverts are about pushing buttons, they're missing mine by miles; they might as well have Anne Widdecombe draped across the bonnet in a bikini for all I care.

Here's the scene: it's night. A weeping man sits behind the wheel of a brand new 4WD and looks at his wallet, a photograph of his wife and daughter. Wiping his eyes the man starts the engine (cue mechanical porn) and begins to drive. He turns on the radio and we hear the ad soundtrack, The Smiths: *there is a light that never goes out*. Cut to a train hurtling through the night. We see the road through the driver's perspective; when you look up into the driving mirror you see his life flash through his eyes in the form of my installation, from an unmarked grave to a crying baby.

In the one I'd produced for Aisha, I'd condensed the whole of my life into sixty seconds, all the images, the covers of my favourite albums, and so on. I didn't *create* it for the advert; they bought it off me. That didn't seem so bad, somehow. Anyway, it won first prize in some advertising awards, the first time I'd come first in anything.

The driver veers off the road, down an impossibly steep incline and onto a train track, where he speeds up the line. Cue rough-gravelled voiceover: "A lot can happen in a lifetime. Some good, some bad. But while you've been living, loving, working and sleeping, we've been working on a new kind of vehicle. The Fire Horse. In Japan, when fire horse meets fire horse it can mean the apocalypse. But it can also signal a new dawn. This is a new dawn in the motor industry. The Fire Horse: so hard it hurts."

Cut to the train, entering a tunnel. Cut to the driver's view, also travelling into the tunnel. Lights up ahead. We see the train driver, panic as he sees headlights in this impossible darkness. The last cut: the train reverses out of the tunnel, pursued by the Fire Horse.

The end.

"So," I ask Tony casually, like I care, "what do you think?"

"Hum," he replies evasively. "A lot of layers. Lots of images. Less is more in my book."

"Not when you're hungry, Tony. Not when you're at war."

"Why does he cry when he sees the pic of his wife and daughter?"

"Up to you."

"No wonder Theo didn't like it."

He'd have liked it even less if I'd stuck to my original plan and used the photo of Becky and Sarah. In the end I copped out as usual.

As we walk out to the jeep, Tony thinks of something else.

"It's hard to make anything out from the installation itself, and I've never actually seen it, but if it's your life, where *are* you?"

"I'm not in it."

"Nowhere?"

I click; doors open.

"That's just the point, Tony; I've never been photographed."

He frowns, searches memory banks. "What – never?"

"Nope."

I'm about to press 'drive' when I remember the beers in the fridge and go back. Propped against them I find all my credit cards.

There's something wrong with the Satnav; it keeps directing me off precipices, up cul-de-sacs, over clifftops into the sea. In the end I press 'override'. As we turn off the freeway onto a mountain track road, Tony roots for something in his jacket pocket and hands over an old-fashioned cassette tape. As I drive, I stare at it gloomily. Along the spine is one word written by hand: *Mandocantus*. The photograph on the cover is of the four of us – me, Tony, Hermione and Becky in Mallorca, 1988. Daithi took the picture, my head missing.

"Who's Mandocantus? The latest thing?"

"It's a compilation, the best English music – including stuff you might have missed. The country didn't stop when you left, Joe."

"What does it mean?"

"Mandocantus? Literally, it's the order of music. You know when you play a compilation so many times, you start to anticipate what comes next?"

We're crawling behind a huge truck up into the mountains, and I'm able to pull out the cassette, but peering round the futuristic control panel there doesn't appear to be anywhere to stick it so instead I look at the track listing.

"So where's all the new stuff I've been missing?"

Tony smiles ruefully. "There haven't been *that* many good songs since you left."

"Don't blame me, Tony. Blame Simon Cowell. He's the real reason I left England. Well – music generally. Want to know the definition of an oxymoron? The best of Coldplay."

"Can you imagine," mutters Tony, "if oxen were intelligent? Anyway – you left England because of Simon

Cowell?"

I think about the question seriously. "Yes."

"Um… so how long had you been here before finding out he lives in Mallorca?"

"When I landed," I reply through gritted teeth. "There's a big poster of him in Palma Airport."

The jeep negotiates a steep bend; to my right the drop is almost sheer for hundreds of feet to the fracturing ocean. Tony beside me, again.

I once watched a programme about this woman who was so frightened of hospitals she waited until her tumour weighed over twenty stones, and they showed footage of the operation to remove this... *thing*, complete with teeth and hair, this *doppelganger* inside her. Did it also have a beard?

"Anyway," says Tony, "I thought you moved here to be near your mum. Where is she?"

I don't answer; there isn't much to tell. I'd been in Spain (a ferry ride away) for two years when Mum announced she'd left Simon and was moving back to Australia. She invited me along but, having met her a few times, Alona didn't really fancy it. Nor did I: too big, Oz. Not that I blame Mum for leaving. She did me a favour – she helped me escape.

As we drive into the fabric of darkness I feel the foreboding presence of the crossbow on the back seat. We pull off the road and onto the *gerrigue*, the Fire Horse making short work of the uneven ground dotted with clumps of myrtle, bracken and Aleppo pine. The short, hard grass is dotted with wildflowers in summer, marigolds, gladioli and cyclamen, but now the headlights pick out ghostly scrub.

Parking up I take the crossbow and pack from the back seat, then go to the boot for our heavy coats and wraps. After winding a scarf round his face Tony follows me over rough ground towards the mountain.

It's a cold, crisp night; up on the mountains the air is clear and bright, the temperature several degrees colder than the coast. I'm reminded of the Yorkshire moors, apart from all the colour, all the life. But then, the moors of my youth hadn't always been empty – that timeless feel was an illusion. Once there had been forests, boar, *Baba-Yaga*. The common folklore of the North.

My flashlight finds an old *sitja*, a charcoal hearth left by peasants, the size of a beehive and smelling of mould, and we sit for a freshener with our backs against it. Tony passes me a beer so I put down the crossbow.

"What are we hunting, anyway?" asks Tony, shivering into his muffler.

"Whatever comes along."

"I never had you down as a hunter."

"I don't often hit anything, and when I do I eat it."

This is almost true. In fact, although I'm a fine shot I've never killed anything; I just like being out here, crossbow in hand, watching animals play in this world without people. When I fire off a bolt it's only a warning so they can fly, run, hop away – melt, shine, rustle, sing.

It feels warm and protective inside my coat; the ground's soft from rain and I doze, thinking about nothing. Then I hear a rustling sound in the grass a few yards away, and open my eyes. The *campo* is motionless; it must have been a gecko or a snake. Yawning and rubbing my eyes I stand, stretch, and look over at Tony, cradling the crossbow, a sad, faraway look in his eyes.

1998

Alopecia has its advantages. Only having to shave every ten or fourteen days means despite my height I've always looked about fifteen; for years I had the fervent hope that life couldn't touch me, gravity couldn't mould my porcelain skin, life's melancholies wouldn't steal the juvenile sparkle from my zealot's eyes.

Yet that afternoon I had looked in a shop window and saw myself pixelated on a computer screen and realised I wasn't immortal after all. A less confident, less happy dreamer might have felt some doom, shared some dark premonition with the Soho street, but I was apart somehow, floating towards the future. Even age couldn't daunt me now. Even death; even 2000.

When I entered the Admiral Duncan on Great Portland Street it was my first time inside a pub for months. I'd decided to quit drinking, and sobriety hadn't been quite as bad as I'd expected – just so long as I smoked bushes of skunk and didn't go out between elevens am and pm. I'd lost a few pounds and felt fighting fit, but quaked at the prospect of spending time with Hermione. For the first time in ages I had a violent urge to take a drink.

It had been Hermione's idea; just a phone call, casual, as if we saw each other every week rather than once every decade. It was arranged for mid-afternoon, as if she was scared I'd turn up slaughtered. I was early, and sipped coke and ice.

Apart from our brief encounter in the alley it was years since I'd seen her, yet I entertained this ridiculous belief that I knew her like no-one else ever would – not even Tony, her partner in crime.

More to the point, I believed that she knew me, that she'd still laugh at the same things, felt the same pain. Even if she *was* 'in property'.

The place was quiet; some old queen in the corner gave me a smile. That's the thing I resent about gay people: their *optimism*. Satchmo came on the jukebox: what a wonderful world. I'd always found the song ironic; for the first time I wasn't so sure.

When Hermione entered my artificial darkness with some of her busy friends, our eyes seemed to lock on each other, two sets of headlights in a game of chicken. As she approached I took in again her body, its slightness, its tightness, her tiny breasts and hips. Her black hair was long and well-styled, her eyes emanated light, and she wore tight trousers and a conservative white blouse through which I could see her dark lace bra. At what age *could* you be classified a dirty old man?

"Hello," said Hermione, doing her usual northern impression that sounded Bangladeshi, "it's Joe Broke."

"Hello Hermione," I smiled, "let me get a drink in." I noted the way my accent became more pronounced, as if that was what she wanted.

"No," said Hermione, "I'll get *you* one. What's that, whisky?"

"Just coke. Long story."

Hermione feigned surprise, though I knew Tony would have told her I was dry. One of her friends (all shirt, teeth and Compton coiffures) intervened jokily. "I say Hermione, I knew you were a goer, but trying to pull in a poof's palace?"

"Joe's an old friend," smiled Hermione. The shirt pumped

my hand, squeezing too hard. I smiled evenly. Herm left and I was forced to listen to her friends: tedious, moneyed, but at least they weren't fake liberals. The men were rugby-shirted fools and the women wore beads, and all seemed to think it a real hoot to be meeting in a gay joint in town.

Herm watched nervously from the bar, and I had to fight the urge to give her my gormless thumbs-up sign. Finally, she walked over with a tray as if carrying plutonium.

"Here we are," said Hermione. "Drinks all round and coke for the baby."

She put down the tray and I grabbed the coke, desperate for energy.

"Where's Tony?"

Hermione dropped her eyes, colouring. "He's gone to Yorkshire. We had a row."

"What about?"

"Oh," said Hermione vaguely, shrugging, "the usual."

When had they argued? When she had casually mentioned she was meeting me? Or had he stormed out so she gave me a call? Either seemed significant; catching Herm's eye I gave her a wink and she actually smiled. There was a sheen of confidence about me, one that made my skin shine. A few months earlier I'd been commissioned to make a series of short, dogma-inspired short films called *Island Apes* about the white tribes of England, now showing at some ungodly hour known only to VideoPlus.

"I saw *The Railway Children II*," smiled Hermione. "What's the next one about?"

"Growing up in seventies' Yorkshire – again."

"Sounds good! What's it called?"

"*Last of the Summer Meths*." Hermione frowned, puzzled, her eyes soft and huge; not wishing to see her unhappy even for an instant I felt compelled to explain. "Don't worry – there's a distinct lack of old men going down hills in baths."

Already the films seemed like ancient history. Much of my time recently had been devoted to another art project: Sue-Zen. As a comment on consumerism I'd done an exhibition composed entirely of fake allegations and faked images of the famous in the hope of being sued. It had worked: one minor TV 'personality' had sued my arse off and I'd been made a bankrupt, the notice of which became the centrepiece of my show. Hence my new nickname: Joe Broke. The taxman was under-impressed, as were the press. I took a small thin package from the pocket of my Top Shop jacket.

"Anyway, I bought you a birthday present."

Hermione looked excited, until she opened it. Her face fell. "*Westlife*?"

"Well, I know how much you love your Irish music."

"Not exactly Planxty, is it?"

"Herm, it's a *joke*. You know your problem: you work too hard. You want to lighten up a bit, have some fun."

Hermione's face brightened and then events swept us along. Her friends were loud and annoying and she seemed embarrassed, though whether by me or them I wasn't sure. I looked like a tramp but some had heard of me, though of course nobody recognised my face. All the cokes were making me nauseous and when Hermione wasn't looking I stepped outside for a breather.

Men passed by hand-in-hand, the last weak sunlight of the day glaring off shop windows selling leather and PVC: ninety-three million miles and eight seconds to illuminate fetishwear. I was about to go for a walk when I heard Hermione's voice in my ear.

"Come on. Let's go."

"Where?"

"You can walk me home if you like. And don't get your hopes up."

As evening fell we walked through smarmy Soho, up between the twin video banks of Tottenham Court Road to sterile Euston, along the cement chasms of the Euston Road to determinedly dreary King's Cross, and then up York Way, arm-in-arm, chatting comfortably like an old married couple.

This was what it would have been like – Hermione was showing me what it would have been like. Not magic but just solidity, permanence, tedium. But it wasn't working. I was wanting my past back, wanting a different story to that which had been told.

I got a shock when we turned the corner to find the street demolished. Even the Churchill had been levelled; all that remained was a row of ghosts. I shivered and grasped Hermione's arm tighter. It was cold and she was warm, and I was afraid of being alone as I had essentially been these last five years. We walked under the viaduct and through the new complex to her door. Herm stopped and looked at me, fear or tragedy or some other emotion in her eyes.

"Where are you living, again?" said Hermione.

"Marylebone. I have a flat there."

"Stay, if you like. You can sleep in Daithi's room. He's kipping at a friend's."

Despite my vow of temperance I quickly formulated an ingenious plan: to drink all Tony's best brandy and then seduce his missus. But Hermione seemed tired and sad, and went to bed, so instead I lay in Daithi's room, debating whether or not to wipe my arse on his Arsenal duvet, listening to the sound of the springs as Hermione lay down on her bed through the thin wall. Both lying alone, I imagined, lonely and wanting, for no good reason; only scruples, morality, conscience.

After some hours I heard a few minor bumps and thought I heard her cry; my cock hardened. There was a tiny knock at the door, as if she didn't want to wake me.

"Joe," said Herm in a small voice, "it's Stig."

I leapt up to open the door to find her in pink pyjamas, tears on her cheeks. I followed her into her bedroom in boxers and t-shirt, vainly trying to hide my erection. Stig was curled up in his box beneath Hermione's bed as always, apparently asleep. I stroked the old cat, his fur already stiff and cold. To my amazement tears came, and I could hear Hermione crying on the bed; for once, just this once, I wasn't the cause of a woman's pain.

Hermione found a shovel so we walked up the hill to Hampstead Heath, Stig over my shoulder in a pillow case, where we buried him in the bushes beneath Parliament Hill. I re-planted a flower; Hermione wept.

Dawn found us sitting in silence watching clouds come alive in the fragile light of morning, shins devoured by insects in the long grass. Then, because she didn't want to go home, to see his basket and wash out the cat bowl, we got a cab to Marylebone, Herm asleep lightly on my shoulder, me looking furtively at the streetlights skimming through her hair and tenderly, tentatively, wondering what was happening.

It was six in the morning, time to answer unformed questions. I had no furniture and slept on an old mattress in the living room. It seemed to be expanding as we swapped pleasantries over tea, until it filled the room. I said Herm should sleep on the mattress, and she said I should; that timeless courtship dance.

Finally we agreed it would probably be okay to both sleep on the mattress, so we lay an exaggerated distance apart watching a square panel of sunlight climb across the room. And then Hermione said something. She said, "Oh, give me a hug…"

She rolled over and pulled me towards her, put her warm arms about me and we froze; we froze time. Sex seemed almost indecent: why the haste? So we lay there still as the dead, bodies touching primly. Doubts resurfaced: what if this were simply the next level of friendship, some obscene test devised by Plato?

Herm's hand stroked the small of my back; her lips touched my neck, kissed my throat. Even the traffic tiptoed passed. It felt like a culmination of events, as if all points had led here and only now could I recognise the pattern, the inexorability of the fates and the winds. Me and Herm, Herm and me, a lifetime of shared pain experienced apart.

I'd never had plans, not solid ones, ones you can measure – just that simple elusive thing called happiness. Hopes, maybe: not to be poor anymore, to make the world a better place, to save the polar bears; but, over and above all, to be and to make others happy. How disastrously I'd failed.

I then remembered that those ancient, roughly-sketched plans had included her.

"I had a dream last night," said Hermione, quietly, finally, into my shoulder. I pressed my motionless lips against her milky neck.

"Did you?"

"Mm."

"What happened?"

She was silent for a long time, and I knew if she let go I couldn't. But then she just said, "This."

She kissed me on the lips: soft, profound, almost chaste. After a few sweet moments I raised my head and looked into her eyes, seeing the sombre reflections of love, and smelled her breath sweet on mine.

The greatest comedy sketch of all time is by Dave Allen. This middle-aged couple are in the archetypal suburban bedroom, he in pyjamas, she in her winceyette nightie – very Terry and June. They're bickering: she's bemoaning the fact he's been saying the same thing for twenty years, he's saying she's nagged him his whole life. Suddenly they hear a noise from downstairs and they look at each other in alarm. Finally, the woman puts her hand over her mouth in horror. "Oh my god, it's my husband!"

That's a bit how it was with Hermione that Indian summer; although we'd never been lovers it seemed like we knew each other too well. Sometimes over the course of those weeks I'd wake in the night to feel our bodies entwined, twitching comfortable secrets in some ancient, mysterious language of their own.

She stroked my bald head like other lovers had; unlike the others she said it was like a skinful of soul. When that happened, I almost felt guilty about spending what little money I had on topical immunotherapy, Minoxidil, exotic dung.

But it didn't work; it could never have worked. Despite the fact we steered clear of their names, in case they were summoned, Tony and Becky were everywhere. It was like cheating on the blind and on the dead.

Tony was away a lot that summer, and we saw each other when we could. But I knew it was pointless – like fighting history. I kept reminding Herm of her vow, to marry me at forty, but she only made faces from the past that I thought she'd forgotten.

Even as it happened that particular day had a terrible, ominous air: Tony's job up north had ended and he was coming home for good. Autumn had fallen; we walked in the park in the wind and had coffee before returning to the flat to discover the heating was cut off. Fucking ourselves warm we huddled beneath a mountain of ancient duvets.

Hearing Hermione's delightful piggy snore, her soft breast on my arm, I looked out of the window. Hard-edged air. I wanted to do a Windows '95, to airbrush the sky blue. All the leaves had fallen from the Rousseau-tree outside, and twigs bisected the grey cloud so it seemed like that oppressive shell had been shattered with a great hammer, fragments carelessly put back together in a mosaic.

Hearing the unhappy fridge still and dead, I went to get a beer, pulling one from the four pack, balancing the rest on the window ledge where they'd stay cold. I'd been hoping the meter would last until Hermione left, but luck had run out. When I turned back into the dark room she was looking at me.

"How can you live like this?" asked Hermione.

I frowned. "Like what?"

"I mean, look at this place. You don't even have any furniture. You don't even have a sofa. How *old* are you?"

"Not *that* old..."

"Over thirty, no furniture, no electricity..."

"I did have. I told you – I got *sued*. But it's not forever."

"Why don't you buy this then sell it?"

I shrugged, knowing my protestations would seem hollow to anyone, let alone someone in her position, who had sold her flat the first chance she got.

"I don't need to do that. I'll get a deposit –"

"Joe, *I'll* give you the deposit. You could buy this place at a discount, sell it and make fifty grand."

"For a profit."

"Does it matter? You could do anything you wanted. What *do* you want?"

I thought about this: about what I wanted. I thought I'd found it. Other needs had never really been considered. I thought of something else.

"I want to move to Spain."

"So move to Spain."

"I want you to come with me, Hermione. We don't need money. We can live in a cave somewhere, make love beneath the lemon trees."

"You know I can't do that. Tony –"

"You weren't bothered about Tony before."

Hermione bit her lip angrily. "You're pathetic. Living like some sort of bohemian. There's nothing glamorous about poverty, Joe – especially when you have a choice."

"Some choice."

"You have plenty of choices. Aisha says you could make a fortune by letting them use your work on this advert. That way you could scrape your deposit together – *and* have a drink."

"That's not a choice – it's capitulation."

Hermione shrugged, and it was as if something cold had taken her over. This was it, her get-out clause, her way of saying goodbye: by making me hate her. She rose, her small breasts still floating; did I really want to see them droop, watch the nursing veins spread from her nipples like Danish blue, to wither and dry and wrinkle? I rose too, went to the window naked, took a can of beer and opened it. Herm pulled on her panties (chosen for me) and looked for her bra. The silence was deadly. I broke it. "When's Tony back?"

"Tomorrow. Early."

"So this is it, then."

"I suppose it is. I should get home –"

"For Tony." Giving up on her bra, Hermione pulled on my old t-shirt. "Do you want to know something, Herm? Remember that time, back at the squat, when we were so close to kissing? You wouldn't, then, because of Tony. And do you know what he was doing? Fucking Becky."

Hermione's pale eyes filled with hurt; I watched with sad fascination as her pain shone through.

"Liar."

"No Herm, why bother? Why lie, now? What would I gain?"

"Revenge?"

"On who?"

"Becky, Joe. She ran from you and you want to hurt her. Don't you? So you spoil her to her best friend."

When I shrugged angrily Hermione went to the bathroom. She came back seeming happier, resolved; decisions had been made. Herm always stuck to her decisions. She even kissed me and called in a Chinese while I went to buy candles with her money. After we'd eaten we made love again, sadly, without fury, and after I plopped outside of her she hopped out of bed. It was cold; pulling on my boxers and t-shirt she started rooting through her bag.

In order to reinforce her Irishness Hermione practised the penny whistle. She propped her music book up against the windowsill and tootled some interminable reel, while behind her I shivered and pulled the duvet to my neck like a virgin bride, watching her frightened rabbit eyes reflect off the still-steamed glass.

I once saw an episode of *Star Trek* where the bald Yorkie captain is zapped away from his ship without warning to an alien planet where no-one believes who he is. In the end he marries, settles down, has a huge family, and lives quite happily for hundreds of years. He even learns to play the flute. But at the moment of his death he's zapped back to The Enterprise, where only twenty minutes have passed since he was spirited away. In order to prove to himself he hasn't gone completely insane, he picks up a flute. The final shot shows him playing a sad tune as he stands at a window looking out at the vast emptiness and the stars.

In that moment Hermione looked the same – wearing my old t-shirt and boxers, her hair unkempt – looking out of the window at the baleful moon, the indifferent night, and I wondered if the episode was a metaphor for a novel, in which a whole life could be lived in a day; or perhaps life as a novel joke, your death the predictable punch line.

I called to her from the bed. "Can you play *A Day in the Life*?"

Herm stopped playing and looked at me in the glass. Or perhaps she wasn't looking at me, seeing the candles glitter all around the bed, but at herself, her glittering city, our melancholy universe.

"No."

"'*Somebody spoke and I went into a dream.*' Put it on my tombstone, will you, Herm?"

Hermione gave me a stern look through her tear-filled eyes of blue, then began to play as she had once sang to her father, drifting back to her ancestral heritage, where familial spirits danced in steaming marshes full of bones.

1999

A tabloid hack found out that the allegation I'd made against the minor TV celeb in my exhibition turned out to be true, mostly. A lawyer counter-sued (to my bemusement) and I received a large cheque and some grim publicity. Fortunately it wasn't considered a big enough story for the paparazzi to hound me.

My life-in-30-seconds installation was complete, but Aisha couldn't or wouldn't look at it, and, despite a series of short films under my belt, commissioning editors wouldn't bite. The cheque dwindled. I avoided anonymous sex – for me a screw without love has always been like a screw without a Rawl plug: dusty, loose, temporary. So what could I do? I drank.

You might have gathered by now that I like a drink. But I wouldn't class myself as an alcoholic, and do you want to know why? Because I'm too lazy. Hands up: if I woke up with a staggering hangover and there was a can of cider to hand, I might drink it. But would I get up and go to the Turkish offie for a can? Rarely.

Alcohol isn't my addiction: it's my fetish. Without booze I'd never have slept with Becky or Julie. If it wasn't for booze, the birthrate in this country would plummet.

My year of abstinence was over and I made up for it in spades. I took to wandering the streets, camera in one hand, Tennants Super in the other, pointing. When mothers passed with children they unconsciously held the toddler's hand, called their child's name.

How dirty I felt, itching and scratching through street-battered clothes. I was alone and I acknowledged it, wallowed in it. Everyone's afraid of the new bad wolf, the single man.

Among other things Herm had complained at the heat I radiated, said I was too clingy, needing to be held, that I moaned and groaned too much in the night, thrashing about like a dolphin on a hot Japanese deck. But I could only remember those tube-tunnel dreams when sleeping alone, head under the duvet, waking in cold terror, blood in my veins like iced jellied eels, cold sweats and a thudding heart. When I was with Herm that fear went away, and she could sense that, she knew how much I needed her and so she left me to stew. She'd come and was gone like a little summer breeze, leaving me empty and cold.

Then just after midnight I returned from some unspeakable pub to find Herm sitting on my 12th floor doorstep, shivering with what I assumed was the cold. As she heard me approach she stood and I saw tears in her eyes; she wore a long white coat and a party dress, her heels bringing her to my shoulders. She held out her arms and rested her head on my shoulder. I could smell the cleanness of her hair as if she'd never been away.

"I've left him."

I said nothing, just closed my eyes and held her close. Hermione sobbed, so I led her inside and turned on the light. I noticed that she looked round, saw the flat contained furniture now, and I wondered if that made a difference. She sat on the sofa and smiled ruefully as she sniffed. I sat next to her, noticing the way her long coat split, her naked legs and heels. Producing a hankie Herm blew hard, making me jump.

"*Why'd* you leave him? Why now, a year later? I mean –"

"Why do you think?"

"I think all sorts of things, why don't you tell me?"

Hermione reached out and took my hand; pulling it to her mouth she kissed it. I was astonished; I hadn't seen her, or spoken to Tony, since our brief affair. If I didn't see him, he couldn't see through me. Ominously, nor had Tony called *me*. But there was no time to question Hermione now, just time to hold her, to kiss her again, to hear more secrets and dreams.

"I remember you telling me a story," said Hermione. "About a boy who was locked in a sound-proofed room until he composed music which had never been heard before." I said nothing, trying to remember when I'd told her that same story I'd told Becky. "I was thinking about it the other day and I realised you were really talking about love: starve a child of love and it will magic up its own unique strain."

"Are you *drunk*?" I hoped so.

"No, Joe. I'm not drunk; I'm driving."

Hermione led me to her car and drove through the night. Now and then I tried to make conversation, but she said little and so I drifted into sleep, convinced and almost hoping she'd smash into the back of some truck from Dusseldorf.

When I awoke we were in unfamiliar countryside and it was morning, and Hermione was chewing gum with grim determination, eyes bright with some drug. My head was banging and I slept on, feeling safe. Only be a passenger if the driver has something to live for.

After a few more hours, we turned off the surprisingly busy 'A' road and into a field full of hippies and druids, pulling up in front of a bush that reminded me of Bertrand Russell. I looked around at the uninspiring environs.

"Is this *it*? What's going on?"

Still silent but smiling evangelically Hermione produced a bottle of *Cava* and led the way up some scabrous path that petered out in a rotten field. I following her rear, too fatigued even to appreciate the view. We reached a clifftop, and stood and faced the sea. I wondered if we were at Beachy Head, the end of the road.

Then Cornwall fell into temporary darkness, and it was all the fault of the moon. Seagulls screeched and wheeled in their confusion then returned to precarious nests on the rocks, believing it was night. Down by the shore waves swept in, oblivious; flashing cameras recorded the eclipse for future generations who'd open photo albums and wonder why the night was so *photogenic*. I didn't have my camera, but wondered how you take a photograph of nothing.

The clifftop resounded to the whoops and champagne corks of the lucky few who had made it through the snarl-ups. As the fire lit up the sky over the ocean, I felt Herm's hand slip into mine and tears pricked at my eyes, my tongue too swollen to drink the cheap wine, and together we watched the day's second dawn while the seagulls raucously cried. Then Hermione's fingers gripped harder, and when I looked she was staring with horror to a figure on the cliffs to our left, watching us both. After a moment it turned and was swallowed by the horizon; it had looked a lot like Tony.

After the eclipse we went back to the tent and at Hermione's insistence made love. I didn't have any condoms, but she had brought a Femidom. I shuddered as I entered her; it felt like that packet of Monster Munch. I knew it was her birthday and wondered if I was her present as I'd been Becky's. The thought almost put me off my stroke, so I had to revert to my Darkest Sexual Fantasy to achieve a priapic state: Me, Rebecca Front and Kathy Burke embark on a rambling holiday to North Wales. But, unbeknown to us all, the girls have inadvertently pitched their tent in a dry riverbed. That evening, while we're enjoying a quite reasonable ploughman's lunch in a local pub, a heavy deluge causes the girls' tent to be washed away and – I rarely get further than this.

As we slept, the sun, angry at being upstaged by the upstart moon, came out to play. Hermione drove us into the nearest village, a chintzy place with fishing boats bobbing in a stone marina and pubs by the water. The sun was warm on the stones. Men dressed as Wurzels attempted to entertain an unimpressed crowd – hard to compete with a total eclipse. Hermione swiped at a fly on her cheek and closed her eyes.

The sun shone: *here I am*.

After some difficulties with language, bodyspace and the bar staff, I emerged from the pub seething with rage carrying two pints of fake scrumpy, to find Hermione sitting with her legs dangling over the water with a sorrowful look in her eyes, kicking her shoes on the mossy stones like the child she had never been. I placed the glasses on the uneven stone between us. Tony might have disappeared from the clifftop, but I knew he'd turn up soon enough; he always did.

"Here you are – happy birthday."

"I didn't think you'd remember. Why would you? I don't even know when yours *is*. We don't know each other that well really, do we?"

"I think we do."

I sipped sour liquid; Herm shook her head and looked out to sea.

"No, Joe. We nearly snogged fifteen years ago, didn't *see* each other for ten. A fling last year, a fuck just now. I don't even know why I *brought* you here."

"Herm, don't do this. Tony –"

"Tony knows me, Joe, in ways you never will. I'm just – a delusion, a romantic notion. You know what scared me most? When we fucked last year? When I came to your flat I went into your drawer to borrow a t-shirt and you still had mine. The one I gave you all those years ago. Smelled like it hadn't been washed in twenty years. I'm not a person to you: I'm a – shrine, a saint."

"You're real to me. Always were. You know how I've always felt about you."

"No, Joe, I don't know if I do. How can you *know* me? You don't know anything *about* me. What's my mother's name?"

"I don't know – or care."

Herm sipped her drink, winced, took a deep breath and looked at me fiercely. "But you *have* to care, don't you see? Know me, know my history."

"None of it matters."

"It *does* matter, Joe! Because it's still here with us. Still making waves, changing plans. I almost didn't come last night because of Daithi. Part of my past, part of my future – you don't even know who he is."

"Of course I do! We went on holiday –"

"He was *four years old*, Joe – he's fifteen now. He told me he saw you down the Angel once, in some pub, and you didn't even recognise him."

"I'm sorry, Hermione, but I don't see how all this matters."

"Because it's my history Joe, it's *who I am*. How can you love someone you don't know? I think it was when you asked me to come to Spain last year I realised you didn't know who I *am*. Didn't care about me, my plans, my life. I'm just a – dream."

"No. You're real. You're here. When I hold you it's not a dream, when I hear you snore or come it's not a dream." Hermione shrugged angrily and swallowed cider, wincing again and almost gagging.

"All right," I said. "All right. Make yourself real to me. Tell me things. Tell me about who you are, where you've been – I promise you nothing can change how I feel."

Hermione put down her glass on the stone; it leaned at an angle, the sun within like a lemon, and I waited for it to fall into the ocean. She lit a fag.

"Do you know why we *really* left Ireland? Because after Dad died, his brother Sean took a fancy to Mum. Wouldn't leave her alone. She tolerated it; he gave her money for drugs. Once I walked in and caught her in bed with him; the shock sent me deaf. Anyway, my hearing came back on the boat over and all the pissed up paddies in the bar thought it was a miracle. I wanted to be a singer, before reality set in. Mum wanted to come here to have an abortion, but then she couldn't go through with it – hence Daithi."

"It sounds to me like she knew exactly what she was doing. She brought you over, had Daithi, then abandoned you both, went home and left you to bring him up."

Hermione said nothing. I looked out over the black still water, hard waves beyond the estuary. Young boys jumped the twenty-feet from the quay. An octogenarian surfer plodded through the pub crowds, his naked, scrawny body coated in bleached hair. Hermione appeared to be waiting for something but I couldn't speak.

But then, when she glanced sideways and smiled, I saw it in her eyes; I was finally winning her over, winning her love. She touched my hand, leaned over, and when her lips touched mine I was shaking, almost nauseous. This was no dream; this was real. Her lips, her hand in mine, the warm sunshine on her face. Then a shadow.

"Fancy meeting you here," said Tony. We pulled apart and looked up at him. He didn't appear angry, just smug, his whole countenance one of confirmation.

"You two look great together, really great," he smiled. Hermione stood up and straightened herself. I stood too, tense and ready to fight for her. Herm looked nervously at me, and then back to Tony.

"How did you find us?" she asked.

"I followed you. All the way. To Joe's, then here. It was

pretty obvious where you were going, Hermione. Don't you remember we talked about coming here when you were pregnant?"

Hermione lit a cigarette with shaking fingers. "You shouldn't have come, Tony. We're finished."

"I don't doubt it," laughed Tony. "Do you really think I'd drive three hundred miles to beg you to come back?"

"Then why did you come?" I asked him unsteadily. I'd never seen Tony look like this: cold, confident, so much in control. He glared at me then back at Hermione, and I could see him attempting to disguise his love for her, and so revealing his weakness. A cold wind snapped off the sea and I shivered, goosebumps rippling on my arms.

"I thought it only fair that Hermione knows what she's getting involved with. What he's done."

"I think she already knows, Tony. We have no secrets."

Hermione looked from me to Tony and back to me.

"What's he talking about, Joe? *What* have you done?"

A succession of images flashed through my head like lightning exposures in the dark, but there was nothing Tony could say that would change what was happening. I put my arm round Hermione's shoulders, and Tony looked from me to her with contempt. He pointed at me while looking at Herm.

"He killed Becky – *and* Sarah."

My fists clenched and I looked at Hermione, who appeared stunned, confused.

"Tony, what the fuck are you on about?"

Tony didn't look at me; just Hermione.

"He didn't push them under the train. But it was his doing."

Hermione turned to me, doubt fracturing her peace of mind.

"What's he talking about, Joe? Why's he saying this?"

I said nothing. Tony laughed. "Remember that time Joe disappeared in Manchester? Becky brought Sarah round and he never showed up? Know where he went?"

I stared at him in warning.

"Shut up, Tony."

"All the way back to Millmoor, back to Julie. Joe's first love."

"Shut up, Tony."

"Fucked her, didn't you Joe? Your old flame – a crackhead. How low can you get? Then Becky found out – the same day she died."

I appealed to Hermione, who was looking at me calmly.

"Herm, he's got it all wrong. I swear."

"Did you go back to her, Joe?"

"Well – yes, but –"

Hermione punched me full in the face, harder than I'd ever been hit. I keeled over backwards into the water, a voltage of cold through my body. A part of me wanted to stay down there in that violet silence, but after a decent interval I surfaced and began a slow breast stroke to the ladder, my clothes pulling me back into the depths; the rowdy drinkers on the quayside started to laugh. Hermione watched me dully for a moment then finished her pint, put down her glass and walked away. I watched, kicking water, as Tony looked down at me and shook his head wryly, then disappeared after her.

When I emerged cold and shivering from that Cornish dock I realised that I had no means by which to return to London. In the rush from the flat with the love of my life I'd not taken my wallet, and possessed neither credit card nor chequebook to buy a ticket.

As I boarded the train at Penzance and hid I realised I'd had enough of it all, this powerlessness, this reliance on the whims of others; I'd been a decontrol freak for too long and it was time to take charge of my destiny. And for that I needed money.

This is what capitalism does, this is its genius: it sucks you in. Even if you try and remain outside it expands, changes the rules of gravity, so you're impelled to become a part of it all. Sucked back into the city as if against my will, money calling, recognition calling, not destiny but destination calling, not unwillingly but unavoidably, irrevocably sucked back to town to speak to men in suits.

Aisha said she'd try to fix up a meeting. In the meantime I needed money. I'd had enough of being on the outside, nose against the glass. So I took a job with a local authority, as a publications and film resourcer or something; in other words, polishing turds. If Tony could do it, anyone could. One of my film slogans (a joke) even became the council's new tag-line, and can still be seen on headed paper and border signs all over the borough: '*A Community in Harness*'.

Now I knew why the office environment never suited me: staple jokes, single-entendre comments about filing cabinet flings. Sometimes a mushroom flashback would engulf me and I would imagine the office floor was expanding crazily in every direction, a vast plain of plainness, a plateau of platitudes.

I've never been one for talking really. My pronunciation lets me down, as does my self-education – it wasn't until I was 32 that I discovered *wrath* rhymes with *broth*. Long and clever words sound peculiar when spoken with a Yorkshire accent; imagine Geoff Boycott saying '*tautology*'.

So in my mind I always talk quietly about those silent days. Having bought and sold my flat I'd decided not to buy some other box so instead asked Mother to invest my profit margins in Spain and went to live in a Travelodge in West London. I'd rise, eat a solitary breakfast watching Jane Hill, crush myself onto a packed tube train, all of us silent, heads buried in the same old news, then take the dockland railway that weaves between the ghettoes of the rich and poor.

London in winter is so grey that when passengers embark onto the DLR train from a platform it's like they step from a black-and-white film into one of colour; their jackets, scarves, the books they read acquire warm new hues. The ones who get off become so many shades of newsprint – the old newsprint, *Pathe News*, the ones that were still showing on cinema screens when I was born.

My DLR station didn't have a ticket office, just an empty lift, ghostly stairs. I'd enter the building, swipe my card, sit at a desk, eat a sandwich from a trolley, take a train back to my rented room, eat a microwave meal, drink cheap plonk, masturbate, sleep. It became a point of honour not to say more than two-dozen words a day. Sad, in all senses of the word, that was me; I remember reading one night that *Question Time* was going to be on and punching the air with joy.

Then they introduced prepaid cards you could recharge on the net, and removed the kettle to make way for a hot tap. They sacked the sandwich girl and installed a catering machine. That chocolate dispenser in the sterile, windowless office kitchen reflected my life. You pay your money, it dumps your reward, No surprise, no ceremony. Ten thousand years ago the office boys would have caught a goat and sat round a fire – this is the trade-off we've made. I could live with that; I'd eat aspirin if it meant I could live ten thousand years. Maybe.

They introduced hot-desking and flexitime, the purpose of which was supposedly to make life easier but of course only made things trickier, less personal; the women couldn't put monsters on their pencils and line managers lost their floors. I loved it: I did a 2-10, 7-11, 3am till 9, off home as the old-timers staggered in from Basildon and Grays.

In this way, by working nights and weekends when I could (the vast empty canyons, the baffled security guards, the photographs of children pinned to PCs like murder-memorials), I managed to get my words-spoken total down sometimes to zero; only some minor mishap (a spilled coffee, a toe trodden on, that chicken-style right-of-way dance in doorways) could induce a smile, a few words, a snarl.

I had another problem: office etiquette. If a woman was walking behind me in a corridor, each time I reached a swing door I'd have to make a snap decision based on clothing, facial expression and other factors whether to hold the door open. Some were outraged if you did, others if you didn't. Sometimes it was the opposite response from the same person, depending on the position of the moon.

What I really hated were the ones who'd open the door for you when you were still halfway down the corridor, so you'd have to do a hundred-yard dash in an odd sort of walking-run with a strange grateful expression on your face.

Anyway, that's where I actually met a temp called Alona. Alona liked boots, pints and pipes, but she remained feminine; she wore pinstripe trousers, lines like runway lights. On her first day I was following her down this endless corridor in my own seething world. Even though she was miles away Alona held the door open; as I hobbled towards her she smiled and then let go.

I didn't get the chance to speak to her until the Christmas party. I don't generally attend office parties, being the superior sort who finds them tedious, embarrassing and hypocritical; but I hadn't spoken to anyone for more than a paragraph for almost a month.

I was trying to locate the corkscrew when she came over, heels high.

"You're quiet today," said Alona.

I didn't understand; I was *always* quiet. I had nothing to declare, except my paralysis. Why did I tell Tony I met her in Barcelona? Maybe it just sounded better, more romantic than a few suits with desks making imprints in their arses, Lambrini in plastic cups, racy jokes by, for and about imbecility. I no longer hated suits, but I didn't belong there. Nor did Alona – we had that in common, and common attractions, common needs.

There was a grim wine bar built into the complex but it would be full of office whisperers, so instead I took Alona to a victimised pub full of Millwall fans, hemmed in on all sides by impenetrable glass: unvisited by officers, unfrequented by executives, unlistened-to by elected members. Alona loved it. Later I walked her to the DLR and she kissed my cheek.

It wasn't so much a whirlwind romance as a tsunami, just go with the flow and hope to float. Did Alona want to come with me to Spain? Did she want to go home? She did.

Aisha was incommunicado so I made arrangements; Alona flew back to Spain to lubricate my entry into her country. No word from Mum but it didn't matter: I'd be seeing her soon enough. On Christmas Day I sat alone in my Travelodge with a bottle of Jameson and a tab of ecstasy and found myself wishing Noel Edmonds was up the post office tower. Then there was that disorienting void between Christmas and Millennium Eve, most of which I spent on the phone to Alona, and to ancient prostitutes, and to impossible Aisha.

On Millennium Eve I stepped into the offie round the corner from the Travelodge and something made me cry. A blubbery, stubble-chinned bloke, in his forties, with an old smelly t-shirt, bought four two-litre bottles of 8.4% cider, a can of Fray Bentos and another of own-brand cat food. Here was someone lonelier than myself. I was about to invite him to spend midnight together when it struck me: at least he had a cat.

Somehow I missed midnight; my grandfather's watch was slow, my PC fast, and I couldn't hear the countdown from the river because there wasn't one. There were no rivers of fire that night and England fizzled out.

That's the thing, about life: anything can happen, but it usually doesn't.

2000

All alone in Spain, Alona was becoming impatient; Aisha wasn't coming through with the deal. Winter collapsed into Spring. It was time to take control. On 1st May, the same day public schoolboys tormented burger boys and Hermione dropped Millie, I wrote my final press release.

Aisha was still out of town and I was convinced that deals were being done behind my back. Meanwhile I was running out of money and caves don't heat themselves. I needed to get to Spain – not *from*: *towards*. So I walked out to meet the advertisers alone.

Just as England was winding down, heaving a heavy sigh of relief (we made it), I was pulling out. And as I walked along Chancery Lane in the gathering dusk I realised that it wasn't Spain that had brought this fresh promise, this sense of new sunlight; it was the leaving behind. The ghosts of Becky, and Sarah, and my former selves, dissolving like mist.

As I walked, I wondered where all the love went: the great romances, the grand passions, the agonies, the tears, the joyous ecstasies and the doom. For no love, no matter how important or how low, has ever lasted more than a hundred-and-fifty-years. Then it's gone on the wind, smote like dust, in ghostly wraiths, never again to burn and to transcend, its beauty gone on the tides like a message in a bottle no-one will ever read; perhaps that's its beauty.

For so long it had seemed my twin miseries were

ineluctable: England and sadness. But that day I felt almost sheltered from the diaspora of miseries gathered about me: there the dreadlocked white boy, with his dog and his education; here the Kosovan tramp, arms stretched from dangling beneath lorry axles; above all the cameras, watching and refusing to intervene, judging without knowledge and witnessing without pity. Everywhere I looked there were New Labour signs telling me what I couldn't do (but then, who needs *permission*, right?) The only thing it seems you can do and be thanked for is to spend some money. But it doesn't seem enough on which to base a strategy for living, for happiness.

And yet did I have other plans, other strategies? Not really, just security, the desire to sit beneath orange trees, to entertain the foibles of others who might have better ideas than I had. That had to do for the moment.

My sombre spirit lifted and briefly I was warmed, then I remembered the time and place and shivered as the rainy wind shuddered around my shoulders, stung my face; I wasn't in Spain yet. England: hidey-hole of the egg-eater, the seed-sucker, the arse-licker, Thatcher's abortions and Blair's stillborns. This was what I was leaving behind.

They were still mopping up the mock riots when I reached Hatton Garden, weaving between the Bridgets and Allys (and Hermiones), with their one too many G&Ts at the office Christmas party, their inadequate but well-dressed boyfriends, and the coerced delights of celery salad boxes all wrapped up.

When I was photographing food I discovered that the richest man in the country was some faceless overlord who had the bright idea of wrapping everything up. Everything that doesn't move, he wraps. If it moves, he'll stop it and wrap it up. Video cassettes, nappy sacks, slices of cheese, all separated by invisible barriers, impossible-to-remove film to protect them from life. We are a world of ten billion countries, each with their own imports and exports, customs and war zones.

London was full of killers. I saw them now, with their Bosnian eyes and Rwandan smiles, World War memories, Vietnam secrets: all the angry men. Out of the woods and stomping city pavements, looking for victims and finding only fresh problems killing can't solve.

According to the papers we were bombing somewhere new; I wondered if Campbell would be so keen on war if he'd been the son of a Vietnam rather than Keighley vet. Yet I felt as if *I'd* been at war: with my country, myself. Maybe I had some disease, like those bubble-children you heard about who were allergic to the 20th century. Maybe they were like me, missing that invisible skin. The 21st century had coughed politely and there was still no cure.

Still early so I dawdled. Walking past that hotel, the one Granddad told me about in his only war story.

"I was on leave, and went into town to see a show, meet a few girls, that sort of thing. This hotel called *Café du Paris* had a dance band on every night with some black guy, 'Snake Hips' Johnson I think he was called. But, the night I was due to go, something kept me back at the air base so I arrived in town late. It turned out pretty lucky as the hotel had taken a direct hit from a V2. I went inside and it was carnage, over a hundred were killed in the blast."

The odd thing, Granddad said, was that in a far corner of the enormous ballroom, the mirror ball still spinning its light over the dust, and faded crimson velvet splashed with gore, there was a table that looked relatively untouched. Four men sat around it in evening suits, their heads slightly forward as if they'd nodded off. The blast from the bomb had killed them instantly, but there wasn't a mark on any of them.

I knew the non-feeling – relatively free of scars and scrapes, yet underneath a mess of short circuits and faulty wiring. Women bustled past in the rain, umbrellas flaring like the frill-necked lizards of Australia. Cider Mary staggered into the road, a car honked and swerved; *Death Race 2000*, a dark obelisk will be found on the moon, clanged on by Clangers with soup dragon's bones.

Darker now, freezing, and the rain showed no signs of stopping. Along High Holborn I wandered, the cultural desert between the City and the West, between the cerebral and the material, the creative and the industrial, great grand buildings on an inhuman scale, built for architectural awards – containing nothing of interest to anyone with humanity in their soul.

Post-riot Covent Garden: fools on stilts and opera-goers pissing on the poor's chips, smug vegetarian cafes selling groovy sarnies for a fiver, crystal and candle shops and, worst of all, kite shops. Again I was in India and the fragrant warmth of the sub-continent heated my cold, wet skin.

When Tony and I arrived in Delhi it was 3am. As the plane descended neither of us knew what to expect, and looked out gloomily at the huge darkened city, bonfires pin-pricking the darkness. After being swamped by hollering beggars in the airport we caught a windowless bus full of drunk Australians into town, then took a cycle rickshaw through living streets, piles of rubbish that moved and groaned, the only sound the squeak of the wheels and the man's laboured breathing.

We knew we looked absurd – our identical green backpacks glowing, luminous – and tried to make a joke by pretending to jab a pin in the Indian's bony arse – faster, bearer. He took us to his brother-in-law's hotel in Paharganj and we were woken by a cacophony at five as if somebody had flicked a switch: birds, horns, bulls and rickshaw raspberries.

Shaken by what we witnessed there, we took the roof of a bus to Agra, arriving late at night. A signboard outside the hostel proudly announced '*views of the Taj*'. I didn't believe it, didn't really care, and then in the morning I went up to the roof of the hostel and there it was, sending shivers down my neck as if Diana herself – my first love in her newsprint blouse – was sitting there by the fountain.

The novelty soon wore off; after all I'd seen it a million times on curry house walls, and I was only there with Tony. Hermione was thousands of miles away and some symbol of true love this was; true, the Shah Jahan had erected it as a tribute to his wife, and true also that when he died he had plans to erect an identical one in black (man's black heart) opposite, but thirty thousand slaves had died in the making, and its Italian architects were blinded so they could never do anything of the same majesty again. To me that wasn't love but pride, like the pyramids, egos like the thrusting great towers of the docklands that would one day crumble to dust.

No, what struck me about the view from the roof in the scorching heat of early morning was that in the other direction, over the corrugated slums, where among the clusters of vultures and crows circling mugging monkey gangs, fluttered shiny bits of paper on string. The children of the slums made the kites out of scrap paper and flew them to taste the freedom they were never likely to taste themselves, and I watched with racial pride as the kites flew free of the ghetto into the shimmering wide space of sky.

Unfranked memo to self: don't glorify poverty. I could never understand why people just back from India are so damn *smug*; I was devastated.

I got lost between Covent Garden and Leicester Square as I always had, a mental roadblock guarded by some balaclavered thug of the night's unconscious; riot cops prowled but I was wearing a suit. Emerging as usual by the church in Trafalgar Square (its witty billboard: '*The Ten Commandments is not a multiple choice question*'), a thousand miles from where I wanted to be: reading Scheherazade on the sunshine-baked deck of a ship tavelling from Spain to Mallorca, with a cold beer, a warm heart and Herm on my lap.

An old man shouted as I passed; he shouted yesterday and would do so again tomorrow. He wore worn charity rags and the frightened scowl of an animal trapped in a world without food. He didn't want to be there; I could see in his haunted eyes that all he wanted in his scorched heart was to flee to the forest, to lie down on the earth, to melt, shine, rustle, and sing.

Dark now as night fell with the rain on the bubbling streets. I wandered past some gallery where forgotten faces peer out into the eternity of night, past Scandanavo-tourists huddling with inch-square backpacks strapped to their backs like randy marmosets. The millennium wheel turned my heart on the horizon like an upturned UFO but instead I took a sharp left up the no man's land alley that leads to Chinatown and then Leicester Square, the most godforsaken part of central London, worse even than the bankrupt auctions and golf sale placards of Oxford Street.

Moving quickly through the crowds queuing for the latest Hollywood extravaganza I crossed Shaftesbury Avenue and stumbled into the relative safety of Soho through the empty crowds, the faceless nobodies.

No – they were just ordinary Joes and Josephines, enjoying a film. Enjoying normality. I'd been outside the mainstream for so long, nose against glass, I no longer knew how it felt to do normal.

Pulling off my tie I went with the ebb and flow of the crowd-tides, along faggot alley, to Charing Cross Road, past

Molly Moggs and Macari's Musical Instruments, to Tottenham Court Road. Centrepoint pointed pointlessly and in Ann Summers Alley dealers on BMXs waited with satchels and itchy feet to sell Dexys to night-clubbers needing an extra something to get them through the night. I didn't need anything now; I'd killed enough time, so instead I meandered up the brick back alley into Soho Square.

The Seal Club was full of the usual boozehounds and balloonheads. I liked the place because it had a subterranean feel, despite being on the first floor. It was always open and the staff were always surly. The laconic, bespectacled barman nodded and poured me a Guinness; behind me loud, braying laughter. I turned.

There was some sort of party going on, all oysters and champagne, three suits and three dresses in Tory uniform – the men in dark blue shirts with white pinstripes and matching white collar, confidently florid ties; the women in identical blouses, collars peeking up over thousand pound jerseys. As I watched, one of the men staggered over to the barman.

"One of your ancient whiskys, please. The best in the house."

Authority in the man's voice; the barman named a brand.

"Wonderful."

"It's... one-hundred-and-twenty pounds a glass."

The man looked him squarely, if unsteadily, in the eye. "Give me the bottle."

The barman shrugged, unimpressed, and the suit put a drunken hand on my shoulder. That was it: trapped. Like a fly in onyx.

"My good man. It *is* Noone, isn't it? Your description... Might I offer you a drink?"

I shrugged the hand away. "All right. I'll have a pint."

"Have a chaser! Have one of these wonderful whiskys. Champagne! Anything you like."

"Just a pint."

The man shrugged and the barman poured me another drink. I looked deep into the black heart of the glass. My father's grave, my mother's tears, my sweetheart's fist. This was what it all came down to: failure.

"So," said the suit, "what time did you say Aisha would be here?"

"She isn't coming – there's no need. There's nothing to negotiate."

The suit registered surprise, and already I could see new deals, hard calculations, torn contracts. It didn't matter. I knew what I wanted.

"You've... changed your mind about the deal?"

I looked at him, then around the room – just people, laughing, drinking, enjoying life in their mysterious ways, their fashions. There was no need to be like them, but nor was there any reason to despise them. In ten billion years the universe would collapse into a blank dense cloud of zeros.

I muttered a figure; without argument the suit shrugged and took out a contract. I signed it; we shook hands. I let him buy me another drink, and when he offered me a hundred in cash I took it with thanks. Then I left the club and went back to the Travelodge, taking the phone off the hook so Aisha couldn't reach me. When the cheque cleared I took the plane to Spain.

I never looked back.

2007

It's gone midnight: stars shine bright and cold. The smile on Tony's face is set, rictus-like, unreadable. I decide to let him say whatever it is that brought him out here. After all, he has the crossbow. The best way to get the truth out of somebody isn't to point something lethal at them; let them point it at *you*.

Unable in this uneasy darkness to make out if the safety catch is on, I sense the competing tensions of wood and wire. But Tony's aim is poor, his eyesight weak, and I don't think he wants to kill me, despite it all; surely he could have done that back in Cornwall, when his passions still ran hot?

I'm right. He snorts with some private amusement and points at an old Marxist carob tree fifty yards off to the south, picked out by chance in my hunting light. Tony pulls the trigger and there's a click. The arrow stays put in its polished track; he never was cut out for the role of cupid.

"Let me show you how it's done," I tell him gently. Tony shrugs and hands it over carefully, eyes downcast. "I wouldn't know where to start."

Releasing the safety catch, I hand the crossbow back to Tony with a look of power. He looks away and squints as he takes aim at the tree. The usual form is that you explain how to shoot: to squeeze, to point above your target to allow for the pull of gravity on the speeding arrow, but I don't feel like helping him anymore.

Tony pulls the trigger: a vicious snap, a savage click and a small splash of sand kicks up ten yards from the tree. He hands the weapon back and slumps against the *sitje*.

"My bloody eyes."

I say nothing; he's getting at me. He wouldn't wear glasses for years after I struck him with the snowball and his eyes suffered as a result. That's Tony: why blame your own vanity when you can blame someone else?

Loading the second arrow I point carefully at the tree. Now I know how William Tell felt, or William Burroughs. I fire, knocking off Marx's nose; a small chip of bark flies into the air as the arrow twangs, wood into wood, made of the same substance but different densities, different velocities. If I was Clint Eastwood in a shawl maybe I could hit the bark as it falls to the earth, but they don't make heroes like that anymore, so instead I put the crossbow in its case and pick up my drink.

"That reminds me," jokes Tony, making light, "I could murder a pint of cider."

"They call it *sidra* here. Why did you come, Tony? Where's Herm?"

"Where do you think she is?"

Sudden cold fear grips me. "Is she dead?"

Tony laughs sadly. "No, she's not dead. Except to me."

"You split up. I'm sorry Tony."

"No you're *not*!" An unexpected rage comes into his eyes, and now I'm glad the crossbow's packed away. "You don't care that I've loved Hermione for over twenty years, lived with her, held her, became a dad to Daithi, then –" Tony stands to give his rage some purchase. "All you care about is your selfish version of love, your little ideal. Despite all those women you wanted *her*, and even when you *got* her it wasn't enough."

"It *was* enough – for me." I speak quietly, to neutralise his loudness, to ensure we leave no footprint here.

"Then why turn her down?"

I frown at him. "I didn't – what are you on about?"

"She offered to buy your flat, and if you'd taken it she'd have gone anywhere you wanted. So why didn't you? Was it that you didn't really love her after all?"

"I didn't know *what* I wanted then. Some modicum of pride, respect –"

"So she came back to me. I became second-best. Thanks for that, mate. Then, when things got tough, she came back to you. How do you think I felt following you to Cornwall? Seeing you there in the car, wondering what you were saying to each other?"

"We weren't talking about you," I murmur softly.

"No. Tell me something, Joe. Have you ever loved anyone? Really, really loved them?"

I have to think about that one. I loved Alona's reflection; Becky when she slept; Julie when she wasn't there. Maybe love's the wrong word, because I've only found that once. A chill descends from the slopes and I shiver, zipping up my jacket.

"Why did you *really* come here, Tony?"

Tony swigs his beer. I know his bottle's empty; he puts it on the ground.

"Remember I told you about all the miscarriages Herm suffered? Naturally, being a man, I blamed her – her lifestyle, her family, her fucking will to procreate. After five went down the pan we both had tests and it wasn't her; it was me. Something called a balanced translocation, apparently."

The silence is immense; it's just me and him out on the mountain. My heart hurts, my brain's racing and my scalp itches.

"So what are you telling me?"

Sadly, Tony takes the photo of Millie from his wallet and passes it over; in the harsh light I study the snap of the young girl afresh. Herm's nose and sky blue eyes: beautiful, a miracle. Except I don't believe in miracles, life flayed them all out of me. I don't believe in mathematics, either, but with a pen and paper I can do the sums:

11 August 1999 + 266 days = Wednesday, 3 May 2000.

Except, according to Tony, Millie was born two days earlier – May Day, her birth brought on by a minor riot, by public school boys with dreadlocks attacking immigrants who work in McDonalds. I'm trying to look at Millie's beautiful face but my eyes are watering with the wind off the mountains.

Now I finally succumb and allow this great joy back inside me, cosseted and kissed by a benevolent universe; it scares the hell out of me because I know where happiness can lead. My Millie. I also feel afraid and wonder what I'll say to Herm; if Millie will accept me as a father.

"How does Herm feel about me? I mean, the last time we met she chucked me in the sea. Does she still blame me for Becky's death? For Sarah?"

"I think she blames everyone. Including me."

"What did you have to do with it?"

"I was the one who reported her. Julie. About her kids. I think she thought it was you."

"But why, Tony?"

He smiles, grimly. "I grew up in a big house, Joe, not like you. A house with a name. That name was pain."

Shivering, he takes a swig of a new beer. "Anyway. Your question. Why don't you go and find out?"

"Maybe I will."

Grey dawn sneaks over the horizon like grey goo; ecophagy's another of my nightmares. Night drains away from the mountain like a receding flood. As I look out over the rough *campo* I find I'm wondering again, my wonder is returning. Tony zips up his coat with a sort of finality and drains the last of his beer. I remain seated and look up at him, wondering whatever the hell will become of him. Tony hoists up his bag and squints at me.

"One last thing. You never did tell me. Why *did* you throw that snowball? Why did you have it in for me?"

I sigh and smile pacifically. "There was a rumour going round town that you'd read a book."

Tony thinks about this then bursts out laughing. Shaking his head, he turns away and begins walking across the rough grass towards the rising sun. I have a feeling that this is the last time I'll ever see him, and I wonder what he'll do next.

"Tony?"

He looks back.

"I'll leave the keys to the cave under the stone on the porch. It's yours."

And, to his credit, he just smiles and waves in thanks.

England has changed since I left, despite the best efforts of Messer Blair; the green lattices of Berkshire are dotted with swimming pools. In my dealings with pools (few and far between) it's always been my way to close my eyes and jump – don't check the depth, don't even check to see if there's water in the pool, just close your eyes, hold your nose, jump and hope for the best. And look where it's brought me.

There's a moment just after the plane lands, before the brakes fully engage, that you know you're out of control and your fate is out of your own hands. I always liked that moment: subject to the whims and winds. Then the brakes kick in and you slow down and, at some critical point, you know if the plane crashes you'll still have a chance, you might just make it.

Not that I believe in fate, or gods. The closest I get to a religious experience is that bit in *Miss Sarajevo* where Pavarotti's voice dives and soars, the peaks and the troughs of human existence. Maybe you just need to believe in something, in anything; that's why there are so many conspiracy whackos about. Someone must be running things, if not God then the CIA.

The customs people don't seem at all keen on letting me in, but finally understand they have no choice: I am a snowball, nothing can divert me. When I emerge sweating into Heathrow I make for the bar, to welcome myself home.

Being stupid and usually wrong I've missed the cut and thrust of London pubs, that anarchic, archaic hubbub, the Autumnal colours, purples and browns, the smoke inhaled and porter sucked with ambiguous reverence, harsh light refracting through lager glasses, crunchy carpets where sodden dreams and Murphy's ashes are ground underfoot. But this is an American version of an English pub, so I only have two, and a chaser.

Replenished, I pop into the duty free shop and buy myself a camera. They don't seem to have real ones, so I have to make do with a digital. I haven't taken a photo for seven years and I start with something small. The shop has acres and acres of a book bearing Julie's image: fifteen, unsmiling under her ginger bush and over-made up in her school uniform, that poster of Ozzy Osborne behind her – our front room, but I didn't take it; my father did. The book is called *Hell and Back*; I would've thought *A Dog's Life* might be more appropriate.

A whole life in 300 pages: imagine. I flick through it but in this final, edited version I don't see my name, don't even get a mention, despite the fact I was her first love, and despite the fact that when she was at her lowest ebb I came back, even if it wasn't planned for her. She lied to Tony; we did fuck that night. You'd think she was ashamed. Or maybe she was worried I might kiss and tell the tabs about her exotic breakfast menus.

The book's dedicated to her childhood sweetheart: Tony. Apparently, they met again at her book launch and hit it off. She quite fancied him in glasses. Again I flick from the back to the front but there's nothing. I nick the book and a *Quaedian*, and head down to the tube.

It feels surprisingly thrilling to be back in Blighty, everyone walking round with this look of cowed malevolence. The women are all stalking around in these weird trousers with tights beneath like some weird dominatrix insect – a demented look, I feel – but, then, I always felt vaguely cheated when confronted by women in culottes.

At regular intervals along the Piccadilly Line there are enormous billboards advertising the Fire Horse, bursting from a dark tunnel. As the tube dives beneath a scabrous scrawl of old buildings I remember how much I've missed London. Although there's always been a vast difference between town and country – you can have one without the other, and many people do. But under New Labour they began to merge, to co-exist in ways I didn't like: Londoners got the conservatism, the provinces got the drive-bys.

My mind has always leaned towards the lateral, nodes cutting corners and jumping gaps, like the tube I'm riding, which misses out Stamford Brook and Ravenscourt Park. Despite the fact it's a Saturday, the train hurtles past legions of grey-suited commuters waiting patiently for trains that never come; suburbia's terra cotta army.

I doubt I'll stay long. Aisha once told me angrily that if I even set foot in the country she or the taxman will mow me down. But it really doesn't matter that I'm back for these few small, unimportant hours; all that matters is that despite the diabolical mess I have created, the upheavals and pain and unnecessary hurt, I have another chance.

Because I'm worth it.

I've always prided myself on knowing where to alight on the tube to be opposite the exit on disembarking, but things have changed, superficially – the Northern Line trains are smarter and still running late. I get off at the wrong end of the platform and feel lost, then once more I'm waiting at Euston for the northbound train.

There's the same poster on the tube wall: '*what have you got to look forward to?*' A few years ago I visualised vultures, volcanoes, now I see orchards and blossom… well, not quite. Doubtless more problems lie ahead.

Nothing matters at this particular instant: our bitterness, our politics, the music we like; strangely, even the future doesn't matter now. The last time I saw Hermione I was treading water; now I can swim, carrying Millie on my good strong back. And Herm, if she'll let me. I'll know when I see her eyes.

In the paper I read about a girl who will never grow up – disabled, operated upon – to live a normal life span as a child clutching her teddy bear. Sometimes I wonder if that's what I've done to Sarah: kept her safely sealed and innocent in my mind. I'll never let go, but maybe I'll let her breathe again.

My reflection in the tube window shears the creases off my face; seeing my blurred double image through squinting eyes I look fifteen again, angry and afraid. Then I see an apparition. The City line tube comes into view, all the disconnected faces, a machine full of ghosts. One of the faces looks my way and seems familiar, though I can't quite place his pale ghastly face; he seems to know me, though, and waves.

Ascending the escalator at Camden Town, I leave by the Lock exit and look around. The rain has cleared and cars hiss on the skiddy streets. Looking up I see a CCTV camera follow me, reminding me why I left London.

But then out comes the sun from behind its cloud and spotlights her over the way, on the corner of Britannia Junction, Millie peeking out from beneath her long coat, Herm's old beret and straggly hair falling over her eyes. The 6th of January is known in Spain as the epiphany, so here is mine. If love is not dogmatic, it is not love.

In this dream, as Hermione turns my way and looks into my eyes she smiles radiantly as the demure English sunshine shines on her incandescently beautiful face. Even as my lip quivers and heart explodes the smile becomes a little laugh, as if she's beaten me across the traffic.

It seems all points have come to this, all roads, to this point where time stops and the lights are changing to red. But as I go to cross the street I temporarily forget where I am and look right. Stepping out, I realise my error and look sharp left as a 4WD bears down; I'm sure I hear Herm scream over the traffic but that's impossible. The book you read rushes through my head. So it *was* the past, and not the future, after all.

But then the car (with its 600 horse power hydraulic actuator super all wheel control brakes) stops an inch from my gut. Holding my breath I put my hands on its bonnet and look through the driver's window and recognise the face within. I wonder if he's looking at me, or in his mirror, and I wonder what he sees. He smiles in recognition; the man I might have been, were I richer, stronger, more hirsute.

I move out of his way and he zooms away north. Now I hurry across the street to the far corner, where Herm shivers and shudders in her long cream coat, deep within which Millie waits uncertainly for the man she has heard is her father. We stand a few inches apart; the last of the sickly January sun lights up the tears and uncertainty on Herm's beautiful face.

"So," I say to Hermione, still uncertain, still scared, "here you are."

And Herm smiles and nods, wipes away her tears, whispers: "Here I am."

Legend Press

Independent Book Publisher

This book has been published by vibrant publishing company Legend Press. If you enjoyed reading it then you can help make it a major hit. Just follow these three easy steps:

1. Recommend it
Pass it onto a friend to spread word-of-mouth or, if now you've got your hands on this copy you don't want to let it go, just tell your friend to buy their own or maybe get it for them as a gift. Copies are available with special deals and discounts from our own website and from all good bookshops and online outlets.

2. Review it
It's never been easier to write an online review of a book you love and can be done on Amazon, Waterstones.com, WHSmith.co.uk and many more. You could also talk about it or link to it on your own blog or social networking site.

3. Read another of our great titles
We've got a wide range of diverse modern fiction and it's all waiting to be read by fresh-thinking readers like you! Come to us direct at www.legendpress.co.uk to take advantage of our superb discounts. (Plus, if you email info@legendpress.co.uk just after placing your order and quote 'WORD OF MOUTH', we will send another book with your order absolutely free!)

Thank you for being part of our word of mouth campaign.

info@legendpress.co.uk
www.legendpress.co.uk

ZOMBIES

ZOMBIES
A CULTURAL HISTORY

ROGER LUCKHURST

REAKTION BOOKS

'The blancs are blind,' he said, 'except for zombis.
You see them everywhere.'

Herard Simon in Wade Davis,
The Serpent and the Rainbow (1985)

Published by
Reaktion Books Ltd
Unit 32, Waterside
44–48 Wharf Road
London N1 7UX, UK

www.reaktionbooks.co.uk

First published 2015

Printed and bound in Great Britain
by TJ International, Padstow, Cornwall

A catalogue record for this book is available from the British Library

ISBN 978 1 78023 528 8

Contents

Introduction 7

1

From *Zombi* to Zombie:
Lafcadio Hearn and William Seabrook 17

2

Phantom Haiti 44

3

The Pulp Zombie Emerges 58

4

The First Movie Cycle:
White Zombie to *Zombies on Broadway* 75

5

Felicia Felix-Mentor: The 'Real' Zombie 97

6

After 1945: Zombie Massification 109

7

The Zombie Apocalypse:
Romero's Reboot and Italian Horrors 137

8

Going Global 167

References 197
Select Bibliography 213
Acknowledgements 217
Photo Acknowledgements 218
Index 219

Note on Usage

This book explores how key terms are transformed by translation, so the spelling and usage of certain words vary throughout this book. All quotations preserve the original spelling, but I use *zombi* for the term that was used across the Caribbean in different local dialects and 'zombie' for the American concept, which first entered into popular usage in America in the 1920s. Similarly, the word Vodou is preferred for the complex religion and ritual practices in the Caribbean, while Vaudoux and later Voodoo refers to the Western fantasies about those practices.

Introduction

You know what a zombie is.

The zombie is that species of the undead that returns by some supernatural or pseudo-scientific sleight of hand. Zombies are speechless, gormless, without memory of prior life or attachments, sinking into an indifferent mass and growing exponentially. They are a contagion, driven by an empty but insatiable hunger to devour the last of the living and extend their domain until we reach the End of Days. Zombies are the Rapture with rot.

And you know how the zombie got here.

The zombie starts out as the decomposing poor relation of aristocratic vampires and mummies, the outlier undead of horror film. It shuffled out of the margins of empire, from Haiti and the French Antilles, making the leap from folklore to film in Victor Halperin's *White Zombie* (1932), a rewrite of *Dracula* set in a hallucinated Caribbean. This production, significantly enough, was a low-budget, independent shocker in the year that the Universal studio in Hollywood crowned Count Dracula, Frankenstein's Monster and Imhotep the Mummy as the unholy trinity of the undead. The zombie rotted a bit more from neglect, lurking unnoticed in graveyards, sinking into the shudder pulps and horror comics of the 1940s and '50s. Then another group of filmmakers completely outside the studio system in Pittsburgh clubbed together to fund George Romero's *Night of the Living Dead* (1968). After years on midnight movie and cult circuits, the reimagining of the zombie as a form of mass contagion began to seep into horror films in the

1980s. The remorseless zombie attack was bedded down as a familiar Gothic trope after Romero's *Dawn of the Dead* (1978) in a nasty outbreak of 'cannibal holocaust' films that chewed their way out of Italian grindhouses and reinfected American production. It leaped host again in 1996, when the Japanese computer giant CAPCOM released the video game *Resident Evil*, initially under the name *Biohazard*. This was conceived by designer Shinji Mikami, who coined a new term for the genre: 'survival horror'. Since the late 1990s over twenty different versions of the *Resident Evil* game have been released (along with an associated film franchise). These commodities have made billions of dollars of profit, and have been one of the main vectors ensuring that the zombie has become a truly global figure – and arguably the central Gothic figure for globalization itself. In 80 years, the zombie has ground down the bones of the opposition and lurched out of the shadows to become the dominant figure of the undead in the twenty-first century.

It is now impossible to move without stumbling over zombie apocalypse films, comics, novels, TV series, computer games and cosplay. Zombie parades began as a local phenomenon in Sacramento, California, in 2001, but have become an annual feature of many cities around the world. A television adaptation of *The Walking Dead*, an episodic, open-ended comic series, has become one of the most successful cable TV series ever made, surrounded by a host of imitators such as *Dead Set* and *In the Flesh* in Britain and (a little more dubiously) *The Returned* in France. The global reach of the zombie figure is represented not just by the colossal budget of Hollywood disaster films like *World War Z* (2013), but in the way it has fused with very local supernatural tales of the undead around the world, in Africa, Asia and Latin America.

'Zombie' has become a standard adjectival modifier, too: we are in a world of zombie computers, zombie stocks and shares, zombie corporations, zombie economics, zombie governments, zombie litigation, zombie consciousness, even zombie categories (concepts or terms that are dying out but still lingering on). These things all become zombified because they are marked by loss of agency, control or consciousness of their actual state of being: they are dead but don't yet know it, living on as automata. They are the perfect emblem of decline coupled with denial: the zombie condition of the Western world unwilling to face itself after the peak of its power. It comes to something when an official government agency, the Office of Public Health Preparedness and Response of the American Center for Disease Control and Prevention, issues a 'Zombie Apocalypse Preparedness' kit (including posters and comics for schools), believing this was the most efficient way to educate the public in preparation for emergency. In 2011 the Wellcome Trust for medical research similarly funded the 'Zombie Institute for Theoretical Studies', a project to engage young people in Glasgow in 'zombie science', looking at risks of infection and treatments in a fictional disease outbreak. So extensive is this range of reference that the zombie is, as Jennifer Rutherford has observed, 'a mass metaphor', a metatrope, 'a figure that binds together other figures in a dense network of meanings'.[1]

Because of this ubiquitous presence, you also know what the zombie *means*. There are several basic interpretations of this creature that circulate in different registers, from the often highly informed but informal online discussion boards among fans to the arcane worlds of competing academic schools of thought. Zombies are what the anthropologist Victor Turner calls 'threshold people', those anomalies that straddle crucial cultural boundaries, 'necessarily ambiguous, since this condition and these persons elude or slip through the network of classifications that normally locate states and positions in cultural space'.[2] The most obvious boundary breach of the zombie is between the seemingly definitive states of life and death. Nearly every culture on the planet elaborates stories about the undead as a means of negotiating the perilous biological, cultural and symbolic passage between these two states. Like the North African *ghoul* or the Eastern European *vampyre*, zombies are also marginal folkloric creatures, clinging on in the uncertain zone between ancient belief and modern knowledge systems, who prey on those loved ones who hang around in cemeteries too long. They all act as a warning to observe the proper social protocols of mourning and avoid the risks of too much melancholic lingering of the living among the dead. These creatures transgress but in the end help uphold cultural categories of purity and pollution, the sacred and the profane, the living and the dead. The zombie tests the limits of kinship and attachment where these are placed under severe pressure, as in systems of slavery or conditions of extreme economic dispossession and migration. The zombie is the loved one who has somehow catastrophically *turned*, in the same body yet a stranger to themselves and their kin. They can be (in Haiti) a pathetic figure of a long-dead relative who wonders forlornly into their home village years later, or (in Africa) a bewitched migrant whose labour destroys a fragile economic and social balance, or (in American and European horror films) the ravening wife, husband or child who has forgotten all emotional and social ties and is intent only on devouring their own kin(d).

The real question is why it is that this particular figure of the undead has become so all-pervasive. There are still large numbers of doomed aristocratic vamps around, of course, despite Buffy's repeated 'dustings', or operatic announcements of the exhaustion of genre, like Jim Jarmusch's enervated film *Only Lovers Left Alive* (2013). A good deal of North American real estate nowadays seems to be the subject of vengeful spectral returns (and not only from the enraged ghosts of long-dead mortgage providers). An occasional mummy, bad-tempered pagan elemental or even Old Nick himself still stirs his stumps once in a while. The unique twist the zombie offers, though, is massification: the undead as a multitude. Thus it is very common by now to interpret zombies as a distinctly modern contribution to the Gothic tradition, not archaic survivals from a ghastly past we thought we had superseded, but products of our industrial modernity, 'mirrors and images of modern mechanical processes'.[3] The zombie mass is a figure of the 'statistical society' that fully emerged in the late nineteenth century, in which government actuaries discard individuals for analysis of the peaks and flows, the appetites and risks, of abstracted populations. The zombies do not do the cultural work of monstrous others, slimy tentacular aliens or ancient cephalopodic gods raised from the deep. Instead, they are simply us reflected back, depersonalized, flat-lined by the alienating tedium of modern existence. They are the pressing problem of the modern world's sheer number of people, the population explosion, bodies crammed into super-cities and suburban sprawls, demanding satiation beyond any plan for sustainable living. Survival horror is the crisis of the last representatives of rugged Western individualism trying to wrest themselves from the unregarded life of the anonymized mass.

It is then a short step to reading the zombie as the symbolic figure for contemporary capitalism. The zombie is 'the official monster of the recession', a relatively new addition to 'the capitalist grotesque', one shouty Marxist tome declares. 'What is striking about capitalist monstrosity', David McNally continues, 'is its elusive everydayness.'⁴ Karl Marx didn't have the zombie metaphor to hand, but he did sometimes write of capital as vampiric, sucking dead labour from living bodies. Now that contemporary capitalism has become both massively more extensive (reaching around the globe) and intensive (penetrating and commodifying body and mind), this seems to make the zombie horde the privileged emblem of globalized hyper-capitalism, a runaway world always on the brink of apocalypse. Zombiedom as contagion, as sparking off exponential viral vectors through the communication networks of the global village, is only another figure for representing the risky interconnection of the world's economy. The zombie is the Gothic version of the catastrophe that haunts what sociologists call 'the risk society'. 'The deepest pleasure of the zombie story', another radical critic declares,

> lies always in its depiction of the break, that exhilarating moment of long hoped-for upheaval: the fulfilment of a sometimes avowed, sometimes disavowed, desire to see power at last unmade, laid finally to waste and torn limb from limb – and our structures of dominion and domination replaced finally and forever with Utopia, if only for the already dead.⁵

This hellish zombie 'utopia' is so deeply ambiguous for Marxists because, as Slavoj Žižek never tires of putting it, with neo-liberalism rampant after the collapse of the ideological blocs of the Cold War, 'it is easier to imagine a total catastrophe which ends all life on earth than it is to imagine a real change in capitalist relations.'[6]

Since the overt satire of George Romero's first sequel, *Dawn of the Dead*, in the late 1970s, where the zombies roam the world's first indoor shopping mall, ambling without purpose around the stores to jaunty muzak, this reading of zombie culture is less an allegory to be teased out, less subtext, than overt text. It is a blindingly obvious thing to say because it repeats what the zombie text itself already says so fulsomely. But through this reading, abject pulp fictions acquire the sheen of political critique. Even if it might only be a nihilistic gesture of refusal, the phantasmagoria of the zombie apocalypse reveals the deathly logic of contemporary capitalism. To the barricades! Occupy the Necropolis!

These things we know about the zombie. Indeed, so fixed is this understanding of the genre that some people get rather upset when there are slight changes or innovations in the zombie figure. Although it is perhaps hard to recall now, there was a shocked collective intake of breath among the first audiences of *28 Days Later* (dir. Danny Boyle, 2002) when Cillian Murphy finally encountered the undead in a church after wandering the empty London streets; they sniff out their prey with sudden predatory alertness and *begin to run*. Gone was the quintessential zombie shuffle, the lumbering remorselessness of the undead crowd. Uproar ensued: could Danny Boyle's victims of the 'rage virus' even be considered zombies at all? Even as this device was picked up and conventionalized (the zombies are *really* fast in the remake of *Dawn of the Dead* (2004) and there is a discussion of how to outsprint the undead with cardio training in *Zombieland* (dir. Ruben Fleischer, 2009)), traditionalists objected. Simon Pegg, co-writer and star of the 'rom-zom-com' *Shaun of the Dead* (dir. Edgar Wright, 2004), cried in agony:

> ZOMBIES DON'T RUN! I know it is absurd to debate the rules of a reality that does not exist, but this genuinely irks me. You cannot kill a vampire with an MDF stake; werewolves can't fly; zombies do not run. It's a misconception, a bastardisation that diminishes a classic movie monster.[7]

Since about 2010, some zombies have also been acquiring a flickering of consciousness, intelligence, halting speech and conflicted emotional lives, soliloquizing and even falling in love. Isaac Marion's novel and film *Warm Bodies* (2013) is a zombie rewrite of *Romeo and Juliet*; S. G. Browne's novel *Breathers: A Zombie's Lament* (2009) is an account of a dead man coming into possession of his true zombie state; M. R. Carey's *The Girl with All the Gifts* (2014) focuses on a child who seems to be a hybrid between human and zombie. In fact, this coming into consciousness is an old story, for zombies have been narrators since at least early 1950s comics: 'I cannot rebel, for I have *no* will!', Morto explains in the opening panel of the front story of *Adventures into the Unknown*. 'I can only obey for . . . I AM A ZOMBIE!'[8] Even so, people can get pretty cross about this contemporary trend, even those who understand that genres evolve in a spiral, repeating tropes but also constantly modifying them. Genres are unfolding processes in constant alluvial flow, not typologies with fixed categories to tick off like a game of bingo.

This becomes even more important when you realize that an answer to the question 'What is a zombie?' can be accurately answered with any of the following responses. A zombie is a noisy child; a three-legged horse; a homeless person; a wretched dog too weak to bark; a male spirit that haunts tree-lines; a potent rum cocktail invented in California in the 1930s and made famous at New York World's Fair in 1939; a female spirit with a broken neck; a Guédé god, Capitaine Zombi being part of the Vodou pantheon; the soul of a person caught in a bottle (this is a bodiless soul, a *zombi astral*, as opposed to a soulless body, a *zombi cadavre*); a person with catatonic schizophrenia expelled from their community or found wondering alone; a person poisoned by a sorcerer and left in a state of suspended animation, to be revived by an antidote; the outcast of the social justice exercised by the community's secret societies; a bewitched slave or indentured labourer or guest worker, forced to work on plantations away from home or in the gardens of large houses or the back rooms of bakeries (because bakers work late at night); a foreigner; a young, free and single urbanite; a coughing spectre that spreads tuberculosis; an entranced person easily returned to 'life' by eating salt; a being easily recognized by a nasal tone of voice. You don't always know what a zombie is.

The point of this eclectic list is to emphasize that while there is a familiar history of the emergence of the zombie, this needs to be situated in a host of other cross-currents. The zombie is in fact one of the most unstable figures in the panoply of the undead, and has never stayed fixed for long. This is not surprising when you realize that 'zombie' is a word that emerges from the grim transports of populations between Africa, Europe and the plantations of the Caribbean and the American South. The word originates from a belief system that is a product of the slave trade plied between Africa, Europe and the Americas from the sixteenth century onwards. The zombie is rarely stable because it is a syncretic object, a product of interaction, of translation and mistranslation between cultures. Possible African linguistic candidates for the origin of the world include *ndzumbi* ('corpse' in the Mitsogo language of Gabon), *nzambi* ('spirit of dead person' in the Kongo language of the Congo) and *zumbi* (a fetish or ghost in the Kikongo and Bonda languages). In the Caribbean, speculations on the origins of *zombi* include sources in Arawak (*zemi* means spirit) or even a Kreyòl derivation from the French *les ombres*. It also bears some relationship to the words 'jumbee' and 'duppy', more familiar from Jamaican folklore as umbrella terms for a wide array of ghosts, spirits and changelings. The passage of the French Caribbean *zombi* to the North American pulp fiction zombie in the 1920s and '30s is also a complicated but crucial story to tell.[9] The American zombie is a mistranslation and weird creative elaboration of the Caribbean *zombi*, yet all the time it keeps an undertow of violent colonial history in plain sight.

The zombie, in other words, is a product of what has been called 'the circum-Atlantic world': 'Bounded by Europe, Africa, and the Americas, North and South, this economic and cultural system entailed vast movements of people and commodities to experimental destinations.' This created what the theatre historian Joseph Roach terms 'an oceanic interculture' marked by the hybridization of peoples and beliefs.[10] It also creates a *poétique de la relation*, a cross-cultural poetics.[11] A crucial part of the story, then, is that the zombie is a result of the Black Atlantic, 'a webbed network, between the local and the global', a dynamic interaction of far-flung points on the map, brought into contact through centuries of maritime trade and colonization that produces unpredictable forms of cultural mixing or *métissage*.[12] The meaning of the zombie changes radically from point to point, time to time, twisting and turning, constantly subverting, reverting and inverting itself, sometimes a positive belief held in a magical or theological frame, just as often a negative projection of primitive superstition onto others.

If the zombie emerges in the slippage *between* cultures, all the same this is not a preface to celebrating the zombie as some kind of sliding signifier that can mean anything we want it to mean. Wherever it comes to stop, the zombie is still branded by the murderous history of slavery and colonial dispossession that underpins its origins. It remains connected to the meaning of Haiti and the islands of the Antilles to the modern world, and the systematic violence, expropriated labour, rebellion and revolution in those areas, however far it travels. What is complex about the figure is often the way this atrocious undertow is at once avowed and disavowed as the zombie stumbles through very different cultures.

This book is an attempt to reveal the very specific cultural history of a liminal Gothic monster and the path it has travelled from the speechless subaltern world of slavery into the heart of the American empire and the networks of globalized popular culture. It means sifting material from a diverse range of sources, from travel narratives to colonial histories, anthropology and folklore, legal and medical case studies, pulp fiction, anti-colonial political polemics, gaming culture, comics, high art and lowly modern horror film, in order to accumulate the proper range of resonances the term zombie now carries. I'll unfold this history in eight chapters, following the story chronologically from the first appearances of the elusive *zombi* in nineteenth-century travel narratives to its global pervasion 100 years later.

Let's start, then, with a bewildered traveller on Martinique in 1889, who turns to the daughter of his landlady and asks in some confusion: 'What is a *zombi*?'

Welcome to Zombieland! *Zombie Flesh Eaters* (aka *Zombi 2*, 1979).

I

From *Zombi* to Zombie: Lafcadio Hearn and William Seabrook

How the obscure and fragmentary superstitions about the *zombi* began their journey out of the local regions of the Caribbean and became the global zombie can be put down to the influence of two extraordinary travel writers who published books 40 years apart.

In 1887, the bohemian writer and journalist Lafcadio Hearn (1850–1904) was hired by *Harper's* magazine to write picturesque pieces on the French West Indies. Hearn, who was of mixed Irish-Greek parentage but had been educated in France and England, had travelled to America at nineteen in his first headlong flight from bourgeois European life. Hearn was a curious mix. He was a journalist in Cincinnati and New Orleans who reported on working-class and African American life in lurid terms, but he also spent his time translating the French decadent prose poetry of Théophile Gautier and Pierre Loti. His impressionistic reportage from New Orleans included records of the deaths of Marie Laveau, a Vodou queen, and Bayou John, 'the last of the Voudous', a Senegalese-born 'obi man', 'the last really important figure of a long line of wizards or witches'. 'Swarthy occultists will doubtless continue to elect their "queens" and high-priests through years to come', but Hearn mournfully reflected that 'the influence of public school is gradually dissipating all faith in witchcraft.'[1] This was a classic antiquarian's lament, trying to capture the fragility of the exotic as the modern world bulldozed every last enchantment. Hearn soon began producing books that focused on artfully retold folkloric tales, stories captured on the brink of dying out. He favoured ghost stories and superstitions transposed into crystalline, decadent prose. He wrote to a friend: 'I have pledged me to the worship of the Odd, the Queer, the Strange, the Exotic, the Monstrous.'[2] He is most celebrated for his collections *Some Chinese Ghosts* and *In Ghostly Japan*, and his obsession with Far Eastern folklore led to life, marriage and assimilation in Japan, where he lived from 1890 and adopted the name Koizumi Yakumo.

His two-year stay in Martinique from 1887 was an escape from a brief sojourn in New York, which he hated: 'Civilisation is a hideous thing. Blessed is savagery!', he declared.[3] He wrote two books about Martinique, one a historical novel set during the slave rebellion of 1848, the other an episodic travel narrative titled *Martinique Sketches*. Martinique was known as *le pays de revenants*, meaning either the country so alluring it always compelled visitors to return or, more ominously, the country of ghosts. The place did seem to teem with stories of exactly the kind of 'weird beauty' Hearn loved to collect. Like a good folklorist, Hearn dutifully records the ephemeral super-stitions of the country from his informants, racing to capture these wisps of oral culture in stylized written form before their vanishing.

'Night in all countries brings with it vaguenesses and illusions which terrify certain imaginations', Hearn reflects, 'but in the tropics it produces effects peculiarly impressive and sinister.'[4] Martinique was so superstitious, though, that the local Kreyòl has the common saying: '*I ni pè zombie mêmn gran'-jou* (he is afraid of ghosts even in broad daylight) ... Among the people of colour there are many who believe that even at noon – when the boulevards behind the city are most deserted – the zombis will show themselves to solitary loiter-ers.'[5] These lofty reflections, however, get stuck on the word that Hearn has confidently translated as 'ghost', as if aware he has not quite caught all the local resonances of the term. And thus he starts a conversation with his landlady's daughter Adou, in which halting translation is at the core of the exchange.

'Adou,' I ask, 'what is a zombi?'
    The smile that showed Adou's beautiful white teeth has instantly disappeared; and she answers, very seriously, that she has never seen a zombi, and does not want to see one.

'*Moin pa té janmain ouè zombi, – pa' lè ouè ça, moin!*'

'But, Adou, child, I did not ask you whether you ever saw It; – I asked you only to tell me what It is like?' . . .

Adou hesitates a little, and answers:

'*Zombi? Mais ça fai désòde lanuitt, zombi!*'

'Ah! It is Something which "makes disorder at night." Still, that is not a satisfactory explanation. 'Is it the spectre of a dead person, Adou? It is *one who comes back?*'

'*Non, Missié, – non; cé pa ça.*'

'Not that? . . . Then what was it you said the other night when you were afraid to pass the cemetery on an errand?' . . .

'*I said, "I do not want to go by that cemetery because of the dead folk; – the dead folk will bar the way, and I cannot get back again."*'

'And you believe that, Adou?'

'Yes, that is what they say . . .'

'But are the dead folk zombis, Adou?'

'No; the moun-mò are not zombis. The zombis go everywhere: the dead folk remain in the graveyard . . . Except on the Night of All Souls: then they go to the houses of their people everywhere.'

'Adou, if after the doors and windows were locked and barred you were to see entering your room in the middle of the night, a Woman fourteen feet high?' . . .

'Why, yes: that would be a zombi. It is the zombis who make all those noises at night one cannot understand . . . Or, again, if I were to see a dog that high [she holds her hand about five feet above the floor] coming into our house at night, I would scream: *Mi Zombi!*'[6]

Frustrated by this odd exchange in which *zombi* constantly slips away from definition, leaping from noun to noun, lost in translation, Hearn then returns to Adou's mother for clearer answers. Things only get worse, however:

'*I ni pé zombi*' – I find from old Théréza's explanations – is a phrase indefinite as our own vague expressions, 'afraid of ghosts,' 'afraid of the dark.' But the word 'Zombi' also has strange special meanings . . . 'Ou passé nans grand chimin lanuitt, épi ou ka ouè gouôs difé, épi plis ou ka vini assou difé-à pli ou ka ouè difé-à ka màché: çé zombi ka fai ça . . . Encò, chouval ka passé, – chouval ka ni anni toua patt: ça zombi.' (You pass along the high-road at night, and you see a great fire, and the more you walk to get to it the more it moves away: it is the zombi makes that . . . Or a horse *with only three legs* passes you: that is a zombi.)[7]

Hearn makes it plain how he senses that there are 'strange special meanings' of the word which he cannot access without incorporating the act of translation into his very discussion. He cannot parse the difference between the *zombi* and the *moun-mò*, or keep the referent stable at any point. He might not have known that the 'three foot horse' also featured as an instance of Jamaican duppy lore, but here it is confidently called a *zombi*.[8] Hearn wants to incorporate this brand of supernaturalism into his appetite for global instances of the exotic and strange, but finds the *zombi* oddly resistant to his urge for definitional knowledge.

Much deeper into the *Sketches*, Hearn introduced another informant, Cyrillia, lovingly slotted into the libidinal economy of Martinician women built in the book. She also provides commentary on the supernatural, and again the meaning of *zombi* is a riot of confusion. Hearn declares:

> *Zombi!* – the word is perhaps full of mystery even for those who made it. The explanations of those who utter it most often are never quite lucid: it seems to convey ideas darkly impossible to define, – fancies belonging to the mind of another race and another era, – unspeakably old.[9]

This assertion is indebted to Victorian anthropological notions that superstitious beliefs are 'survivals', fragments of beliefs or customs that have failed to die out in the process of cultural evolution. 'Survival in Culture . . . sets up in our midst primaeval monuments of barbaric thought and life', Edward Tylor declared in 1871.[10] Whereas Tylor regarded his function as an ethnographer 'to expose the remains of crude old culture which have passed into harmful superstition, and to mark these out for destruction', Hearn's quest for the weird and strange was exactly the reverse: to preserve its last traces.[11] He is happy to let his informants multiply senses of the word rather than providing any stable accumulation of meanings. This passage continues:

> One form of the *zombi*-belief – akin to certain ghostly super-
> stitions held by various primitive races – would seem to have
> been suggested by nightmare, – that form of nightmare in which
> familiar persons become slowly and hideously transformed into
> malevolent beings. The *zombi* deludes under the appearance
> of a travelling companion, an old comrade . . . or even under
> the form of an animal. Consequently the creole negro fears
> everything living which he meets after dark upon a lonely road,
> – a stray horse, a cow, even a dog.

Hearn then records Cyrillia's narrative of her regular encounters with *zombis* in her bedroom at their favoured hour in the dead of night, gently rocking in her rocking chair. This charming set of superstitions, transcribed by an indulgent Hearn, is given yet another kind of status in his last paragraph on the subject, however. There is a 'source and justification' for many peasant superstitions: the baneful influence of the 'negro sorceror', with his array of poisons and dark occult influences. Martinique has burned witches in the ignorant, pre-modern past, 'but even now things are done which would astonish the most sceptical and practical physician.'[12] This is typical of Hearn, who eroticizes the mixed races in exact proportion to the extent that he demonizes African blacks. It also oddly shifts the status of folkloric tales into a different order of reality, hinting at an objective truth behind the fragile splinters of local legends and lore. It is a final moment of hesitancy between the natural and the supernatural, scientific and folkloric explanations, that typifies writing on the *zombi* in the Caribbean.

Hearn was a pioneer in transporting words between languages: English owes him the word 'tsunami', for instance.[13] If he was one of the first travellers to name the 'zombi' in his travel narrative, then this first lesson is that it seems to defy the essence demanded of the question 'What is a zombi?'

Forty years later, a second traveller from America ventured not to Martinique but to Haiti. The self-mythologizing journalist, alcoholic, occultist, primitivist, sadomasochist and exotic traveller William Seabrook (1884–1945) bravely credited himself with porting the word from Kreyòl to English in his autobiography, *No Place to Hide*:

> Zombie is one of the African words. I didn't invent the word zombie, nor the concept of zombies. But I brought the word and concept to America from Haiti and gave it in print to the American public – for the first time. The word is now part of the American language. It flames in neon lights for names of bars, and drinks, is applied to starved surrendering soldiers, replaces robot, and runs the pulps ragged for new plots in which the principal zombie instead of being a black man is a white girl – preferably blond. The word had never appeared in English print before I wrote *The Magic Island*.[14]

There is no doubt that Seabrook's breathless account of his travels and initiation into the Voodoo cult in the mountains of Haiti, published in 1929, was hugely influential, although he was surfing the crest of a much larger trend, as we shall see.

Seabrook was an American writer who grew up in the South, among plantations and black servants. He claimed that his grandmother, nursed by a 'black Obeah slave-girl from Cuba', had passed on a few occult tricks. After a dissolute early life as newspaperman, advertising executive, tramp and ambulance volunteer in the Great War, Seabrook committed to the life of a travel writer of exotic locales and became – despite his alcoholism – one of the highest-paid feature journalists of the era. He moved among the Modernist, occult and bohemian circles of New York, Paris and London in the

Lafcadio Hearn with his Japanese wife Koizumi Setsu, before 1904.

1920s and '30s. He spent time with the black magic 'Anti-Christ' Aleister Crowley, publishing a short piece about their 'experiments' together in 1921, and also knew the circle in Paris of Maria de Naglowska, a practitioner of ritualistic sex magic who wrote several books on the subject. Seabrook later collected his occultist adventures together in a book called *Witchcraft*. Seabrook himself had a kink for tying up women, something he discusses openly in his Freudian autobiography. In France, he hung out on the fringes of Surrealism, and was published by Michel Leiris and Georges Bataille in their journal, *Documents*. Leiris was a great admirer of Seabrook's *The Magic Island*, a copy of which he carried with him during his own journey to Dakar, as he recorded in *Phantom Africa*. Seabrook's rubber fetish photos of his masked and bound wife appeared in *Documents*, while Man Ray photographed Seabrook doing various sadistic things to his lover, Lee Miller, herself a celebrated Surrealist and documentary photographer. Seabrook knew Jean Cocteau and Thomas Mann, and once travelled the length of France to meet the Modernist doyenne Gertrude Stein, convinced she could cure him of his alcoholism once he had realized 'I'd become like one of my own zombies.'[15]

Seabrook was immersed in that strand of Modernism that expressed its disgust of bourgeois civilization after the Great War by embracing what it perceived as the 'savage' vitality of the 'primitive' black world as an answer to Western decadence and decay. This 'negrophilia' stretched from Picasso's famous use of African masks in his seminal painting *Les Demoiselles d'Avignon* (1907) after visiting the ethnographic display in the Musée d'Ethnographie du Trocadéro, to the craze around *La Revue nègre* in Paris in 1925, which made a star of the near-naked black dancer Josephine Baker. Paris in the 1920s was a city 'in the grip of a *virus noir*'.[16] Michel Leiris delighted in another African American revue, *Black Birds*, declaring that it shattered the polite tedium of bourgeois art by reconnecting with 'our primitive ancestry', and exclaimed that the show was the perfect exemplum of 'why we have so little esteem left for anything that doesn't wipe out the succession of centuries in one stroke and put us, stripped of everything, naked, in a more immediate and newer world'.[17] Seabrook was the same: he wished to 'escape modernity through initiation into blackness'.[18]

This cult of black inversion culminated in Nancy Cunard's oddity, *Negro: An Anthology* (1934), a vast collection of images and essays on racial conditions around the world, denouncing America's Jim Crow laws and record of lynching, examining the state of Africa, and including essays on 'Obeah: The Fetishism of the British West Indies' and a section on Haiti (with essays mostly translated from the French by Samuel Beckett). Cunard, daughter of the heir of the shipping family, had been disowned and disinherited by her father for her relationship with the black jazz musician Henry Crowder. Seabrook, who met Cunard, shared this problematic equation of black culture with virile primitivism to some extent. There is a very funny account of Cunard meeting Seabrook and his wife at the Café Select in Paris in 1929 just before he went to Africa, in which Cunard disdains their ignorance of actual blacks. Nevertheless, even Cunard thought the 'part about the dead Zombies rising from the grave ... seems the most authentic – as a document has the priority over fiction'.[19] Seabrook travelled the world in search of the wild savagery that would shake the prison of his white identity. Most often, though, he found this in the bottom of a bottle, and he wrote a remarkable memoir of his treatment for alcoholism, *Asylum*.

In 1927 he published *Adventures in Arabia*, which included an account of his stay among the Yazidi 'devil-worshippers' (a 'cult' among the Kurds sometimes evoked in Lovecraft's horror stories). *Jungle Ways*, in 1931, was a book in which Seabrook recounted his attempts to find cannibal tribes and the 'panther men' of West Africa. The second part of the book was called 'Cannibals', and Seabrook claimed to 'have brought back, among other things, a number of recipes'.[20] The book was the result of the Paris-based writer Paul Morand commissioning Seabrook to find a cannibal cult, join it and eat human flesh. At the end of *Jungle Ways*, Seabrook does just this, explaining that human flesh tasted 'like good, fully developed veal, not young, but not yet beef'.[21]

The actual story was that the French colonial authorities so controlled native life on the Ivory Coast that Seabrook could only find monkey meat used in native rituals there. It was only in a Paris morgue that Seabrook could buy a hunk of fresh human flesh to fulfil his bargain with Morand. This reversal – the 'civilized' colony and 'savage' metropole – neatly illustrated the kind of inversions Seabrook perversely embraced. In his study *Witchcraft* of 1941 he delighted in claiming that London 'houses more strange cults, secret societies, devil's altars, professional "sorcerors" and charlatans than any other metropolitan area on earth', including 'goat worship, cults of cruelty, tree cults, cults of the horrible, Rosicrucians, Thugs, ghost circles, Black Brothers and Grey Sisters, suicide societies and mummy-worshippers'.[22] He also recalled a case of belief in persecution through a Voodoo doll, a story shared over dinner with Jean Cocteau and Luigi Pirandello among the bohemians of the Côte d'Azur.

His journey to Haiti to penetrate the cloud of rumour and myth that had grown up around the Vodou cult was therefore part of a larger continuum of explorations into virile primitivism. Seabrook reported all these exotic encounters in a tone that deliberately suspended judgement, expounding rational and psychological explanations of the power of the supernatural, yet also allowing for the authentic reality of extreme experience. It leaves the savage supernatural resting on the cusp between folktale and objective knowledge, the perfect place for sensational reportage. Seabrook arrived in the capital of Haiti, Port-au-Prince, to the cliché of the Voodoo drums sounding in the hills and the thrill of his native informant (his servant Louis) telling him that 'we white strangers in this twentieth-century city, with our electric lights and motorcars . . . were surrounded by another world invisible, a world of marvels, miracles, and wonders – a world in which the dead rose from their graves and walked.'[23]

Much of *The Magic Island* involves Seabrook's attempts to find and gain entry into 'secret' Voodoo rituals, presented as if he is a fearless participant observer (rather than, as was most probable, experiencing a package set up for the wealthy adventurous tourist). Eventually he does work his way into a place where he can witness the sacrifice of a goat and the ritual drinking of blood. He graduates to his own 'blood baptism' and even a feeling of 'possession' by one of the local gods. He proclaims these savage rituals vastly superior to 'a frock-coated minister reducing Christ to a solar myth'. 'I believe in such ceremonies', Seabrook says: 'I believe that in some form or another they answer a deep need of the universal human soul . . . Let religion have its bloody sacrifices, yes, even human sacrifices, if thus our souls may be kept alive.'[24] Just like Hearn's decadent

William Seabrook, author of *The Magic Island* (1929).

bohemianism, Seabrook's Modernist primitivism embraces precisely what Victorian anthropologists of superstition and colonial authorities had vocally condemned. Seabrook admires the 'dark depths no white psychology can ever plumb', although in the same sentence declares the Haitian peasants 'naïve, simple, harmless children' with conventional lazy racism.[25]

Woodcut of 'dead men working' by Alexander King,
from William Seabrook's *The Magic Island* (1929).

What follows is Seabrook's introduction to a magic that hides
behind Voodoo, a 'black sorcery' that is much harder to access.
Seabrook's fame rests on a short chapter called '. . . Dead Men
Working in the Cane Fields', which is mostly filled with second-
and third-hand reports of superstitions about 'a baffling category on
the ragged edge of things which are beyond either superstition or

Alexander King woodcut from *The Magic Island* (1929).

reason'.[26] These relayed stories involve the vampire, the *loup-garou* or werewolf, and, most elusively, the *zombie*, a term that always appears in italics, as if resistant to incorporation into American English. In contrast to the slippery confusion of Lafcadio Hearn, Seabrook offers a precise definition:

The *zombie*, they say, is a soulless human corpse, still dead, but taken from the grave and endowed by sorcery with a mechanical semblance of life – it is a dead body which is made to walk and act and move as if it were alive. People who have the power to do this go to a fresh grave, dig up the body before it has had time to rot, galvanize it into movement, and then make of it a servant or slave, occasionally for the commission of some crime, more often simply as a drudge around the habitation or the farm, setting it dull heavy tasks, and beating it like a dumb beast if it slackens.[27]

Seabrook collects a number of folkloric tales about zombies, detailing how they can be brought back to a paradoxical consciousness of their 'true' dead state by eating salt. The awakening of a zombie to its true condition through the agency of salt is a constant in these early accounts. It is a superstition linked to the one in Europe, where spilled salt is thrown over the left shoulder in the Devil's face: salt is a preserver and purifier. Seabrook is then told that the zombie is not simply a marginal peasant belief, but has been enshrined in the Penal Code of Haiti, in a clause first added as early as 1864. Article 249 declares:

Also shall be qualified as attempted murder the employment which may be made against any person of substances which, without causing actual death, produce a lethargic coma more or less prolonged. If after the administering of such substances, the person has been buried, the act shall be considered murder no matter what result follows.[28]

This ambiguous legal formulation seems to confer the imprint of reality on zombification beyond merely folkloric whispers. The Penal Code was concerned to objectify and outlaw *sortilèges*, 'sorceries' exercised beyond, behind or in parallel to religious practices. Could the zombie be the product of a secret shamanic knowledge of a pharmacopeia used for inducing catatonic states? Could this be the material base for this elusive state?

It was precisely Seabrook's use of detail from the authority of medicine and law that was picked up in *White Zombie* in 1932, a film that leaned heavily on Seabrook as a source. This clause from the Penal Code is laboriously read out by the local doctor; Article 249 was also reproduced on posters for the film, as if it were a legal guarantor of 'true' horror. In 1936, the feverish pulp novel *Damballa Calls* by the German writer Hans Possendorf started and ended by quoting this same article of law, commenting: 'This gruesome paragraph, which is surely not to be found in the penal code of any other country, seems to be good evidence for the existence of "zombies".'[29]

Fifty years later, in the 1980s, the exotic adventurer and 'ethnobiologist' Wade Davis revived this old theory, claiming to have found both the poison that induced this catatonic state – derived from the puffer fish – and its antidote, thus finally 'solving' the mystery of the zombie once and for all. He published an academic paper, 'The Ethnobiology of the Haitian Zombi' in 1983, followed by a more sensational popular account of his adventures among the occultists of Haiti in *The Serpent and the Rainbow*. The book (and subsequent TV specials) presented 'actual' zombies created by the profound but secret skills of poisoners. They had proper names and case histories, these zombies. Clairvius Narcisse had 'died' in 1962, but was filmed by a BBC film crew in 1981. He later told Davis that he remembered being conscious but rendered completely immobile through his own funeral. Francina Illeus was being treated in a psychiatric institution for catatonic schizophrenia. Wade's theory was that these people had been poisoned with a potion used as a form of social policing by Haiti's secret societies. This theory created controversy and was largely dismissed by his fellow researchers.[30] In another echo of Seabrook, Davis's account, which wanted to claim a serious scientific basis, also became the source material for a sensationalist Gothic horror film, Wes Craven's *The Serpent and the Rainbow* (1988).

Seabrook starts collecting zombie stories as soon as his ear is attuned to this elusive being from the 'ragged edge'. These seem to be folkloric tales of the vengeance of these unquiet dead on the greed that drives their gangmasters or owners to extract unholy quantities of labour. One story he is told refers to a gaggle of workers employed under a headman for HASCO, the Haitian American Sugar Company, an American enterprise then faltering at trying to reintroduce large-scale plantation farming back into Haiti. The rhetorical device is to link a native superstition to the machinery of modern American industrialism. Even more miraculously, his native source dismisses any hesitancy about the status of these stories by immediately offering to show Seabrook zombies actually at work in the fields. 'I did see these "walking dead men", and I did, in a sense, believe in them and pitied them, indeed, from the bottom of my heart', Seabrook declares with significant ambiguity at the opening of his description. He adds:

> My first impression of the three supposed *zombies*, who continued dumbly at work, was that there was something about them unnatural and strange. They were plodding like brutes, like automatons . . . The eyes were the worst. It was not my imagination. They were in truth like the eyes of a dead man, not blind, but staring, unfocused, unseeing. The whole face, for that matter, was bad enough. It was vacant, as if there was nothing behind it.[31]

Seabrook experiences a twist of 'mental panic' at this apparently incontestable empirical proof of the existence of the undead, only to rationalize what he sees as 'nothing but poor ordinary demented human beings, idiots, forced to toil in the fields'.[32] The chapter ends, however, in suspension between natural and supernatural explanations, with Seabrook quoting the authority of a respected Haitian scientist who reads out Article 249 of the Penal Code to hint at 'something in the nature of criminal sorcery' behind the zombie. A gripping yarn about the exotic uncanny must always be left unresolved, the zombie shuffling beyond any single frame of reference.

It is only in later chapters that Seabrook provides any proper context for his visit, when he travels to the island of La Gonave to meet its famous 'White King'. Faustin Wirkus was the American Marine Corps sergeant promoted to effective governor of this island in the Gulf of Gonave, 30 miles from Port-au-Prince. Wirkus 'ruled' this territory as the lone white American representative on the island. After Seabrook's visit, Wirkus became something of a celebrity in America, published his own memoirs and went on the lecture circuit with his 'exotic' films of Haitian life. Seabrook praises the Marine for weaving himself into peasant structures of belief and justice, rather than trying to impose foreign values: this is how Wirkus is crowned 'King', symbolic companion to the native Queen.

The key point is that in visiting Wirkus, Seabrook's travelogue finally acknowledges that his whole trip is made possible by the occupation of Haiti by American forces in the period between 1915 and 1934. His impressions of Haiti are entirely dictated by this act of colonization, and this context is central to understanding how the Caribbean *zombi* made the leap to become the American zombie.

The occupation of Haiti was part of a larger series of American interventions in the Pacific and Caribbean in the early stages of America's imperial expansion into its sphere of influence from the 1890s: the annexation of Puerto Rico in 1898, the occupation of Cuba and Honduras, the creation of Panama, the troops sent into Mexico in 1914. Haiti occupied a unique position in the Caribbean in that it had been an independent republic since 1804, changing its name from Saint-Domingue to the indigenous Arawak name Haiti. It was the only state to be built from a successful slave rebellion at that time. This revolt began in 1791, started by a group of 'Black Jacobins' inspired by the rhetoric of universal liberty promised by the French Revolution; it had to defeat French, Spanish and English troops and a last Napoleonic attempt at reinvading the island before winning final independence.

Saint-Domingue had been the most profitable colony in the French empire, pouring vast wealth into French port cities like Brittany and Marseilles from rich harvests of sugar and coffee. The wealth of a substantial portion of the French bourgeoisie depended on the output of this single colony. Its profits were so vast because the plantations exercised a brutal system of slavery that slaughtered hundreds of thousands of African slaves throughout the eighteenth century in the relentless pursuit of maximum return.

The infamous newly independent black republic wrote a constitution outlawing foreign ownership of land. For this and other outrages, Haiti was demonized in white Europe and America for a century as an affront to benign accounts of the civilizing virtues of imperialism. The fledgling post-colonial state was virtually crippled from birth by the huge reparations of 150 million francs it was forced to pay in 1825 to foreign plantation owners for loss of income in return for limited trading deals. Haiti has been in debt dependency ever since.

In July 1915, the u.s. intervened in Haiti, ostensibly to restore political stability and avoid civil war following the murder of the president Guillaume Sam, who had been torn apart by his own citizens. The Americans depicted themselves in paternalist terms, and Haiti as its savage, childish 'ward' requiring benevolent guidance. American capitalists had actually been steadily securing control of Haiti's Banque Nationale over the previous decade, and the finances of the country had effectively been taken over by the New York City Bank before the u.s. Navy arrived. Haiti was again a pioneer, this time in experiencing the neo-imperialism of global finance at the start of the twentieth century.

American diplomats installed a new puppet president and forced the passage of a constitution which allowed for foreign ownership of land again. Much of the constitution was drafted by Assistant Secretary to the Navy Franklin D. Roosevelt. A $40 million loan secured from New York banks in 1919 further indebted Haiti. American capital then set about reconstituting large plantations. New business ventures, such as HASCO, were investment opportunities that promised large returns to their investors. Improvements in the infrastructure of the immiserated state of Haiti were funded by heavy taxes; most Haitians could not pay in cash and were forced to do so through the supply of their indentured labour. The return of the *corvée* gang within a year of American occupation, working on roads and railroads, was seen by many as the return of slavery.

The Americans fought a long-term insurrection by guerrilla rebels (known as *cacos*) and also, alongside the Catholic Church and Protestant missionaries, a war against 'native superstition', which involved attempts to systematically dismantle any Vodou religious worship among the peasantry. This resulted only in a black-market trade in 'Voodoo drums' seized from *honforts* (ceremonial spaces) destroyed in police and army raids. In 1920, allegations about atrocities allegedly committed by Marines, reported by the black American journalist James Weldon Johnson in *The Nation*, resulted in an American Senate Committee inquiry that undermined the discourse of paternalism. Haiti became a political focus for black civil rights and Negritude movements across the interwar period. By 1922, HASCO was in financial collapse and had to be recapitalized. During this slump, tens of thousands of Haitians travelled to neighbouring Dominica; up to 25,000 of them were later slaughtered in the ethnic massacres of 1937 known as *El Corte*, 'the cutting', thousands of macheted bodies of Haitian workers flung into the Massacre River. There was also mass migration to find work in Cuba, some estimating that nearly a quarter of the male population moved in this period. A shift in American foreign policy after the election of 1933 ensured the end of the occupation in the context of non-intervention. The U.S. withdrew from Haiti on 15 August 1934.

Seabrook's visit came towards the end of the occupation, at a time when the euphemistically named 'Hygiene Service' of the occupier was engaged in yet another major drive to disrupt an insurgency they closely associated with Vodou worship. They were being assisted by a very active Catholic Church campaign against peasant beliefs. The weirder and more sunk in superstition savage Haiti was, the more the language of Empire and Church as bringers of enlightenment justified intervention. Seabrook's Modernist primitivism clearly disliked any pious Christian interference with savage energies (his rejection of Christianity was wrapped up in his rejection of his father's evangelical ministry). This is why he approved of the king of Gonave's decision to merge with local customs rather than try to eradicate them, and why he embraced with typical colonial melancholy what he believed were the last traces of authentic rituals and customs before modernity swept them away.

But Seabrook was also blind to the conditions that created his 'dead men working in the cane fields'. The cultural resistance to slave plantations, from a century of building nationalist myths commemorating the violent refusal of the white masters, meant that the large HASCO plant in Cul-de-Sac found it very difficult to find labour for its revival of large-scale harvesting. Gang bosses brought in outsiders under duress; they were referred to locally as *zombis*. If slavery is, as Orlando Patterson has evocatively put it, a form of social death, to be returned to slavery by the American occupiers was an uncanny return after a century of freedom: no wonder the 'undead' roamed the HASCO fields. 'The essence of slavery is that the slave, in his social death, lives on the margin between community and chaos, life and death, the sacred and the secular. Already dead, he lives outside the mana of the gods and can cross the boundaries with social and supernatural impunity.'[33] So the imbecilic state Seabrook diagnosed could just as well have been the exhaustion of *corvée* work, and the shuffling gait might have come either from being in chains or from a distinctive way of moving that slaves developed to conserve energy. There is a reason why so many African American dances are based around ideas of 'the shuffle'. What Seabrook thinks he sees as a savage survival is actually a product of the very industrial modernity he believes he is leaving behind. 'Could there have been a more fitting image of and inclusive commentary on the proletarianization of the displaced Haitian peasant sharecropper than a crew of *zombies* toiling in the HASCO cane fields?' one historian asks.[34]

While Seabrook might have resisted many aspects of American modernity, his help in transferring the *zombi* into the zombie only retrenched a vision in the colonial centre of a series of immiserated margins creeping with supernatural beings set on vengeance. The malignant ancient Egyptian mummy starts awake in the British Museum with murder on its mind only after the British begin their military occupation in 1882. In the Roaring Twenties, American power is to be haunted by its own imperial revenant, one that will eventually bring full-scale and repeated apocalypse down on the American empire until it stands in imagined ruins – again and again and again.

What do these first brushes with the *zombi* in Hearn and Seabrook teach us? These books show us that it is important to grasp geo-political differences of emphasis as the *zombi* circulates around the circum-Atlantic world. The Martinician *zombi* is different from the Haitian *zombi*. They seem to have a different slant from the tales of *zombi* devilry collected in Dominica in the 1920s by folklorist Elise Clews Parsons, for instance, and different again from accounts of 'spirit thievery' associated with the Obeah tradition (Obeah being a term more familiar in Anglophone colonies in the Caribbean like Barbados and Jamaica, the word perhaps derived from the Igbo term *obia* for that figure that lies somewhere between doctor and priest).[35] In turn, these zombies vary from the American undead of Louisiana or, further north, from the zombies spewed out of New York pulp publishing houses in the 1920s and '30s.

The very different colonial histories of Caribbean islands contribute to these shifts of meaning. Lafcadio Hearn's elusive encounter with the meaning of *zombi* in Martinique anticipates a more expansive range of metaphorical resonances there. Unlike the revolutionary struggle for independence crucial to the identity of Haiti, Martinique, despite several slave rebellions since its colonization by the French in 1635, remains to the present day a 'department' of the French state, never having undergone full decolonization. This continued sense of dispossession in the native population has made Martinique a significant location for the emergence of anti-colonial theory that condemns this subjection in terms that often use the zombie as metaphor.

It was in Fort-de-France in Martinique that the revolutionary thinker Aimé Césaire, author of *Discourse on Colonialism*, taught Frantz Fanon, who went on to train in medicine and psychiatry and become a key intellectual in the struggle against French colonialism in the Algerian war of independence and elsewhere in North Africa. When Fanon published *The Wretched of the Earth*, the preface by Jean-Paul Sartre saw it as an epochal book in the reversal of power between white and black, colonizer and colonized. Sartre declared to his European readers of these 'wretched':

Their fathers, shadowy creatures, *your* creatures, were but dead souls; you it was who allowed them glimpses of light, to you only did they dare speak, and you did not bother to reply to such zombies . . . Turn and turn about; in these shadows from whence a new dawn will break, it is you who are the zombies.[36]

Fanon's book, as a manual for building revolutionary consciousness, actively denounced the 'terrifying myths' of 'leopard-men, serpent-men, six-legged dogs, [and] zombies', typical of what he called the 'occult sphere' of under-developed nations (he was not very careful in separating out the locality of these beliefs, either, as this mixed list attests). 'Believe me, the zombies are more terrifying than the settlers', Fanon said, arguing that these only reinforced the subjection of 'the native, bent double, more dead than alive', stuck in 'pseudo-petrification' under a 'death reflex'.[37] Even as Fanon urges revolutionary youth to 'pour scorn upon the zombies of his ancestors', the idea that settler colonialism can only create 'cultural lethargy and the petrification of the individual' very clearly borrows from the notion of the zombie, as if he cannot quite shake it himself.[38] In his psychiatric case studies of disorders produced by the violence of subjection and the traumas of his patients resulting from war, imprisonment and torture, the metaphorical zombie rears up again in his account of psychosomatic conversion hysterias, although he never uses the term:

It is an extended rigidity and walking is performed with small steps. The passive flexion of the lower limbs is almost impossible. No relaxation can be achieved. The patient seems to be made all of a piece, subjected as he is to a sudden contraction and in - capable of the slightest voluntary relaxation. The face is rigid but expresses a marked degree of bewilderment.

The patient does not seem able to 'release his nervous tension'. He is constantly tense, waiting between life and death. Thus one of such patients said to us: 'You see, I'm already stiff like a dead man.'[39]

This description produces a very different undertow of meaning for the contemporary zombie.

Another significant Martinician writer and intellectual, Édouard Glissant, was also prone to use the zombie as a metaphor for the divided consciousness of the colonial subject. In his essay 'Dispossession', Glissant argued that Martinique suffered a very specific form of colonial melancholia, never having been in control of the economics of the plantations, even at the height of slavery, since the market was always determined elsewhere, by other islands or by the colonial centre. There was no density of island culture or identity. After centuries of colonialism and the neo-colonial assertion of Martinique as an Overseas Department of France in 1946, Martinician culture was marked only by pseudo-production, paralysis, 'technical automatism' and 'mental automatism'.[40] In a companion essay, Glissant reflected: 'Just as the Martinician seems to be simply passing through his world, a happy zombi, so our dead seem to us to be hardly more than confirmed zombis.'[41]

Subsequently, these intellectuals provide the basis for a generic portrait of the colonized self as a kind of zombification that extends to other Caribbean writers. Jean Rhys, the expatriate writer at the centre of Modernist Paris and London in the 1920s and '30s, was born in Dominica. At the end of her life, she rewrote the story of the first Mrs Rochester from *Jane Eyre*, a Caribbean Creole, in her novel *Wide Sargasso Sea* (1966). The story mixes the bewilderment and confusion of the last surviving rump of Creole planters after the end of slavery with Rochester's newcomer nightmares of being 'buried alive', 'the feeling of suffocation' and a dread of being poisoned by his servants. Early in his visit, Rochester looks up 'Obeah' in a travel book called *The Glittering Coronet of Isles*, reading: 'A zombi is a dead person who seems to be alive or a living person who is dead. A zombi can also be the spirit of a place, usually malignant but sometimes to be propitiated.' The same entry warns, however, that the Negroes 'confuse matters by telling lies', making this superstition difficult to pin down.[42] From these suggestive hints at native beliefs that exceed rational reduction, Rhys constructs a portrait of selves zombified by the weight of colonial history and doomed expectation, and it spectacularly revises a reading of Brontë's Bertha Mason as a metaphorically zombified colonial subject.

Similarly, the Jamaican writer Erna Brodber, a scholar long interested in folklore and superstition, uses the notion of 'spirit thievery' in her novel *Myal* to depict the pressures on a young girl caught between her Irish father and Jamaican mother, between passing for white and being abjected as black, and between the allegedly enlightened values of her adoptive family of Protestant missionaries and the traditional beliefs of the peasant village steeped in Obeah lore. Her slow decline into 'vacant staring' and increasing phases of catatonic shutdown leaves a chorus of voices to diagnose her condition:

> – . . . He gives them no mind. He has . . . –
> – Zombified them. That's the word you need. –
> – Meaning –
> – Taken their knowledge of their original and natural world away from them and left them empty shells – duppies, zombies, living deads capable only of receiving orders from someone else and carrying them out . . .
> – Have you been zombified?[43]

This slippage around the zombie in generic post-colonial discourse 'creolizes' the *zombi* into a metaphor of colonial and post-colonial torpor. This is in distinct contrast to what happens in Haiti, however. The Haitian *zombi* has accrued a much more fixed set of cultural identifications and meanings. As my reading of William Seabrook's *The Magic Island* has begun to suggest, this is down to the very specific role that the black republic of Haiti has played in the colonial imagination of Europe and America since independence in 1804.

Seabrook's sensational story of the zombie needs to be understood as the story of a creature emerging from a long history of demonization of Haiti, which was focused for decades on overheated fantasies of Voodoo, cannibalism and black magic. Once this sense of historical undertow is in place, we can begin to place Seabrook as merely one voice in the cacophony that unleashed the zombies that poured into American popular culture in the last years of the colonial occupation in the late 1920s and early 1930s.

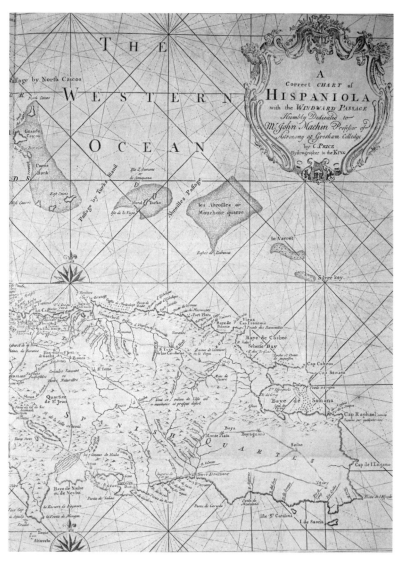

Map of Haiti, *c.* 1800.

2

Phantom Haiti

In 1685, Louis XIV signed into law the notorious Code Noir, the document that formed the official legal framework for slavery and the enforcement of order in the French colonies. The first article expelled all Jews from French colonies; the second article required all planters importing African slaves to baptize them as Catholic within a week of arrival or else face a fine; and the third edict forbade any other public exercise of religion, regarding all other congregations among the slaves as 'illicit and seditious'.[1] In the colony of Saint-Domingue, later to become Haiti, this produced a century of detailed elaborations of the Code, outlawing slave assembly first for dances, then for drumming ceremonies at night, then the practice of *sorciers*, the uses of magic charms and talismans, and, in 1758, all 'superstitious assemblies'. This followed a rebellion led by the maroon (fugitive slave) Makandral, rumoured to be a sorcerer who had poisoned French planters and exerted uncanny influence over his followers. In the 1780s, when Mesmerism became fashionable in Paris, it was immediately banned in Haiti. The law and the spirits are symbiotic: the Code's interdictions shaped and validated the very occult forces it was trying to eliminate.

The first European travel narrative about Saint-Domingue, Louis-Élie Moreau de Saint-Méry's *Description topographique, physique civile, politique et historique*, appeared in 1797, in the midst of the slave rebellion. The book spoke of 'disgusting' savage rituals and warned that 'nothing is more dangerous from all reports, than this cult of Vaudoux, founded on this extravagant idea, which can

44

Haiti's interminable wars of independence: January Suchodolski's
The Battle at San Domingo, 1845.

be made into a very terrible weapon, that the ministers of the being
that is decorated with this name are omniscient and omnipotent.'[2]
It was strongly rumoured that the group that instigated the slave
rebellion of 1791 did so over a blood sacrifice. Boukman, the first
leader of the rebels, was widely believed to be a *papaloi* or Vaudoux
priest. Throughout the nineteenth century, Saint-Méry's fantastical
account of secret serpent worship in gatherings in the mountains
was rehashed as the authoritative truth that was hidden beneath
the surface of the black republic of Haiti. This is how the journey
from the French *Vaudoux* to the Louisiana Creole Voudou to the
modern American Voodoo begins.

The word *vodun* in the African Fon language loosely translates
as 'spirit', the invisible spiritual energy that entwines itself through
all human affairs, binding together past and present, mundane and
ultramundane spheres. Historians of Vodou religion speculate that
the French took slaves in such large numbers from the kingdom of

Dahomey (now Benin) that they transported much of their spiritual beliefs with them wholesale. Across the Caribbean, different slave ancestry produces slightly different local religions: hence Obeah in Anglophone colonies, Vaudoux in Saint-Domingue and Santería in Cuba. The French operated their most profitable colony with such brutality that the planters rarely bothered to 're-educate' their slaves, given the short life expectancy. Yet if Vodou is a partial link back to ancestral origins, it is also undoubtedly a syncretic set of beliefs, fusing with the official Catholic religion of the French colonists in Saint-Domingue in such intricate and ingenious ways that the Church authorities have found attempts to separate orthodox and unorthodox religious belief in Haiti impossibly self-defeating. Vodou is not a fixed doctrine, but a dynamic array of rituals and practices, so the Vodou *lwa* (or spirits) constantly mutate and transform in and beyond the Catholic panoply of saints. It also adapts very locally, often down to individual *honforts* (places of worship), and no two schematic descriptions of the cosmogony ever quite match up.

Under slavery, Vodou operated secretly in defiance of the Code Noir. But even after independence, the ruling elite in Port-au-Prince tended to regard Vodou practices as a peasant superstition that blocked progress and development towards modern statehood, adopting a European Enlightenment model of the nation. It was only in the 1920s that leftist political intellectuals like the anthropologist Jean Price-Mars suggested that Vodou could form the basis of a new indigenous national identity in Haiti. Most anti-colonial thinkers – like Fanon – continued to regard superstitious belief as a regressive force, a marker of subjection, not liberation.

Secret and disavowed before and after independence, Vodou steadily acquired a monstrous and phantasmal status in nineteenth-century travel writing. Vaudoux was an elusive cult mentioned only marginally before 1850 (and not at all in Thomas Madiou's four-volume history of the republic, published in 1848).[3] Yet it started to be the *defining* element of the Haitian republic in the 1850s, when the politics of race and slavery became incendiary during the American Civil War. In this context, an independent black state only a little bit further away than the American slave states in the South required ideological demonization by the enemies of abolition. Black autonomy had to indicate depravity and credulity. When the ex-slave and soldier Faustin Soulouque became president of Haiti in 1847 and ruled as Emperor Faustin I between 1849 and 1859, Haiti was portrayed as returning to a savage African state of bestial cruelty and superstition. It was emphasized that Soulouque was a 'pure' black African who had massacred the mulatto ruling elite in Port-au-Prince on coming to power, eliminating the last traces of white influence. The scientific racism of Count Gobineau's notorious *Essay on the Inequality of the Human Races* (1853–5) used Haiti as the exemplar of race degeneration. A lurid depiction of this savage state, *Soulouque and His Empire*, was published by Gustave d'Alaux in French in 1856 and translated into English in 1861. Towards the end of the American Civil War, there was also propagandistic use of the Bizoton Affair, a trial in a place near Port-au-Prince that appeared definitively to link Vaudoux with human sacrifice and cannibalism, the basest marker of savagery imaginable in Western thought. This was hugely important in further darkening the reputation of Haiti.

A detailed account of the Bizoton trial was published in English in Spenser St John's *Hayti; or, The Black Republic* in 1884, some twenty years after the fact, suggesting the story still carried a lot of cultural freight. St John was a career diplomat who had served as the British consul in Haiti from 1863 to 1875. Although when in the Far East he had scandalized his fellow colonial rulers by openly acknowledging his three children with his Malay mistress, his disdain for black Haitians was absolute. In his chapter 'Vaudoux Worship and Cannibalism', St John suggests that the arrival of Soulouque made Vaudoux effectively the official religion of the rulers of the republic, and that this dark alliance was continued by Soulouque's successors after he was deposed. St John detailed rituals that included 'the adoration of the snake', sacrifices of animals and the 'goat without horns' (which St John understands as meaning the sacrifice of human children). The ceremony of the snake, St John asserts, using second- and third-hand accounts, 'is accompanied by everything horrible which delirium could imagine to render it more imposing',[4] a formulation that has no content but positively invites the reader to fantasize horrific things.

The Bizoton trial develops directly from these stories; the record of the law is again supposed to provide objective truth value of an horrific tale. In December 1863, the court heard, the labourer Congo Pellé had sought intercession from a Vaudoux *papaloi*, who had demanded a human sacrifice. Congo's niece was delivered; she was strangled, decapitated, her head cooked for soup and her flesh for a stew, with some body parts eaten raw, participants later confessed in court. The disappearance of another child in the area for a second sacrificial ritual had exposed the horrific plot.

St John is contemptuous of the process of the court (modelled on the French, not British, system), where the fatal confession had obviously been beaten out of the defendants and testimony was whispered to the judge by those too terrified to attest in open court. Yet he points out with dogged empiricism that 'there, on the table before the judge, was the skull of the murdered girl, and in the jar the remains of the soup and the calcined bones.'[5] Eight members of the *honfort* were condemned to death, and St John's account contains an intriguing last detail:

> The Vaudoux priests gave out that although the deity would permit the execution, he would only do it to prove to his votaries his power by raising them all again from the dead. To prevent their bodies being carried away during the night (they had been buried near the place of execution), picquets of troops were placed round the spot; but in the morning three of the graves were found empty and the body of the two priests and the priestess had disappeared.[6]

Presumably, if the word had been available to him, St John would have said something about the *zombi* at this point, but his account never uses the term. St John rationally dismisses the story as an act of collusion with the gendarmerie, a further indication of how sunk in superstition Haiti has become. A few pages later, however, St John quotes from an official French report of 1867 about a disturbed grave and the occupant found 'killed' a second time, stabbed through the heart. The report hints at 'a sleeping potion' used to place victims in a drugged state that doctors mistake for death. After the funeral, the bodies are disinterred, killed and their body parts used in rituals. St John picks up the phrase *li gagné chagrin*, local Kreyòl for 'a sort of anaemia of the mind' that is affected by this drug. This is tantalizing, but St John offers no further details.[7]

This was still the case as late as 1913, when a tale can be told about Haiti in Stephen Bonsal's *The American Mediterranean* about the poisoning, burial and snatching from the grave, without having the word *zombi* available. Bonsal, in rampantly racist terms, relates a story personally known to him from his time in the Black Republic of a man declared dead and buried, but found semi-conscious and bound to a tree in the midst of a hastily abandoned Voodoo rite. 'The unfortunate victim of Voodoo barbarity recognised no one, and his days and nights were spent in moaning and groaning and in uttering inarticulate words which no one could understand.' The 'unfortunate wretch' never recovered from his 'mental decay': the authorities colluded by refusing to admit his actual identity, and he was left in this half-life hidden away on a prison farm.[8] Bonsal believes poisoning by the Voodoo cannibal priests who secretly run Haiti is the truth of the case. The outline of a narrative is slowly emerging, although this case is framed as proof of the prevalence of human sacrifice in Haitian Voodoo.

These anecdotes suggest the beginnings of the Haitian *zombi* that crystallized in Seabrook's account 50 years later, but the elements have not yet found their arrangement in the modern form. Instead, both the St John and Bonsal accounts are dominated by the scandal of cannibalism, a trope central to defining Europe's savage Others. This association was of course invented in the Caribbean. On his famous voyage that entirely misread the terrain of the West Indies, Christopher Columbus was told in November 1492 by his Arawak informants of a land of 'people who had one eye in the forehead, and others whom they called "canibals." Of these last, they showed great fear, and when they saw this course was being taken, they were speechless, he says, because these people ate them and because they are very warlike.'[9] This was the first use of the word 'cannibal' in a European language. Columbus later landed on Hispaniola (the first name for Haiti) and had a very brief exchange with a profoundly 'ugly' native that the admiral judged, without any material evidence, 'must be one of the Caribs who eat men'.[10] Peter Hulme's analysis of this invention of the cannibal suggests that Columbus's crew merely slotted the man-eating Caribs into the phantasmatic place of the savage 'Anthropophagi' race that Herodotus imagined to lie somewhere beyond the edge of ancient Greece. Barbarians always devour human flesh.

As the maritime British Empire expanded, cannibalism became a particular obsession in English colonial discourse. 'Cannibalism is for the British something that defines the Savage as such, an atavistic tendency that even middling civilization cannot overcome.'[11] British explorers were obsessed with finding proof of cannibalism, whether among the Maoris in New Zealand and the aborigines in Australia or in the tribes of Hawaii (who were alleged to have eaten the morcellated body of Captain Cook). Later, West Africa, particularly Dahomey, was regarded as teeming with cannibal cults. By the 1890s, the spectacle of Dahomey cannibal tribesmen was one of the biggest draws of the 'human zoos' that were built for world's fairs and expositions around the world.[12] Since Haitians were descended from West African slaves, Vodou was bound up in this feverish set of associations. In each region, an obsessive prosecution by colonial authorities means that, as one legal historian puts it, 'law and cannibalism produce each other', because legitimation for colonial rule comes through the attempt 'to correct the excesses of atavism by applying the restraint of law'.[13] It is therefore no surprise that an English consul would refract savage Haiti almost entirely through the lens of cannibalism. Meanwhile, the American Stephen Bonsal says of Haiti that 'there is no place in the world where you could so easily satisfy a cannibalistic craving as this land' and believes that child sacrifice is at the core of all Vodou ritual.[14] The book, published just a few years before the American occupation, justifies intervention because without 'supervision and control' of the black population, 'the task of civilisation has only been half accomplished.'[15]

The critic Gananath Obeyesekere has argued that the British spent so much time anxiously inquiring at first contact about cannibalism that natives began to reflect back in various ways the act that so clearly terrified their invaders. And if the cannibal can be understood as a paranoid projection outwards onto the Other, that is because acts of cannibalism among shipwrecked and stranded sailors at the very limits of empire were common. The notorious 'raft of the *Medusa*' incident, which took place off the coast of Senegal in 1816, in which the desperate survivors were known to have eaten men as they died, haunted the nineteenth-century imagination, as did the suspected fate of Sir John Franklin's disastrous expedition to find the Northwest Passage in the 1840s (Charles Dickens was particularly enraged by speculation that Franklin's noble crew must have got stuck in the ice and resorted to cannibalism). And in the very year that Spenser St John published his account of savage Haiti's Vodou cannibalistic cult, 1884, three English sailors were prosecuted for the act of eating a fellow survivor following the shipwreck of the *Mignonette*.[16] The outrage about this case was rather more concerned with the fact that a code among British mariners *in extremis* had been brought to court in the first place; this was a formalized act of survival, and although the perpetrators admitted their guilt, they were pardoned shortly after imprisonment. The cannibals, in fact, were us, not them.

Three years after St John's *Hayti*, the journalist and fiction writer Grant Allen published 'The Beckoning Hand', a lurid Gothic short story about an Englishman's fatal obsession with a mixed-race actress, soon revealed after their marriage as a Haitian quadroon whose matrilineal African inheritance pulls her back to Haiti and to Vaudoux, 'the hideous African cannibalistic witchcraft of the relapsing half-heathen Haitian negroes'.[17] This biological taint cannot be superseded: black blood and its savagery will out. This new kind of 'colonial Gothic' used the spurs of imperial travel to reinvigorate a notable revival in supernatural fiction: Allen had been embittered by his failure at an idealistic university experiment to educate the natives in Jamaica and returned to his home in England to write fiction that harped instead on biological determinism and racial degeneracy.

Haiti was evidently part of this Gothic palette. In 1899, the big-game hunter, explorer and novelist Hesketh Hesketh-Prichard was commissioned by the *Daily Express* to travel into the interior of Haiti, a place that he claimed had been a 'sealed land' to whites since the last massacre of planters in 1804. His book of this trip, *Where Black Rules White* (1900), was written, he said sarcastically, 'in the hope of seeing with my own eyes those hidden things which the negroes had accomplished in their hundred years of opportunity.'[18] What it consolidated was only St John's demonic portrait of Haiti and Vaudoux. 'Vaudoux, Juju, Obi, or some analogous superstition seems to belong to the bottom stratum of black nature', Hesketh-Prichard authoritatively explained.[19] He continued: 'Vaudoux is cannibalism in the second stage. In the first instance a savage eats human flesh as an extreme form of triumph over an enemy . . . The next stage follows naturally. The man, wishing to propitiate his god, offers him that which he himself most prizes.'[20] The *papaloi* dominate civil society not with magic but with poisons: 'secret poisoning pervades the scheme of Haytian life.'[21] These poisons – 'which seems at present to lie outside the white man's range' – include one that 'can produce a sleep which is death's twin brother' and is often used to procure the bodies of children from graveyards for ritual sacrifice.[22] Again, Haiti is portrayed as a land 'netted over with fear, fear of vague and occult potencies', but the *zombi* has not quite yet emerged.[23] Hesketh-Prichard concludes his journey by remarking that Haiti provides only evidence that the Negro is quite incapable of self-rule, just four years before the Americans landed in Port-au-Prince and took command of the state machinery.

This paranoid vision of savage Haiti as a den of conniving cannibals was reproduced wholesale during the American occupation. Richard Loederer's *Voodoo Fire in Haiti*, for instance, published in New York in 1935, is breathless about 'secret cults, black magic, and human sacrifices'. These have been woven into the thread of the black republic from the beginning, Loederer claims, explaining that 'from out of these sexual orgies grew the atavistic impulse towards cannibalism.'[24] A native informant has told him the story of the Bizoton Affair, now sensationally retitled 'the "Congo Bean Stew" trial'. This material is clearly just lifted from St John's 50-year-old book. Another invented informant is given the words of William Seabrook, which shows how quickly the older cannibal fantasy started to incorporate zombies in the 1930s where they had been entirely absent before: 'Voodoo is strong; stronger even than death. The Papaloi can raise the dead. He breathes life into corpses who get up and behave like men. These creatures are bound forever to their master's will. They are called "zombies."'[25] From very early on in America's engagement, the depiction of Haiti is largely a palimpsest of recycled textual fantasy.

Another example of this American view was John Houston Craige, a u.s. Marine who was transferred to train the Haitian police force for three years and published *Cannibal Cousins* in 1935. Rebellion and Vodou are as usual tied together in Craige's sketch of the republic, and Vodou is routinely associated with cannibalism from the earliest days of independence. Craige records a general disbelief of these stories among American Marines, but cites the legal case against Papa Cadeus, who had been an important figure in the Cacos Rebellion against the American occupiers, and a Vodou *papaloi* long rumoured to use cannibalistic rituals involving the 'Goat without Horns'. Craige reports (second hand) that human bones had been found buried around the Cadeus *honfort*, and that the priest had been sentenced to death by the court in the early 1920s, a judgement foolishly commuted at a time when the Americans were under scrutiny for their own alleged atrocities. In a later chapter titled 'Doctor Faustus, Cannibal', Craige charts the 'marvellous tale' of a lowly black peasant from Marbeuf who rises to become the chief of police in Port-au-Prince by virtue of his deal with a Vodou priest.[26] It is said, Craige reports, that his rise came at the cost of the sacrifice of one baby a year for over 40 years. This is recirculated gossip: a patina of savagery rubs off, and even if untrue it serves to abject Haitians as credulous fools for believing such a story. It also deflected any critical attention from the organized political and guerrilla opposition to the occupation.[27]

This demonization continued long into the post-occupation era, particularly under the dictatorship of François 'Papa Doc' Duvalier (who came to power in 1957), in part because this brutal regime carefully cultivated fear and obedience among the population by associating Duvalier with Vodou and occult secret societies. Duvalier, who trained in medicine, was closely associated with the scholar of Vodou Lorimer Denis and they co-wrote the study *The Gradual Evolution of Vodou*. In the 1960s, when gruesome news of Duvalier's atrocities began to circulate (helpful material in an era of violent anti-colonial wars against Western powers), the details mixed atrocity, Vodou and supernatural doings in the presidential palace. After a failed rebellion in 1963, Duvalier was alleged to have ordered the leader's 'head to be cut off, packed in ice and brought to the palace in an Air Force plane. News spread around Port au Prince that Papa Doc was having long sessions with the head; that he had induced it to disclose the exiles' plans.'[28] Through stories of sorcery, Duvalier became associated with the Guédé *lwa*, the Vodou spirits who preside over death and the cemetery, and he deliberately dressed to echo the signature style of Baron Samedi in a black hat, dark glasses and funeral suit: a figure to preside over a funeral. In an odd feedback loop, Duvalier survived by exploiting American fantasies of Haitian cannibalism and supernaturalism, reimporting them to terrorize his own population.

Meanwhile, familiar tropes of travel narratives about Haiti continued into the 1960s. Graham Greene had first travelled to Haiti in 1954, and seen his first Vodou rituals as a tourist. Once Duvalier came to power, Greene returned to report on his 'reign of terror'. 'Some strange curse descended on the liberated slaves of Hispaniola', Greene reported. 'The unconscious of this people is filled with nightmares; they live in the world of Heironymus Bosch.'[29] In his novel *The Comedians* (1966), Greene used the Haiti of Papa Doc's regime of murder squads superficially as an exotic objective correlative for his usual wearisome dramatization of Catholic angst among expats. Zombies are mentioned in passing, but simply as part of a black culture paralysed by fear and superstition: they are now reference points for the Haitian exotic.

For the anthropologist Francis Huxley (great-grandson of the Victorian man of science), Haiti in the 1960s was summed up in this way: 'Notorious for its voodoo and its zombis, it can indeed be fascinating and beautiful: but its poverty is disgusting, its politics horrible, its black magic a matter for dismay.'³⁰ An obligatory search for zombies takes him directly to the Psychiatric Centre, where many patients suffer 'voodooistic hallucinations'. Many patients offer him sincere accounts of (un)dead girls returned from the grave: 'Such stories are endemic', Huxley explains. 'The girl is always recognized by her bent neck – because her coffin was too small, and her head had to be jammed down to fit her in – and a scar on her foot, where a candle had overturned and burnt her when she was laid out.'³¹ Huxley considered *zombi* stories 'an epiphenomenon of possession', psychologizing the folklore as a subset of Vodou's practice of ecstatic dancing and the ritualistic loss of self.

The Vodou context might have fallen away to a large extent from the cinema depictions of the zombie since the 1970s, except here and there in the framings of films like the blaxploitation horror Paul Maslansky's *Sugar Hill* (1974) or Lucio Fulci's Louisiana-set *The Beyond* (1981). Yet the trace of this long history of fantasies about savage Haiti survives in the mindless drive of the modern zombie to devour living human flesh. The cannibalistic act remains the index of savage otherness to Western civilization, just as it has since the ancient Greeks, and survivors of the zombie apocalypse can slaughter the undead hordes in such massive numbers because they are modern representatives of the subhuman barbarians at the gates. In the zombie TV series *The Walking Dead*, the worst imaginable menace is less the undead than the other groups of survivors who have resorted to cannibalism, thus severing the last connection to pre-disaster American values.

In the 1980s, cannibalistic fantasies specifically about Haiti returned again, this time with catastrophic humanitarian consequences. In the very early years of the AIDS pandemic, it was a common speculation that the syndrome was invading American shores through African or Caribbean carriers. Signs of the syndrome were particularly rife in the immigrant Haitian population in New York. In 1982, AIDS was considered 'an epidemic Haitian virus' and a year later the association with 'Voodoo practices' was first made.[32] In 1986, the august *Journal of the American Medical Association* published a letter from a doctor voicing the hypothesis that those attending Vodou rituals 'may be unsuspectingly infected with AIDS by ingestion, inhalation or dermal contact with contaminated ritual substances, as well as by sexual activity', citing Wade Davis as the sole authority. The journal titled the contribution 'Night of the Living Dead II'.[33] The drinking of blood invoked four centuries of an association with the eating of flesh, cannibalism and magic. The high incidence of AIDS among Haitians, one reporter declared, was 'a clue from the grave, as though a zombie, leaving a trail of unwinding gauze bandages and rotting flesh' had appeared at the doors of the hospital.[34] There was no recognition that it was sexual tourism between America and the Caribbean that was the most obvious source of infection.

For the historian Laënnec Hurbon, Haiti and its Vodou practices have long been sites of American projection, places where travellers 'find in Vodou their own fantasies'.[35] It is generally agreed that while ritual anthropophagy (the eating of human flesh) can occur in highly ritualized circumstances, the 'cannibal' is an invention of colonial discourse. What testimonies of Vodou rituals involving the eating of flesh are most likely to be are literalizations of highly metaphorical practices. Vodou is, after all, a practice of possession and dispossession, of roles and masks, where one thing stands in for or displaces another and the metaphysical transposition of identities is at the core of events (just as the transubstantiation of the 'body of Christ' is at the heart of Christian ritual). In a discussion of the Kreyòl term *mangé moun* ('eating man'), Erika Bourguignon noted its extremely flexible metaphorical range in Haiti, where greed and envy, domination and control were translated into talk of oral aggression or acts of devouring, and the metaphorical transpositions of animal and human flesh.[36] Deftness in both language and ritual practice outwits leaden visitors, particularly if they filter what is witnessed through a pre-prepared grid of interpretations about 'savages', witch-doctors or cannibals.

This longer historical perspective on Haiti in the Western imagination offers the broader context for now concentrating on the crucial years in which the Caribbean *zombi* translated and transformed into the zombie in American culture.

3
The Pulp Zombie Emerges

The zombie was invented in the vast surge of anonymous discourse that poured out of the printing presses of America's pulp printing houses. The pulps – so-called because of the cheap untreated wood-pulp paper they were printed on, in contrast to the upscale 'slicks' – established a format of short melodramatic fictions breathlessly told with the arrival of Frank Munsey's monthly magazine *The Argosy* in 1894. The golden era of the pulps was the 1930s, when it is estimated that over 30 million Americans were reading nearly 150 titles per year by the outbreak of the Second World War. Differentiation in a crammed market produced many of the commercial genre distinctions we still use to categorize popular fiction. It was in this era that the magazine entrepreneur Hugo Gernsback invented the term 'science fiction' in *Science Wonder Stories* in 1929, for instance. The pulps also twisted traditional Gothic into modern horror fiction in magazine, like *Terror Tales*, *Horror Stories* and *Unknown*. There were also strange fusions between horror, science fiction and mystery, creating odd hybrids such as *Weird Tales*, from 1923, and whole genres like the weird menace stories that thrilled readers in the 'shudder pulps' of the 1930s.

Pulp fiction was an unashamedly commercial mass culture industry, driven by the mechanical production of sensation. It was designed to jolt tired nerves, always pushing at the boundaries of acceptable taste by toying with taboos around sex, race and death. The editorial in the first issue of *Terror Tales* justified itself somewhat disingenuously by arguing: 'today, in a generation protected and coddled by the artificial safeguards of civilization, the average citizen finds scant play for those tonic bodily reflexes which are so largely caused by primitive fear. Thrills, we believe, fill an important, necessary function in any normal, healthy human life.'[1] The exotic zombie was an exemplary creature to shuffle out of this context.

I want to trace how the zombie emerged in the pulps, sampling a few crucial representative writers and tales. These are the stories that, alongside Seabrook's *The Magic Island*, directly underpin the more familiar story of the arrival of the zombie in American cinema just as the category of 'horror film' was emerging in *White Zombie* in 1932.

Pulp fiction seeks to stimulate the reader through extreme physiological reactions: the thrill of excitement, the tears of sentiment,

Original film poster for *Voodoo Devil Drums* (1944).

the prickling of fear, the shudder of revulsion. The ambition to produce unmediated bodily reaction is the reason why it is rarely considered proper art. Gothic fiction was condemned from the start as a dangerous stimulant, generating 'the shocks', as Coleridge said of the scandal about Matthew Lewis's blasphemous romance *The Monk* in 1797, that 'always betrays a low and vulgar taste'.[2] The Gothic began in graveyard elegies, melancholy over mouldering remains, and soon mined a rich seam for its horrific effects by continually transgressing the boundary taboo that separates the living and the dead.

That later American Gothic scoundrel, Edgar Allan Poe, was in no doubt that '*no* event is so terribly well adapted to inspire the supremeness of bodily and of mental distress, as is burial before death.' In relishing the ghastly anecdotes that make up the first part of his short fiction 'The Premature Burial', Poe's narrator argues that 'We know of nothing so agonizing upon Earth.' To come round and find oneself alive yet trapped in the grave evokes 'a degree of appalling and intolerable horror from which the most daring imagination must recoil'.[3] In 'The Facts in the Case of M. Valdemar', Poe would cross the border from the other direction in a tale where a man suspended in a Mesmeric trance at the moment of dying is held there for seven months to then speak from beyond death: '*I say to you that I am dead*', that entirely impossible utterance. He is released from his trance and disintegrates into 'a nearly liquid mass of loathsome and detestable putrescence'.[4]

Throughout the nineteenth century, Gothic fiction continued to toy with this taboo, breaching it in every abject way. There were tales of body snatchers who haunted cemeteries for low-rent anatomists. Varney the Vampire launched a penny dreadful serial of unending undead returns. Victorian newspapers obsessed about every true-life incident of premature burial. Many of these obsessions recurred in the twentieth-century horror pulps. In H. P. Lovecraft's lurid early serial fiction 'Herbert West – Reanimator', a pulp Victor Frankenstein rootles around in graves, morgues and abattoirs for his vivisections, and so sets the tone for the obsession with unruly corpses in *Weird Tales*. A later example was Henry Kuttner's story 'The

Graveyard Rats' (1936), featuring the gruesome yet fully deserved end of a gravedigger who pilfers valuables and body parts from graves; he is eventually trapped in a system of tunnels in the cemetery dug by giant rats only to confront 'the passionless, death's head skull of a long-dead corpse, instinct with hellish life', which eats him alive.[5]

Weird Tales was established by J. C. Henneberger in 1923 out of an admiration for Lovecraft's brand of pulp horror. It nearly collapsed by sailing close to censorship with the necrophiliac tendency of C. M. Eddy's story 'The Loved Dead' a year later, a crisis that brought the influential editor Farnsworth Wright to the journal. Wright fostered the mighty weird trio of Lovecraft, Robert E. Howard and Clark Ashton Smith, although just as famously turned down some of their strongest works: he was a quixotic editor.

The influence of *Weird Tales* on the other horror pulps set up a nexus of concerns that produced the perfect conditions for Seabrook's 'dead men working in the cane fields' to flourish instantly in American popular culture. *Weird Tales* was generically slippery, hovering between supernatural and science fiction, a magazine that early on carried on its cover the promise of stories of 'the bizarre and unusual' or 'startling thrill-tales', but also 'pseudo-scientific tales'. Early editions mixed up pulp horror with reprints of Charles Baudelaire, Théophile Gautier and Percy Bysshe Shelley, as if seeking to invent its own literary tradition of decadence and outrage. Lovecraft himself came to define the weird tale as something beyond the clanking chains of mere Gothic sensation, a striving to convey 'a certain atmosphere of breathless and unexplainable dread of outer, unknown forces' and 'a subtle attitude of awed listening, as if for the beating of black wings or the scratching of outside shapes and entities on the known universe's utmost rim'.[6]

The weird tale therefore often used far-flung, exotic settings and Orientalist colouring. The stories were suffused with paranoia about foreign menace and fears of invasion or subversion. This was the era of the 'Yellow Peril' from China and the 'Red Scare' from the immigrants pouring into America from Eastern Europe, bringing socialism or Bolshevism (or – almost as bad – Catholicism) with them. White Puritan America, from the solid, reliable stock of

A quintessential pulp cover: *Weird Tales* (July 1929).

Northern Europe, faced 'a racial abyss' or the prospect of 'race suicide' as the blood of the nation was diluted by these weaker races, conservatives argued.[7] Lynchings continued in the South as tolerated forms of social policing, and the Ku Klux Klan reinvented itself and peaked as a national mass organization in the 1920s. Meanwhile, groups like the National Association for the Advancement of Colored People pushed harder for equality of civil rights. American colonial ambitions in the Caribbean and Pacific brought a military dimension to these speculations, one which carried an undertow of anxiety about reverse colonization and fantasies of race revenge.

Pulp fiction often reflected back these racial anxieties, seeking populist approval. Sax Rohmer sold millions of his Fu Manchu stories, moving from England to America to be closer to his market. The 'Yellow Peril' – the fear of the Chinese masses – had become a Western obsession by the late nineteenth century, stoked by writers like Rohmer and the Caribbean-born pulp author M. P. Shiel. American pulp science fiction was obsessed with lost races in the last unexplored interiors of Africa or the Amazon, or else imagining futures in explicitly racial terms (Buck Rogers fighting Ming the Merciless, or the race wars on Mars depicted by Edgar Rice Burroughs). In the *Weird Tales* roster, both Lovecraft and Howard were pathological racists, directly linking the Gothic form they embraced to the biological inheritance of the white, Nordic north. These pulp writers wrote hypnotic race fantasies, dripping with the weird menaces threatening to undo the last scions of white manhood in a delirium of miscegenation and monstrosity.[8]

The Caribbean *zombi* knotted together these elements into a single pulp figure. It was a being that hovered between life and death, the natural and the supernatural, and toyed with the gruesome prospect of being buried alive by nefarious native conspirators. It rose up in that indeterminate zone of rumour in the colonial margin, and when the threat was transposed to the imperial centre it offered a shivery instance of infiltration and exotic menace. The Master of the *zombis*, exercising a demonic hypnotic power over the weak-willed, was fused with a long-established melodramatic narrative about foreign mesmerists and their threat to white women, and therefore to the purity of the race. The Haitian *bokor* (or 'witch-doctor'), was but a new version of the threat represented by Count Dracula or Svengali in the 1890s. If the Gothic romance shadows geopolitical shifts, and mocks the discourse of bringing light and enlightenment with its countervailing dark fantasies, then America's occupation of Haiti after 1915 only reinforced the allure of this Caribbean inflection of the supernatural. Its force in the Gothic imagination was redoubled after America's withdrawal in 1934.

There are several anthologies of fiction that can be used to trace the history of the emergence of the pulp zombie, before and after the publication of Seabrook's *The Magic Island*. Otto Penzler's soberly titled compendium *Zombies! Zombies! Zombies!* collects classics from Poe, Lovecraft and Kuttner, and doubtful borderline cases like Sheridan Le Fanu's 'Schalken the Painter' and Thomas Burke's often anthologized 'The Hollow Man', about a murdered man reanimated by African cultists and returning to London to seek out his murderer.[9] The first cluster of recognizable pulp zombie stories is in the late 1920s and early 1930s, from magazines like *Weird Tales* and *Thrilling Mystery*. They follow Seabrook very closely. Seabury Quinn, inexhaustible author of Jules de Grandin detective stories for *Weird Tales*, actually dramatizes the shift in 'The Corpse-Master' (1929), when his Fu Manchu-like Chinese villain, who presides over a harem of transfixed, languorous women, proves to have 'resided long in Haiti, and that there he mingled with the *Culte de Morts*'.[10] De Grandin efficiently educates the reader in the conventions they need to know about this dastardly new enemy: 'In Port-au-Prince and in the backlands of the jungle they will tell you of the *zombie* – who is neither ghost nor yet a living person resurrected, but only the spiritless corpse ravished from its grave, endowed with pseudo-life by black magic and made to serve the whim of the magician who has animated it.'[11]

Ten years later, in Thorp McClusky's 'While Zombies Walked', the narrator sees men with severe head wounds labouring in a cotton plantation 'like soldiers suffering from shell-shock', but comes to a belated understanding (much later than the reader) when 'there flashed across Tony's brain a confusion of mental images that he had acquired through the years – an illustration from a book on jungle rites – a paragraph from a voodoo thriller – scenes from one or two fantastic motion pictures he had witnessed.'[12] By 1939, the zombie is recognized by its embedded references in American popular culture, rather than through obscure colonial folklore.

The early stories in this cluster start by repeating the same folkloric elements about a Voodoo spell that holds the zombie in thrall to its master, but which can be broken if the victim is given salt. This traces back to G. W. Hutter's story 'Salt is Not for Slaves', first published in *Ghost Stories* in 1931, which reads like the transcription of a folklore story from Haiti, which it essentially is. The substance of the story is narrated by an ancient servant, Marie, who tells of a French plantation owner who controlled slaves in the fields with witchcraft up to the eventual triumph of the 1804 revolution. The story never uses the word *zombi* or *zombie*, as if it is not quite yet secure in the language. Marie seems to recall vividly scenes from over a hundred years before, explaining how these abject slaves are deliberately fed salt to awake them in revolutionary times to their (un)dead state. The tale ends with Marie's own horrifying dissolution, for she too has been in this suspended state for over a century: 'That face! The flesh melted away under my terrified gaze. Nothing was left but the grim bones of the dead.'[13] Perhaps because the framing has a certain ethnographic tone of authority, the elements of the story were recycled by others: salt wakes the enslaved undead of a visiting Haitian revue in London in Charles Birkin's 'Ballet Nègre', for instance. G. W. Hutter's influence was far more substantial in another way, though. Presumably because of the authority of 'Salt is Not for Slaves', Hutter, the pseudonym of Garnett Wilson, became the scriptwriter for *White Zombie* the following year, in 1932.

Once the film had further lodged 'zombie' in the language, the pulps rapidly absorbed it. By 1933 it had already crossed the Atlantic. Vivian Meik's short story 'White Zombie' of 1933, published in his collection *Devil's Drums*, is set in the English colonial context of West Africa, centred on a plantation on the edge of the terrain where administrative authority begins to run out and something has gone very wrong after the death of the white owner. Aylett, sent to investigate, realizes that the 'pitiful automatons' who still work the fields labour unto and beyond death at the command of a sinister gangmaster: 'zombies, the natives called them in hushed voices'. The story finishes off the zombified white owner with a crucifix that reduces him to 'greyish powder', suggesting a rapid fusion of Seabrook's Haitian zombie with European vampire conventions.[14]

Some pulp writers did not merely exploit the tropes of the latest horror trend, but relied on more detailed knowledge of Haiti. One of the most celebrated pulp writers of the 1930s was Theodore Roscoe, who wrote serials for *Argosy* and later sensational crime journalism for Hearst's *American Weekly* (he only published two stories in *Weird Tales*, because their hack rates were too low for one of the most successful pulp writers of the day). Roscoe added authentic grit to his exotic pulp fictions by travelling in the late 1920s and '30s to far-flung places, journeying across the Caribbean islands for several years, including Haiti. His travel notes from 1930 mention: 'But five days down from New York lies an island where the law was only recently passed that a man must wear pants in town. Black Haiti.'[15] The stench of Port-au-Prince ruins its picturesque poverty. He hears the drums at night, listens to stevedores steeped in Voodoo belief, and implies that savagery is only just kept at bay by the presence of 500 American Marines. This was the first of several trips to Haiti before Roscoe went further afield to research the French Foreign Legion at war in Morocco and Algeria, and later to explore the Leopard Man cults of West Africa.

In 1931, Roscoe published *The Voodoo Express: A Haiti Novelette*, the cover story in *Argosy*, about the myth of a phantom train that hurtles through the Haitian jungle, said to be full of Spanish gold protected by the undead. It is full of melodramatic clichés, of the jungle as a 'weird' primordial space, of secret Voodoo gatherings that are a 'blood ritual dating from the dawn of time', of a witch-doctor who 'was a high priest of the dreaded Cultes des Mortes; master of Petro and Legba rituals – the weirdest of all Haitian creole voodoo'.[16] The place is also a tumble of superstitions, including the zombie, somewhat confusingly presented:

While our early Pennsylvania Dutch believed in *hex* and the backwoods Gumbo Ya-Ya Cajuns of Louisiana have all kinds of fetishes and charms, the Caribbean creoles have this black-magic witchcraft called *obeah*. Haiti reeks with that sort of business. Ghosts. Haunts. The Haitians have their own special version. You know about *zombies*. The 'undead dead' they call them. Corpses who've been dug up and set to work like mechanical slaves.[17]

The breathless action seethes with anxiety that Haiti 'will bring out what's already in a fellow's blood', pulling the rational visitor down into primitive superstition: 'If it's born in a man he'll revert to type in the tropics.'[18] It is set in 1915, significantly right at the start of the period of American occupation. Although much of the mystery is rationally (if improbably) explained in the end, preserving the American protagonist from this reversion, the zombies that ride the train are left deeply ambiguous, suspended between natural and supernatural explanation.

During a lengthy trip through Haiti in 1934, Roscoe also wrote the serial *A Grave Must Be Deep: A Chilling Mystery of Haitian Black Magic*, composed, he said, on his travel typewriter partly in Cap Haitien, Gonaives, and by candlelight in a cemetery near Léogâne. Roscoe's plot transports a Greenwich Village bohemian to a plantation on Haiti, as she is declared one of the heirs to the recently murdered white planter owner, her Uncle Eli. The shenanigans at his funeral – deep burial in a hardwood coffin beneath a heavy stone, completed by a metal stake through the heart – suggest that knowledge of these superstitions have some purchase. 'He is afraid they would get him for a *zombie*', one Haitian nevertheless helpfully explains.[19] The plot kills off the heirs one by one, maintaining a vaguely spooky air before the book reaches a truly delirious finale. Uncle Eli rises from the grave to announce himself the White King of the Zombies and agitates to revive the Caco insurrection against the fragile grip of the authorities. The chief of police refuses to believe in the zombie, yet anxiously explains: 'the mountain blacks are of the most fanatic. This story spreads like the disease.'[20] The ploy is all unsubtly telegraphed and laboriously explicated in the last

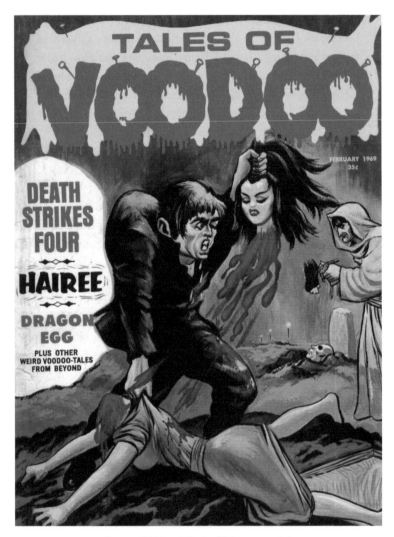

Cover of *Tales of Voodoo* (February 1969).

chapter. This is an exercise in the 'explained supernatural': Uncle Eli's death was staged and the zombie trappings used manipulated the credulous natives, of course.

Roscoe's follow-up serial adventure for *Argosy* was called *Z is for Zombie* (1937), a title that neatly suggests how soon 'zombie' entered the pulp ABC of horror. The story is another detective fiction, starting

68

out in Port-au-Prince before heading into the superstitious hills beyond the town. By the late 1930s, Roscoe is able to toy with the knowledge his readers have of zombies, although the term is still written in italics as if it remains an unassimilated loan word. The plot includes corpses vanishing from graveyards, apparent medical experiments in resuscitating the dead conducted by suspect German scientists in remote hospitals in the jungle, and even the possibility of undead German spies left over from the Great War. Roscoe also indirectly evokes the details of Seabrook's description of dead men in cane fields, as his hero reflects:

> It was no time, either, to recall the story a French consul in Port-au-Prince had once told him about the dead men they'd found working at the Hasco plant . . . Hasco stands for Haitian American Sugar Company, and you can buy Hasco Rum today in any good liquor store in the United States. You wouldn't expect the un-dead in a modern industrial plant under Yankee capital, but the rumour persisted that *zombies* had been seen there.[21]

For a serial adventure that requires constant convulsions in plot development, these instances of reflection – which cost his editor two cents a word – are telling. At another moment, the protagonist Ranier reflects on the ghosts of atrocious history that haunt Haiti and personify its uncanny night as 'a ghost, fuming and blowing, trailing its gauzy veils across field and road, stalking in moist white cerements through the jungle'. This purple patch ends very oddly: 'The ghosts here were American. Ghosts from the days of Benoit Batraville and Guillaume Sam and the Caco insurrections. Shades of Smedley Butler! . . . Ranier almost listened for a faint bugle echo to summon phantom stalwarts of the Corps . . . charging the fog with reckless bayonets.'[22] The spectres conjured are of the beginning of the American occupation and the war conducted by the American Marine Corps against the Caco insurgents from 1915. Smedley Butler had been awarded the Medal of Honor for his assault on a Caco stronghold in November 1915, making him the most decorated soldier in American history. Yet Roscoe, who wrote extensively on American naval history after the decline of the pulps, must have known that by the early 1930s, Butler had become, in his retirement, a prominent peace campaigner and ardent critic of American warmongering and colonial profiteering in its sphere of influence. Although Roscoe's zombies again all turn out to be explicable ruses in *Z is for Zombie*, the hesitation expressed in the plot is not just about the explanatory power of the supernatural, but a register of the ambiguous legacy of American foreign policy.

The most sustained engagement with the Caribbean supernatural in the pulps can be found in the short stories of Henry St Clair Whitehead. Whitehead published consistently in *Weird Tales* throughout the 1920s, but also in other pulp venues like *Black Mask* and *Strange Tales*. He became a friend of H. P. Lovecraft, who long admired his contributions to *Weird Tales*. Lovecraft corresponded with him, assisted him with rewriting rejected stories and eventually visited him for a fortnight in 1931. He came away admiring 'one of the most fascinating personalities I have ever encountered'.[23] When Whitehead died quite suddenly in 1932 before publishing a collection, Lovecraft mourned a writer whose 'best work is among the finest weird writing of the present time'. Whitehead was the exemplary weird writer because he stuck to rigorous rules: 'avoid all extravagance, freakish or capricious motivation, redundancy of marvels, and the like, and to follow absolute realism except for the *single* violation of natural law.'[24] In deference to Lovecraft's high opinion, Arkham House, which was set up in 1939 to publish the fiction of H. P. Lovecraft and his circle, published two Whitehead collections, *Jumbee and Other Uncanny Tales* (1944) and *West India Lights* (1946).

Whitehead could evoke an authority about the world of the Caribbean supernatural because many of these tales were written, rather extraordinarily, while he was the Protestant Episcopal Church's archdeacon of the Virgin Isles, living on the island of St Croix between 1921 and 1929. He had a PhD in philosophy from Harvard and contributed ethnographic commentary on the local dialect to American academic journals. Whitehead was a senior cleric at a time when both Catholic and Protestant churches from North

America were waging war against superstition in their colonial holdings in the South, and he was in St Croix soon after it had been sold to America for $25 million by the Danish government. St Croix had been Spanish, then French, and was held by the Danes from 1733 to 1917. This was a place of extensive migration where English was spoken with a Dutch accent and 'Crucian Creole' had been invented by Moravian missionaries to communicate with their slaves. Whitehead said he was bringing news from what he called 'the newest colonial possession of The United States'.[25]

Whitehead's stories have the studious, diffident air of M. R. James. Their melodrama is often effectively distanced because they are framed as stories of local superstitions collected as exotic ethnography by a scholarly alter ego, Gerald Canevin. This collector of supernatural tales has a clubbable air, listening to stories coaxed out of informants, their tongues loosened by generous rum swizzles. An early story for *Weird Tales* called 'Jumbee', published in 1926, indicates that we are in the matrix of Anglophone Caribbean superstitions. An American Southern gentleman, wintering in St Croix because of lung damage from mustard gas in the Great War, is determined to get an authoritative fix on the meaning of 'jumbee'. Like a latterday Lafcadio Hearn (who is mentioned in the opening paragraphs), Mr Lee interrogates the local populace, but they determinedly displace the belief, all offering the united front 'that the Danes had invented Jumbees, to keep their estate-labourers indoors after nightfall'. Dissatisfied, Mr Lee 'had been reading a book about Martinique and Guadeloupe . . . and he had not read far before he met the word "Zombi". After that, he knew, at least, that the Danes had not "invented" the Jumbee.'[26] This implies that jumbee and zombi are identical forms, although the story that unfolds demonstrates that they are rather different.

Mr Lee finds his native informant, Jaffray Da Silva, a man 'educated in the continental European manner' but who is 'one-eighth African' and who speculates 'that everybody with even a small amount of African blood possesses that streak of belief in magic and the like'.[27] His story of the jumbee starts out as a tale of 'crisis apparitions' – a theory among psychical researchers at the time that ghosts are projections of psychic energy released in moments of crisis, often said to be broadcast during the death throes. Da Silva 'sees' his Danish neighbour, Mr Iversen, but knows it is an apparition and an announcement of the man's death in a house a mile or so away. And so it proves to be. As Da Silva journeys to Iversen's house, he runs across 'the "Hanging Jumbee"' on the road: three black ghosts suspended in the air, like sentinels marking death. This appearance is described in an oddly casual manner, the discussion first framed by noting that the apparition conforms to their appearance in another textual account of the Hanging Jumbee. This is not a melodramatic ghost, but evidential confirmation that jumbees are associated with recent deaths. The way in which the spirits are described inevitably recalls the fate of slaves hanged from branches: 'They are always black, you know. Their feet . . . are always hidden in a kind of mist along the ground whenever one sees them.'[28] Another species of vengeful ghost, this time an old black woman, sits on the steps of Iversen's house, who turns into a *sheen* – a dog (*chien*) or werewolf. Whitehead's tale ends abruptly with the refusal to explain much of what has just happened, never clarifying the causal relationships between Iversen's death and these native spirits. It is enough, for Canevin, to have merely collected the testimony. This is a storytelling device that enhances the sense of immersion in a set of local supernatural beliefs that shapeshift beyond your limited grasp. Just to be even more bewildering, another jumbee tale, 'The Projection of Armand Dubois', is offered as 'a gem, a perfect example', 'typically, utterly West Indian', yet the manifestations here bear no resemblance to those in 'Jumbee'.[29]

In 'Black Terror', Whitehead's narrator Canevin notes that 'here in Santa Cruz the magic of our Blacks is neither so clear-cut nor (as some imagine) quite so deadly as the magickings of the *papalois* and the *hougans* in Haiti's infested hills with their thousands of *vodu* altars.'[30] Whitehead's expert local knowledge thus picks the careful path of the ethnographer through local island variations. 'Black Terror' is one of his most overt stagings of the spiritual battle undertaken in the colonies, of Christian belief against the 'primitive barbarism' and psychological pressure exerted on the population by black *papaloi*. If the Christian priest wins this local battle against sympathetic magic, it is only because of the greater institutional power behind the padre's particular account of the ultramundane world. The same priest recurs in 'The Black Beast', called in to counter a vengeful haunting on a white planter's family home. Father Richardson, Canevin comments, 'had spent a priestly lifetime combating the "stupidness" of the blacks', and Christian exorcism wins out over Damballa, the 'Guinea Snake' God.[31]

The specific supernatural world of Haiti appears in 'The Passing of a God', first published in *Weird Tales* in 1931 (and claimed by Lovecraft to be Whitehead's best work). It is a narrative communicated by Dr Pelletier, lately arrived in St Croix from Haiti. It is significant that it begins with a lengthy discussion about the impact of William Seabrook's *The Magic Island*, the doctor noting 'that there have been a lot of story-writers using his terms lately.'[32] The exchange continues:

'Have you read Seabrook's book, *The Magic Island*, Canevin?' asked Pelletier suddenly.

'Yes,' I answered. 'What about it?'

'Then I suppose from your own experience knocking around the West Indies and your study of it all, a good bit of that stuff of Seabrook's is familiar to you, isn't it? – the *vodu*, and the hill customs, and all the rest of it, especially over in Haiti – you could check up on a writer like Seabrook, couldn't you, more or less?'

'Yes,' said I, 'practically all of it was an old story to me.'[33]

Precisely because of this familiarity, Whitehead eschews the world of Seabrook's zombies to pick up instead on the account of spirit possession by one of the Vodou gods, delivering a bizarre tale of an American businessman whose cancerous tumour is worshipped by the local Haitian population as the earthly incarnation of one of the Vodou gods. The doctor who excises the growth sees two eyes staring back up at him on the operating table, 'something incredibly evil, something vastly old, sophisticated, cold, immune'.[34] Again, a story ostensibly about black credulity is read more compellingly as an account of the literal incorporation of native superstitions by occupying settlers, including those professional agents of colonial enlightenment, doctors and priests.

Another remarkable story of incorporation, 'The Lips', is set in 1833, significantly just after a slave uprising on St Jan had been violently suppressed (although the text does not mention that 1833 was also the year the British parliament passed the Slavery Abolition Act). It concerns a slave-ship captain bitten by a female slave as she is sold. The suppurating wound will not heal and develops into 'blackish-purple, perfectly formed, blubbery lips' which open to reveal 'great shining African teeth' that bite at his fingers and whisper to him relentlessly until the captain kills himself.[35] It is written for the bravura pulp horror of this denouement, but the story also presents an unconscious registration that colonial violence will burrow under the skin of the perpetrator and lead to self-destruction. And isn't this what happens when the *zombi* leaps from local Caribbean traditions to become the American zombie? The transition is an act of cultural incorporation, which makes the zombie less a spectacle of black abjection than a measure of the deathliness that comes with imperial power.

Whitehead published in the pulps, yet the ethnographic authority of his stories derived partly from his refusal of the generic tropes that popular fiction relied upon (Canevin proves equally dismissive of high art, taking aim at the inaccuracies in Ronald Firbank's decadent fantasy compounded of Cuba and Haiti, *Prancing Nigger*, which came out in 1924). There is no standard zombie business in Whitehead's work; he conveys instead a certain complexity of local superstitions across the Caribbean. Whitehead might have had more influence on how this world was portrayed had he not died in 1932, the year in which the Halperin brothers brought the zombie to cinema.

4
The First Movie Cycle:
White Zombie to *Zombies on Broadway*

White Zombie (1932) was scripted by pulp writer Garnett Wilson and took its main inspiration from Seabrook's *The Magic Island*. It was an independent production by the Halperin brothers, experienced Poverty Row filmmakers in the 1920s, who made it in eleven days for $100,000. It was a typical piece of opportunism. In 1931, the son of the Universal Studio head, Carl Laemmle Jr, had produced Tod Browning's *Dracula*, followed nine months later by James Whale's *Frankenstein*. The sensational impact of these films prompted a boom in 'weird' pictures that in the course of 1932 began to be described as horror – the British Board of Film Censorship introduced the classification 'H for Horrific' that year. The Halperins somehow persuaded the star of *Dracula*, Bela Lugosi, to effectively repeat the role of Count Dracula as the mesmerist Murder Legendre in *White Zombie*. He received a pitiful fee, which Lugosi himself later claimed was only $500. The plot also essentially followed the Browning *Dracula*: a young white couple due to be married, the woman imperilled by a foreign desire exercised through super-natural means, her fiancé temporarily unmanned but aided by a Van Helsing type to vanquish the un-Christian foe. The sense of déjà vu was intensified by the recycling of sets in *White Zombie*, which were hired at night from Universal Studio, from scenes leftover from *Dracula, Frankenstein, The Hunchback of Notre Dame* and *The Cat and the Canary*. The film was released in New York to critical ridicule yet much ballyhoo at the Rivoli Theater, where hired zombies shuffled across the awning above the entrance to illustrate 'THE LEGION OF

The first cinematic glimpse of 'dead men walking'.

SOULLESS MEN' (as the posters explained) at the horrifying core of the film, causing mobs to gather on Broadway. Although only modestly successful, the crowds falling away after its first couple of weeks, *White Zombie* made a twenty-fold return on the initial investment. Unusually for an independent production, it had been picked up for distribution by United Artists. So began the shuffling, disreputable B-movie life of the zombie.

In fact, Seabrook's 'dead men working in the cane fields' had already appeared in a short section of *Walter Futter's Curiosities* in 1930, a compendium of exotic documentary footage that claimed to catch visual evidence which confirmed Seabrook's account. This was another crucial context for embedding the heady mix of horror and erotic allure associated with Haiti, Vodou and zombies in early sound cinema. There was a craze for sensational expeditionary films that brought back footage from far-flung savage lands. Martin and Osa Johnson did this entirely legitimately, releasing titles including *Jungle Adventures* (1921) and *Head Hunters of the South Seas* (1922). However, *Africa Speaks!* (dir. Walter Futter, 1930) and the scandalous

The white woman, zombified.

Congo film *Ingagi* (dir. William Campbell, 1930) were soon exposed as frauds, lurid fictions largely composed of stock material and foot-age shot on Hollywood lots and at Los Angeles Zoo. By the time Seabrook's old friend the White King of La Gonave, U.S. Marine Faustin Wirkus, returned from Haiti to tour his documentary film, *Voodo* (1933), it was presumably rather difficult to tell the difference between fact and fiction. Wirkus's *Voodo* happily mixed both in its 36-minute running time, including footage gathered at Voodoo cere - monies on La Gonave, but it ended with an entirely fictional rescue of a young girl from ritual sacrifice, to conform to melodramatic structures.

Ingagi claimed to be about the kidnap of a woman by gorillas, with that spicy blurring of black sexuality with animal bestiality that was soon to be explicitly staged on Skull Island in *King Kong* (1933). *Ingagi* was an exploitation film: early viewers soon spotted that the topless girl in the arms of a gorilla was an aspiring actress in Los Angeles, not an African native, and the actor playing the gorilla, Charlie Genora, was quickly found by the press, as were several of the black kids from Los Angeles who had been drafted in as African pygmies. The film's documentary truth claims prompted the wonderfully named American Society of Mammalologists to issue a formal complaint, declaring their members 'unanimous in deploring its numerous fictitious features'.[1] There is an ironic echo of all this in Josef von Sternberg's *Blonde Venus* (1932), when Marlene Dietrich climbs out of a gorilla suit in front of some nubile Nubians singing 'Hot Voodoo – black as mud / Hot Voodoo – in my blood / That African tempo makes me a slave / I'd follow a caveman right into his cave.'[2] There were many other exotic exploitation films circulating in the early 1930s, from *Blonde Capture* (1932) to *Wild Women of Borneo* (1932), *Jungle Virgins* (1932) and *Gow* (1932), the last of which promised its audience 'SAVAGE ORGIES OF MAN-EATING HUMANS'. The spuriously educational premise of showing naked Balinese young women was entirely about stoking desire, but the darker the skin of the natives and the closer one got to Africa, the more menacing the plots became.[3]

The horror cycle constantly used the promise and threat of inter-racial sex, most notoriously in *The Island of Lost Souls* (1932), an adaptation of H. G. Wells's *The Island of Doctor Moreau*, with Charles Laughton playing the mad scientist vivisecting animals into beast men as a lascivious pervert intent on engineering a sexual liaison between beast and man. This, in addition to the depiction of a successful insurrection on the island against the white master (the beasts led by Bela Lugosi, again), caused the film to be banned for many decades.

The erotic allure of miscegenation was all the more transgressive because of the arrival of the Production Administration Code in 1930. Also known as the Hays Code, this was meant to hold Hollywood cinema to strict moral guidelines, banning the representation of vices, 'impure love' and (explicitly) mixed-race relationships. Amendments had to catch up with the emergence of the horror film, putting vague limits on the representation of 'gruesomeness'. The Code, written by a Jesuit priest and Catholic editor, was constantly invoked by purity campaigners but unenforced by the studios, until the extensive nudity in *Tarzan and His Mate* (1934) caused panic and ushered in a regime of strict enforcement. The zombie film therefore also emerged in this strange 'pre-Code' era, in which the law was marked out precisely by the extent to which it was ignored.

In this early context, then, *White Zombie* is obviously tilted towards the transgressive erotics of the encounter between white and black, living and dead. It also needs to be placed in a wider array of films about Haiti and the Caribbean than zombie film histories usually allow. What followed were heady melodramas where Voodoo and magic (but not necessarily zombies) feature strongly, such as *Black Moon* (1934), *Chloe, Love is Calling You* (1934) or *Drums O' Voodoo* (1934). *Black Moon* was a Columbia Studio feature set on the island of San Christopher – an island declared to be somewhere off Haiti, perhaps meant to be St Kitts – where a recently married white French Creole woman feels compelled to return to her family plantation; away from her modern New York life. There, she is secretly pulled into a sacrificial Voodoo cult as its queen, happily plotting to kill her own child for a culminating magical ritual. The racial ambiguity of the Creole is her death sentence: she is shot by her own stricken husband, who fortunately has the pure white Fay Wray on hand to marry instead (the film has exactly the same plot as Grant Allen's 'The Beckoning Hand'). *Chloe, Love is Calling You* and *Drums O' Voodoo* were both based in Louisiana, and staged the struggle to modernize the belief of local black populations against the last traces of Voodoo.

Ouanga (1936), though, also marketed as *The Love Wanga*, was set in Haiti. It had the strap-line 'Dramatic Dynamite for ADULTS ONLY' and involves the mixed-race star Fredi Washington playing a Haitian plantation owner, Cleli, a light-skinned octoroon who tempts her pure white neighbour Adam across the colour bar, something he steadfastly refuses ('Your white skin doesn't change what's inside you. You're black'). Washington had started out as a dancer in the same revues as Josephine Baker; her light skin seemed to intensify the temptation to transgress in the racial logic of the time. Adam's refusal (he has his pure white Eve as a fiancée, after all) prompts Cleli to revert to native 'wanga' (the generic American term for African-inflected witchcraft in these films) for her revenge. Cleli's love charms fail, so she moves to raising a couple of black zombies to menace her rival, along lines borrowed from Seabrook.

The production of *Ouanga* was somewhat doomed, with an over-optimistic plan to take the whole production crew down to Haiti to recruit authentic dancers and drummers. This was hastily abandoned when local *papaloi* forcefully objected, and the filming moved to Jamaica where a cyclone destroyed sets and killed two of the crew. *Obeah*, an independent production from 1935 and presumably set in Jamaica, featured an explorer and his daughter imprisoned by a cult and scheduled for ritual sacrifice, but the film has not survived.

These films ensured the steady accumulation of depictions of savage witchcraft and sexual abandon that fixed the representation of the notorious Black Republic in early Hollywood cinema. 'Haiti entered the dominant, twentieth century imagination by way of B-horror', one film critic has argued.[4]

White Zombie wears its debts to the European Gothic heavily. Lugosi plays Legendre as a sardonic monster able to dominate the wills of others by natural and supernatural hypnotic powers, exerting his own implacable will at a distance with luminous eyes and a weird 'zombie grip'. He is of indeterminate race and portrayed as a *bokor*, a witch-doctor and master of subtle poisons and mental powers. Legendre is a pitiless victor over his enemies on the island; he has transformed into lifeless zombies his old master of the dark arts, a captain of the gendarmerie, the Minister of the Interior and even the High Executioner with a touch of poison and an imperious command. This feeds the American view that Haiti cannot govern itself, with every element of society corrupted by superstition.

Legendre's desire is all-encompassing too: not only does he long for the white beauty Madeline, but he openly expresses his desire for the white plantation owner Beaumont. 'I have taken a fancy to *you*, monsieur' – Lugosi delivers the line with his typically odd emphasis, perhaps making it sound camper than it was intended to be. *White Zombie* repeats much of the perverse threats in the *Dracula* plot. It borrows the unholy lust and penetrating eyes of the foreign Mesmerist from John Barrymore's depiction of the Mesmeric

The zombie hits the big screen: *White Zombie* (1932).

monster *Svengali* (1931), a film based on George du Maurier's sensational romance *Trilby*, in which a white girl singer is the puppet of a swarthy European Jew. Indeed, *Variety* magazine called *White Zombie* 'the Trilby of the Tropics', suggesting how carefully the Halperins worked to fuse the film with established conventions.

Yet *White Zombie* also goes to some lengths to establish for the audience precisely what a zombie is. The opening titles launch the word across the screen a letter at a time: Z-O-M-B-I-E, over the monotonous chanting of a group of blacks at a graveside. In this opening scene, a beatific white couple, Madeline and Neil, recently arrived in Haiti and on their way to marry, witness a burial at a crossroads and soon after encounter Legendre with his shuffling group of workers behind him, a gang that terrifies the driver and prompts him to shout out: 'Zombies!' The driver is played by eminent African American actor Clarence Muse, a writer, composer and actor who wrote Louis Armstrong's signature song 'Sleepy Time Down South' and later worked with Langston Hughes on the film *Way Down South* (1939). Here, he plays the credulous native, who laboriously explains: 'They are not men, monsieur. They are

81

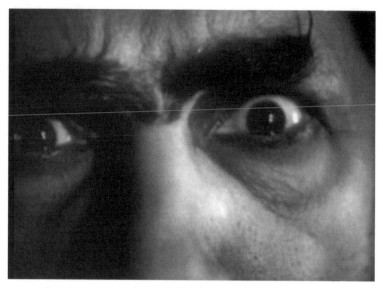

Bela Lugosi as the hypnotic Voodoo master Murder Legendre.

dead bodies. The living dead. Corpses taken from their graves and made to work.'

The iconography of the line of undead workers descending the hill is directly borrowed from the woodcuts that accompanied Seabrook's text in *The Magic Island*. The pressbook for the film, given as an aid to journalists, also directly quoted Seabrook in a contextual section called 'What Writers Found', although it leaves him uncredited.[5] This hillside scene begins to establish the filmic conventions of the zombie: blank eyes, slow pace, stiff limbs and a deathly white pallor (even on black faces). Further direct debts to Seabrook come in Doctor Bruner's lengthy explanation, delivered in a cod-German accent and in a sinuous single take, that zombies must be real to the extent that they are present in Haiti's Penal Code. The clause, number 249, transcribed by Seabrook and spoken by Bruner, was also reproduced in some of the advertising for *White Zombie*, designed to place the film in a zone of uncertainty between the exotic expeditionary documentary and the horror film.

The scenes of the zombies in the mill are highly evocative, as the workers are portrayed in a deathly silence, adopting the slave shuffle of the socially dead. Even the gangmaster looks zombified, indifferent as one of the workers topples into the millstones relentlessly being fed the cane. Legendre's cynical indifference to their fate – 'they work faithfully and are not worried about long hours' – evokes Seabrook's description of the HASCO workers, yet also entirely displaces the context of the new labour laws installed by the American occupation. At the end of the film, Legendre's mountaintop retreat is surely meant to evoke the Citadel built above Cap Haitien by 'King Christophe' at the cost of thousands of lives between 1805 and 1820. Christophe was the 'savage' dictator continuously evoked in the first years of the American occupation, the Citadel called by one history 'the most impressive structure ever conceived by a negro's brain or executed by black hands', although its construction was soaked in blood.[6] The Citadel was the place where, legend has it, the emperor ordered his soldiers to march off the edge of the cliff when they displeased him, in a manner echoed in the final scenes of *White Zombie*, as Legendre's band of walking dead men tumble off the parapets and onto the rocks below. The film is torn about acknowledging the American presence – the hapless groom is an

Zombified factory workers, *White Zombie* (1932).

83

American banker down from New York, after all – but ultimately works hard to displace all the violence and cruelty onto Haiti itself, erasing the American 'modernizing' presence on the island.

In the end, *White Zombie* is significant mainly for dropping the paraphernalia of Voodoo to focus on the body of the zombie itself. The emphasis in Legendre's band of undead slaves is on physiological transformation into empty husks indifferent to pain or bullets – as in the memorable last scene. They are relentless agents of a demonic will, and so are little different from vengeful reanimated mummies (Karloff as *The Mummy* also appeared in 1932) or Count Dracula's abject servant, Renfield. The transformation of Madeline is somewhat different. Hers is a purely hypnotic enslavement that renders her catatonic, like someone suffering from tropical 'sleepy sickness', but easily returned to life (she is a *zombi astral* as opposed to the *zombi cadavre*). Madeline, her name perhaps an echo of Poe's Madeline Usher, was played by silent-era star Madge Bellamy, struggling to keep her place in cinema in the transition to sound. Her voice is thin and reedy, her gestures in the silent pantomimic mode

The Citadel, Haiti, Murder Legendre's fortress in *White Zombie* (1932).

Zombies plummet from the Citadel, *White Zombie* (1932).

already old-fashioned, although the film reverts to silence for much of the running time. Some critics unkindly suggest that Bellamy is so poor 'that the audience is unable to differentiate between her acting living and dead'.[7] Oddly enough, I think this works in the film's favour. Zombification is a kind of fatal return to the dumbshow of the silent era, the victim deprived of language and reduced to fumbling, exaggerated gesture. The technology of cinema itself, in the transition to sound between 1929 and 1932, contributes another level to *White Zombie*'s commentary on modernity and the supersession of the old.

On announcing their plans to shoot *White Zombie*, the Halperins were unsuccessfully sued by the playwright Kenneth Webb, whose play *Zombie* appeared on Broadway for only 21 performances in February 1932. No transcript of the play survives, but it was presumably also reliant on Seabrook's *The Magic Island*. When the Halperins decided to return to the zombie theme for *Revolt of the Zombies* in 1936, they avoided Haiti to set the story in Indochina, playing on the legends associated with the tyrant who built the

Angkor Wat temple with an army of slaves in the twelfth century. Still, they were sued again, this time over the copyright of the term 'zombie'. *White Zombie* was reissued in 1936, and one of the original investors, Amusement Securities Corporation, claimed proprietary rights on the word to protect their first film. In a written ruling, one of the judges stated:

> It seems that the term 'zombie', though the term be considered descriptive, is subject to exclusive appropriation as a trade name. A word which is not in common use, and is unintelligible and nondescriptive to the general public, though it may be known to linguists and scientists, may be properly regarded as arbitrary and fanciful and capable of being used as a trade mark or trade name.[8]

In their appeal, the Halperins tried to show that the word 'zombie' was in prior use before *White Zombie* and had entered *Webster's Dictionary* in 1935. Nevertheless, they were forced to pay damages and legal costs, resulting in the odd situation that Amusement Securities Corporation appeared to own the word 'zombie' in the 1930s.

The judge was presumably not a reader of pulp magazines or a drinker of zombie cocktails, and although the Halperins were asked to pay damages, the ruling was otherwise unenforced. Zombies were in fact already being folded back into Haitian melodramas, becoming the central horrifying detail where they had been almost absent only a decade before. In Hans Possendorf's *Damballa Calls: A Love Story of Haiti* (published in English in 1936), for instance, someone tries to dismiss the zombie as 'a fairy-tale created by some crazy newspaper man', only to be corrected: 'On the contrary, they are the most terrible fact in all the world.' Yet, just to keep the perspective realistic, this authority adds: 'This devilish art is, thank God, practised only on very rare occasions. So far as I am aware, no white man has ever yet had to endure this terrible fate.'[9]

The Halperins almost killed off the zombie with the poor melodrama of *The Revolt of the Zombies*, in which the 'Secret of the

Zombies' is held by Cambodian priests at Angkor Wat. A battalion of undead soldiers is seen advancing on a European front, indifferent to bullets, followed by a hasty gathering of Europe's generals determined to destroy this new weapon, which surely threatens the survival of the White Race if the dastardly Orientals rediscover it. In Cambodia, the secret is put to use not in the service of such a grand plan, but rather to further a dreary love triangle. Those superimposed hypnotic eyes that create a zombie army, the only memorable sections from the film, are recycled directly from *White Zombie.*

Lugosi himself, meanwhile, was condemned to repeat the witch-doctor role to the end of his career. He kidnapped American women off back roads and turned them into a bevy of *zombis astrals* in the rudimentary B-movie *Voodoo Man* (1944). Lugosi wears a cape embroidered with magical symbols, typical of a magus of ritual magic, and Haiti has dropped entirely from the context. The film is far keener to evoke the fantasies of sexual abandon that swirled around the world of ritual magic, which was being practised in Southern California at that time by the bizarre circle of science fiction writers, rocket scientists and occultists gathered around Jack Parsons.[10] In *Voodoo Man*, the kidnapped women are dressed in the white robes of initiates and shuffle around the basement with absolute compliance while Lugosi experiments with transferring their minds into the body of his undead wife, who has been in a zombified trance state for twenty years. Rescue comes in the midst of a culminating magical ceremony. Lugosi appears again as a voodoo man in *Zombies on Broadway* (1945), although by this time he is merely a cameo to mark out a certain frame of supernatural reference. 'Those voodoo drums – that's the death beat you know', he reflects, but he remains almost entirely marginal to the comic plot. Lugosi's last role, notoriously, was in Ed Wood Jr's *Plan 9 from Outer Space* (1959), often given the plaudit of being the worst film ever made. The plot involved aliens reviving the human dead as their agents on Earth. Almost as soon as filming began, Lugosi died, only to live on in the film, replaced by a hopeless stand-in. Even in death, he was held by the zombie grip.

After the failure of *Revolt of the Zombies*, the figure was doomed for a rapid revival for comic effect, as in the Bob Hope and Paulette Goddard vehicle *The Ghost Breakers* of 1940. In the film, Goddard inherits a Gothic pile that looms on 'Black Island' off the coast of Cuba and is said to be haunted down the generations by the slaves who once laboured there. Bob Hope tags along as a self-declared 'ghost-breaker' (a less catchy job title than ghostbuster) with his comic black sidekick. They are warned off by the threat of various malignant ghosts and zombies. These still require some explanation: 'It's worse than horrible because a zombie has no will of his own', explains a local expert. 'You see them sometimes, walking around blindly with blank eyes, not knowing what they do.' 'You mean like Democrats?' Hope asks. In fact, Hope's character knows the pulp origins of the zombie. When he arrives at the spooky mansion, his opening gambit with the old woman caretaker is to ask: 'Could we interest you in a subscription to *Weird Stories* magazine?' The zombie that features in *Ghost Breakers* is actually a figure of pity rather than fear, which prefers its ghosts old-school Gothic and Spanish. Once again, it is Hollywood history rather than the film itself that provides the telling detail. The zombie is played by Noble Johnson, one of the first African American film producers and actors, who ran his own film company in the 1910s. He acted consistently through the 1920s, playing a range of exotics, but was also able to pass as white. Johnson led the tribesmen of Skull Island in *King Kong*. In *Ghost Breakers* he is reduced to a mute shambler, barely featuring in a plot that superimposes the European Gothic onto a Caribbean context.

Ghost Breakers produced a cluster that further embedded the zombie as one element in American supernatural conventions. *King of the Zombies* (1941) was a Monogram Pictures vehicle for the successful black vaudeville comic Mantan Moreland to play up his stereotype of the mouthy manservant spooked in a haunted house. 'What's a zombie?' someone asks. 'Dead folks what's too lazy to lay down', he replies. When he is zombified by the disdainful lead Nazi, he continues his quicksilver backchat. 'Zombies can't talk!' the kitchen maid objects. 'I can't help it if I is loquacious',

A pitiful zombie in *The Ghost Breakers* (1940).

Moreland snaps back. In a dim echo of the old folklore, as soon as Moreland eats salt he recovers his senses, such as they are. Set on an indeterminate West Indian island and involving a dastardly German plot to use hypnotism and Voodoo to torture war secrets out of a kidnapped American admiral, the plot continually digs at German racism while fully demonstrating Hollywood's own rigid racial logics.

Mantan Moreland was back again in another Monogram film, *Revenge of the Zombies* (1943), an anti-German B-movie in which a mad scientist played by John Carradine thinks he has succeeded in creating 'an army of the living dead' amid the swamps of Louisiana to ensure German mastery (quite what he's doing there is left unclear). He has achieved this by indifferently experimenting on his wife Lila, all in the service of the greater glory of the Fatherland. Moreland plays another black servant who keeps running into zombies long before his white boss grasps the true story. In the end, Carradine's evil Nazi cannot control the will of his zombies and he sinks beneath the swamps in the clutches of his vengeful undead

Darby Jones as Carrefour, *I Walked with a Zombie* (1943).

wife. These films underline the link of Nazi Germany and zombies, established early in the pulps by Theodore Roscoe, which continues up to the present day in films like *Dead Snow* (2009). The roots of this connection lie partly in American finance capital's attempt to keep German interests out of Haiti just prior to the occupation and the start of the Great War.

Nothing in these comic films quite prepares the way for the extraordinary lyrical masterpiece of Jacques Tourneur's *I Walked with a Zombie* (1943). The film was a product of Tourneur's collaboration with Val Lewton, who had just shot *Cat People* (1942) as the first production in RKO's justly admired 'horror' film unit, B-movies given strict $150,000 budgets and usually developed, shot and delivered in a three-month cycle. The indirection and oneiric oddity of *Cat People* had been disliked by the studio, for Lewton was a suspiciously high-cultural type, but it proved immensely popular. Lewton told an interviewer early on that his team had 'tossed away the horror formula right from the beginning. No grisly stuff for us. No mask-like faces hardly human, with gnashing teeth and hair standing on end. No creaking physical manifestations. No horror piled on horror.'[11] This seemed to refuse every element of the physical horror that had been established for the zombie film.

Just as *White Zombie* had relied on Seabrook, the scriptwriters for *I Walked with a Zombie* were given a piece of sensational journalism written by Inez Wallace in *American Weekly* which had been optioned by the studio: 'I have come to look upon the weird legend of the zombie – those dead men and women taken from their graves and made to work by humans – as more than a legend.'[12] The story that Wallace relates, about a recently married white woman zombified (with secret poisons) by a spurned Haitian rival, advances Seabrook's sensational account considerably, although this report is clearly filtered through a decade of American shudder pulp fictions. Lewton was compelled to work with this optioned essay and was forced to use the lurid title by the boss of RKO, Charles Koerner. He initially despaired before coming up with the idea of using the suggestive West Indian backstory from *Jane Eyre* to transform the material. Lewton then added a detailed file of research cuttings he had mined on Haiti and Vodou ceremonies to the writing process, such as Rex Hardy's photographs in *Life Magazine* published in 1937, the year of the Massacre River genocide.[13] From this material, the scriptwriters Ardel Wray and Curt Siodmak, along with Tourneur, transformed their pulp sources into something wholly different.

I Walked with a Zombie rewrites *Jane Eyre* (as Jean Rhys would do in *Wide Sargasso Sea*), in this case sending a naive nurse to the Caribbean island of San Sebastian to look after Jessica, the catatonic wife of the plantation owner. Precisely what occurs on the island is elliptical and odd, the narrative never coherently settling for natural or supernatural explanation. Is Jessica suffering from the after-effects of a fever, mental illness, the guilt of betraying one brother for another, or something stranger? If she is a zombie, then who is her master? Is Jessica actually the zombie of the title, or not? The film radically fractures any settled point of view and the narrative is studded with sequences intent only on evoking haunting atmospheres, the sinuous camerawork providing a confounding chiaroscuro. The first encounter with the entranced Jessica is when she glides away from her room, out from under a reproduction of Arnold Böcklin's *Isle of the Dead* that hangs over her bed. She stalks through the shadows of the plantation, evoking uncanny dread, as does the long night-walk of Betsy and Jessica to the *honfort*, traversing a sequence of liminal spaces in a series of lateral moves and dissolves conducted in virtual silence to the hypnotic rhythm of the drums.

Voodoo superstition on the island is demystified by the Western rationalism of Mrs Rand, the doctor who is the hidden hand behind the native witch-doctoring, which she manipulates for ostensibly benign medical effects. Her authority is undercut by her unresolved Oedipal jealousy of her son's wife, however. The destructive mesh of desire at the heart of the Holland family plantation is subject to the ironic commentary of the calypso singer Sir Lancelot, who acts as the black chorus to a colonial family tragedy. Lancelot is half in and half out of the fictional frame of the film, being a famous Trinidadian calypso star in the States, well known for his radical left politics (Sir Lancelot also helped Lewton source the Haitian musicians who play the ritual drums on the soundtrack). The film ends with an unattributed black voiceover, almost the communal voice of

Zombie shadows, *I Walked with a Zombie* (1943).

the blacks on the island, the former slaves, which entirely displaces nurse Betsy's initial framing of the story. It is hard to think of another Hollywood film of the era that cedes narrative authority in this way, and the film's formal oddity acts perfectly to convey how narrative authority slips from white command. The audience is left bewildered by the film's puzzling dream logic: *I Walked with a Zombie* has been called a 'sustained exercise in uncompromising ambiguity'.[14]

Tourneur later claimed that the film's sympathetic portrayal of the former black slaves on San Sebastian got him placed on an unofficial Hollywood 'grey list' that blocked his career. The Office of War Information, the wartime censor, certainly took an interest in seeing the film, worrying that the depiction of the racial divide on the plantation undercut their request for images of integration – however fictive.[15] RKO certainly made it difficult for Lewton and Tourneur to collaborate again.

The most memorable figure in the film is Carrefour, the towering and silent black man with blank eyes who stands as sentinel and stalks the margins of the film (his name means 'crossroads', and is a deeply symbolic locale for the meeting of worlds in Vodou theology). It is this figure we see in the opening shots of the film, with Betsy, on the edge of the water, the liminal space where sea meets sand. His ambiguity – is he living or dead, agent of civilization or savagery, protection or threat, a zombie or not? – contributes again to the persistence of *I Walked with a Zombie* in the memory, a film that lingers like the after-image of a fever dream.

Almost as if to pull the zombie down from these heights of weird menace, *Zombies on Broadway* brings the figure crashing back to the B-movie gutter. This crass comedy from the same studio returns to San Sebastian and features Sir Lancelot's calypsos and Darby Jones reprising the role of Carrefour, but this time played for laughs. The plot features a gangster Ace Miller opening a nightclub, The Zombie Hut, in New York, and for the hullaballoo of the opening night Ace sends two saps down south to the islands to grab a 'real' zombie. This is the excuse for the vaudeville double act of Alan Carney and Wally Brown (RKO's low-rent Abbott and Costello) to indulge in some comic turns. Zombification is openly about *becoming black*, about minstrelsy, as Carney is inadvertently blacked up in the jungle ('You're so scared, you've turned black!') and then subject to one of Lugosi's injections, which thickens his lips, bulges his eyes and renders him a passive mute. Becoming black is, fortunately, an entirely reversible condition – for Carney at least. Abbott and Costello killed off every Universal horror monster in their dire horror comedies starting in the late 1940s, but Carney and Brown had already terminated the place of the zombie in the RKO cycle by 1945.

Zombies on Broadway signals the complete passage from *zombi* to zombie in American popular culture. The nightclub in the film, 'The Zombie Hut', suggests the craze for tiki bars in the 1930s, selling cocktails in exotic, vaguely South Pacific settings. Don Beach, who started the revolution with his Beachcomber Café in Hollywood in 1934, was also the inventor of the Zombie cocktail, a fruit punch so heavily laced with various Caribbean rums that it 'zombified' the drinker. Just like the composition of the *bokor* poisons in Haiti, the recipe for the first Beachcomber Zombie was kept strictly secret. The chain of bars became known as 'The Home of the Zombie: The World's Most Potent Potion'. The drink became world-famous when nightclub impresario Monte Proser opened a tiki bar that sold the Zombie at the New York World's Fair in 1939. Famously, the Beachcomber restricted customers to a maximum of two Zombies per night (although on at least one occasion Val Lewton claimed to have drunk three or four in a desperate attempt to find inspiration to appease his Hollywood bosses). In the com - edian Billy Connolly's famous routine 40 years later, the Zombie results in the drinker getting drunk from the legs up before the effect seizes and entirely disables the brain.

The Zombie cocktail retains a direct tie back to its Caribbean origins: rum, from the word *rumbullion*, meaning 'great tumult' among the West Country settlers in Barbados, emerged on the sugar plantations of the Caribbean because it was distilled by slaves from the 'spillings' of sugar-cane processing for which the planters initially had no use. Known also as 'Kill Devil', these improvisations of consolation for the intolerable conditions of slavery have since

Carioca Rum marketed the first bottled Zombie drink in the 1940s.

become a multibillion dollar industry owned by large multinational corporations.[16]

'Do do / that Voodoo / that you do / so well', the Cole Porter song went – first composed in 1929 before becoming a standard. Within ten years, the zombie shuffled out of whispered folkloric beliefs on the colonial margin of the American empire and into the sensational newspapers, pulp magazines, songs, nightclubs, lurid B-movies and radio serials like *The Shadow* that were at the brash heart of the American popular culture industry. But if the zombie seems to have been thoroughly decoupled from its Caribbean *zombi* by this point, at the same time a different cultural stream was pulling it back firmly to the Caribbean.

The 1920s and '30s was the peak of Modernist experiment, and among the writers of the Harlem Renaissance – the flowering of black writers in New York – Haiti and its culture were key reference points. To get a full picture of the zombie in 1930s American culture, we need to recognize how crucial Haiti was in avant-garde circles too. It was Theodor Adorno, the most trenchant critic of the arrival of mass culture in the early twentieth century, who recognised that this kind of lowly pulp fiction had to be seen in relation to high art: they are but 'torn halves' of each other.[17] In the 1930s, these came together in the writing of Zora Neale Hurston. During her nine-month stay on Haiti over the winter of 1936, the novelist and anthropologist met, photographed and recorded the first encounter with an actual, real-life zombie.

5
Felicia Felix-Mentor: The 'Real' Zombie

Zora Neale Hurston was one of the writers associated with New York's Harlem Renaissance in the 1920s and '30s, that fantastic flowering of black cultural forms in music, theatre, dance, art and writing that intersected with but was entirely distinct from Modernist 'negrophilia'. The political motivations of black activism at the time made Haiti, with its proud tradition of independence currently under the heel of the American occupation, a key point of reference. There was a distinct Black Atlantic element to the politics of various Negritude movements, with Marcus Garvey moving between New York, London and Jamaica, for instance. The poet Langston Hughes, at a point of crisis in his work, travelled to Haiti and reported for the *New Masses* journal in 1931, writing that 'All of the work that keeps Haiti alive, pays for the American occupation, and enriches foreign traders – that vast and basic work – is done there by Negroes without shoes.'[1] Hughes grasped the economic logic of HASCO far faster than Seabrook. Communist activist and actor Paul Robeson starred in Eugene O'Neill's play *Emperor Jones,* inspired by Haitian history, on stage and in the film version in 1933. Three years later, a twenty-year-old Orson Welles directed an all-black version of *Macbeth,* set in Haiti, at the Lafayette Theater in Harlem, and a play called *Haiti* was staged at the Lafayette in 1938 before going on national tour to black theatres.[2]

Zora Neale Hurston moved in the same circles and shared the same patrons as writers like Langston Hughes. She had grown up the daughter of a Baptist preacher in Eatonville in Florida, one of

Zora Neale Hurston palying a Haitian Vodou *maman* drum, 1937.

the first all-black incorporated towns in America, an unusually free environment in the South. But Hurston was different from other Harlem Renaissance writers in two important respects. First, she was a political conservative, regarding the American occupation of Haiti as an unequivocal good. Second, she had professionally trained in anthropology at Columbia University under Franz Boas and had done fieldwork collecting folklore on 'Hoodoo' in Louisiana in the late 1920s before gaining a two-year Guggenheim grant to study Voodoo in Haiti in 1936. This made for a completely different level of engagement.

Boas, Hurston's teacher, was a crucial figure in shifting anthropology from armchair theory to practice in the field, and from the Victorian evolutionary model, which regarded tribal societies as survivals of earlier man, to a much more liberal and relativist model of cultural comparativism. His injunction in his famous lectures *The Mind of Primitive Man* was that 'the student must endeavour to divest himself entirely of his opinions and emotions based on the peculiar social environment into which he is born. He must adapt his own mind, so far as feasible, to that of the people whom he is studying.'[3] This was a crucial shift away from abstract hierarchies of races to valuing the complexity and contingency of the field. Participant observation came with attendant risks, though: there was still a view that fieldwork was not a 'gentlemanly activity', not least because immersion in another culture revived the old fear of losing perspective and 'going native'.[4]

Was this what happened to Zora Neale Hurston? She had far greater authority to speak of Haitian beliefs than any mere tourist, sensational journalist or pulp fiction writer, yet her findings were thoroughly ridiculed.

Hurston was a valuable researcher to Boas because as a black woman she could enter into certain fields in a way others could not. Her extensive transcriptions of rituals, spells and ceremonies published in the *Journal of American Folklore* in 1931 under the title 'Hoodoo in America', came from her extensive training with several Hoodoo priests in New Orleans and elsewhere. The tone of her report begins with an authoritative discussion of the religious syncretism that typifies Louisiana Hoodoo, which she describes as a meeting of the Haitian diaspora with Roman Catholicism, plus the unique local twist of Spiritualism. Much of the report is neutral transcription of magical spells, hexes and curses. The narrative voice slips on occasion, however, into a first-person participant who isn't able to exercise a full level of control. Under the tutelage of Samuel Thompson, a 'Catholic Hoodoo doctor' who claimed to be the grand-nephew of Marie Laveau (the 'Last of the Voodoos' celebrated by Lafcadio Hearn), she endured several ceremonial initiations. 'I was full of anxiety', a personal voice breaks through, disturbing the illusion of objectivity. 'After a while I forgot my fears, forgot myself, and things began to happen. Things for which I can find no words, since I had experienced nothing before that would furnish a simile.'[5] The Voodoo gods come down and Hurston states: 'I had five psychic experiences during those days and nights' before the academic voice of reason immediately clamps down: 'I shall not detail them here.'[6] She was also sent by another Hoodoo doctor to a crossroads to call up the Devil. 'It was very dark and eerie', she confesses, and the objective observer becomes a trembling subject again: 'I was genu-inely frightened.' The passage concludes ambiguously: 'It was a very long hour. I hope never to meet its brother.'[7]

Under the instruction of Ruth Mason, another Catholic Hoodoo healer, Hurston took part in a Hoodoo dance that lasted for many hours and was meant to invoke 'death-to-the-enemy', as in these rituals 'death was being continuously besought'. In one short sen-tence – 'I danced, I don't know how' – Hurston again suggests that through her participation she has lost her anthropological distance, her subjectivity erased. The phrase implies that she has, in fact, become ridden by one of the gods, as was the sole aim of ecstatic dancing.[8] Three years later, the New York avant-garde dancer Katherine Dunham, also professionally trained in anthropology, travelled to Haiti and explored the same kind of ecstasy; she in turn would inspire the avant-garde filmmaker Maya Deren to undertake research in Haiti.[9]

Under the heading 'Relation to the Dead', Hurston reported how, through the Southern states and into islands like the Bahamas, 'the dead have a great power which is used chiefly to harm.' The graveyard became the site for 'killing ceremonies', with spells involving grave dust, and she adds:

> It is generally held in the Bahamas that strong obeah men can cause a death-like sleep to fall upon whom they will. The person is buried for dead and then the obeah sends his helpers to dig him up and he, or she, is put to work . . . If he is given salt he regains his mental powers and revolts.[10]

In the Bahamas, these (un)dead workers are said to be sent away to pick coffee on plantations. Collected in 1928, and published in 1931, it is striking that Hurston does not use the word *zombi* here, as if it had not been heard in that particular field of inquiry, or else that she simply considered the word too local or unimportant. By the time she published *Tell My Horse* in 1938, however, about her researches in Haiti, there is a whole chapter called 'Zombies' and a lot of rather sensational material.

Tell My Horse is considered a great embarrassment of a book, even by Hurston's admirers. It was a confusing mix of modes, the *Saturday Review* complained: 'the remembrances are vivid, the travelogue tedious, the sensationalism reminiscent of Seabrook, and the anthropology a mélange of misinterpretation and exceedingly good folklore.'[11] She was mocked in the press that 'after eleven months in the dark jungles back of Port-au-Prince, chanting voodoo chants, drinking the blood of the sacrificial goat and worshipping with descendants of the African slaves whose people were bred in the Congo, Miss Hurston returns a believer in voodooism.'[12] Perhaps this reflected the tug of different audiences and patrons. It was published as a trade book by Lippincott's, so the anthropology had to entertain, while Hurston remained indebted to her 'negrophile' backers Charlotte Osgood Mason and the writer Carl Van Vechten (who had written *Nigger Heaven*) to write a thrilling account of energizing 'savagery'. The title translates a Haitian saying that suggests that when possessed, 'the loa begins to dictate through the lips of his mount.'[13] More than one critic has suggested that this is

Original cover
of Nora Zeale
Hurston's *Tell
My Horse*
(1938).

what happens in the strange mix of tones and genres; the book is
possessed by many gods.[14]

Hurston had travelled to Haiti intending a lengthy and immersive research trip. While she established contacts among Vodou
practitioners, she spent the first seven weeks in Haiti writing her best-
known novel, *Their Eyes were Watching God*. Then, as in Louisiana,
she began her training in a local *honfort*, learning to navigate the
complex rituals and cosmogony of the Vodou gods. In June 1937,
only nine months after arriving, Hurston hastily left the island with
a serious gastric illness, something she ascribed to poisoning by
those unhappy with an American outsider dabbling in sacred secrets.

Tell My Horse follows this darkening trajectory, with sections on Jamaica and Haiti that mix the authority of systematic anthropological reportage with the lazy opinion of the travelogue by an American in support of colonial occupation. 'The Haitian people are gentle and loveable except for their enormous unconscious cruelty' is a typical ridiculous sentence.[15] Part III, 'Voodoo in Haiti', works harder than most travelogues to explore and explain the panoply of Vodou gods, although it is an inevitably local and partial snapshot of a constantly moving hierarchy of deities. Then, as the element of closer participation becomes more prominent, Hurston records that at a renowned *honfort* in a place called Arcahaie she saw the body of dead man suddenly sit up in the middle of the funeral, 'and it was so unexpected that I could not discover how it was done'.[16] The local explanation is that one of the *loa*, the gods, has taken possession of the body. Later in the same ceremony, 'the thing of horror happened': Hurston seems to share entirely the feeling of the gathered congregation that an 'unspeakable evil' entered when a man was possessed by a demonic spirit, his face lost beneath 'a horrible mask'.[17] The panoply of Petro gods, a particular branch of Voodoo, Hurston continues, 'demand sacrifices' and 'in some instances' worshippers 'have been known to take dead bodies from the tombs'.[18] This brings the reader to unlucky chapter Thirteen, 'Zombies'.

'What is the truth and nothing else but the truth about zombies?' Hurston begins, as if on oath but not quite willing to get the wording exactly right. She addresses the different levels of belief in Haitian society (peasant conviction versus elite denial), before disarmingly stating her own position:

> I had the good fortune to learn of several celebrated cases in the past and then in addition, I had the rare opportunity to see and touch an authentic case. I listened to the broken noises in its throat, and then, I did what no one else has ever done, I photographed it. If I had not experienced all of this in the strong sunlight of a hospital yard, I might have come away from Haiti interested but doubtful. But I saw this case of Felicia Felix-Mentor which was vouched for by the highest authority. So

I know that there are Zombies in Haiti. People have been called back from the dead.[19]

Hurston lures the reader in with the promise of a direct encounter with what is evocatively called 'the broken remnant, relic, or refuse of Felicia Felix-Mentor', but then veers into a discussion that mixes folklore about the zombie with allegedly 'proven' historical cases, such as the case of 'C. R.' in Cap Haitien in 1898, or the apparently famous case of 'Marie M.' in 1909. These read like the cases collected by the Society for Psychical Research, with the same drawback. A well-attested anecdote remains just that: an anecdote. It proves only that such stories have the fascination to circulate widely, not that they must have a basis in truth. But in November 1936, the Director General of Haiti's Service d'Hygiene invited Hurston to visit an actual zombie now residing on a mental hospital ward.

What Hurston describes is immensely moving and distressing, a woman in a hospital yard who 'hovered against the fence in a sort of defensive position ... and showed every sign of fear and expectation of abuse and violence ... The doctor uncovered her head for a moment but she promptly clapped her arms and hands over it to shut out the things she dreaded.'[20] Hurston's act of photographing this 'remnant' of a person is perhaps the closest one can get to believing the idea that the camera can, after all, steal the soul, or in this case, whatever is left of the soul:

> I took her first in the position that she assumed herself whenever left alone. That is cringing against the wall with the cloth hiding her face and head. Then in other positions. Finally the doctor forcibly uncovered her face. And the sight was dreadful. That blank face with the dead eyes as if they had been burned with acid. It was pronounced enough to come out in the picture. There was nothing that you could say to her or get from her except by looking at her, and the sight of this wreckage was too much to endure for long.[21]

The real zombie:
Felicia Felix-Mentor
in Zora Neale
Hurston's *Tell My
Horse* (1938).

Told to Hurston by her doctors, Felicia's story – if this is who this woman was – was that she had come from a small village, married young and died in 1907. In 1936, a naked and distressed woman was found stumbling along the road towards the farm where she claimed her father had lived. Her brother appeared to recognize his long-dead sister, and Felicia's former husband, under duress, was compelled to make the same identification. The village believed – as was standard – that Felicia's master must have finally died, thus freeing her from bondage to wonder back as an utter ruin of a person to the only life she had known, just as zombies who eat salt usually return to their graves. As was also standard, the village refused to accept her back into the community and she was cast out, eventually ending up in a mental hospital.

For Hurston, the zombie Felicia Felix-Mentor is a brute fact, demonstrating the power of Voodoo. Felicia's condition is created, she is convinced, by the use of poisons concocted to a secret recipe handed down in a clear lineage of descent from African witch-doctors. In the following chapter she gets on the trail of the 'Sect Rouge', a secret society that causes great fear and evasive tactics among her native informants. Fully invested in conspiratorial logic, Hurston suggests that behind even this sect is another very secretive Petro-worshipping group, the 'Cochon Gris', which, she is told, is 'banded together to eat human flesh'.[22] The further the modern anthropologist explores, the closer she seems to get to the myths of cannibals long circulated in Western texts about Haiti.

This presumably explains her odd attack at the end of the book on the common source of information on these occult matters in Haiti, 'Dr' Reser. Reser was a white American who was in charge of the insane asylum at Port Beudet (never mind that he had never been a doctor, only a pharmacist's assistant in the u.s. Navy). Reser was a celebrity because he also happened to practise as a Voodoo priest. 'Everyone who goes to Haiti to find out something makes a bee line for Dr Reser', Hurston says, but separates herself from these 'lazy mind-pickers': 'I consider myself amply equipped to go out in the field and get it myself.'[23] In the end, she was asserting the anthropological authority of the trained fieldworker. Nevertheless, Hurston was shortly to leave Haiti, believing that the secret societies had targeted and poisoned her.

Hurston provides the model for the sensational anthropological account that would be repeated 50 years later by Wade Davis, who explored the same theory of exotic poisons and secret societies in a similar uneasy mode of writing situated somewhere between anthropology, botany and sensation fiction. Wade could also produce his own real-life zombie, in this case Clairvius Narcisse. Even at the time she was writing, however, Hurston was ridiculed by her fellow anthropologists. Her timing was unlucky. One of the leading intellectuals in Haiti, the anthropologist Jean Price-Mars, had in his book *So Spoke the Uncle* (1928) taken the revolutionary position that the religion and folklore of Haiti should be embraced as a point of national identification rather than as something to be suppressed in shame, or explained away as the psychoneurosis of a whole nation. Even as Price-Mars explored Vodou seriously, he dismissed stories of cannibalism and zombies as 'heinous rubbish'. Price-Mars sighed:

THE NEW YORK TIMES BOOK REVIEW, *October 23, 1938.*   23

VOODOO *as no* WHITE PERSON *ever saw it!*

THE amazing experiences of an *actual initiate* of Voodooism, whose race enabled her to witness secret ceremonies seemingly incredible in these modern times. Writes William Seabrook: "I must tell you how terrifically excited I am by this new book of Zora Hurston's. Papa Legba opened wide the gate for her — and Zora has come through as no white ever could." Says George Stevens in his Book-of-the-Month Club Recommendation: "For general color, life and readability, *Tell My Horse* is hard to beat. She tells some hair-raising stories." 24 remarkable photographs. $3.00

TELL MY HORSE
VOODOO LIFE IN HAITI AND JAMAICA
by Zora Neale Hurston

An advertisement for Hurston's *Tell My Horse* taken out
in the *New York Times Book Review*, October 1938.

'Not a year, not even a month passes that we do not hear recounted authoritative details of the most bizarre stories about people who have been found dead for a certain period and had been found living again in some place or another.'[24]

Just the year before *Tell My Horse* appeared, Melville Herskovits, another Columbia University anthropologist trained by Franz Boas, had published *Life in a Haitian Valley*, an immersive account of three months of fieldwork designed to discredit the 'condescension and caricature' heaped on Haiti since Spenser St John's cannibal fantasies. Herskovits, who knew Hurston and at first encouraged her in her anthropological work, explores Haitian religion and magic in detail, suggesting a literate and scholarly interaction with European occultism, rather than voodoo being just a case of 'African survival'. The tone is sober and detached, unlike Hurston's melodramatic account. Herskovits erases himself with professional legitimacy rather than being ridden by the local gods. Sudden or unnatural deaths do produce accounts of the *zombi*, Herskovits says, but he deplores the way that this 'has been presented in recent years with unjustifiable sensationalism to the reading public' and situates it in a lengthy folkloric tradition.[25] Another serious folklorist, Harold Courlander, published *Haiti Singing* in 1939, again a careful treatment of the ritual and religion of Vodou.

Louis P. Mars, professor of psychiatry and eventually Haitian government minister, directly addressed Hurston's findings in *Man*, America's leading anthropological journal. He discussed Felicia Felix-Mentor as 'evidently a case of schizophrenia' and expressed frustration that at the end of the war, in 1945, 'tourists believe that they will be able to see zombis roaming through villages.' Hurston is dismissed as just another American tourist: 'Miss Hurston herself, unfortunately, did not go beyond the mass hysteria to verify her information.'[26]

Hurston was more in tune with the pulps and B-movies than the direction of pre-war anthropology, but *Tell My Horse* strongly evokes the complex situation ten years after Seabrook's *The Magic Island*, in which the Caribbean *zombi* is never quite shaken off in its translation to European and American Gothic conventions of popular culture. It retains an uncanny power precisely because it is at once a laughable and ridiculous Hollywood generic icon by 1940 yet also a 'real', if disputed, anthropological object. The emergence of the zombie in American popular culture is not just a simple case of colonial appropriation and the stripping out of original contexts. This very particular and variegated Caribbean history is a consistent undertow to its New World meanings and resonances.

All the same, something shifts profoundly in the representation of the zombie in the post-1945 era. The zombies stop coming in ones or twos, elusive or vanishingly rare fugitive creatures, squinting in blind terror down the lens of a camera. Instead, they start massing at the gates, coming in hordes to announce the end of the world.

6

After 1945:
Zombie Massification

The most striking change in the representation of the zombie after 1945 is that it is no longer always a lone figure or a gang of pitiful slaves under a single master. Instead, the zombies come in an anonymous, overwhelming mass. The key scene of the zombie film since George Romero's *Night of the Living Dead* (1968) is of the horde pressing in on the Last Redoubt, feeble defences giving way under the sheer dead weight of reanimated bodies pushing in from the outside. They have no strategy, no intelligence, merely the advantage of number. This nightmare of engulfment by the mass is constantly repeated, reflected in titles like *The Horde* (dir. Yannick Dahan and Benjamin Rocher, 2009), and perhaps reaching its apotheosis in the swarms of infected zombies that devour downtown Philadelphia in the spectacular opening minutes of *World War Z* (dir. Marc Foster, 2013).

How did the zombie move from a rare and elusive oddity to become one of the exemplary allegorical figures of the modern mass? In the 1930s, the pulps and American cinema had already begun transporting the *zombi* from the colonial margin to the imperial centre. *Revolt of the Zombies*, the feeble 1936 follow-up to *White Zombie* by the Halperins, innovated by extending the notion of slavery and control to whole armies – the most eye-catching moment is when the camera pans across the faces of an implacable zombie army. But the real transformation began to take place, I want to propose, in or immediately after 1945. The lone Caribbean *zombi* never goes away – indeed, it is very important to retain all the historical resonances that I have excavated so far, as these will continue to underpin later developments. But the zombie finds a whole new set of contexts and media ecologies in which to thrive after 1945.

As if the catastrophic military and civilian losses to a global war over six years were not enough, the last months of the conflict produced two profoundly ruptural moments. In April 1945, British and American forces advancing over the German border came across the Bergen-Belsen concentration camp, discovering 60,000 starving prisoners on the verge of death and surrounded by 13,000 unburied corpses. Although the vicious system of imprisonment of enemies of the Nazi state was well known, and intelligence had reported systematic murder in some camps, this was the first highly traumatic encounter in the West with the extent of the catastrophe. As Susan Sontag eloquently testified on seeing a book of images from Belsen that year, 'one's first encounter with the photographic inventory of ultimate horror is a kind of revelation, the prototypically modern revelation: a negative epiphany.' She was left, she said, 'irrevocably wounded'.[1] The advancing Soviet troops had found something even worse in the liberation of the Auschwitz-Birkenau camp on 27 January 1945: a vast factory machine dedicated to the liquidation of entire peoples, particularly the Jewish population of Europe. The extent of this genocide (the term coined for a 'crime without a name' by Raphael Lemkin in 1946) gradually became known over the course of 1945.

Then, in August, the war in the Pacific was abruptly ended by the American use of a devastating new bomb, which wiped out the Japanese towns of Hiroshima and Nagasaki. The Japanese high command surrendered the following day in the face of this overwhelming destructive force. The nuclear device that detonated over Hiroshima, product of the top-secret Manhattan Project that also invented the 'military-industrial complex', inaugurated a new age of terror. The atom bomb realized the prospect for the first time in history of a weapon with genuinely global reach. There was nowhere on the planet left to escape its deadly technological embrace. Within days of the news of the use of this super-weapon, American culture was flooded with the recognition that it could just as easily be turned on American cities. Fantasies of destruction – of New York or Chicago levelled within 30 minutes of a declaration of war – flooded the American imagination.[2] This was before anyone knew much about the second deadly element of a nuclear detonation. The American government denied the fatal consequences of atomic radiation for years, but by the 1950s the culture was drenched in dread at the prospect of an insidious wave of poisonous radioactive clouds that would advance inexorably across the world, either killing or horribly mutating everything in its wake. Nevil Shute's bestselling novel *On the Beach* (1957) was set in faraway Australia, its protagonists doomed to await the fatal wave of radiation as it sank south. It spoke to everyone forced to share in this new planetary consciousness.

This double trauma created new types or states of being. In a famous editorial published on 14 August 1945 entitled 'Modern Man is Obsolete', Norman Cousins announced 'the violent death of one stage in man's history and the beginning of another'.[3] Many felt that they were suspended in an odd liminal state between life and death. One of the most influential psychologists and public intellectuals dealing with these new 'massive traumas' was New Yorker Robert Jay Lifton. Lifton examined the psychological condition of the Hiroshima *hibakusha*, poorly translated as 'survivors', the more literal meaning being 'explosion-affected persons'. In subsequent books, Lifton detailed his work with Korean War veterans, large-scale disaster victims, Holocaust survivors and perpetrators, and his advocacy in the 1960s and '70s on behalf of the psychologically damaged soldiers returning from the Vietnam War was crucial in developing the notion of post-traumatic stress disorder, a diagnostic term first officially recognized in 1980.[4]

In his key book on Hiroshima, *Death in Life*, Lifton argued that the atom bomb had produced 'a sudden and absolute shift from normal existence to an overwhelming encounter with death'. He suggested that in the wake of the detonation, those who clung on miraculously in the ruins experienced 'a widespread sense that life and death were out of phase with one another, no longer properly distinguishable'.[5] He aimed to categorize the psychological condition of the *hibakusha*, which he argued was marked initially by a defensive 'psychic numbing' and then later by a 'survivor guilt'. Numbing deadened the mind following immersion in mass death, but the *hibakusha* also began to feel that they they were '"carriers of death", who take on a quality of supernatural evil', suffering what Lifton called 'contagion anxiety', as if their survival was a vector of transmission for more mass death to enter the world.[6] Survivors felt either harassed by or came to identify with the 'homeless dead', the vengeful ghosts of those who die dishonoured in the Japanese folkloric tradition. 'Survivors', Lifton later said, extending this condition beyond Hiroshima, 'feel compelled virtually to merge with the dead.'[7]

We have been carefully trained to avoid appropriating the suffering of others vicariously, but in this early work Lifton had no compunction in seeing the *hibakusha* as emblematic of a new, universal condition of a post-nuclear world. The atomic survivor was 'representative of a new death immersion' and 'we all share it', he said.[8] It was Lifton's message throughout his career: we lived now under the imprint of mass death, saturated in its symbolism.

In the B-movie science fiction and horror boom of the 1950s, which flowered as an effect of the breaking of the Hollywood studio monopolies, atomic bomb blasts or the insidious radiation threat became a catch-all explanation for the arrival of the Bug-eyed Monster, from the new mutant to the disturbed prehistoric beast, from the gigantic (*Godzilla* or *Them!*) to the miniature (*The Incredible Shrinking Man*, steadily diminishing owing to exposure to radiation). Zombies were typically subsumed into this superficial exploitation of nuclear anxiety. *Creature with the Atom Brain* (dir. Edward L. Cahn, 1955) featured radio-controlled atom-powered zombies, commanded by a fugitive mad Nazi doctor (obviously). There is some impressive looming at the camera by the unfettered zombies at the end of the film, although they are easily suppressed by the local army. The B-movie maestro Cahn returned to more traditional zombie representation in *Zombies of Mora Tau* (1957). At the end of the decade, *Teenage Zombies* (dir. Jerry Warren, 1959) involves an experimental gas that enslaves the protagonists of also being trialled by ex-Nazis on a remote island, using fears of germ warfare and radiation. In these B-movies, the threat is of a potential mass extension of new nuclear-age technologies that 'zombify' in the simple sense of human agency being dissolved by a *bokor* (replaced by a generic mad scientist), although these plans are thwarted. They tend to be one-note exploitations of contemporary anxiety, but we shouldn't dismiss all 1950s cinema zombies outright, since some examples from the period accrued subtle and ambiguous layers of meaning.

If the living dead *hibakusha* staggered out of the ruins of Hiroshima perpetually haunted by the imprint of death, then it was the figure of the 'Musulman' that assailed the memory of those who survived the concentration camps. This prison slang term associated with Auschwitz, variously spelled, was an 'exotic' and 'foreign' word that was awkward on the prisoner's tongues and which derived from the German word *Muselmann* (Muslim). It named the final stages of the condition of 'utmost inanition', beyond starvation, beyond life, beyond reason, indifferent to pain and suffering, utterly abject and scorned, but not yet dead.[9] Since 'Muslim' derives from the Arabic meaning 'submission to God', it was presumably evoked by prisoners as a slang term for resignation to fate (other camps had different, equally contemptuous terms for exactly the same terminal condition). In Primo Levi's account of his year in Auschwitz, he defines the Musulman as 'the weak, the inept, those doomed to selection' for inevitable death in the gas chambers. Levi continued: 'Their number is endless', forming 'the backbone of the camp, an anonymous mass, continually renewed and always identical, of non-men who march and labour in silence, the divine spark dead within them, already too empty to really suffer. One hesitates to call them living: one hesitates to call their death death, in the face of which they have no fear, as they are too tired to understand.'[10] The impossible interval occupied by the Musulman, the 'non-human who obstinately appears as human', is the focus of Giorgio Agamben's philosophical commentary on Levi's work in *Remnants of Auschwitz*. These 'mummy-men' or 'living dead' are aporia – irresolvable contradictions – who demand memorial and witness but precisely cannot remember or speak for themselves.[11]

Wolfgang Sofsky's description of the *Muselmänner*, those 'persons destroyed, devastated, shattered wrecks strung between life and death', is much more visceral:

> In a final stage of emaciation, their skeletons were enveloped by flaccid, parchment-like sheaths of skin, edema had formed on their feet and thighs, their posterior muscles had collapsed. Their skulls seemed elongated; their noses dripped constantly, mucus running down their chins. Their eyeballs had sunk deep into their sockets, their gaze was glazed. Their limbs moved slowly, hesitantly, almost mechanically. They exuded a penetrating, acrid odor; sweat, urine, liquid feces trickled down their legs.[12]

Testimony from other survivors describes their slow 'shuffle in clogs', that they 'used to sway in a peculiar fashion, sitting or half-sitting. The movement was monotonous, horrifying.' They were described as 'giant skeletons', 'strangely alike', feral, with shining eyes, obsessed with food, driven beyond all taboos by hunger, even to eat corpses.[13] Before their final physical death they suffered social death, expelled from the community as pariahs, abused for their apparent laziness and lack of dignity. They offended because they presaged everyone's future fate: this was the inevitable conclusion of camp logic.

In Sofsky's view, 'The Muselmann is the central figure in the tableau of mass dying – a death by hunger, murder of the soul, abandonment; dead whilst still living.'[14] And it is the *massification* of death that produces the major challenge: 'Individual death leaves the existence of the collective unaffected. By contrast, dying in massive numbers involves a fundamental disorientation . . . [that] shatters the concept of the peaceful continued existence of society.'[15]

The ethical questions that crowd around how to represent this unprecedented Holocaust always make this fraught cultural terrain. Critics frequently challenge any routinization of Holocaust representations, insisting either on a kind of 'traumatic realism', broken forms that register the shattering of mimetic language or narrative, or an aesthetic of interruption, fracture, difficulty, and a refusal of anything approaching narrative pleasure or generic repetition.[16] This is perhaps why only the abjected mass-cultural form of the horror comics in the early 1950s dared to equate concentration-camp victims with zombies. An extraordinary six-page comic-strip called 'The Living Dead', published in *Dark Mysteries* in 1954, told the story of Ivor Blau, lost in the Black Forest at dusk. He finds shelter in a fairy-tale house presided over by a beautiful young girl, who cares for a group of young men and women who sleep the sleep of the dead upstairs. In a jaw-dropping plot development, it is revealed that this group of sleepers are the products of concentration-camp medical experiments by Ivor's father, Klaus, 'the Nazi scientist who disappeared' at the end of the war. 'Soon we'll have these scum back to life with my formula!' he cackles in flashback over his selected camp prisoners. 'Now, they are half-dead zombies who cannot die.'[17] Using the merciless rough justice of the comic world, the son pays with his life for his father's sins. He is pursued and killed by the wakened zombies: 'Boney arms enveloped the terror stricken ex-Nazi youth . . .', and they laugh with vengeful glee over his dead body in the final panel of the story.[18]

It is rare to find such explicit treatments, but Jim Trombetta's fascinating account of the brief flare and accompanying moral panic about horror comics between 1949 and 1954 in his anthology *The Horror! The Horror!* compellingly suggests that the camps were one of the contexts for the consistent use of skeletons, rotting corpses and zombies returning singly and then increasingly in hordes. The comics depicted whole cities of the living dead, masses of zombies creeping across the panels. The horror that an enlightened Western power had rationally planned the manufacture of the Musulman cannot be far beneath these abject depictions.

My sense is that while there remains a taboo on explicitly eliding the dead of the concentration-camp system with the zombie mass, the trace remains with the continued cultural obsession with Nazi zombies. This became popular with Robert Anton Wilson's cracked conflation of conspiracy theories in *The Illuminatus! Trilogy* (1975) – about the time trashy 'Nazi sexploitation' films were pushing at the boundaries of acceptable taste. One late sequence in the *Trilogy* involves an attempt to reanimate battalions of undead Nazis that slumber beneath Lake Totenkopf in Bavaria. Shortly afterwards, the American horror film *Shock Waves* (1977) involved a Nazi 'Death Corps' of seemingly unkillable, undead ss men who surface from a Second World War shipwreck to menace John Carradine and Brooke Adams, and the idea was recycled again in Jean Rollin's *Zombie Lake* (1981), where the 'lake of the damned' near a French village once occupied by German forces hides a nasty secret of wartime atrocity. These are among the most reviled zombie films ever made, with good reason, but the idea has returned again and again, in Steve Barker's film *Outpost* (2008), for instance, or in the delirious splatter of Tommy Wirkola's *Dead Snow* (2009), in which a crack German Einsatzgruppe (the 'mobile killing squads' that pioneered mass liquidations in the East) have become frozen zombies under the Norwegian ice, but are disturbed by teens in their ski cabin. There has also been a Nazi zombie version of the video game franchise *Call of Duty: World at War* (2009): killing already dead Nazis in a shoot-'em-up seems to appease some parents' anxieties about the violence of video games.

The zombie Nazi simply conflates two unqualified mass evils. It stays away from the 'living dead' of their starved and tortured victims, but evokes them by inversion, switching victims for perpetrators. Viewers are morally freed twice over to enjoy the spectacle of (re-)killing. Nazis, after all, come in masses too. Totalitarianism, in Hannah Arendt's view, was a phenomenon of the masses rather than a specific class fraction, and German fascism answered a longing for 'self-abandonment into the mass'.[19] Zombification becomes a post-war metaphor for this willed abandonment of the will under the Mesmeric gaze of a Führer who commands the *Volk* to ever more exorbitant acts of violence. There is also a German connection that keeps us tied to the Haitian context. Long before the Second World War, in pulp fiction like Roscoe's *Z is for Zombie*, it is the Germans who lurk in the hills of Haiti, using the screen of native superstition to conceal their nefarious plans. Part of the impetus for the American occupation in 1915 was to quash increasing

Nazi zombies, *Dead Snow* (*Død snø*, 2009).

German financial control of Haitian banks and markets. This history does not vanish: it means, rather, that the zombie accrues ever more complex layers of meaning.

The initial colonial context for the emergence of the zombie far from disappeared after 1945. Indeed, one of the crucial consequences of the shift in world power that became evident after the Yalta Conference in February 1945, when Roosevelt, Stalin and Churchill met to discuss the future of Europe, was the American demand for the dismantling of the protected markets of the British Empire. Britain, economically broken by the war and saddled with steep debt repayments to the American banks, began to release itself from the costs of colonial occupation and administration and to divest itself of its empire. The year 1945 inaugurated an era of decolonization, although it was a disavowed, elongated and often violent process for many European empires. This was an absolutely immediate post-war problem: on 8 May 1945, the day the Nazi regime surrendered in Europe, French gendarmerie fired on a crowd of Algerians celebrating the end of the war and holding up anti-colonial banners in Sétif, killing an estimated 6,000 people over the next few days.

As we have already seen in the Introduction, nationalist and post-colonial theorists have repeatedly figured the dead hand of empire and its woeful legacies as a form of zombification. Under fascist Vichy rule in the French colony of Martinique and then later during the Algerian War, Frantz Fanon evoked the zombie in his writings on colonial subjection in *The Wretched of the Earth* (1961). He had learned this from his teacher in Martinique, the radical intellectual and poet Aimé Césaire. In his *Discourse on Colonialism* (1950), Césaire influentially argued that the murderous logic of Nazism had been actively trialled in Europe's colonies for decades, and that the atrocities perpetrated in the European camps just reimported these tactics from the edges of empire. The English had invented and named the 'concentration camp' during the Boer War (1899–1902) and the Germans had deliberately and systematically murdered the Herero and Nama in southwest Africa (1904–7). For this barbarism to recur in Europe was a logical consequence of the dehumanization of the perpetrators. Césaire called this 'the boomerang effect' (although in his commentary on Césaire, Michael Rothberg prefers the more literal translation of *un choc en retour*, 'the shock that comes back').[20] This was also the thesis of Hannah Arendt's *Origins of Totalitarianism* (1951), where she proposed that imperialism's 'machine of death', which possesses territories, materials and peoples through destruction, was the test-bed for the liquidations in Germany and the Soviet Union. Arendt also understood the war and the camps as 'the much-feared boomerang effect upon the mother countries'.[21]

For Césaire, colonization was a process that degraded the colonizers too, turning them into objects or dead things. 'It is not the head of civilization that begins to rot first', he said: 'It is the heart.' To further the analogy, Césaire envisaged the European bourgeoisie, who had driven imperialism and then embraced fascism, as the walking dead. In staccato, poetic sentences, Césaire saw them as 'A sign that feels itself mortal. A sign that feels itself to be a corpse. And when the corpse starts to babble' – Césaire does not finish the horrible thought.[22] Much later, when the zombie had become an established cultural trope, the Tunisian post-colonial theorist Albert Memmi mournfully regarded the psychological condition of the displaced, immigrant, decolonized sons of the nationalist liberation movements under the title 'The Zombie'. 'The son of the immigrant is a kind of zombie, lacking any profound attachment to the land in which he was born', Memmi said.[23]

After 1945, mass decolonization did not terminate the colonial contexts in which the enslaved zombie shuffled into popular culture. If anything, it transmitted them back to the centre in intensified form. In the year 2000, Michael Hardt and Antonio Negri argued in *Empire* that we had reached a truly global extension of capitalism, which exerted a 'biopolitical power' through which life itself could be manipulated. Globalization extends the state of metaphorical zombification to us all, commanded by abstract, international flows over which we have no control. In 60 years, we moved from World War II to *World War Z*.

The implacable Cold War blocs that emerged at the end of the Second World War provided another important context in which the mass zombie entered American popular culture. This was an era of large-scale geopolitical reordering of the world by the Soviet Communist and American capitalist blocs. Once the Soviets tested their own atomic bomb in 1949, the strategy of Mutually Assured Destruction locked the world in an icy embrace, trembling on the brink of global disaster. The first major proxy war between these ideological foes had been shaping up on the Korean peninsula since 1945, with American troops openly committed to fighting to protect the South against the Communist North from 1950. This engagement escalated when Mao Zedong sent vast numbers of the Chinese People's Liberation Army to support the Communist push south to capture the capital, Seoul. After initial losses, the American forces pushed back, dug in and became deadlocked until an uneasy peace was signed in 1953.

The Korean War supplies two essential elements for popular imagery of the post-1945 mass zombie. The first relates directly to the tactics of the Communist forces in the early months of the war: the use of the 'human wave'. Mao Zedong long advocated this tactic of sending forward thousands of barely armed infantry to overwhelm better equipped professional armies through sheer force of numbers. When half a million Chinese troops entered North Korea through Manchuria and attacked in October 1950, they forced the shocked

American army into major retreat. The American command had underestimated numbers and was aghast at this new 'mobile warfare', which thrived on chaos and accepted its own mass body count. It was even speculated that the piles of corpses mown down as they advanced were meant to demoralize the Americans, who would be disgusted by their own slaughter. Unable to compute numbers, a joke circulated among the American press corps that 'three swarms equals one horde, two hordes equal a human wave, two waves equal a human tide, after which come the bottomless oceans of Chinese manpower.'[24] The initial success of this tactic – although it was soon abandoned when the losses became too high – cost the American war hero General Douglas MacArthur his command.

Military books that came out of the Korean War had titles like *Red China's Fighting Hordes* by Robert Rigg, and even a memoir written 60 years later by a British brigadier on the United Nations forces in Korea used the title *Chinese Hordes and Human Waves*, as if this were the most striking detail of the war. The 'disregard for human life' as the hordes advanced stayed with the brigadier.[25]

The Asian hordes, *Revolt of the Zombies* (1936).

It is possible that the human wave proved so successful because it reinforced a central racist stereotype of the 'Yellow Peril' that had been established in American public discourse since at least the Chinese Exclusion Act of 1882, a law passed in panic to restrict Chinese immigration. The prospect of an annihilating wave of anonymous masses from Asia was a staple of invasion fantasies from the 1890s, as in M. P. Shiel's *The Yellow Danger* (1898) or Jack London's 'The Unparalleled Invasion' (1910). The nefarious plots of Fu Manchu in Sax Rohmer's novels sold in their millions; Flash Gordon fought 'Ming the Merciless', a dastardly Oriental mastermind. In the paranoid context of the Cold War, where infiltration and invasion fears were stoked high by 'Red Scare' rhetoric, the Reds and Yellows were conflated: 'Communism is an Asiatic theory of government. It grows out of heathenism and barbarism ... By the "yellow peril" we mean the organizing of Orientals into a force that seeks to destroy all white men from the face of the earth', warned the Christian Republican Dan Gilbert in 1951. The 'mass slaughters' to be expected from these ruthless infidels rising from the East were fully predicted in the Book of Revelation, Gilbert continued.[26] This is a sign of the fusion of political paranoia with Christian apocalyptic thinking, crucial to the later development of 'zombie apocalypse' narratives.

The trauma of those early months of the Korean War and of the defeats under this relentless mass attack retains an echo in later American zombie fictions. Sometimes, you don't have to fish for it: the title of Cy Gunther's novella *Zombie Outbreak, Korea, 1950* (2014) says it all. This unedifying tale shows Communist cruelty extending to deliberately killing and reanimating South Korean civilians to send into American positions in the early stages of the war.

The second element that emerged from the Korean War to influence the development of the post-war zombie was a far less physical image. What was the ideological force of Communism that so compelled the Chinese hordes into this terrible, mindless sacrifice? The answer lay in a term that was coined in 1950: brainwashing. The Chinese Communist tactic of 're-education' or 'thought reform' to adjust citizens correctly to the new collective was called *hsi nao*. The journalist and CIA agent Edward Hunter suggested something wonderfully sinister in translating this as brainwashing. In the 1950s, the term became rapidly elided with the idea of the will-less, enslaved zombie, ensuring that zombification became a powerful metaphor for deeply paranoid times. It was a strange echo of the idea of the *zombi astral,* whose soul is captured by the *bokor,* leaving the empty shell of the body to labour in utter servitude.

The true terror of the Korean War for Americans was ultimately focused not on the battle front but on a tiny handful of American POWs who had been captured and sent to camps in Manchuria, where they were taken through re-education programmes by Chinese and Russian interrogators. The alarm was raised when a handful of soldiers and airmen issued public confessions that they had engaged in germ warfare – illegal under international law. Confessions like this were familiar from Soviet show trials and easily dismissed as propaganda. More alarming was the group of 21 POWs who refused to return to America after negotiated prisoner exchanges: they had reformed their thought and embraced Communism. There was consternation that Americans might willingly choose a 'Slave World' over the 'Free World'. Edward Hunter explained what had happened in a set of articles started in 1950 and culminating in his book *Brain-washing in Red China* (1953). 'The intent is to change a mind radically so that its owner becomes a living puppet – a human robot – without the atrocity being visible from the outside. The aim is to create a mechanism in flesh and blood.'[27] In the *American Journal of Psychiatry* in 1951, the psychiatrist Joost Meerloo called the technique 'menticide' (on the model of genocide) for this 'condition of enslavement'.[28] After the war, once the POWs had returned, they were treated with deep suspicion, feared and suspected of having been secretly 'turned' by their cunning captors. A number were court martialled and disgraced. They were emblems of a post-war softness, of a decadent liberal democracy that was unable to provide sufficient ideological strength of conviction to counter the lure of Communism. They were probed, psychoanalysed and pilloried in studies like Eugene Kinkead's *Why They Collaborated* (1959).

Chinese Communists brainwash U.S. troops in
The Manchurian Candidate (1962).

This material was fictionalized in the celebrated novel by Richard
Condon *The Manchurian Candidate* (1959), in which apparent
Korean War hero Raymond Shaw is imprisoned, indoctrinated by
a fiendish master brainwasher in Manchuria called Yen Lo, and
returned to America as a 'sleeper' agent, to be activated like a machine
by post-hypnotic suggestion to assassinate a presidential candidate.
Shaw proves a perfect subject for this experiment due to his unresolved Freudian hang-ups (Condon's target is as much castrating
mothers – the suffocating American culture of 'momism' – as evil
Communists). The technique does not quite work on his fellow
captive Marco: 'What do you think I am – a zombie?' he asks, disgusted.[29] Marco slowly pieces together the truth through the haze
of hypnotic amnesia and mental blocks. 'You are a host body and
they are feeding on you', he warns Shaw. He is intent on depro-
gramming his commander, 'sort of removing the controls, ripping
out the wiring', he says, searching for the right metaphor.[30] Images
of robot command and automation tend to predominate over those
of the zombie in Condon's novel, it has to be said, although critics
often discuss Shaw using the terms 'zombie' and 'robot' interchange-
ably. *The Manchurian Candidate* offered such a potent myth of what
was becoming known as the 'paranoid style of American politics' that
Frank Sinatra, who starred in the film and owned the rights, hastily

withdrew the film version after the assassination of John F. Kennedy a year after its release. It was a decision that of course only intensified its conspiratorial reputation.[31] The film is sometimes also held to reveal the American national security state's own profound interest in developing the psychological techniques to create their own 'prefabricated assassins'.

Brainwashing does not initially suggest a mass, but rather a single individual put under severe and sustained psychological pressure, like Shaw in *The Manchurian Candidate* or Harry Palmer in Len Deighton's *The Ipcress File* (1962). Hallucinatory disorientation and brainwashing techniques were the culminating scenes of Sidney J. Furie's film version of the novel in 1965. Aside from these individual cases, there are, however, repeated fantastical images of collective brainwashing in popular American fiction and film where the metaphorical stitching is looser. The most compelling example from the era is Don Siegel's film *Invasion of the Body Snatchers* (1956), perhaps because its plot invites so many potential allegorical readings. It is not a zombie film, but it is a film entirely about zombification in the post-war paranoid style.

Invasion was shot in a matter of days on a low budget, faithfully adapted from Jack Finney's 1954 serial for *Collier's* magazine. The film takes us efficiently from a small-town idyll, where the local doctor Miles Bennell knows everyone in town and traditional social order binds the community together, to the nightmare of an insidious takeover of Santa Mira by alien beings. Miles can't quite cope with local cases of hysterical delusion, the conviction in a number of patients that their loved ones have been replaced by identical but somehow emptied-out robotic doubles. 'There's no emotion. None. Just the pretence of it', a patient explains (this was recognized as a psychiatric disorder related to hysteria in 1923, but is now understood more neurologically as Capgras syndrome). The local psychiatrist declares these cases to be 'a strange neurosis, evidently contagious. An epidemic of mass hysteria.' Bennell soon enters this delusion himself, briefly persuaded that he has only imagined seeing a corpse-like double in the dark of a basement, growing into the form of his girlfriend, Becky. The material evidence grows, however, as does the paranoia, until Miles and Becky recognize that they are the only humans left in town: the police and all local authorities are part of the conspiracy. The secret is that alien seed-pods, an interstellar parasite, have landed in Santa Mira and have quietly absorbed and reproduced their human hosts down to a cellular level. The psychiatrist Kaufman, speaker for the pod people, celebrates the new collective, always speaking in the third person, presenting a communistic vision of a rational shared life: 'Accept us!' he exhorts Miles and Becky. All the wasted energy of human emotions will be erased; gone will be the tiresome struggles associated with American individualism. In Finney's written version, these body doubles are acknowledged to be merely temporary hosts for a rapacious parasite: 'We can't live, Miles. The last of us will be dead . . . in five years at most.'[32] The film was to end in an open way, with the demented Bennell reaching the highway alone, screaming at the cars: 'You're fools! Can't you see you're in danger? They're here already! You're

The pod people take over, *Invasion of the Body Snatchers* (1956).

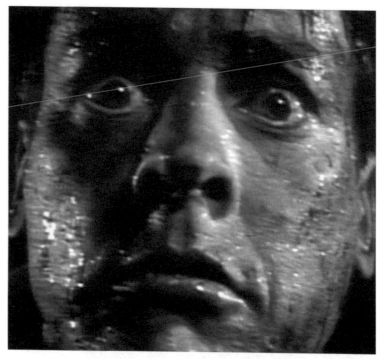

'I didn't know the real meaning of fear until . . .

next!' The complacent small-town doctor has had his social reality entirely disassembled. It was reframed to include a last scene where larger federal agencies appear finally to be swinging into action to counter the threat.

Invasion of the Body Snatchers feeds directly on Red Scare anxiety. Although Senator Joseph McCarthy's exorbitant claims of Communist infiltration of the Washington establishment had crashed with his disgrace in 1954, the director of the CIA, J. Edgar Hoover, had yet to publish *Masters of Deceit*, in which he would declare Communism to be a threat to 'the safety of every individual, and the continuance of every house and fireside' in America.[33] Hoover detailed the insidious tactics of infiltration and warned citizens to be vigilant for the tiniest signs. 'They want to make a "Communist man", a mechanical puppet, whom they can train to do as the Party desires', he warned all right-thinking American citizens.[34] In the

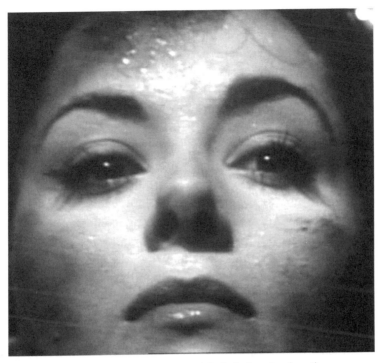

... I kissed Becky', *Invasion of the Body Snatchers* (1956).

film, it is significant that the pod people seek first to *persuade* Bennell to embrace them, scenes that are exercises in 'thought reform' and only distantly undergirded with the threat of forcible conversion. That this transformation takes place during sleep, when ego defences are suspended, also hints at fears of hypnotic invasion and control. By the end of the film, it only takes a moment of sleep for Becky to be converted. She becomes a cold and mechanical creature. With blissful pop-Freudian relish, Miles's voiceover thunders, 'I didn't know fear until . . . I kissed Becky.' Physical and mental states of zombification lurk in this whole nexus of associations.

But *Invasion* endures more than most B-movie alien invasion fantasies of the 1950s because of its marked ambiguities. Siegel was conservative (as was Finney), but such films 'reflected not one but several warring ideologies'.[35] As most commentators note, the ambiguity of *Invasion of the Body Snatchers* is finely balanced, for the coercive conformity of Santa Mira might not be a Communist threat so much as the constricting forces of American post-war consensus. These new normative pressures, according to several liberal commentators, had produced profound changes in the American character. David Riesman famously argued in *The Lonely Crowd* (1950) that many were increasingly 'other-directed', concerned to fit in with their neighbours and friends, suppressing their inner selves for 'close behavioural conformity' in nearly every public and private aspect of life.[36] Automation and the new consumption economy mass-produced machine-tooled people living in identikit suburbs and working for identikit corporations. This was the bland 'Organization Man' (the title of another bestseller of the time), with a personality obsessively trained, tested and policed for any worrisome deviations from the norm. By the late 1950s, fears about brainwashing and hypnotic control were targeted at the new culture of American advertising and hyper-capitalism. 'No one anywhere can be sure nowadays that he is not being worked upon by the depth persuaders', Vance Packard claimed, detailing how the new supermarket environments induced soporific trance states in young women shoppers while advertisers reshaped the nation's unconscious desires.[37] Juvenile delinquency was fuelled by mass culture and consumption, teenagers shuffling around dance halls like zombies, Packard said in his later book *The Status Seekers* (1959); shades of *Teenage Zombies* again.[38] These are the seeds for the satire of Ira Levin's robotic *Stepford Wives* (1972) or the indoor shopping mall populated by listless zombie consumers in George Romero's *Dawn of the Dead*. Fiendish tactics for so long ascribed to America's enemies rapidly experienced their own curious boomerang effect to resurface at the heart of the American Dream. This is how the mechanism of paranoia works: fears projected outward return as demonic persecutions.

The open allegorical grid of a film like *Invasion of the Body Snatchers* allows for the accumulation of many different possibilities. It is often claimed that these forms of science fiction and horror were able to escape an era of media censorship and control – once Hollywood became the target for anti-Communist witch-hunts – because any social criticism was displaced through genre trappings. More likely, they were simply ignored. Susan Sontag, usually more attuned than other cultural critics, regarded the B-movie science fiction boom of the 1950s as entirely devoid of ideas, expressions only of 'primitive gratification' in spectacles of destruction.[39] This was culture that did not contribute to the public sphere, but actively degraded it.

The last element we need to explore in this period is the reception of the *forms* of mass culture themselves. For many leading intellectuals in the 1940s and '50s, the splurge of American mass culture of 'crime, science fiction and sex novelettes' (as Richard Hoggart put it) was an annihilating tide of worthless rubbish.[40] In the influential collection *Mass Culture: The Popular Arts in America* (1957), one of the editors, Bernard Rosenberg, warned that these mass products of a 'machine civilization' created a 'dehumanized' and 'deadened' population, resulting in a 'stupefaction'. At its worst, Rosenberg continued, 'mass culture threatens not merely to cretinize our taste, but to brutalize our senses while paving the way to totalitarianism.'[41] This stance might have been expected from commentators on the cultural right (Ortega y Gasset had long warned of the 'coming of the masses' that would overwhelm the excellence of the high culture of the elite). But this critique also came from the left, a radical like Dwight MacDonald condemning 'the deadening and warping effect of long exposure to movies, pulp magazines and radio'.[42] The German Marxist Theodor Adorno, exiled in America, also routinely condemned the idiocy of 'the culture industry'. In a crucial way, then, the thematic *content* of the zombie mass, that resonant image of mindless shuffling hordes, was also one of the strongest reflections on the abjected *form* of mass culture. The zombie was one of the most abjected products of the American mass culture industry because it became a commentary on *massification itself*. Perhaps this is why the zombie found its most persistent presence in this era in the most widely read yet most reviled cultural form: the horror comic.

The comics industry was huge: with the expansion of the market at the end of the Second World War, it was estimated that there were 60 million copies bought in America each month (with each copy likely exchanged and read by another three or four people). In 1948, there was a notable shift in tone and a boom in violent and gory horror comics began to emerge. Bland titles like *Teen Comics* or *Joker Comics* turned into *Journey into Unknown Worlds* and *Adventures into Terror*. In bold four-tone colours, with shrill and arresting cover images of death and dismemberment, comics companies tried to outdo each other to stand out on news-stands. The height of the boom was between 1950 and 1954, with nearly 150 titles, including memorable runs of *Black Cat Mystery*, *Weird Mysteries*, *Black Magic* and, most notoriously, *Tales from the Crypt*. As the titles suggests, these comics picked up on the lurid end of pulp fiction, kids' stuff but with added twists of sexual torture, perversity and unhinged criminality. Crime themes were incredibly popular, with outrageous bad faith titles like *Crime Does Not Pay* selling millions. As in *Weird Tales*, there was an obsession with the vengeful dead, victims rising from the grave, skeleton gangs exacting punishments on their killers, the decaying dead crawling out of the ground to drag their killers down to hell. It was an exorbitant world with Jacobean levels of bloodthirsty revenge, the gore so extreme that it regularly tipped over into hilarity. A title like 'Horror of Mixed Torsos', featuring an unscrupulous gravedigger finally attacked by the composite muti-lated corpses of the cemetery dead, suggests the deliberate courting of bad taste and disgust.[43] But there were oddly Surrealist elements too. The comic *The Strange World of Your Dreams*, for instance, offered readers the chance not only to have their nightmares illustrated by legendary artists like Jack Kirby, but to have them psychoanalysed by 'dream doctors' in the comic too.

'The fifties world was haunted, all right, but not by ghosts. A ghost is a spirit without a body, but what possessed the fifties was the reverse: a body without a soul – a zombie.'[44] The comics teemed with zombies and the restless undead. Titles like *Voodoo* and *Black Magic* kept the tie back to the 1930s anxiety about colonial monsters from the margin, crossing over with a whole subset of 'jungle comics' which revelled in pulp primitivism, cannibalism and witchcraft among savage tribes. Evil priests continued to mesmerize victims in the old-school Haitian manner. The story 'I AM A ZOMBIE!' in

Adventures into the Unknown, for instance, portrays the abject tale of 'Morto' the zombie, cruelly commanded by the *mamaloi* Mother Harana to do her evil bidding. In flashback, Morto remembers his life as ruthless oil executive Roger Hanks, illegally throwing poor homesteaders off their land in the Louisiana bayou, even resorting to murder to secure his drilling rights. The killing of the voodoo witch Mother Harana results in his eternal servitude to her: 'You are one of the *undead*, Roger Hanks . . . *forever!* You have no will now . . . only mine! Obey me . . . for I am your master!' The 'impossible' narration of the dead Morto allows for a simple reader identification with the punished man and another lesson rammed home in the moral universe of the comics: that 'No one cheats death. No one escapes retribution.'[45]

Many comics featured these basic 'boomerang' stories, of a death exacted for a death by the rotting corpses of returning victims. Significantly, though, the comics zombie also evidenced the kind of massing up that I have been examining in this chapter. In March 1954, *Voodoo* comic included the story 'CORPSES . . . COAST TO COAST', framed as the dream of a nervous undertaker, initially unconcerned about a national strike leaving thousands of unburied corpses across America. This, however, is only the first plank in the secret plan of the demagogue 'The Big Z'. In a kind of oneiric reversal of the Holocaust, the corpses are collected in their thousands and taken to processing centres where they arrive as dead but leave as a marching army of the undead. What is established is the UWZ – the United World Zombies – who in a rapid succession of panels take over the White House and the Senate, then the Kremlin, France and the world. The resisters are herded into 'Rehabilitation Camps' and turned into zombies, 'just like human adding machines! They work 24 hours a day, and never need any rest!' The plot is foiled by atomic attack: luckily it turns out that 'zombie tissue doesn't stand up well under blast and radiation!' This nightmare somehow collapses the mass movements of Nazism and Communism while also mocking the American rhetoric of exporting the values of the free world, one of the last panels cynically celebrating 'making the world safe for zombiocracy'.[46] It is an impressively nihilistic vision. The story

'MARCHING ZOMBIES', from *Black Cat* in 1952, is set in 'the *desolate wastes* of an obscure Asian desert', where two adventurers find a city entirely populated by the living dead. This is a more conventional lost world story, where the threat is contained by the inaccessible city where the relation of life and death is reversed, but the last panel offers another vision of massified zombies, a vast column of the undead trailing through the night, 'a *weird* procession of marching zombies, doomed *never* to rest but to wander like *lost souls* through the long pathways of *eternity*.'[47]

Daniel Yezbick has argued that in the wake of the Second World War and amid the onset of the Cold War, the horror comics were 'designed to debase, disturb, or destroy all manner of conventional, orthodox, or conformist perspectives with gallows humour and gratuitous helpings of violence, psychosis and fetishism'. Deeply contentious, they 'simply went further than most media dared in their sour deconstruction of the American dream'.[48] This is why they became the subject of a moral panic that resulted in their denunciation by liberal criminal psychologist Fredric Wertham in his bestselling jeremiad *Seduction of the Innocent* (1954). A catastrophic defence of the 'good taste' of horror by the owner of EC Comics Bill Gaines before the Senate Subcommittee on Juvenile Delinquency in April 1954 led to a new industry Comics Code in November 1954 that effectively destroyed this whole first wave of horror comics culture in a matter of months.

Commentators started to complain about the moral opprobrium of the post-war comics almost as soon as they appeared. In 1949, Norbert Muhlen noted the 'mass preference' for this new form, and asked what effect 'may this endless tidal wave of terror have on our national life?' He pointed to apparent copycat crimes performed by young children, and worried that the celebration of crime and sexual perversity would corrupt a generation, contributing to the rise of 'godless, totalitarian man' and helping 'the trend toward the robotization of the individual'.[49] The form and content of this mass culture united to zombify the nation's youth. This was typical liberal commentary, most of which followed the lead of the implacable opponent of the comics, Fredric Wertham.

Wertham was a liberal psychologist who analysed the origins of delinquency in poverty, ran a free psychiatric service in Harlem and was a major expert influence in the court cases that ended racial segregation in schools. In comics, however, Wertham found only moral and psychological corruption: 'This is a new kind of harm, a new kind of bacillus that the present-day child is exposed to.'[50] Children simply imitated the violence they read from tales that reinforced the allure of crime, violence and sexual sadism. Comics were gateways: 'All child drug addicts', he insisted, had first been 'inveterate comic-book readers'. Meanwhile, all superheroes were antidemocratic and fascist: looking at the 'S' on Superman's outfit, he commented 'we should, I suppose, be thankful it is not an ss', and he fulminated against this nefarious Nietzsche in the nursery.[51] Comics revelled in racist, white supremacism. It was somewhat rich of the authorities to accuse the comics of racism, since it has been documented that in the last years of the Second World War, the Office of War Information encouraged comics companies to amplify racial stereotypes of the Japs and the Huns, while fictionalizing the extent of racial integration on the home front.[52] Wertham was only one element of a notable shift in suspicion of children and teenagers in the 1950s, a mutant generation of bad seeds and rebels without a cause, intent on defying all authority. Intellectuals found Wertham's comics stance vaguely ridiculous. Robert Warshow wrote a thoughtful reflection on his son's own addiction to EC Comics, arguing for the place of humour, distance and subversion in the child's imagination. Warshow did not think it was desirable for culture to be 'entirely hygienic': on the other hand, he rather hoped Wertham succeeded in banning these disturbing horror comics.[53]

Wertham's book appeared in early 1954 and in April he presented his case to the Senate Subcommittee on Juvenile Delinquency. He was followed by the owner of EC Comics, Bill Gaines, whose disastrous testimony effectively ended the boom in a few short minutes. Shown the cover of one of his comics with an axe and the severed head of a woman held up in glee, he was asked by the committee chair whether this constituted 'good taste'. 'Yes, sir, I do', Gaines replied. 'A cover in bad taste, for example, might be defined as holding the head a little higher so that the neck could be seen dripping blood from it.'[54] In November, the Comics Magazine Association of America issued a Comics Code. Under 'General Standards' it stated: 'No comics magazine shall use the word horror or terror in its title', and also declared that 'Scenes dealing with, or instruments associated with, walking dead, torture, vampires and vampirism, ghouls, cannibalism and werewolfism are prohibited.'[55] The era of the zombie in horror comics came to a sudden end. Gaines had to pour his vitriol into the satire of *Mad* magazine instead.

The suppression of the horror comics reinforced the abject status of its emblematic mass monster, the zombie. It remains the case, I think, that the zombie exemplifies the mindlessness of mass culture, since it is an orphan creature without the legitimating literary forebears of Baron Frankenstein or Count Dracula. One recent history of the Gothic ends by judging the zombie film to actively 'aspire to dismissive critical notice, gesture towards their own disposability', unable to free itself from this redoubled 'creative slavery of mass culture'.[56]

Later, horror comics returned with adjustments to the Code, with *Tales from the Tomb* (from 1962), or the innovative *Eerie* and *Creepy* comics (from 1964), and particularly from the early 1970s, when another major horror boom developed. There were reprints from the lost 1950s era, but also revivals and elaborations of characters, as in Marvel's *Tales of the Zombie* (1973–5), which focused on the melancholic figure of Simon Garth, sacrificed in a voodoo ceremony but revived in an agonized liminal state. Garth 'The Zombie' shuffles intermittently through other series, but nothing featuring zombies quite matched the Gothic elaboration of vampire or superhero mythologies, at least until the independent release of *Deadworld* in 1987, one of the first post-apocalyptic zombie comic narratives (which is still ongoing). It took a third horror comics boom in the early 2000s, long after the demise of the Comics Code, for the zombie to find centre stage: the phenomenal success of Robert Kirkman's *The Walking Dead* (started in 2003) was conceived from the start as open-ended and episodic, 'the zombie movie that never ends', focusing less on horror and gore and instead on human characters in 'extreme situations' after a disaster ends modern American life in a matter of weeks.[57] 'We will change! We will evolve. We'll make new rules – we'll still be humane', the protagonist Rick Grimes agonizes early in the series, although his terrible losses continue to accumulate. Kirkman's sober rendition of the apocalypse trope, focusing on the survivors and pushing the massification of zombies into the background, proved highly influential. The mass presence of the zombie horde becomes the new norm, the permanent emergency. Kirkman then had his fun in the *Marvel Zombies* series (2005–6), in which leading superheroes are infected by a zombie virus, crave human flesh and start to rot horribly ('Oh, Jeez!' says Zombie Spiderman, 'I broke my leg – like – in half'). Commissioned artists also set about 'zombifying' iconic Marvel covers from the past, in delighted acts of desecration. The sight of the Marvel canon of superheroes indulging in cannibal orgies across lovingly detailed splash pages suggested the extent of the zombie infection of the comics universe in the first years of the new century. Many of these later zombie comics retained the resonances of the first post-war boom. In the comic *'68*, the jungles of Vietnam at the height of the war hide not just the Viet Cong but an outbreak of zombies. The Asiatic horde, the massified undead intent on murderous attack, returns in the form we have now thoroughly excavated.

The first horror comics boom was brief but had an enduring effect on the kids that first encountered it and a huge influence on the trajectory of horror that followed. Two of these '50s kids would pay their respects to the world of EC Comics in the anthology film *Creepshow* (1982): the scriptwriter Stephen King and the director George Romero. *Creepshow*, framed by a kid's voodoo doll revenge on a brutish father who has thrown away his 'worthless' comics, contained two classic sequences of the restless dead returning from their graves to exact revenge. King wrote extensively about the influence of EC Comics on his own fiction, calling them 'the epitome of horror, the emotion of fear that underlies terror', and the simple moral universe of the comics colours everything King has written, for better or worse.[58] The influence on George Romero – those panels of massed zombies that climb out of the wreckage of 1945 – would utterly transform the idea of the zombie, and send it on the path towards world culture domination.

The Zombie Apocalypse:
Romero's Reboot and Italian Horrors

We have finally arrived at the zombie that everyone thinks they know: the horde unleashed by George A. Romero's *Night of the Living Dead* (1968), but only really consolidated ten years later with its sequel, *Dawn of the Dead*. Romero spawned an army of imitators, particularly in the European horror industry. It is in this sequence of films, from horror cinema's glorious decade of perverse wonders, that the zombie came together as a relentless, devouring, cannibalistic creature driven by insatiable hunger to turn living flesh into dead meat.

Night Falls

Strictly speaking, Romero's *Night of the Living Dead* is not a zombie film. The lone cadaverous creature hanging around the cemetery in the first scene is another exotic: a *ghoul* (the Arabic term for soulhungry spirits that haunt graveyards). In the film, no one knows quite what to call these dead that walk again. Early on, the radio refers to 'unidentified assassins', but by the end the sheriff just shrugs, 'They're dead – they're all messed up.' Romero's key source was the film *The Last Man on Earth* (dir. Sidney Salkow and Ubaldo Ragona, 1964), an adaptation of Richard Matheson's brilliant novel *I Am Legend*, about a blood disorder that turns the whole population into vampires that nightly assail the last human left alive in shambling, ineffective crowds. Sure, Romero's brain was crammed with the undead from a thousand EC Comics he had read as a child, and

Night of the Living Dead (1968).

he had watched the progressive multiplication of zombies revenging themselves on mad scientists in the 1950s B-movie cycle. But it was only when Romero was persuaded to return to the same scenario ten years later that this became a sequence of zombie films. *Dawn of the Dead* also assiduously avoids the 'z' word, but was released as *Zombies* in Britain and *Zombi* in Italy and elsewhere. It was a global hit and raised the legion of imitators that just keeps on coming. It was only retrospectively, then, that *Night* became a zombie film – indeed, one of the single most transformative texts in the entire history of the zombie figure.

Like most influential films, the impact of *Night* was entirely unforeseen. It was produced by a group of industry outsiders in Pittsburgh, funded by a group of ten friends in the advertising business who kicked in start-up funds (the film was eventually made for $114,000). Pittsburgh was a long way even beyond the low-budget independent outfits like American International Pictures, home to Roger Corman's atomic monsters or florid Poe adaptations. This group was entirely off the map. Romero only gradually emerged as the director and others ended up taking the key acting roles in a project that they gave the dismissive working title of *Monster Flick*. It was an accident, they always say, that the main role of Ben was played by black postgraduate student Duane Jones – he was simply the most accomplished actor among a bunch of mostly amateurs. It was significant, though, that this team were professionals who owned their own film equipment: it was shot cheaply on black-and-white film at night and on weekends, but Romero had the time to edit and synch the sound to polished levels. Its highly accomplished, frenzied montage contributed to its impressive visceral effect.

Nevertheless, the crew kept the references very local to South Pennsylvania because they figured that in the worst case they could at least sell to local drive-ins and recoup some costs there. The finished film was shown to the distributors Continental Releasing in brutal times, the day after Robert Kennedy had been assassinated live on TV. Continental were marginal players, with a reputation for arty and controversial films, and they took the film on. They retitled it *Night of the Living Dead*, but in doing so forgot to add a copyright declaration at the beginning of the movie, meaning that Romero and his crew would for years see very little money from making such

The first attack, *Night of the Living Dead*.

a seminal film (this was why many of the same team gathered to remake the film in 1990). It is oddly appropriate that this film was effectively public property from the start, given that it seemed to have a direct channel into the collective unconscious.

On its first release, *Variety* considered that 'This film casts serious aspersions on the integrity of its makers ... and the moral health of filmgoers who cheerfully opt for unrelieved sadism.'[1] Notoriously, booked unseen, it was shown on Fridays and then repeated in the Saturday matinee slot for kids, where it was watched by the appalled critic Roger Ebert, surrounded by traumatized children with nothing to 'protect themselves from the dread and the fear they felt'.[2] With this kind of reputation, it began to achieve note across bewilderingly diverse audiences. It was shown in inner-city neighbourhood theatres in double bills that were often targeted at black audiences by being paired with *Slaves*, Herbert Biberman's 1969 historical drama about an 1850s slave revolt. It featured in city grindhouses but also became one of the first cult 'Midnight Movies' shown at the countercultural Waverly cinema in Greenwich Village to students and radicals. In 1970, it was dragged out of the exploitation circuit and showcased in the first film slot in the august precincts of the Museum of Modern Art in New York. The cultural temper of the times was to 'cross the border – close the gap' between high and low art. *Night* was the exploitation movie that was claimed by the political avant-garde. This was radical outsider art: cutting edge 'art-horror', sticking it to The Man.[3]

Night retains many of the crucial historical resonances of the Haitian *zombi* and American culture's post-war massification of the zombie. Yet it deserves its reputation as an epochal film. Romero crystallized, with mythic simplicity, the plot formula that was the logical conclusion to all this massing of the undead: the narrative of what we now call the *zombie apocalypse*. The film follows a relentless path from the open spaces of the hillside cemetery and Johnny's mocking mastery of all he surveys down to the cramped confines and utter dethronement of all human value in the basement of a boarded-up farmhouse. Johnny's disdain for the empty ritual of paying respect to the dead father marks a generational shift, no less

Building the Last Redoubt, *Night of the Living Dead.*

than his mockery of decades of domesticated horror by imitating Boris Karloff in the most famous line of the film: 'They're coming to get you, Barbara.' Barbara's catatonic reaction to her brother's sudden, vicious death and her headlong flight through bland fields and trees hints at raw emotional states uncontained by routine movie melodrama. What you want from a horror film is a dangerous sense that rules will be broken. *Night's* toxic celluloid clattered through the gate like there were no rules at all.

The film makes the farmhouse, the Last Redoubt of the handful of survivors, a place of bitter quarrel, murderous infighting and stupid escape plans that steadily deplete the last remaining human resources. Race tensions flare: the white paterfamilias Harry Cooper itches to shoot Ben, the uppity black boy. In a truly incendiary moment, it is Ben who shoots Harry – and with evident pleasure. This was in the year when riots broke out after the assassination of Martin Luther King, and the Black Panther Eldridge Cleaver composed the essay 'Requiem for Nonviolence'. 'That there is a holocaust coming I have no doubt at all', Cleaver said. 'The violent phase of the black liberation struggle is here, and it will spread. From that shot, from that blood, America will be painted red.'[4] Following the escalation of the Vietnam War in early 1968, and a major extension of the draft, students too were turning to violent revolutionary tactics – in France, in Mexico and around the world. American student radicals would turn to violence modelled on an understanding of its revolutionary necessity to overthrow imperial power, as outlined in the writings of Frantz Fanon, the Black Panthers and others. They staged 'Days of Rage' and three of the Weather Underground terrorist group blew themselves up in a Greenwich Village bomb-making factory in 1970, not far from the Waverly. Stalinism offered little hope either: Soviet tanks crushed the Prague Spring in the late summer. The radical filmmaker Chris Marker always suggested that 1967 was the really revolutionary year: 1968 was the curdling of those hopes.[5]

In *Night*, courage, love and sacrifice – all the noble human virtues – are stamped on and destroyed. Tom and Judy, the teenage couple who would have foiled the dastardly plan in cahoots with benign cops ten years earlier in *Teenage Zombies*, are killed by a stupid mistake by Ben, the ostensible 'hero' of the film. Love does

Engulfment, *Night of the Living Dead*.

not conquer all; it gets you fried in a jalopy. In the next scene, *Night* takes the vengeful dead from EC Comics and re-injects them with all the cannibalistic terror that underwrote colonial fantasy. There is no coy turning away from what the ghouls devour: a group sups on ropes of intestines pulled from the fried corpses, while another contemplatively eats a finger-licking good severed hand. Ben Hervey's excellent examination of *Night* is right to suggest that this ghastly aftermath scene has been 'the single biggest influence on a new strain of horror film: the "splatter" or gore film, the "meat movie".'[6] The Last Redoubt is the model of the fragile ego, menaced from without, but every zombie film after *Night* will incorporate a scene of a literal breaking open of the 'skin-ego', the ruination of bodies opened by frenzied crowds of ghouls. After *Night*, all zombies seem solely motivated to devour the living without purpose, to turn the world into an undifferentiated mass of deadened sameness.

Family will not save you either. The basement is where, finally, the family unit will spectacularly turn on and devour itself. The Coopers have been nursing their stricken daughter Karen down there. The fatally wounded Harry Cooper stumps down the steps into the arms of his reanimated daughter. She is discovered moments later munching on the severed arm of her father, and advances on her mother to stab her an unblinking fourteen times. At a young age, Romero had worked on the set of *North by Northwest* (1959), one of Hitchcock's many weird reflections on stifling mother love. *Night*'s explicit slasher scene sets out to show everything hidden in the cuts of *Psycho*'s frantic murder montage just eight years before.

In the end, Ben's cack-handed carpentry constitutes no defence against what Elliott Stein called 'a symphony of psychotic hands' that push through the windows and doors (something Romero borrowed from Polanski's vision of schizophrenia in *Repulsion*, from 1965).[7] This is the spectacle of the final engulfment of the living by the dead, another major influence on the development of the genre, a scene opened out from *The Last Man on Earth*. Barbara is shocked out of her own zombified traumatic state to fight briefly before she spies her brother Johnny among the crowd, come back to get her. Hadn't she denied him candy in the first scene? Now his hunger has

The cannibal feast, *Night of the Living Dead.*

become incestuous, insatiable. Her surrender to him and to the horde tips the balance from horror to a kind of willing masochistic ecstasy of release. It makes *Night* the purest form of kinetic cinema, at least according to Steven Shaviro: 'All cinema tends away from the coagulation of meaning and toward the shattering dispossession of the spectator.'[8] Romero's zombie cinema exemplifies this insight, the thrillingly perverse thirst for annihilation. It was *meant* to sound pompous and jarring when one of the leading film critics of the day, Robin Wood, dared to suggest that the progressive but disordered horror films like *Night* and *The Texas Chain Saw Massacre* (1974) had the 'force of authentic art' in their rigorous nihilism.[9] This was a grand, transgressive statement to make at the time: these nasties mostly subsisted in a world far beyond the taste of the cinéaste.

Night also has a rigorously bleak coda, with a bitter EC Comics twist, that sets off yet more political firecrackers in an era of revolutionary violence. The screen frames a comically banal television interview by actual Pennsylvania TV star Bill 'Chilly Billy' Cardille with a redneck sheriff leading a posse. The report is designed to

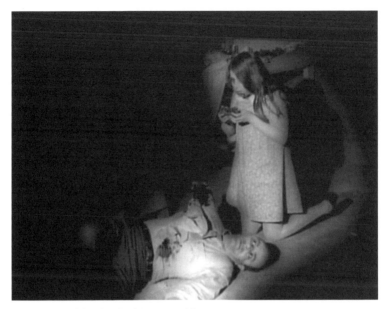

The family devours itself, *Night of the Living Dead.*

parody the bland propagandistic news reports on 'Search and Destroy' missions in Vietnam (even down to the 'kill' statistics at the end), but it also drips with segregation iconography, and Romero used local groups of hunters who brought their own guns for these scenes. This irregular company or lynch mob is on a mission to clear the territory of the undead, offered in the calm tones of a mopping-up exercise after the crisis has passed. They move across the fields in a ragged line seen from a helicopter, deliberately meant to echo the ambling beings they pursue. The increasingly declarative message of Romero's film sequence will be: the zombies are us.

At the farmhouse, they calmly target and shoot the last living survivor, Ben, as he clambers out of the basement. Survival has been an epic struggle; it is cast away worthlessly. They drag his body out of the rubble with meat hooks to burn it on the fire. This is done over the closing titles in still images, photographs explicitly used to echo the photos of murdered blacks that were often taken by lynch mobs and circulated as mementos. The survivor of a 1930 lynching remembered seeing his two friends, torn and bleeding, hanging from the trees: 'they vied with one another to have their pictures taken alongside the tree.' He was up next, for a crowd driven crazy by bloodlust: 'I was already dead', he thought.[10] Imagine how this scene played alongside *Slaves* in black neighbourhoods, or among an anti-war movement on the verge of advocating violent resistance to the militarized state. The National Guard started gunning down students at Kent State University in May 1970.

The meaning of this closing scene therefore kept changing, in lock step with the bitter end of the 1960s. By the time it was a Midnight Movie in Greenwich Village, these images now evoked the mass slaughter perpetrated by American troops in Vietnam. The scandal of the My Lai village massacre, when up to 504 unarmed civilians were killed by u.s. infantry, was exposed after a year of denials when Ronald Haeberle's reel of colour photographs surfaced in November 1969. Images of the massacred dead were constantly circulated by the anti-war movement for the next few years. At the time *Night* was released, the Pittsburgher Tom Savini, who would become the legendary special effects maestro for *Dawn of the Dead* and beyond, was in Vietnam as a combat photographer, recording damaged battlefield bodies. There was no 'subtext' here for him, or for many of Romero's crew: the war spills out on screen in the lurid guts. For every viewer since, though, the last scenes of *Night* rendered explicit the explosive *allegorical* potential of the zombie trope for commentary on the contemporary world.

While Romero's outsider status gave kudos to the countercultural force of *Night*, he has struggled throughout his career to find a stable way of making films within the studios and on their margins. A couple of non-horror films failed in the early 1970s, while other filmmakers explored the allegorical potential of the undead ghoul. Bob Clark's *Deathdream* (aka *Dead of Night*, 1974) featured an undead Vietnam veteran returning to prey on his family, in a mode somewhere between vampirism and zombiedom. The criminally overlooked *Messiah of Evil* (1973) by Willard Huyck and Gloria Katz continued that strange fusion of art-house existential angst and low-budget horror. This film has unnerving scenes of shopping malls abandoned and empty but for the crowds of fiends cramming raw meat into their mouths at the deli counter. It explains little or nothing in scenes disordered by dream logic, and is all the better for it. The Europeans, as we shall see shortly, took *Night of the Living Dead* to be a serious political film, and cooked up an entire sub-genre of considerably more dubious political intent. Romero's *The Crazies* (1973) should be considered integral to his zombie sequence, not just because the anti-statist, anti-military satire becomes broader and much cruder in this film, much more hectoring, but because the ghouls are driven to murderous frenzy by the accidental leakage of a germ warfare virus, inexpertly covered up by the secret state. Romero sketches out the script for a million bio-medical horror imitations.

The Crazies directs the same poisonous energy at paternal authority (fathers are everywhere psychotic and rapine), with the iron chain of military hierarchy receiving the most contempt. The antidote for the outbreak is found, but lost in the bureaucratic parameters of the secret state, bent on containing the flow of information. The President is briefed to prepare a hygienic nuclear strike: slowly but surely, normalcy and lunacy switch places. *The Crazies* also develops Romero's signature buzz of confused and competing voices that overlap on the soundtrack, from TV, from radio, from the phalanx of talking heads and advisers – a welter of noise that is his figure for the last days of the public sphere in America. It features again in the radio talk show discussions that bombard the audience through his very fine revisionist vampire film, *Martin* (1977). The chaotic vision of the public sphere intensifies throughout the zombie series, but finds its first and strongest articulation in *Dawn of the Dead* (1978).

Dawn was a hybrid American-European production, mainly because Romero absolutely resisted compromise with potential backers, refusing to consider delivering a tame 'Restricted' rated film, pinning his oppositional principles to an 'Unrated' shocker. The film was therefore part-funded by Italian horror producers, who agreed to part-finance the film on the understanding that it would be chopped up and fed to the Eurotrash exploitation markets. It was recut for the Italian market by the Italian horror maestro Dario Argento, who greatly admired Romero's *Martin*. As a result of this financing, the Italian *Zombi 2* appeared only a matter of months after Romero's renamed *Zombi* was released. *Dawn* was made for a low-rent $650,000 but made an estimated $55 million across the world. The film is an odd mix: a one-off that was far more important than *Night* in establishing the whole genre of the zombie apocalypse in modern cinema, and a movie that wears its politically progressive satirical aims openly on its sleeve, but also boils with crudely regressive tendencies that ultimately disable much chance of social critique.

Dawn begins in the utter chaos of a TV studio, competing talking heads shouting contradictory theories about the murderous outbreaks in the city. The confident containment at the end of *Night* has not worked: the strange contagion has spread. The TV director (played by Romero himself) is unable to control the disputes in the studio. Meanwhile, troops seek to concentrate potentially infected populations – Hispanic and black slum-dwellers – trying to flush them out of tenements as the dead reanimate. It is another explosive racial representation of civic disorder. There is no meaningful rational discourse on display anywhere, only suicidal strategies and murderous disagreements. Out of this chaos, four people escape in a helicopter, including a pregnant woman, Fran, and a black soldier, Peter. Fran makes up for the passive or catatonic women of *Night*, and the series henceforth contains strong female survivors.

The next last redoubt: the shopping mall, *Dawn of the Dead* (1978).

Zombies go shopping, *Dawn of the Dead*.

This group eventually makes it to the Monroeville shopping mall east of Pittsburgh. The mall was one of the first self-enclosed suburban shopping centres completed in America: it becomes this film's last redoubt for the survivors. As always, their survival strategies prove pretty stupid; avarice and boredom invite the inevitable invasion from nihilistic bikers who only bring the zombies back in behind them, wrecking the defences. The film was scripted to end with the zombie horde closing in on Peter and Fran; Peter was to turn the gun on himself, Fran to decapitate herself on the helicopter blades. This nihilistic end was rewritten with a tiny loophole: Fran and Peter taking off to seek yet another last redoubt, left unseen and perhaps unimaginable amid these last scenes of engulfment.

Dawn is the central film for cultural critics to declare that the zombie is a 'capitalist monster', the exemplary figure of late capital's invasion of every last public space, a contagion that speeds through the body politic and 'turns' every last consciousness into zombified slavery. Robin Wood long ago offered this reading in his Freudian Marxist advocacy of the radicalism of 1970s horror, but Romero has remained the poster boy for progressive readings up to the present day, the last bearer of a flame amid the darkness of vacuous American horror.[11] The zombie, after the 2008 global financial crash, has been declared 'the official monster of the recession', the image of the

Overrun again, *Dawn of the Dead*.

suckered global poor.[12] All of these readings are ultimately rooted in the heavy-handed satire of *Dawn*'s shopping mall sequences, when the muzak, fountains and escalators are turned back on and the dumb zombies totter around the shops in a shambolic instinctual repetition of ingrained habit. This sequence is played for laughs under harsh strip lights, no longer for terror in the chiaroscuro of a dank basement. 'This was an important place in their lives', Peter muses, looking down on the zombie hordes from the mall's roof. 'They're not after us. They're after *the place*.'

This reading of *Dawn* is hardly the unearthing of a brilliant ideological subtext: it is openly avowed on the surface of the text. For a progressive critic, the film is often just a narcissistic mirror. But aside from nudging out of the picture the complex colonial history of the zombie, it is also important to recognize how the film's critique of consumption is thoroughly part of its historical moment – and necessarily limited by it. The post-'68 analysis of the containment of youth revolt was that the era rapidly looked less like a revolution and more 'profoundly adaptive to the system's productive base', a disruptive seizure in the West's shift from a production to a consumption economy.[13] This was the 'Society of the Spectacle', Guy Debord's pessimistic pronouncement on a new level of extension of capital in everyday life, a book that first appeared in

1968. Perhaps this is what the bikers, the third term between humans and zombies, are meant to represent in *Dawn* – the emergence of adaptive possessive individualism with a nihilistic edge rather than any collective opposition. They are not easy riders, but post-Altamont Hell's Angels, here to bring the world to an end.

The Pittsburgh area, which Romero's zombie films always heavily reference, felt this economic transition particularly keenly. Pittsburgh had been the centre of America's steel industry, with Andrew Carnegie's mill towns built around the regional centre in the late nineteenth century. Job losses and closures began dramatically in the early 1960s and were finally completed in the vicious union-breaking struggles of the '80s, leaving de-industrialized ghost towns and vast populations of the structurally unemployed. Romero made the melancholic post-industrial wreck of the town of Braddock a key part of *Martin*'s demystification of the vampire, and one of his key collaborators, Tony Buba, has made a number of documentaries on the industrial decline of the Pittsburgh area. With neat circularity, the local union activist Carol Bernick said in 1991: 'Braddock is like the land that time forgot. It looks like somebody just bombed it and didn't clean it up . . . People look like zombies.'[14] The rise of shopping malls in de-industrialized areas is the starkest emblem of a shift from Fordist production to low-wage, de-skilled service industries floating on the whims of international capital.

This is a powerful undertow in *Dawn*, but there remains something problematically smug about the subject position the film invites the viewer to adopt: by definition, *you* are not a zombie, *you* are not fooled by this ideological mystification or a part of this mindless mass, *you* can resist this interpellation into the casino of consumption capitalism. Romero's view of the shopping mall masses echoes Vance Packard's *The Hidden Persuaders* (1957), where the immersive, soporific world of the shopping centre lures the off-guard and unsuspecting into consumption. Cultural theorists still talked about malls as zones of mass *distraction* into the 1990s, dreamworlds of capitalism, from which to awake required the jolt of radical critique.[15] For all the assertion that Romero's message is 'the zombies are us', this mode of survival horror often flatters the

Opening nightmare, *Day of the Dead* (1985).

exceptionalism of its audience, reinforcing a sense that it is possible, with the appropriate exercise of cynical reason, to see behind and demystify 'false consciousness' and stay humanly alive.[16] Yet this is a very 1970s stance on ideology critique.

There is considerably less optimism on display in Romero's third film, *Day of the Dead* (1985), a darker and even more despairing vision in which the zombie apocalypse is presumed to have spread virtually everywhere. Romero made the film with Laurel Entertainment, a production company set up with the express aim of capitalizing on the economic success of *Dawn* by producing another sequel. By 1984, however, Romero had done poorly with *Knightriders* (1981) and *Creepshow*, and his backers declined to fund his epic vision for *Day*, particularly as he once again refused to deliver a Restricted certificate film, holding out for an Unrated. The decision cut the budget in half and the film was scaled back to a gruesome ensemble piece, dominated by Tom Savini's gory special effects and largely filmed underground in a disused cement mine and a decommissioned missile silo site in East Pittsburgh. In the culturally conservative 1980s, and in the wake of 'Video Nasty' panics, the circulation of *Day* was limited and eclipsed that year by the comic rendition of the zombie trope by another EC Comics nut, Dan O'Bannon, in *Return of the Living Dead* (1985).[17]

Day markedly shifts the sympathy towards the undead, who are pacified and corralled in a secret research centre like concentration-camp prisoners, where they are experimented upon by a mad scientist protected by a much diminished military guard. Dr Logan's vicious vivisections and his arguments with the murderous brutes that protect him leave no doubt as to who are the lower species in these last days of the contagion. The central figure of *Day* is the zombie Bub, who appears to show 'the bare beginnings of social behaviour', being trained painfully slowly by Logan to recover simple actions: shaving, saluting, picking up a Stephen King novel. His military commander thinks only in genocidal terms, though, and Logan's conception of the human is such an impoverished form of behavioural training that it takes only a little more zombie 'development' to overthrow their masters. We last see Bub remembering how to use a gun and leaving the military commander Rhodes fatally wounded, doomed to be pulled apart and eaten.

The film repeats the same basic trajectory: the last redoubt, accelerating dissent and disorder, the final breach, engulfment, a cannibalistic feeding frenzy and another final loophole escape. Romero's marginals are this time a woman, a Jamaican pilot and an Irish engineer, who escape the implosion of the military-industrial

Teaching the zombie Bub, *Day of the Dead*.

complex in a helicopter. In the last shot of the film we see them on an island beach, perhaps the very Caribbean island the pilot had long pressed for as an escape plan. It is another stub of utopian possibility, although ironically on the islands where the notion of the zombie first emerged.

A trilogy has a certain formal elegance, and Romero left this sequence alone for nearly twenty years – many of those outside the business entirely – before he compromised with financiers on *Land of the Dead* (2005) and produced an 'R'-rated film with a bankable star (Dennis Hopper). Romero returned on the wave of the zombie apocalypse genre he had started: he was backed because of the box-office success of Zack Snyder's 2004 *Dawn of the Dead* remake. In *Land*, zombie education has now progressed to a rudimentary political intelligence: 'they're learning how to work together'. 'Big Daddy', a zombified black garage mechanic, grasps the nature of their servitude and leads the masses on a march to target their exploitative human masters, now holed up in a luxury mall where all of America's class inequalities have been preserved intact. The iconography of the film happened to resonate uncannily with the Katrina disaster in New Orleans that took place in the year of the film's release. A column of dispossessed poor and black zombies wade through swamp waters towards the human zone of privilege, seen rising above the flood plain. There are distant echoes of the Black Jacobins in this image. This context invested the film with a punchy contemporaneity, as a commentary on the Republican administration's indifference to the fate of poor black populations: Romero has said that Hopper's character was based on Donald Rumsfeld, then Secretary of Defense in George Bush Jr's team. It is also a significant echo of the roots of the zombie in slavery, figuring the dispossessed as 'proletarian pariahs' who 'make visible a phantom history'.[18] As ever, the last redoubt is overrun, the privileged engulfed. The only possibility of human survival is seen across the border in Canada.

Romero has since made two very low-budget late additions to the series, digital technology making it possible to return to the smaller-scale, more guerrilla productions of his youth. *Diary of the*

The horde overruns the Last Redoubt again, *Day of the Dead*.

Dead (2007) swings back to a focus on media addiction to atrocity, abandoning any interest in the zombies themselves. It is a film that seems caught up in an odd self-loathing about violence and the compulsion to repeat, centred as it is on a filmmaker unable to stop filming the disaster as his hokey horror film turns into documentary. 'All that's left is to record', he says, even unto his own death. Although there is some human organization (notably among urban blacks long prepared for survival), the film ends on the last survivors shutting themselves in a panic room: there is no possibility of getting out here, only a shutting in. 'Are we worth saving?' the female narrator asks over the last seconds of footage that again echo the worst images of lynch mobs in the series since the end of *Night*; 'You tell me.' Robin Wood thinks we are meant to answer this last question with a resounding Yes; I am not so sure.[19] *Survival of the Dead* (2009) finally situates a drama on that long-imagined island retreat, but only to re-tread *Day*'s exploration of the doomed possibility of teaching zombies to make an accommodation with human survivors. This time, the film ends on an image of two feuding islanders, each now dead, staggering back into undead life to recommence their gun battle, firing empty barrels at each other, presumably for the rest of time, or until their bodies rot away. It is a bitter last image: zombies learn, but only enough to reduce human stupidity to its purest form.

Romero's transformation of the zombie narrative from a marginal horror into a dominant cultural trope has been so influential, I think because it ultimately fuses with the post-war revival of Protestant millenarian thought in America. Although the American state was of course founded by millenarians hoping to establish the New Jerusalem as the last redoubt against a sinful, fallen Europe, the contemporary revival of eschatological thinking has been striking since the success of Hal Lindsey's *The Late Great Planet Earth* (1970). Eschatology has been a presence in national discourse since the late 1960s, Paul Boyer claims, exactly coincident with the production of *Night of the Living Dead*.[20] Romero is not religious (the film *Martin* is Romero at his most staunchly anti-Catholic), but this has not stopped his notion of the zombie apocalypse cross-fertilizing with notions from the Book of Revelation to make a prophetic record of the end times. For many believers, contemporary history is an unfolding apocalypse, the final 'unveiling' of truth, the Last Judgement, and the Rapture is only just around the corner. Certainly, Romero's zombie films have been appropriated by Christian thinkers: in *Gospel of the Living Dead* (2006), Kim Paffenroth asserts his belief that the films 'vividly show the state of damnation of human life without the divine gift of reason'.[21] From a menaced farmhouse in rural Pennsylvania, Romero hatched a plot that fed into these visions of global apocalypse.

The most interesting critique to emerge from Romero's film cycle is his meditation on the nature of the public sphere. In 1962 the German sociologist Jürgen Habermas published his influential study *The Structural Transformation of the Public Sphere*, in which he argued that his idealized model of an enlightened public arena of rational and inclusive debate, established with the modern bourgeois state in the eighteenth century, had been put progressively under pressure by the interference of states and a fracturing of the public into disputatious and irreconcilable voices, prompted by the proliferation of media and communications. In many ways, Romero's films track this collapse of the public sphere in America: by racial division in *Night*, consumerism in *Dawn*, the militarized state in *The Crazies* and *Day*, and by a self-cannibalizing, disputatious media culture in *Dawn* and particularly in *Diary*. Habermas, a cultural conservative, blames crass popular culture as one cause of a debased public discourse. But Romero displays just how eloquent Gothic devices can be for exploring precisely these concerns, even being able to develop a critical *counter*-public discourse. The perpetual disputes in the last redoubt mark the end of a cohesive public sphere, while engulfment by the zombie mass becomes a dramatization of its mute and deathly embrace, yet each loophole escape signals the fugitive chances of a counter public sphere, a different way of living. Romero's series, over 40 years, has become a monumental study of the structural zombification of the American public sphere.[22]

But it is important to emphasize that the series was never simply or straightforwardly 'American'. *Night of the Living Dead* took key inspiration from the Italian Ubaldo Ragona's *The Last Man on Earth*. In turn, the scenes of cannibal feeding in *Night* inspired a whole sequence of European horror films, from Amando de Ossorio's *Tombs of the Blind Dead* (1971) and its several sequels, to Jorge Grau's Spanish-Italian co-production *The Living Dead at Manchester Morgue* (1974), all of which elaborated on the zombie as the relentless and insatiable ghoul, dedicated solely to eating the flesh of the living. Grau's film, which improbably unleashed a horde of living-dead Italian character actors in the streets of Manchester and the Lake District (although the actual locations were Sheffield and the Peak District), used vivid Technicolor to pause lovingly on the entrails and dismembered limbs of their victims. There is a persuasive argument that both Ossorio and Grau saw the allegorical potential of Romero's revision of the zombie and used it as a commentary on the 'living dead' Fascist dictator of Spain, General Franco, then living out his final deathly years in power.[23] Certainly, Grau staged a generational conflict between the hippy male hero George and the repressive police sergeant who guns him down with evident relish, proclaiming 'I wish the dead *could* come back to life, you bastard, because then I could kill you again.' Having sounded off about the permissive society and all these long-haired dead dudes, Sergeant McCormick is duly revisited by George's reanimated corpse and polished off. The revolutionary spirit will come back and bite you.

In turn, these films directly influenced the look and explicit gore of Romero's *Dawn of the Dead*, which was released first in Italy as *Zombi* in 1979. As an immensely successful *Italian* film, *Dawn* became the start of a cycle of films in Italy that are among the most notorious films ever made.

Zombie Apocalypses and Cannibal Holocausts: The Italian Recipe

Horror film production in Italy is one example of what is called *filone* filmmaking. A major cinematic success produced a 'stream' of remakes, imitations, off-shoots and unofficial sequels.²⁴ These were made cheaply and often pre-sold for distribution, making modest profits before films even went into production (hence the studios being rather uninterested in the quality of the finished films, which were hacked up and re-edited for different tastes and the censorship schemes of different national markets). Horror boomed with the *giallo*, the precursor of the serial killer/slasher film, after Mario Bava's bravura shocker, *Blood and Black Lace* (1964), and cresting with Dario Argento's delirious and perverse wonders that started with *The Bird with the Crystal Plumage* (1969) and its many follow-ups. Argento reached the heights of Grand Guignol and stylized supernatural horror with *Deep Red* (*Profondo Rosso*, 1975) and *Suspiria* (1977). Often gloriously uninterested in narrative or logic, these films cross unblinking gore with art-house Surrealism, moving from one spectacularly staged death to another.

These achievements were always surrounded by a vast swirl of opportunistic, gratuitous and unoriginal knock-offs. Nevertheless, in England and America, where film censorship was tighter, the whole genre was given the patina of transgressive promise, fans desperate to see clandestine 'uncut' versions. These became briefly available in the early 1980s with the arrival of video distribution, which was initially left outside the purview of the British Board of Film Censorship, but the 'video nasty' panic of 1984, which focused overwhelmingly on these Italian horror films, ended this access, legally at least, under the Video Recordings Act of 1984. As always, censorship only rarefied the value of the worthless product they withheld. Perhaps recognizing this paradoxical effect, the films were quietly returned to distribution, almost entirely uncensored, with DVD releases in the 1990s. 'Previously Banned!', the covers now plaintively say, surfing on nostalgia.

The large profits associated with *Zombi/Dawn of the Dead* destined its Italian co-producers and their rivals to foster a cluster of immediate zombie sequels and imitations. Lucio Fulci's *Zombi 2* (1979, released in England as *Zombie Flesh Eaters*) proved massively successful too, and resulted in Fulci's return for the diminishing returns (in every sense) of *Zombi 3* (1987). This disaster was probably topped by Claudio Fragasso's *Zombi 4: After Death* (1989). But Romero's revisioning of the zombie as a cannibal meant that the zombie film fused with another Italian *filone*, of horror films set in distant jungles where all tribes are deemed savage and bent on devouring their white explorers. There were many films that followed in the wake of Umberto Lenzi's *Deep River Savages* (1972), culminating in the controversy surrounding Ruggero Deodato's notorious *Cannibal Holocaust* (1980), which was banned for three years in Italy while it was investigated whether the director had actually murdered his actors. This Italian conjuncture reconstituted the historic link in colonial fantasy between the cannibal and the zombie, just as Romero was redirecting the zombie trope elsewhere, so we need to see these genres in tandem.

In *Zombi 2*, or *Zombie Flesh Eaters*, the journalist Peter West accompanies a woman to the Antilles, where she is searching for her missing father. His boat has arrived empty and abandoned in the river off Staten Island in New York, pitching up like the mysterious *Demeter* in *Dracula*, and with its own bloated undead creature on board who slips into the waters, having bitten a coastguard. Peter and Anne eventually arrive on the uncharted island of Matul, the home of white-suited Dr Menard (shades of H. G. Wells's *The Island of Dr Moreau*), where either a strange plague is killing off the last of the whites and the villagers, or else Voodoo magic is reviving the recently deceased who are compelled, in their relentless shuffling way, to take large chunks of flesh out of the nearest living human being. These zombies are no longer trained for labour in the fields, and the film has no interest in portraying the *bokor* witch-doctors that might have commanded them – no interest, indeed, in any local culture at all. The zombies shuffle purposelessly through the ruined and abandoned village, abstracted figures of failed post-colonial development. To stay their advance, gruesome damage to the head is very necessary and carefully depicted: bullets to the body do nothing. The plague escalates. The zombies feast lovingly on gushing jugulars and opened torsos, depicted by special effects ace Giannetto De Rossi. The survivors stagger through a jungle only to find themselves in the midst of an old cemetery of the irritated corpses of Spanish conquistadors dragging themselves from the earth after 400 years. The survivors retreat to the last redoubt but are soon depleted and overrun. Peter and Anne finally escape on a boat, only to hear on the radio that the dead are returning to life in New York. The film ends with a famous image of a vast horde of the dead processing across the Brooklyn Bridge towards Manhattan, with the World Trade Center and the end of advanced civilization looming in the background.

The plot is unusually coherent for the director and the genre. Fulci went on to complete an informal 'zombie' trilogy with *City of the Living Dead* (1980) and *The Beyond* (1981). *The Beyond* in particular is a memorably deranged accumulation of brutal set-piece deaths, built around a vaguely Lovecraftian idea of one of the Gates of Hell being opened under a hotel in Louisiana, old school 'hoodoo'

Zombies return in Lucio Fulci's *Zombie Flesh Eaters* (aka *Zombi 2*, 1979).

Zombies take Manhattan, *Zombie Flesh Eaters.*

style. One set-piece involves an unnerving sequence in a hospital morgue, as autopsied bodies begin to revive. Shrugging off any criticism, Fulci said: 'my idea was to make an absolute film ... there's no logic to it, just a succession of images.'[25] Presumably this is why *The Beyond* involves a good five minutes devoted to tarantulas biting the face off a man in a library. And another scene in which a vat of acid dissolves the head of a woman, her daughter stepping back from the froth of blood spreading across the tiled floor. These scenes clearly try to up the ante on Romero's injunction not to look away. It is no wonder Fulci (following Argento) is so obsessed with portraying damage to the eye. The most notorious moment in *Zombie Flesh Eaters* – the one that got the film listed as a banned 'video nasty' – is the death of Mrs Menard, skewered through the eye on a splint of wood, shown in unflinching detail in a crazed homage to the razor and eyeball in Salvador Dalí and Luis Buñuel's Surrealist film *Un chien andalou* (1929). You will see so much, the scene seems to say, that what you see will blind you.

Deodato's *Cannibal Holocaust* is even more graphic than this, although formally quite accomplished and artfully designed. The film is a nasty trick in trying to persuade the viewer they are watching 'actual' atrocity footage, a sleight of hand many Italian lawyers and judges fell for (it turns out that legal training does not cover simple techniques of montage). The film grows out of the so-called 'Mondo' genre, named after the Italian pseudo-documentary *Mondo*

Bad news in the morgue: *The Beyond* (1981).

Cane (1962), which purports to be exotic travelogue footage of shocking cultural customs and lots of gratuitous nudity from around the world. Many films followed in the same mode, echoing the American tradition we've already explored in relation to Voodoo films in the 1920s and '30s. In *Cannibal Holocaust*, an anthropology professor is persuaded by a New York TV company to retrace the steps of a film crew of four whites who vanished after going into the heart of the Amazon in search of the elusive cannibal tribe the Yanomamo. Professor Monroe eventually finds the eviscerated and ritually displayed remains of the crew, decorated with film canisters. What is in the canisters, which we see as raw and unedited footage continually interrupted by revolted viewers in a New York viewing room, is a shocking tale of violence and degradation as the film crew desecrate, rape and pillage their way through the jungle. They are out to provoke a response that they can offer as primitive savagery, only to end up filming their own evisceration, death and devouring. As with zombie films, the footage captures heads bludgeoned, torsos opened, bodies brutalized, raped and castrated in a rhythm of increasing intensity.

Cannibal Holocaust is clearly meant as a heavy-handed satire on sensational 'Mondo' filmmaking, the rapacity of TV companies seeking 'authentic' horror, and the desire of certain viewers for 'real' snuff movies. *Cannibal Holocaust*'s bad faith problem is that it wants to offer all these sensational delights while finger-wagging at the same time. Others went on to try to outdo the gross-out levels of carnage: Umberto Lenzi's *Cannibal Ferox* (1981) is a film with an equally gruesome reputation. Very rapidly, these two genres fused together in titles like *Zombi Holocaust* or *Zombie Creeping Flesh* (both 1980) to produce a frenzy of exotic zombie cannibal excesses for several years in the 1980s, all given transgressive allure by heavy censorship or outright bans. Precisely because these remain deliberately abject and tasteless films, it has been left to fans to catalogue and document the extent of the genre.[26]

This *cinema vomitif* is of course designed to be disgusting. Disgust is an involuntary physical recoil from things that pollute or contaminate, that leak or ooze, breaching borders policed by powerful taboo. Disgust is 'precisely the emotion that is meant to guard the sanctity of the soul as well as the purity of the body'.[27] As the anthropologist Mary Douglas observed in *Purity and Danger*, some of the strongest taboos surround the recently dead, who must be transported between the rigorously divided worlds of the living and the dead through rituals that manage this fraught transition.

Back in 'cannibal' country, *Cannibal Holocaust* (1980).

Horror and disgust surge around bodies that fall out of ritual place, that are desecrated or defiled. Italian zombie cinema pushes relentlessly on these taboos, the dead biting and breaking open the skin of the living, delightedly pulling the insides out. That this must be compulsively represented is not just a matter of the economics of horror genre filmmaking; it also implies that the films do the cultural work of registering traumas around breached bodily boundaries by continually restaging them.

The problem with disgust is that it cannot sustain an aesthetics. Long ago, the philosopher Immanuel Kant argued that 'disgusting objects present themselves to the imagination with an inescapable immediacy that prevents the conversion of the disgusting into something discernably artistic and aesthetically valuable.'[28] What this means is that films exploring the abject find it difficult to be anything but abjected themselves – as happened with the 'video nasty' moral panic. Whatever the varied ambitions of these films, Italian horror made the zombie an emblem of wallowing in the disgusting and the tabooed. They became the nadir of mass cultural ooze, zombies that zombified their corrupted audiences: the zombie squared.

There are always defences for this phase of zombie culture. What Jeffrey Sconce has called the 'paracinema', which delights in an existence beyond the safe bounds of bourgeois taste, is still, after all, cinema, and always open to cultural reading.[29] Others have argued that Eurotrash genres like Italian horror – films so bad they become avant-garde critiques of cinema itself – can create a Brechtian 'vulgar modernism' or pulse with 'trash vitality' that get their kick exactly by refusing the boundaries of good taste and proportion in art.[30] For Patricia MacCormack, there is a radical liberation in the 'ecstatic excess beyond the need for narrative or comprehensible pleasure' in these films, which opens up a 'cinesexuality' far beyond standard accounts of trauma or loss, because the pleasure is located precisely in the undoing of bounded bodies.[31] Ian Olney is unambiguous in regarding films like *Cannibal Holocaust* and Margheriti's *Cannibal Apocalypse* (1980) as progressive political critiques. In Olney's view, the films restore the colonial contexts of the cannibal and the zombie, lost in the translation to America. They use

Caribbean, Amazonian or Pacific settings to launch searing attacks on American neo-imperialism after 1945. Where American zombie cinema has disavowed this origin, Olney argues that in Italian horror 'the black zombie becomes the perfect embodiment of all that is repressed in the colonialist scenario.'[32]

I would be more persuaded by this if *Cannibal Holocaust* didn't clearly rely uncritically on the deeply contested sociobiological anthropology of Napoleon Chagnon, who used his fieldwork with the Yanomami (the 'Fierce People') in the Amazon to argue for an inherent, genetically encoded tendency to violence in *Homo sapiens* in best-selling books and ethnographic films throughout the 1970s. The critique of the white imposition of savagery is utterly compromised by the exploitation of myths of lost tribes and cannibals. The film remains thoroughly invested in the Chagnon position on innate violence. On indigenous cultures, Deodato and Fulci are a long way from being 'progressive'.

Where the cannibal/zombie films remain of symptomatic interest is in their exorbitant nihilism, an embrace of violent transgression of all human value surely born of the catastrophic crisis of the Italian state in the 1970s, when the republic's democratic institutions were being violently assailed and resisted by terrorist actions from across the political spectrum, from the Red Army Brigade to anarchists and neo-Fascists, including the kidnap and murder of the political leader Aldo Moro in 1978. In the final scene of Fulci's *The Beyond*, the last two survivors of the attacks by various forms of the undead discover that they have pushed beyond the tissue-thin walls of everyday reality and found the hellish, blasted wasteland that lies beyond. It is a vision of the psychotic Real, the complete breakdown of all symbolization. This is an extraordinary metaphysical moment, an instant of *vastation*, that culminating glimpse of a wholly other order of things which results in a 'laying waste to a land or psyche', that reveals that the 'malignant system of the world . . . is tearing you apart.'[33] Eugene Thacker has described modern horror as an attempt to think 'the enigmatic thought of the unknown', beyond all necessarily limiting human categories of thought, where humanity is utterly dethroned on a planet teeming with other agencies.[34]

The Italian zombie backs us into a corner in the last redoubt, with little or no hope of escape, but these films are at their most frightening when the crowd pushes us through the flimsy walls and out the other side, to see not just social apocalypse but the very end of meaning itself.

Romero's zombie cinema established the template for the zombie apocalypse; his Italian imitators dragged it into the margins and wallowed in its annihilating gore. For a time, the zombie looked consigned to rot away unquietly in this state of abject extremity. Yet the zombie was retooled again in the 1990s and blasted out of the margins and into the cultural mainstream in an extraordinarily pervasive way, making it an iconic figure around the world *as* a figure of the condition of the world. Let's now turn to this global apotheosis of the zombie.

8
Going Global

In the last fifteen years, the zombie has reached saturation point. Zombies emerged from the lowest forms of mass culture in pulps, comics and exploitation films but, like the viral catastrophe it so often imagines, they have entered the global bloodstream to become an instantly recognized metaphor around the world. Indeed, the zombie apocalypse is precisely one of the privileged ways of imagining our interconnected global condition. This late in modernity, in what sociologists call the risk society, where 'the state of emergency threatens to become the normal state', the zombie has become a paradigmatic allegorical mode for imagining the multiple disasters that threaten human society and the planet.[1]

Crucial to this change in the last twenty years has been a shift in the locus of experience and identification of zombie culture. In the proliferating zombie video games that emerged in the 1990s from a cultural sector that is now economically larger than cinema, the player is immersed inside the zombie apocalypse, becoming a wired-up and networked participant in the catastrophe, although as a result the relation to the undead significantly shifts. That change is registered in the phenomenon of zombie parades or walks, which first began in 2001 in Sacramento but have since become a global ritual in cities across the world (48 cities took part on World Zombie Day in 2008). No one participates in a zombie walk as a survivor – that would be boring. Instead, much care is taken in assuming the identity of the previously abjected other, the undead. Why this shift of focus? Is this a reflection of the medical and biological revolutions

The World Record for the largest number of people dancing simultaneously to Michael Jackson's 'Thriller', Mexico City, 2009.

Mapping catastrophe: infection spreads out from Tokyo, *Resident Evil: Afterlife* (2010).

that have steadily redefined death? Or is it a process of routinizing the zombie, of domesticating it, as suggested by the stream of TV dramas and even children's fictions that explore not the catastrophe itself but the return to a new kind of normal in the wake of a zombie catastrophe? Perhaps this still depends on where you are located in relation to the profound unevenness and inequities of the processes of globalization. In places of poverty, border insecurity and violence, the old anthropology of the *zombi* is still very much alive, dead and kicking.

Video Games: Survival Horror

In 1996, the Japanese computer game designer Shinji Mikami helped design a quest game for consoles set in a haunted mansion and loosely based on the Japanese horror film (and subsequent game) *Sweet Home* (1989). It was called *Biohazard*, and one key inspiration was Romero's zombie films. 'I saw [*Dawn of the Dead*] as a junior high school student', Mikami said. 'It made me dream about living in a realistic world in which zombies appeared.'[2] The dark doings of the military-industrial Umbrella Corporation and their development of the biological warfare T-Virus, which breaks out in their secret laboratories, was also influenced by the plot of Romero's *The Crazies*. At a late stage, Capcom decided to release the game outside

Alice as medical test subject, *Resident Evil* (2002).

Japan under the name *Resident Evil.* The strapline for the game was 'Welcome to the World of Survival Horror.'

Along with *Alone in the Dark,* which appeared a little earlier in 1992, *Resident Evil* invented a new genre of horror game which then fed back into the cinema and fostered a new wave of zombie apocalypse films, completing the feedback loop by reinforcing the success of a film like *28 Days Later* (2002) and ensuring the remake of *Dawn of the Dead* (2004) by Zack Snyder. *Resident Evil* made the idea of anxious strategizing to survive a global zombie 'outbreak' a narrative with global range. It also largely abandoned supernatural explanations or Voodoo magic for an entirely medicalized explanation of the zombie horror. Zombification becomes a matter of viral contagion – a product of the interconnectedness of the modern world itself, rather than the ancient, primordial return more typical of the Gothic imagination.

Since 1996, there have been over twenty *Resident Evil* games in the franchise, including a remake of the original with more processing power in 2002 and a re-remake in 2015. In 2004, *Resident Evil: Outbreak* moved the game online for the first time, so that players could encounter each other's avatars. This new communality, breaking the isolation of the lone console player, multiplied the risks with all manner of new threats, the technology again reinforcing the sense of the fragility and danger of interconnection. Players could cooperate but the more common route, as predicted in Romero's films, was either to act humanly, like an asshole, or more interestingly, like a zombie. Shortly afterwards, the game *Stubbs the Zombie* (2005) reversed the usual play and made the player a zombie intent on eating human brains and exacting revenge on a whole town built over your grave. Computer games were evidently shifting the axis of identification within the zombie plot in major ways. Mikami returned to design *Resident Evil 4* (2005), which more obviously fused with action and shooter games, with greater player agency motored by greater fire power, making some question the survival of 'survival horror' as a meaningful category.[3] Romero's *Dawn of the Dead* directly inspired the game *Dead Rising* (2006), with zombies roaming through an elaborate shopping mall environment, and another major zombie outbreak narrative, *Left 4 Dead* (2007 and 2009), which zombifies populations after an outbreak of 'Green Flu'.

There are currently six delirious and thunderously stupid *Resident Evil* movies (starting in 2002), starring the supermodel Milla Jovovich as the increasingly post-human, technologically augmented, living-dead heroine, Alice. The plots are openly structured to work through game levels, even using computer models of the buildings to orient the viewer between levels of action. The bullets are limitless and the slaughter of infected zombies and other T-Virus mutant

Trapped by biopolitical machines, *Resident Evil* (2002).

creatures relentless. There is little interest shown for these CGI zombie hordes, except as fodder for the spectacle of mass slaughter.

Holding off zombies is now a multi-billion-dollar, multi-platform industry. The zombie offers transmedial synergies for global entertainment corporations. Again, plots of global zombie infection by faceless corporations uncannily echo the staged 'release' of games across global trading zones by media megaliths like Capcom. *Resident Evil* is now a cluster of texts that can open the question of what it really means for the figure of the zombie to end up going global.

When the zombie moves from cinema to computer screen, this is not a straightforward shift from the masochistic passivity of merely watching horror on film to a new kind of agency, where the gamer is in control. Survival horror was initially about locating the avatar of the player in an extremely anxious situation with scarcely any weapons or defences, in a space seen from a fixed, high angle that emphasized vulnerability, with doorways and voids invoking dread and zombies groaning and shuffling towards you unless you learned to avoid them. 'Be smart!' the instructions said. 'Fighting foes is not the only way to survive this horror.' As a completely useless player, I can vividly recall being repeatedly bitten to death in the very first corridors off the lobby of the mansion as I panicked and failed to master the controls at the first sight of the shambling undead.

In a deliberate subversion of action driven, first-person shoot-'em-ups, the first *Resident Evil* taught you about scarcity, evasion and restraint. Strong on spooky atmospheres, there were long stretches of investigation of spaces and rooms before you hit upon the right clues to advance to the next room (or, in my case, before you got bitten to death and had to start again). Tanya Krzywinska has argued persuasively that the survival horror genre of gaming exploited the technological limitations of memory power to operate on an axis between limited agency and predetermined trajectories, these moments of loss of control, or 'cut-scenes', where the plot is advanced in mini-film animations, only underscoring feelings of inevitability, dread and anxiety.[4]

Some have suggested that this different kind of agency comes from a distinctively Japanese ethos of the first designers. Japanese horror does derive some of its power from the complex Shinto system of the debts and obligations between the living and the dead. Those vengeful ghosts in post-war Japanese film, from *Ugetsu* (dir. Kenji Mizoguchi, 1953) to *Ring* (dir. Hideo Nakata, 1998), are the wronged and dishonoured dead that seek recompense. But the zombie does not fit into this supernatural ethos and there is no native 'zombie' tradition in Japan; it was imported only after Romero's revision of the figure.[5] Perhaps in Japan the game initially echoed the 1995 sarin nerve gas attack on the Tokyo subway, subtended by a deep-seated fear of the radiation effects of the 1945 atomic bombs, but the terror of germ warfare attacks is shared across the globe. *Resident Evil* and the games like it are cultural hybrids, carefully calibrated to appeal to different traditions.

The oddest effect of the translation to gameplay is the readjust-ment of the zombie rules. In early *Resident Evil* games zombies required several pistol shots to be put down, and shots to the body were fine (largely because there was no way to aim precisely at the head). There is no specificity to the zombie in this gameplay: they are merely obstructive pixels – problems to be solved – that could just as well have been rendered as demons, or aliens, or Nazis. The fact that they are already dead means zombies can solve the occasional moral panic about the 'zombifying' effect of video games on the world's youth. *Carmageddon* (1997) was a game that involved running over pedestrians for points, and was initially refused a certificate by the British Board of Film Censorship. The censors relented when the pedestrians were changed to zombies. At a stroke, a reprehensible act became a responsible, even hygienic gesture. This trick, however, did not stop an American judge from excepting games such as *Resident Evil* from First Amendment protection since the games had no 'free speech' or conceptual content worthy of defence. Con-tempt for survival horror put it outside the domain of deliberative democracy – a continuation of the tendency to damn zombies to the outer darkness, beyond the bounds of mainstream cultural taste.[6]

If zombies are almost entirely detached from their history in these games, the biggest change is to the rules of infection of the usually human protagonists. In the post-Romero zombie film, a single bite is fatal, leaving human life extremely vulnerable to accidental (un)death, to cruel and arbitrary fates. In the 'procedural adaptation' of zombies from cinema to game, this rule is necessarily transformed.[7] A player can sustain a bite or two and neutralize their effects with health packs picked up along the way. Only repeated bites, their effect sometimes measured on an on-screen health monitor, result in death. Even so, this death lasts only as long as the game takes to restart from the last save point. This makes the avatar of the player effectively a zombie, subject to repeated deaths and revivals, even as they learn to navigate and 'survive' each level. An irreversible economy of absolute death is replaced by a fluctuating rhythm of hundreds of little deaths. This change, I suspect, has had much to do with opening the way towards new kinds of identification with the zombie. Little by little, the binary opposition of self and other has bled out.

In the computer game, the framing narrative tends to be advanced in cut scenes, preset blocks of cinematic exposition with reduced interactive possibilities. The experience of survival horror gaming is separated from this diegesis and is largely about navigating maze-like environments, evading or confronting zombie-pixels and problem-solving. The frame narratives are rudimentary, built from elements that provide immediate genre recognition: a shadowy corporation, a rogue soldier/cop/spy, a secret military-industrial facility, an experiment gone wrong, an outbreak, a survival mission that twists and turns. The film versions of *Resident Evil* frequently suspend narrative to engage in spectacular shoot-outs, but narrative drive and elaboration remain important to them. Indeed, narratives of zombie apocalypse like *Resident Evil* can help us explore how the zombie figure has been medicalized in the recent apocalyptic imagination.

Medicalization I: The New Dead

The release of George Romero's *Night of the Living Dead* in 1968 and the revision of the zombie proved influential for another reason we have not yet examined. It coincided with the emergence of a significant medical transformation of the boundary between life and death. In 1968, the medical definition of death was changed by a small group of doctors that came together in a group called the Ad Hoc Committee of the Harvard Medical School. This working group was prompted by medical advances that effectively invented new beings inside a brand new technological assemblage, which was called the Intensive Care Unit.

At the core of this newfangled ICU – which brought together a lot of disparate specialisms for the first time – was a new generation of artificial respirators. 'Iron lungs' had been developed amid outbreaks of the poliomyelitis virus in the 1920s as machines to keep paralysed lungs breathing. These were replaced by more efficient devices in the 1950s. Survival rates improved, but in doing so created a novel problem. The success of the mechanical respirator meant that the cardio-pulmonary system could be sustained separately from brain function. There were now patients with a complete absence of cortical activity – who were 'brain dead' – but who continued to live on within the biotechnical apparatus of the ICU. These paradoxical 'living cadavers', as they were first called, were interstitial beings of a new liminal world. They mark a cybernetic disarticulation of the human body into separate systems that can be managed and sustained independently of each other as long as they are plugged into a machine. Other names for these new beings included BHCs (beating heart cadavers), 'potential cadavers' and 'neomorts'.

In 1968, the Ad Hoc Committee wanted to address the 'obsolete criteria for the definition of death' in this new situation.[8] This was because legal discourse still defined death as the cessation of the heartbeat, a fixed and incontrovertible moment in the eyes of the law. It left many doctors risking prosecution for wrongful death if they elected to switch life-support machines off, a decision that in 1968 had very few formalized criteria and was largely determined by individuals in local situations. This was becoming urgent, too, because advances in human transplant surgery were making the living cadaver an object of intense interest as a potential source of organs. Christiaan Barnard had performed the first heart transplant the year before, and early attempts at kidney transplants between identical twins had been made only a few years earlier. In the late 1960s, however, a doctor in Virginia who performed the first heart transplant in the state was prosecuted for the wrongful killing of a patient by the removal of their heart.[9]

As a solution to this crisis, the Ad Hoc Committee set out to relocate death from the heart to the brain and established the criteria for determining what they called 'irreversible coma'. This was marked by a complete absence of responsiveness in both autonomic systems and the higher neocortex. Yet while the recommendations of the report were hugely influential on medical practice in the next decade, there remained problems of definition. If the patient met the criteria for unresponsiveness, brain death could be declared, the respirators turned off and biological death allowed to follow. Or not, as it sometimes turned out. The creation of this interval between brain death and biological death shifted death from a decisive moment to an ongoing process. In the dilation of this space between deaths, not only were a thousand bioethical issues to bloom but a new panoply of liminal creatures were to be born, including the zombie. No wonder you have to shoot these post-'68 zombies in the head to be sure they stay down.

The definition of 'irreversible coma' has proved problematic and subject to a succession of refinements and subtle gradations, further dilating this zone between deaths. One of the criteria for establishing brain death in the Ad Hoc Committee proposals was a flat EEG record. However, it transpires that the brain-dead brain can appear to be disturbingly lively on an EEG monitor, even if these signs are often ICU 'artifacts' – misleading records generated in the complex feedback loops of the bodies and machines.

In 1972, Bryan Jennett and Fred Plum coined the term 'persistent vegetative state' for states of catastrophic collapse of brain function that nevertheless preserve evidence of higher neocortical activity. 'Persistent vegetative state' shifted to 'permanent vegetative state' after twelve months, although neither diagnosis has the same legal standing as 'whole brain death', and thus is constantly caught in legal wrangles when the rights to live and die in relation to the medical care of these states are raised. Plum had also coined the term 'locked-in syndrome' in 1966 for another liminal state in which higher cortical activity is unequivocally preserved amid the catastrophic collapse of the voluntary muscular and nervous systems. These states were considerably livelier than whole brain death, a category confirmed by a presidential commission in 1981 called *Defining Death*, which became the basis for a uniform legal definition of brain death across the United States.

These manoeuvres all took place alongside spectacular and disturbing anomalies, such as the case of Karen Ann Quinlan, the woman who slipped enigmatically into an apparently brain-dead state in 1975. In 1976, her father was successful in being granted the legal right to turn off her respirator to let biological death follow. Instead, Quinlan's breathing stabilized without mechanical assistance and she lived on, without leaving the coma, for another ten years, in a twilight state, becoming a crisis of category for bioethics.

There was another flurry of diagnostic and definitional work in the mid-1990s. In 1994, a neurology task force attempted to shade the scales between persistent and permanent vegetative states, a crucial boundary for declaring brain death. Between 1995 and 1997 an entirely new category, the 'minimally conscious state', emerged. MCS was defined by the Aspen Neurobehavioural Work-Group as a 'severely altered consciousness in which the person demonstrates minimal but definitely behavioural evidence of self or environmental awareness'.[10] This encompassed not just severe physical trauma, but many forms of late-stage dementia. Margaret Lock has termed these new medical definitions a process of 'Making up the Good-as-Dead', and polemically contends it could be read as the cultural work of demarcating ever more categories of social rather than biological death. 'In late modernity', Lock pronounces, 'the numbers of people recognized as candidates for social death have increased exponentially.'[11]

The boom in zombie narratives since 1968 has coincided with this ongoing medical transformation of the definition of death, and the undead are undoubtedly exotic figurations for these new liminal states between life and death. The trauma of being inserted into the technical ensemble of the ICU unit is one of the foundational tropes of the modern zombie film. It is significant how many times a plot is launched from the recovery room of an abandoned ICU unit. This is how *28 Days Later* starts, Jim de-intubating himself after weeks in a coma and walking through the abandoned hospital and out into the London streets. Exactly the same scene recurs in the first post-catastrophe sequence of the TV series *The Walking Dead* (2010–), Rick Grimes waking up and repeating the same bewildered process of discovery. Meanwhile Alice, in the *Resident Evil* series, repeatedly suffers waking into post-catastrophic worlds at the start of each film. She finds that her vulnerable human body has been directly plugged into a torturous medical-corporate system which manipulates the virus that courses through her veins, which either adjusts her biology or carefully induces in her structural amnesia. Alice's entrapment is imaged through her constantly being framed by banks of medical monitoring surveillance screens of the Umbrella Corporation's ICU, or tied down on gurneys in experimental medical facilities.

Coma works narratively in the zombie apocalypse film to locate the protagonist in a position where they must learn the new dispensation at exactly the same speed as the viewer. But at a more fundamental level, do the protagonists thrive in a world of the walking dead because they themselves, as coma survivors, are already one of the many living dead, another of the liminal creatures populating this era of the New Dead?

In the *Resident Evil* films, the least interesting thing is the zombies themselves, at least compared to the bizarre post-human journey taken by the female protagonist, who is progressively less a human being with bodily integrity than a biotechnological device, genetically spliced, enhanced, intermittently controlled by satellite, with irises that now bear the corporate logo of the Umbrella Corporation, and launched as a bioweapon sometimes called 'Project Alice' into a post-contagion world. Underground secret medical facility succeeds underground secret medical facility until the third film unveils the infinite reserve of cloned Alices awaiting deployment. These are all promptly killed off in the opening minutes of the fourth film, Alice suddenly de-augmented and rehumanized again, the reboot to readjust her to human sympathies and identification.

The *Resident Evil* franchise is a conflicted series, at once plaintive about the depredations of the human body and basically revelling in these post-human enhancements. Alice, after all, is little more than the spectator's enhanced first-person-shooter point-of-view, and must experience multiple deaths and revivals before learning how to get through to the next level, the next sequel.

On an individualized level, the zombie may be an emanation of the shifting boundary between life and death, but the zombie *masses*, the ravening horde, also help figure another aspect of the contemporary medical imagination: the epidemic narrative.

Medicalization II: The Outbreak Narrative

In 1989, a World Health Organization conference coined the term 'emerging infections' to name potentially catastrophic new global health threats. After the discovery of the Marburg haemorrhagic fever in the 1960s, the identification of the Ebola virus in the 1970s, HIV in the 1980s and the global panic around the SARS coronavirus in 2003, public health has been anticipating and planning for a lethal pandemic for decades. Fatal mutations in the influenza virus, a threat temporarily held off by antibiotics, can only last so long before a lethal pandemic recurs. It is perhaps the classic disaster scenario for reflexive modernity – that is, a risk that is created and amplified by modernity itself, by the interconnectedness of global transport and communication networks. 'A permanent modern scenario: apocalypse looms . . . and it doesn't occur. And it still looms', Susan Sontag said in her reflections on *AIDS and its Metaphors*. 'We seem to be in the throes of one of the modern kinds of apocalypse.' Not *Apocalypse Now* but *Apocalypse from Now On.*[12]

In the eighteenth century, Enlightenment thinkers defined themselves against supernatural or theological explanations of disaster and plague, for millennia ascribed to the malign influence of unlucky stars (*dis astro* means 'unlucky star'). They sought first natural-scientific explanations for illnesses, and then social ones for their spread. 'Contagion' long referred as much to rumours and dreads as to the disease itself, and it was believed that fear and ideas could kill as much as the mysterious agents carrying the illness. Plague and revolution were thus tightly tied together. When Heinrich Heine described the 'choleric riots' in Paris in 1831, it was unclear precisely what contamination the crowds fought against so frenziedly. What is certain is that the mob resembled the zombie horde:

> One thought the end of the world was coming . . . Woe to those who looked suspicious . . . The people rushed upon them as a wild beast . . . Nothing is more horrible than the people's anger, when the people is thirsty with blood . . . Then the black waves of a sea of men surges through the streets . . . and they howl wordlessly, like demons or the damned.[13]

Through the nineteenth century, disease increasingly became a matter of public health and the disciplinary administration of populations – what the historian and philosopher Michel Foucault called 'the rise of biopolitics'. Yet despite turning disease increasingly into administrative emergencies, outbreaks continually evolved to defy complete rational order and containment. The mutation of Spanish influenza at the end of the First World War killed an estimated 20 million people, and also hid within it an epidemic of encephalitis lethargica (or 'sleepy sickness'), which reduced hundreds of thousands of those who survived the first fever to 'the chilling appearance of a corpse' – living, yet largely comatose.[14] Since sleepy sickness affected tens of thousands of Americans in the 1920s, I sometimes wonder if this isn't one of the secret vectors that transferred the idea of the shuffling, catatonic zombie into American culture, since it was a major epidemic that was never 'cured', and left thousands in a perpetual twilight state.

The zombie really fused with the notion of the virus, though, which was first popularly understood and explained as a distinct entity in the 1950s. They remain an uncanny fit. Wendell Stanley, a pioneer Nobel Prize-winning virologist, explained that viruses were 'entities neither living nor dead, that belong to the twilight zone between the living and the non-living'.[15] Viruses are inert until they enter a host cell and take over its mechanisms, often killing the host

Computer modelling global infection, *World War Z* (2013).

in the drive to reproduce only itself. This is the medicalized notion of the viral zombie outbreak in a nutshell.

The tie of viral epidemics to the history of the zombie was consolidated in the early years of the HIV crisis, when a high preponderance was noted in the immigrant Haitian population in New York and it was called 'an epidemic Haitian virus'.[16] Under the headline 'Night of the Living Dead', the *Journal of the American Medical Association* speculated, entirely fantastically, that HIV was spread by Voodoo rituals using human blood. This simply rehearsed the age-old tactic of marking the migrant and foreigner as fatal disease invader, the demonized carrier, but the modernity of 'emergent infections' in particular resides in how they always trace out colonial and post-colonial pathways.

Modelling epidemiological catastrophe is intrinsically bound up with fantasy. It seems improbable that the Office of Public Health Preparedness and Response of the American Center for Disease Control and Prevention released a 'Zombie Apocalypse Preparedness' pack, including posters for schools, to educate the population on basic measures that would help contain an epidemic outbreak. Yet zombie pulp fictions, films and video games have long been imagining this outbreak narrative. The paradigmatic scene for the zombie pandemic is a computer map of the globe charting the exponential spread of the disease. In *World War Z* (2013) a global map hangs above the command centre, slowly turning red with infection, a counter clicking through the billions killed with exponential spread.

The opening of *Resident Evil: Afterlife* (dir. Paul W. S. Anderson, 2010) zooms out from a single bite on a street crossing in Tokyo, pulling back to see the lights of the city, then the island, and then progressively the globe, go deathly dark. The failure to contain new viral strains within the security protocols of medical facilities is central to the premise of the *Resident Evil* franchise and the 'Rage' virus of *28 Days* and *28 Weeks Later.* The HQ of the CDC in Atlanta is the destination of the ragged band of survivors in the first series of *The Walking Dead,* an empty hope for a solution or cure, it transpires. In zombie-virus fictions like M. R. Carey's novel *The Girl with All the Gifts* (2014), medical researchers end up the allies of viral transmission, placed in the long Gothic tradition of mad scientists.

In turn, epidemiologists have long used the notion of the 'Andromeda strain' for newly emergent pathogens, taking the name from Michael Crichton's novel and film about an extraterrestrial virus that wipes out a small town and then an advanced medical facility. The medical outbreak narrative fantasizes primitive and savage origins, such as Haiti or Africa for AIDS or the jungles of West Africa for Ebola – just as zombie fictions always have. The sheer nastiness of haemorrhagic fevers like Ebola create what Priscilla Wald calls 'an epidemiological horror story' that looks a lot like *The Invasion of the Body Snatchers.*[17] The popular science books that came out after 'emerging infections' were identified as a major global threat had titles like Laurie Garrett's *The Coming Plague,* and in Richard Preston's *The Hot Zone* Ebola is explicitly described as turning the infected person into a 'zombie' or 'a living virus bomb'.[18] As we learned from the outbreak of Ebola in 2014, the virus lives on in the dead body, making the corpse one of the most dangerous sources of infection. Those screened at airports returning from West Africa to Britain and America were asked if they had attended funerals, as a way of alerting authorities to the insidious reach of the lively dead.

'Apocalypse' has come to mean complete catastrophe, but it has also always meant, in the biblical tradition, a revelation, an unveiling of a tremendous Final Truth. Millennialists waiting for the Rapture to signal the beginning of the End Times read emerging infections as portents and signs, just as plagues have always been interpreted. Meanwhile, the 'Preppers', a movement dedicated to preparing for the apocalyptic end of society by developing a survivalist skillset, with self-sufficiency farming techniques and a big arsenal of weapons, can either watch zombie movies or read leaflets from the CDC.

What the zombie outbreak narrative really reveals – as do all epidemics – is the shape of our networks and risky attachments, our sense of an incredibly fragile global ecology. Frank Kermode long ago suggested that disaster narratives served 'our deep need for intelligible Ends' while we were stuck in the confusing midst of things: 'We project ourselves . . . past the End, so as to see the structure whole, a thing we can't do from our own spot of time in the middle.'[19] Medicalized, viral zombie hordes offer us a figure of a properly globalized interconnection.

Figuring Globalization

We read over and over again that the zombie apocalypse is an allegory of neo-liberal globalization, accelerating after the new geopolitical dispensation since 1989, after the end of the Cold War. Perhaps the zombie is less *allegoresis* – a writing otherwise – than a literalization of the capitalist logic of the expropriation of dead labour from living bodies. 'Biopower', the extension of the system's invasive control into bodies and the processes of life (and death) itself, marks a new stage of capitalist development. The zombie hordes are the living-dead proletariat, dying as guest workers on construction sites or in heavy industry or garment factories around the world in their hundreds of thousands. Romero's *Land of the Dead* is not horror but a peculiar new form of social realism. This new empire of capital comes with a 'necropolitics' that Achille Mbembe regards as a renewal of the social death of slavery in neocolonial form.[20]

After the banking crisis of 2008 the system has continued to operate, even after its apparent death throes, further perfecting the analogy. 'Neoliberalism now shambles on as a zombie', Mark Fisher comments, 'but it is sometimes harder to kill a zombie than a living person.'[21] *Zombie Capitalism*, a study of the banking crisis, was one of the last books written by Marxist theorist and agitator Chris Harman, in which he tries to account for this perplexingly lively afterlife.

It has been suggested that science fiction, fantasy and horror are able to capture these aspects of the 'world storm' because they are 'planetary fictions', uniquely aware of the imbrication of story and world in a way that more domesticated realism cannot begin to grasp.[22] Critics have coined the term 'globalgothic' for cultural fictions around the world that share the same conditions but embody them very differently in local superstitions and supernatural conventions. 'In its ghostly form, capital moves outside of what we might have considered a real world. Its disembodied and spectral presence signals something other than an invisible hand conferring or withholding wealth. The new monster operates autonomously, in an inhuman way.'[23] The medicalization of the zombie outbreak narrative already maps the space of flows in this new kind of informational capitalism, because it points up the permanent condition of teetering on epidemiological catastrophe that modern risk society experiences. The big pharma companies, too, are among the largest and most rapacious multinational corporations, seeking profits from patenting the medicines that hold off the emerging infections that course through the channels of the global body.

World War Z, Max Brooks's novel from 2006, which became an overblown $190 million film in 2013, ought to be the logical outcome of this new kind of globalgothic imagination, because the story self-consciously sets out to encompass the globe within an all-encompassing narrative, stretching from Antarctica to the frozen north of Canada. The novel is meant to be a patchwork of eye-witness accounts from across the world, put together by a United Nations representative in the aftermath of the war, a testimony to a threat from the 'Z Germ' now contained after a long struggle away from a near-extinction event. It puts Patient Zero in the depths of China (where SARS was thought to have emerged), and charts its spread through legal and illegal networks of trafficking around the world, to Brazil and South Africa, before going global. There is a satirical edge to this science-fictional future plague, which offers some neat inversions (for instance, a desperate flotilla of boat people

The Arab zombie horde, *World War Z* (2013).

head out from Florida for Cuba, reversing decades of traffic). It also gestures at contempt for the enclaves of the ultra-rich, whose defences are – as always – inevitably overrun. Ultimately, though, the book has a very narrow Western perspective, reinforcing the American way, but only once its liberalism has been toughened up with some brutal 'hard truths' learned from Israeli and South African hardliners, which are passed off as simply inevitable if the human race is to survive. The Israeli interviewee in the novel explains: 'I happened to be born into a group of people who live in constant fear of extinction. It's part of our identity.'[24] This is why the state of Israel holds out longer than anyone else, behind the wall it has long actually been constructing. The white Afrikaaner, who offers another extreme solution based on past policies of apartheid, is also given considerable focus. Humanity survives only once it begins to adopt these tactics, led by the American President after his commanding speech at the United Nations. As is common to the American apocalyptic imagination, the disaster proves a hygienic reboot for a nation that has forgotten its Puritan foundations.

The film is considerably more objectionable, as Brad Pitt, the white hero who discards black, Asian and Hispanic sidekicks with alarming regularity, sets about saving the world through dumb luck (it is never entirely clear why the World Health Organization so cherishes his particular skillset). The abiding memory of the film is the image of the last safe haven on Earth, Jewish Jerusalem, overrun by the frenzied zombie Arab hordes that pour over the wall in their

Defending Israel, *World War Z* (2013).

CGI millions and tear through the city. I suppose some might read this as the liberating 'multitude', the new kind of resistance that is incubated by the logic of globalization itself, a swarm of post-human subjects.[25] To me, it reeks of racial demonization, in accord with an underpinning violent colonial history. In another set piece, the infection breaks out on an aircraft, inevitably starting way back in the economy seats and spreading fast towards First Class. It is a potent communication of the danger of proximity with the diseased poor. Later, Brad Pitt's character learns that the zombies will simply ignore the sick, by injecting himself with a nasty bug in a medical facility in Cardiff. It is another striking image of how the super-rich West might inoculate themselves against the ravening global poor, learning to coexist with them by simply becoming invisible to their toxic touch. The sequence in the medical facility includes a provocative image of a caged lone black woman zombie snapping at the glass. She is being used as an experimental test subject. The image of the woman is reminiscent of the photograph that Zora Neale Hurston took 80 years earlier of the 'real' zombie, Felicia Felix-Mentor, and suggests that the colonial fantasy that rendered that abjected woman a zombie still operates in Hollywood's slick global commodities. It seems highly significant that in October 2014, the image of this caged black woman was doctored and used to spread a hoax news story that Ebola victims were rising from the grave.

The English Ford brothers have filmed *The Dead* (2010), shot in Burkina Faso, and *The Dead 2* (2013) in India, in a conscious attempt

Return of the black zombie, *World War Z* (2013).

to globalize at least the film production of the zombie trope. The films prove rather uninterested in inflecting the narrative to local contexts, however, merely colouring a familiar outbreak narrative from a hundred other films with a bit of exotic local colour. There is a gesture towards local religious conceptions of reincarnation in *The Dead 2* but it does not help reconceive the figure of the zombie: ravening zombies inevitably pour out of Mumbai slums in another set of images abjecting the poor.

Actually, though, it is entirely possible to take a trip around contemporary world cinema to see how the zombie has been adapted into local traditions, illustrating how the multidirectional global trade in genre elements can fashion new kinds of emphasis according to particular national histories. Local horror narratives can offer rich allegorical potential to address specific contexts of national or regional trauma through reworked horror tropes.[26] In India, *Go Goa Gone* (dir. Krishna D.K. and Raj Nidimoru, 2013) was the first Hindi zombie film, where Bollywood genre expectations exerted far more influence than Romero rules. In Japan, also without a native zombie tradition, zombie films have begun to emerge after *Resident Evil*, often with local satirical intent. My favourite remains *Stacy: Attack of the Schoolgirl Zombies* (dir. Naoyuki Tomomatsu, 2001), where teenage girls suffer a brief delirium of Near Death Happiness before returning as monstrously demanding, all-devouring zombies, which are nicknamed 'Stacys'. It is a deranged account of Japan's 'Lolita complex' and schoolgirl fetish. For a truly bizarre reworking of the zombie trope, however, little will match Takashi Miike's *The Happiness of the Katakuris* (2001), which mashes up body horror with an all-singing, all-dancing homage to *The Sound of Music*, but otherwise defies description. In Britain, filmmakers have often sought to merge with American zombie conventions, even in films like Kerry Anne Mullaney's *The Dead Outside* (2008), which was nevertheless heavily invested in using specific Scottish locations to heighten atmosphere. Yet there is also a strand of English bathetic humour in the native film industry, the joke of *Shaun of the Dead* (dir. Edgar Wright, 2004) coming from the translation of grandiloquent Romero drama to the scruffy streets and pubs of North London. If *World War Z* depicts empire at full global reach, *Shaun* is suffused with local and very English post-imperial melancholia. Quite how far the jokes in *Cockneys vs Zombies* (dir. Matthias Hoene, 2012) could travel is unclear, although there is a memorable slow-motion chase of a shuffling zombie after an elderly man with a Zimmer frame, wonderfully emblematic of a decrepit nation's translation of zombie film conventions.

In Europe, Spanish and French directors have revisited their low-budget zombie histories and reproduced the outbreak narrative in films like the *[REC]* films (four since 2007), the first based in a quarantined Madrid housing block, or *La Horde* (dir. Yannick Dahan and Benjamin Rocher, 2009), an anonymous attempt to reproduce the American zombie action model. These films did not do much to transform conventions, only to mimic them. It is a measure of cross-cultural circulation that the British *Shaun of the Dead*, already a parody, inspired the Spanish-Cuban *Juan of the Dead* (dir. Alejandro Brugués, 2011). However, the breakout success of *Les Revenants* (a French film in 2004, then a TV series starting in 2013), suggests that its subtly disturbing narrative of the dead returning to their families and lovers as brute physical presences, markers of stalled mourning or melancholic denial, can twist away from the splatter-gore aesthetic that has predominated since Romero. *Les Revenants* returns to that hesitation between the literal and the figural, the sliding around of meaning that Lafcadio Hearn first encountered in Martinique, *le pays de revenants*.

In Latin America, similarly, the zombie apocalypse has been readjusted and rescaled. The Argentinian films *Phase 7* by Nicolás Goldbart (2011) and *The Desert* by Christoph Behl (2013) are chamber pieces, exploiting the assumption that we now know what the zombie apocalypse looks like and do not need to stage it in the spectacular manner of *World War Z*, instead letting this happen off-screen to focus on the bored and frustrated survivors waiting out the catastrophe. Both use the familiar apocalyptic scenario to offer a critique from the South of the dominance of the North. *Phase 7* contains no zombies, only an outbreak crisis happening beyond the apartment block we never leave. It toys with a conspiracy theory that imagines the viral outbreak is an eventual product of George Bush Sr's New World Order speech in 1991 after the First Gulf War, seen playing on a TV set in a survivalist's den. The film slyly critiques American hegemony and the American-backed insistence on Latin America conforming to the neo-liberal policies of the International Monetary Fund and World Bank, demands that have repeatedly sent the Argentinian economy into crisis, as Sherryl Vint has suggested.[27] *The Desert* is much more oblique, set largely in one apartment with three survivors in a destructive ménage and a chained-up zombie they call 'Pythagoras'. There are sequences where they attempt to get the zombie to return their gaze, finding the Other's lack of recognition intolerable. In this quieter, philosophical rendition the threat to identity and bodily boundaries is marked in a different way: while Ana's body is covered in unexplained scars, Axel spends the film carefully tattooing flies on his skin, ending the film entirely covered in a second skin. It is an insect carapace serving as a second ego-skin that is meant to protect the human but ends up destroying it. The camera ventures beyond the boundaries of the apartment only once, but the apocalyptic consequences are perfectly conveyed by the damaged dynamics of the survivors and their one captive.

Another low-budget chamber piece, this time from Canada, also implicitly turns the zombie apocalypse trope against North American general conventions. In *Pontypool* (dir. Bruce MacDonald, 2008) the zombie virus is a linguistic illness, something that is communicated through the clichés and banalities of public speech. The film is based on Tony Burgess's elliptical novel *Pontypool Changes Everything* (1995), which explains:

> Once infected, the victim produces the virus in the language he or she struggles with ... The victim becomes frantic, rebelling against the onset of the disease by wilfully destroying, ahead of the virus, his or her own normative behaviour. It is a desperate attempt to escape ... Strangers' mouths are the escape route through which the victim attempts to disappear, in a violent and bloody fashion.[28]

In the filmed version, the action is restricted to a public radio station, where the massacres unfold through news reports phoned in by reporters. The jaded talk-radio DJ must learn to reinvent language, avoid empty cliché and do active damage to the degraded currency of talk on the radio in order to arrest or cure any incipient signs of zombie aphasia. Is this a comment on the linguistic colonialism of America's encroachment into the Canadian public sphere, the export of shock-jockery? It is certainly an explicit element of this unfolding apocalypse, for the virus is only carried in the English language. The last scenes include communications and directions issued by French-speaking troops coming in to master the outbreak. This detail is clearly attuned to the local context of the French-speaking Québécois minority's demands for independence within Canada. Burgess's novel and MacDonald's film seem very sensitive to debates about conceptions of the public sphere and whether there remains a possibility of escape from the cultural hegemony of America. The critique is advanced by subverting one of its most dominant exports – the zombie apocalypse – from within.

By tracking these examples across the globe – although my discussion above is by no means exhaustive – it is possible to see how the figure of the zombie has become a planetary icon, a figure for the homogenizing tendencies of global mass culture, but also flexible enough to get embedded in local contexts, accumulating the grit of difference to resist the frictionless circulation of the same. This is not entirely a recent phenomenon: the history of the zombie is one of continual transport, translation and transformation, since it emerged from within the nexus of the transatlantic slave trade and colonial occupation. The zombie is born in transit, in between cultures, and is thus always susceptible to rapid reworking.

If the zombie has reached a certain global extension in the twenty-first century, then this has also been a remarkably intensive phase of cultural saturation. Kids can play free zombie games on their tablet computer (*Plants vs Zombies*), or read about the awkwardness of puberty through the zombie metaphor (the young adult series of books by Charlie Higson, for example). Architects could enter designs for the Apocotecture Awards for the best zombie-proof houses, or at least until the annual competition was closed, as it was considered in poor taste. Meanwhile, art collectors went wild for Dawn Mellor's paintings of zombified celebrities, the undead portraits of Audrey Hepburn, Mia Farrow or Judy Garland. The South African photographer Pieter Hugo has also used hints of zombification in his unnerving portraits of ragpickers subsisting among toxic waste dumps.

The mainstream literary novel has now absorbed the zombie apocalypse. Colson Whitehead's *Zone One* (2011) unfolds in finely honed prose that nevertheless tells the familiar apocalyptic story of the temporary last redoubt on Manhattan being inevitably overrun by the zombie masses, however much the military teams seem to clear and master each zone. Zombification has even extended back and infected literary classics, as in the remarkable success of the mash-up novel *Pride and Prejudice and Zombies* (2009). 'It is a truth universally acknowledged that a zombie in possession of brains must be in want of more brains', it begins.[29] The joke, a simple ramming together of high and low, Austen's genteel moral discriminations with vicious survival logic, rather outstays its welcome, but now includes a full-scale mock-heritage film treatment too. And zombification has extended to a whole slew of other classics, like those of Charles Dickens (who even teamed up with The Doctor to overcome a Victorian zombie plague early in the rebooted *Doctor Who* TV series).[30]

The zombie has infiltrated avant-garde writing too. One of Stewart Home's experimental anti-novels, *Mandy, Charlie and Mary-Jane* (2013), features a fractured, post-modern lecturer in cultural studies teaching fractured, post-modern zombie films like Lucio Fulci's *Zombie Flesh Eaters*, while working on his own Eurotrash horror script, *Zombie Sex Freaks*, and beginning to hallucinate the apocalypse around him – unless the unfolding disaster is simply the normal state of the university. 'The essence of a great genre movie is that it is as much like every other film from its category as possible', the narrator says. 'I'm determined that *Zombie Sex Freaks* will be the greatest undead movie to stalk the horror section.'[31]

If all this is too intense and the local cinema is only showing zombie films, you could go for a walk (if you can avoid any local zombie parades), or a run (but maybe not using Zombies, Run!, the running app designed by writer Naomi Alderman). Or else you could slump in front of the television, except that you might stumble across the zombie episodes in the *X Files*, *Buffy the Vampire Slayer* or *Angel*. Voodoo made a big come back in *American Horror Story: Coven*, which pitted African American Vodou against a more white, Pagan group. By 2010, zombies got their own dedicated TV shows, from the BBC's zombie serial *In the Flesh* (2013–) to AMC's massively successful serial *The Walking Dead*.

We might take *The Walking Dead* as a significant sign of the *normalization* of the zombie apocalypse, the mark of how routine this genre has become. The series was turned down by the main American broadcast channel NBC as being simply unshowable on mainstream, primetime television. In 2010, the subscription channel AMC picked up the first season. Since it is subscription-only, AMC is not bound by the same strict censorship thresholds as mainstream television is, and commissioned a show that every week outdoes Romero's once 'unrated' horror films for the gruesome dispatch of hundreds of zombies, usually through visceral head wounds. The effects are designed by Gregory Nicotero, who had worked on Romero's *Day of the Dead* 25 years earlier. The freedom to depict graphic violence has made the horror genre an integral part of the development of 'American Quality Television' since the 1990s, because it so clearly declares the difference from public channels.[32] Worldwide, *The Walking Dead* was picked up by the multinational media corporation Fox, and is shown in over 120 countries in 30 languages almost simultaneously with its first airings on American TV, making it one of the most successful – or at least pervasive – global television programmes ever made.

As previously discussed, Robert Kirkman's source comic was envisaged as an open-ended episodic tracing out of the post-apocalyptic life of the central character, Rick Grimes. 'I want *The Walking Dead* to be a chronicle of years of Rick's life. We will NEVER wonder what happens to Rick next, we will see it. *The Walking Dead* will be the zombie movie that never ends.'³³ This open-endedness makes it perfect for conversion into the serial form of television. What it also does is switch the focus from the punctual point of the outbreak and catastrophic social collapse to an unfolding condition, Susan Sontag's notion of *Apocalypse from Now On*. There is no origin story (so far) for the outbreak and Rick never defends the last redoubt, only the next redoubt, an endless, ongoing chain of temporary respites. Although the zombies consistently press at the fragile boundaries of whatever redoubt they occupy, the series often ignores them for long stretches to deal with the dynamics of family and group relationships under conditions of barely tolerable risk and danger.

The accumulated losses and weight of grief sometimes push central figures (including Rick) beyond the bounds of human society, and they act in disordered and stricken ways before they find their way back to a diminishing terrain of being human. The series often feels as though it is dealing with an abstracted condition of 'precarity', the ugly shorthand term Judith Butler has coined for the war-torn, supremely violent, uncertain and grief-stricken world which has emerged to ensnare many places in the world after 9/11 and the global 'War on Terror' that came in its wake. Woundedness and grief have become foregrounded as the social bonds that co-constitute a precarious global condition: 'I am as much constituted by those I do grieve for as by those whose deaths I disavow, whose nameless and faceless deaths form the melancholic background of my social world.'³⁴ Butler might as well be talking about the undead who mass beyond the gates and fences.

Rick, a small-town sheriff before the disaster, is a leader struggling with a set of traditional social and moral values, seeking to adapt them to a condition of permanent crisis. The 'walkers' are decidedly *not* there to be identified with in this series – only to be dispatched. The vicious rival human groups they encounter – the fascistic 'Governor' and roving cannibals – do not provide many models either. The series tends to revert to deeply conservative values of Christian family and close kinship, of 'defending your own', even as it registers alarming threats against the survival of these categories. The apocalypse is unending because there is no ability to imagine alternatives. Ulrich Beck declared the notion of the conventional family one of his 'zombie categories', a modern conception that has outlived its usefulness.[35] If that is so, *The Walking Dead* merely pits one set of walking dead against another, in a Southern landscape invisibly shaped by the history of its slave plantations.

The global armies of CGI dead might be an obvious place to end this history, a remarkable journey of a rare, hybrid superstition from the Antilles arriving at complete cultural saturation across the globe in just under 100 years. But the smooth glide of this metaphor of the digital dead as the allegory of globalization feels too easy to dispatch in this way, as if a single interpretive bullet to the head would do the trick. Instead, I want to emphasize again the often highly mobile meaning and local differences in each instance of the zombie, even under the heading 'going global'. Since the zombie developed from the syncretism forced by the slave trade, it seems better to end by following this circulation of meaning back to Africa.

In the North Province of South Africa there was an upsurge in accusations of witchcraft after the collapse of the apartheid regime and free elections in 1994. The dramatic increase in punishment killings led to formal commissions of inquiry and a number of anthropological studies. In the Sotho language, the *setlotlwane* is a person killed by poison or other occult means and revived after death as a mute and docile worker sent to labour day and night. The witch works by first capturing their shadow, then slowly taking over different parts of the body until they have possessed the entire person. Their apparent death and funeral is a trick that bewitches the families and conceals the soul-theft. After 'death', the *setlotlwane* can be magically transported great distances by their masters, and are the secret source for the accumulation of wealth by the privileged few. It is the users of witchcraft that are accused by communities devastated by structural unemployment, the HIV/AIDS epidemic and border disturbances.

This belief echoes elements of Haitian Vodou, but it also transmutes ideas from further north in Africa, ones that have been common in Cameroon (where the *ekong* are revived from apparent death and sent to work on the slopes of magical Mount Kupe) and also in Tanzania, where these beliefs were recorded by police as far back as the 1920s, and may be the folkloric trace of the slavers that traded in Cameroon a century before.[36] These beliefs run in parallel to pervasive ideas about blood-sucking creatures like vampires (called *mumaini* in Swahili) that were associated with the presence of colonial missions and hospitals in Rhodesia (now Zimbabwe) and the Congo in the 1920s and '30s.[37] Under apartheid, the authorities in South Africa had suppressed or rendered complicit the tribal systems for adjudicating accusations of witchcraft, meaning that by the end of the regime local youth organizations were administering immediate rough justice by necklacing hundreds of those who had suspicious good fortune or wealth.

The *setlotlwane* seems self-evidently the idea of the zombie imported and translated to South Africa, part of a 'diasporic flow of occult images' that are communicated through global networks but that get 'spliced into local mystical economies'.[38] The research of Jean and John Comaroff sees this recent emergence of the zombie in South Africa as a result of the profound social and economic disturbances that are the consequence of the new South Africa entering the flows of global capitalism, experiencing major structural unemployment, migration and rapid social transformation.[39] There are even part-time zombies in South Africa, those half-bewitched who wake up exhausted, not knowing that that they have been at work half the night for a secret master. Even the job of the zombie has been casualized with zero-hour contracts.

Zombie witchcraft is a way of thinking magically about the mysteries of the unequal accumulation of wealth (a process so mystical that Marx himself resorted to the language of African fetishes to describe it). Isak Niehaus, however, an anthropologist who spent three years in the field in the same area, warns against making witchcraft an easy *index* of something else, a matter simply of allegorical interpretation. The *setlotlwane* is a real being in the local cosmology, with real social effects. They are not metaphors but 'actual exercises in constructing, rather than merely representing, social realities', he suggests.[40] It might do the cultural work of translating precarious feelings about life, health, family, community, labour, migration and borders, but that is not how such things are *experienced*.

Wherever the zombie travels, it embeds in local belief, mutating in those liminal worlds of rumour, superstition and storytelling. In doing so, it sheds the traces of its transmission, burrowing into local economies of fear and wonder. The zombie is not simply a metaphor, ultimately reducible to a single explanation. Each instance demands attention and a recognition that it would not work to condense such complex social realities if it was instantly interpretable. This is why the zombie has steadily chomped its way into a bewildering variety of practices and discourses, pushed over the fences that mark off disciplinary thought, and devoured so many brains in its relentless advance over the last century. The ambulatory dead are a moving target, an enigma that resists simple capture. If you haven't caught this bug yet, there's only one thing left to say: 'They're coming to get you, Barbara.'

References

Introduction

1 Jennifer Rutherford, *Zombies* (London, 2013), pp. 18, 23–4.
2 Victor W. Turner, *The Ritual Process* (Harmondsworth, 1974), p. 81.
3 Fred Botting, 'Zombie Death Drive: Between Gothic and Science Fiction', in *Gothic Science Fiction, 1880–2010*, ed. Sara Wasson and Emily Alder (Liverpool, 2011), p. 42.
4 David McNally, *Monsters of the Market: Zombies, Vampires and Global Capitalism* (Chicago, IL, 2012), pp. 1, 2.
5 Gerry Canavan, 'Fighting a War You've Already Lost: Zombies and Zombis in *Firefly/Serenity* and *Dollhouse*', *Science Fiction Film and Television*, IV/2 (2011), p. 202.
6 Slavoj Žižek, *Living in the End Times* (London, 2011), p. 334.
7 Simon Pegg, 'The Dead and the Quick', www.theguardian.com, 4 November 2008.
8 December 1953 story, reprinted in *Zombies: The Chilling Archives of the Horror Comics*, ed. C. Yoe and S. Banes (San Diego, CA, 2012), p. 11.
9 These etymological speculations (and others) are discussed in Hans-W. Ackermann and Jeanine Gauthier, 'The Ways and Nature of the Zombi', *Journal of American Folklore*, CIV (1991), pp. 466–91.
10 Joseph Roach, *Cities of the Dead: Circum-Atlantic Performance* (New York, 1996), p. xi.
11 The *poétique de la relation* is a phrase coined by Édouard Glissant in *Caribbean Discourse: Selected Essays*, trans. J. M. Dash (Charlottesville, VA, 1989).
12 Paul Gilroy, *The Black Atlantic: Modernity and Double Consciousness* (London, 1993), p. 29.

1 From *Zombi* to Zombie: Lafcadio Hearn and William Seabrook

1 Lafcadio Hearn, 'The Last of the Voudous', in *Inventing New Orleans: Writings of Lafcadio Hearn*, ed. S. Frederick Starr (New Orleans, LA, 2001), p. 77.
2 Quoted in Adam Rothman, 'Lafcadio Hearn in New Orleans and the Caribbean', *Atlantic Studies*, V/5 (2008), p. 265.
3 Quoted ibid., p. 272.
4 Lafcadio Hearn, *Martinique Sketches* [1938], in *American Writings* (New York, 2009), p. 324.
5 Ibid., p. 325.
6 Ibid., pp. 326–7.
7 Ibid., p. 327.
8 See MacEdward Leach, 'Jamaican Duppy Lore', *Journal of American Folklore*, LXXIV (1961), pp. 207–15.
9 Hearn, *Martinique Sketches*, p. 489.
10 E. B. Tylor, *Primitive Culture: Researches into the Development of Mythology, Philosophy, Religion, Art and Custom*, 2 vols (London, 1871), pp. 15, 19.
11 Tylor, 'Conclusion', *Primitive Culture*, vol. II, p. 453.
12 Hearn, *Martinique Sketches*, p. 493.
13 See Richard Hamblyn, *Tsunami: Nature and Culture* (London, 2014).
14 William Seabrook, *No Place to Hide: An Autobiography* (Philadelphia, PA, 1942), pp. 280–81.
15 Ibid., p. 341.
16 Petrine Archer-Straw, *Negrophilia: Avant-garde Paris and Black Culture in the 1920s* (London, 2000), p. 19.
17 Michel Leiris, 'Civilization' [1929], reprinted in *Brisées: Broken Branches*, trans. Lydia Davis (San Francisco, CA, 1989), p. 20.
18 Susan Zieger, 'The Case of William Seabrook: *Documents*, Haiti, and the Working Dead', *Modernism/Modernity*, XIX/4 (2013), p. 744.
19 Nancy Cunard, typed note 'Meeting Mr and Mrs Seabrook' (Autumn 1929), in Cunard archive held at the Harry Ransom Center, Austin, Texas.
20 William Seabrook, *Jungle Ways* (London, 1931), p. 122.
21 Ibid., p. 172.
22 William Seabrook, *Witchcraft: Its Power in the World Today* (London, 1941), pp. 67–8.
23 William Seabrook, *The Magic Island* [1929], reissued as *The Voodoo Island* (London, 1966), p. 18.

24 Ibid., p. 63.
25 Ibid., p. 91.
26 Ibid., p. 92.
27 Ibid., p. 93.
28 Ibid., p. 103.
29 Hans Possendorf, *Damballa Calls: A Love Story of Haiti*, trans. L. A. Hudson (London, 1936), p. 9.
30 For commentary, see David Inglis, 'The Zombie from Myth to Reality: Wade Davis, Academic Scandal and the Limits of the Real', *Scripted*, VII/2 (2010), pp. 351–69.
31 Seabrook, *The Voodoo Island*, pp. 100–101.
32 Ibid., p. 101.
33 Orlando Patterson, *Slavery and Social Death: A Comparative Study* (Cambridge, 1982), p. 51.
34 Kate Ramsey, *The Spirits and the Law: Vodou and Power in Haiti* (Chicago, IL, 2011), p. 174.
35 See Elsie Clews Parsons, *Folk-lore of the Antilles, French and English*, 3 vols (New York, 1933–43), and also J. S. Handler and K. M. Bilby, 'On the Early Use and Origin of the Term "Obeah" in Barbados and the Anglophone Caribbean', *Slavery and Abolition*, XXII/2 (2001), pp. 87–100.
36 Jean-Paul Sartre, Preface to Frantz Fanon, *The Wretched of the Earth*, trans. Constance Farrington (Harmondsworth, 1985), pp. 11–12.
37 Fanon, *The Wretched of the Earth*, pp. 43, 39.
38 Ibid., pp. 42, 73.
39 Ibid., p. 236.
40 Édouard Glissant, *Caribbean Discourse: Selected Essays*, trans. J. M. Dash (Charlottesville, VA, 1989), p. 40.
41 Ibid., p. 59.
42 Jean Rhys, *The Wide Sargasso Sea* [1966] (London, 2000), pp. 88–9.
43 Erna Brodber, *Myal* (London, 1988), p. 107.

2 Phantom Haiti

1 A full English translation by John Garrigus of the Code Noir is available online at https://directory.vancouver.wsu.edu.
2 De Saint-Méry, cited in Kate Ramsay, *The Spirits and the Law: Vodou and Power in Haiti* (Chicago, IL, 2011), p. 42.
3 See Alasdair Pettinger, 'From Vaudoux to Voodoo', *Forum for Modern Language Studies*, XL/4 (2004), pp. 415–25.
4 Spenser St John, *Hayti; or, The Black Republic* (London, 1884), p. 188.

5 Ibid., p. 202.
6 Ibid., p. 205.
7 Ibid., pp. 217, 221.
8 Stephen Bonsal, *The American Mediterranean* (London, 1913), p. 98.
9 *The Journal of Christopher Columbus*, cited in Peter Hulme, *Colonial Encounters: Europe and the Native Caribbean, 1492–1797* (London, 1986), pp. 16–17.
10 Ibid., p. 40.
11 Gananath Obeyesekere, '"British Cannibals": Contemplation of an Event in the Death and Resurrection of James Cook, Explorer', *Critical Inquiry*, XVIII (1992), p. 638.
12 See Pascal Blanchard et al., eds, *Human Zoos: Science and Spectacle in the Age of Colonial Empires* (Liverpool, 2008).
13 Katherine Biber, 'Cannibals and Colonialism', *Sydney Law Review*, XXVII (2005), pp. 624, 626.
14 Bonsal, *American Mediterranean*, p. 88.
15 Ibid., pp. 112–13.
16 See A. W. Brian Simpson, *Cannibalism and the Common Law: The Story of the Tragic Last Voyage of the 'Mignonette' and the Strange Legal Proceedings to Which it Gave Rise* (Chicago, IL, 1985).
17 Grant Allen, *The Beckoning Hand and Other Stories* (London, 1887), p. 25.
18 H. Hesketh-Prichard, *Where Black Rules White: A Journey Across and About Hayti* (London, 1911), p. xiv.
19 Ibid., p. 106.
20 Ibid., p. 107.
21 Ibid., p. 127.
22 Ibid., pp. 142, 129.
23 Ibid., p. 133.
24 Richard A. Loederer, *Voodoo Fire in Haiti*, trans. D. Vesey (New York, 1935), pp. 2, 17.
25 Ibid., pp. 252–3.
26 John Houston Craige, *Cannibal Cousins* (London, 1935), p. 201.
27 See Laënnec Hurbon, 'American Fantasy and Haitian Vodou', in *Sacred Arts of Haitian Vodou*, ed. D. J. Cosentino (Los Angeles, CA, 1995), pp. 181–97.
28 Bernard Deiderich and Al Burt, *Papa Doc: Haiti and its Dictator* (Harmondsworth, 1972), p. 348.
29 Graham Greene, 'Nightmare Republic', *New Republic*, CXLIX (16 November 1963), p. 18.
30 Francis Huxley, *The Invisibles: Voodoo Gods in Haiti* (London, 1966), p. 9.

31 Ibid., p. 81.
32 See Paul Farmer, AIDS and Accusation: Haiti and the Geography of Blame (Berkeley, CA, 1992), p. 2.
33 William Greenfield, 'Night of the Living Dead II: Slow Virus Encephalopathies and AIDS: Do Necromantic Zombiists Transmit HTLV-III/LAV during Voodooistic Rituals?', Journal of the American Medical Association, CCLVI/16 (1986), p. 2200.
34 Report cited in Farmer, AIDS and Accusation, p. 2.
35 Hurbon, 'American Fantasy', p. 195.
36 Erika Bourguignon, 'The Persistence of Folk Belief: Some Notes on Cannibalism and Zombis in Haiti', Journal of American Folklore, LXXII (1959), pp. 36–46.

3 The Pulp Zombie Emerges

1 Terror Tales, from September 1934, cited in Robert Kenneth Jones, The Shudder Pulps: A History of the Weird Menace Magazines of the 1930s (West Linn, OR, 1975), p. 19.
2 Samuel Taylor Coleridge review of The Monk [1797], reprinted in Gothic Documents: A Sourcebook, 1700–1820, ed. E. J. Clery and R. Miles (Manchester, 2000), p. 187.
3 Edgar Allan Poe, 'The Premature Burial' [1844], in The Selected Writings, ed. G. R. Thompson (New York, 2004), pp. 361–2.
4 Roland Barthes' analysis of this story discusses this moment as 'a true hapax of narrative grammar, a staging of speech impossible as speech: I am dead', in 'Textual Analysis of a Tale by Edgar Allan Poe', in The Semiotic Challenge, trans. R. Howard (Oxford, 1988), p. 285.
5 Henry Kuttner, 'The Graveyard Rats', in Zombies! Zombies! Zombies!, ed. O. Penzler (New York, 2011), p. 162.
6 H. P. Lovecraft, Supernatural Horror in Literature (New York, 1973), p. 15.
7 Influential books from the time included Madison Grant's The Passing of the Great Race (1916) and Lothrop Stoddard's The Rising Tide of Color against White World-supremacy (1920).
8 For Lovecraft, see my introduction to Classic Horror Tales (Oxford, 2013), pp. vii–xxviii. See also Christopher Frayling, The Yellow Peril: Dr Fu Manchu and the Rise of Chinaphobia (London, 2014).
9 Other useful collections include P. Haining, ed., Zombie: Stories of the Walking Dead (London, 1985) and John Richard Stephens, ed., The Book of the Living Dead (New York, 2010).
10 Seabury Quinn, 'The Corpse-master', in Zombies!, ed. Penzler, p. 412.

11 Ibid., pp. 412–13.
12 Thorp McClusky, 'While Zombies Walked', in *Zombies!*, ed. Penzler, p. 309.
13 G. W. Hutter, 'Salt is Not for Slaves', in *Book of the Living Dead*, ed. Stephens, p. 383.
14 Vivian Meik, 'White Zombie', in *Zombies!*, ed. Penzler, pp. 118, 119.
15 Theodore Roscoe's travel notes are excerpted in Audrey Parente, *Pulpmaster: The Theodore Roscoe Story* (Kindle Edition, 2012).
16 Theodore Roscoe, 'The Voodoo Express' [1931], reprinted in *The Wonderful Lips of Thibong Linh* (West Kingstown, 1981), pp. 127, 102.
17 Ibid., p. 83.
18 Ibid., pp. 71, 134.
19 Theodore Roscoe, *A Grave Must Be Deep: A Chilling Mystery of Haitian Black Magic* (London, 1947), p. 17.
20 Ibid., p. 74.
21 Theodore Roscoe, *Z is for Zombie* (Mercer Island, WA, 1989), p. 65.
22 Ibid., p. 79.
23 Lovecraft, letter to Henry Weiss (5 June 1931), in *Selected Letters*, vol. III (Sauk City, WI, 1971), p. 374.
24 Lovecraft, letter to E. Hoffmann Price (7 December 1932), in *Selected Letters*, vol. IV (Sauk City, WI, 1976), p. 116.
25 Henry S. Whitehead, 'Negro Dialect of the Virgin Islands', *American Speech*, VII/3 (1932), pp. 175–9.
26 Henry S. Whitehead, 'Jumbee', in *Voodoo Tales: The Ghost Stories of Henry S. Whitehead* (London, 2012), p. 336. All references are to this collected edition.
27 Ibid., pp. 336, 337.
28 Ibid., p. 341.
29 Whitehead, 'The Projection of Armand Dubois', p. 596.
30 Whitehead, 'Black Terror', p. 6.
31 Whitehead, 'The Black Beast', p. 490.
32 Whitehead, 'The Passing of a God', p. 446.
33 Ibid.
34 Ibid., p. 459.
35 Whitehead, 'The Lips', pp. 617–18.

4 The First Movie Cycle:
White Zombie to *Zombies on Broadway*

1 Quoted in George E. Turner and Michael H. Price, *Forgotten Horrors: The Definitive Edition* (Baltimore, MD, 1999), p. 26.
2 Details in this paragraph come from Thomas Docherty, *Pre-Code Hollywood: Sex, Immorality, and Insurrection in American Cinema, 1930–1934* (New York, 1999).
3 See Eric Schaefer, *Bold! Daring! Shocking! True! A History of Exploitation Films, 1919–59* (Durham, NC, 1999), especially the chapters on the 'exotic exploitation film'.
4 Chris Vials, 'The Origins of the Zombie in American Radio and Film: B-Horror, U.S. Empire, and the Politics of Disavowal', in *Generation Zombie: Essays on the Living Dead in Modern Culture*, ed. S. Boluk and W. Lenz (Jefferson, NC, 2011), p. 50.
5 See Gary Rhodes, *White Zombie: Anatomy of a Horror Film* (London, 2001) for discussion of the press pack and an exhaustive account of the production and release of the film.
6 John Vandercock, *Black Majesty: The Life of Christophe, King of Haiti* (New York, 1933), p. 4.
7 Alison Peirse, *After 'Dracula': The 1930s Horror Film* (London, 2013), p. 80.
8 Opinion of Judge Hoffman, cited in Rhodes, *White Zombie*, p. 173.
9 Hans Possendorf, *Damballa Calls: A Love Story of Haiti*, trans. L. Hudson (London, 1936), pp. 21–2.
10 See John Carter, *Sex and Rockets: The Occult World of Jack Parsons* (Port Townsend, WA, 2004).
11 Val Lewton quoted in Joel E. Siegel, *Val Lewton: The Reality of Terror* (London, 1972), p. 31.
12 Inez Wallace, 'I Met a Zombie', *American Weekly* (3 May 1942), reprinted as 'I Walked with a Zombie', in *Zombie: Stories of the Walking Dead*, ed. P. Haining (London, 1985) p. 96.
13 See 'Black Haiti: Where Old Africa and New World Meet', *Life* (13 December 1937), pp. 27–30.
14 Chris Fujiwara, *Jacques Tourneur: The Cinema of Nightfall* (Jefferson, NC, 2011), p. 87.
15 See Clayton Koppes and Gregory Black, *Hollywood Goes to War: How Politics, Profits and Propaganda Shaped World War II Movies* (London, 1988), pp. 127–8.
16 See Frederick Smith, *Caribbean Rum: A Social and Economic History* (Gainesville, FL, 2005).

17 Theodor Adorno's discussion of the 'torn halves' of the culture
industry and art is in his 'Correspondence with Benjamin', in
Adorno et al., *Aesthetics and Politics* (London, 1977).

5 Felicia Felix-Mentor: The 'Real' Zombie

1 Langston Hughes, 'People without Shoes' [1931], in *The Collected
Work of Langston Hughes* (Columbia, MO, 2002), vol. IX, p. 47.
2 See the chapter on these links in J. Michael Dash, *Haiti and the
United States: National Stereotypes and the Literary Imagination*
(London, 1997).
3 Franz Boas, *The Mind of Primitive Man* (New York, 1916), p. 98.
4 Henrika Kucklick, 'After Ishmael: The Fieldwork Tradition and its
Future', in *Anthropological Locations: Boundaries and Grounds of a
Field Science*, ed. A. Gupta and J. Ferguson (Berkeley, CA, 1997),
p. 53.
5 Zora Neale Hurston, 'Hoodoo in America', *Journal of American
Folklore*, XLIV (1931), p. 358.
6 Ibid., p. 359.
7 Ibid., pp. 390–91.
8 Ibid., p. 370.
9 See Dorothea Fischer-Hornung, '"Keep Alive the Powers of
Africa": Katherine Dunham, Zora Neale Hurston, Maya Deren,
and the Circum-Caribbean Culture of Vodoun', *Atlantic Studies*,
V/3 (2008), pp. 347–62.
10 Hurston, 'Hoodoo', pp. 398–9.
11 Review cited in Robert Hemenway, *Zora Neale Hurston: A Literary
Biography* (London, 1986), p. 251.
12 Journalist Helen Worden, cited in Mary Renda, *Taking Haiti:
Military Occupation and the Culture of U.S. Imperialism* (Chapel
Hill, NC, 2001), p. 293.
13 Zora Neale Hurston, *Tell My Horse* (New York, 1938), p. 234.
14 Amy Fass Emery, 'The Zombie in/as the Text: Zora Neale
Hurston's *Tell My Horse*', *African American Review*, XXXIX/3
(2005), pp. 327–36.
15 Hurston, *Tell My Horse*, p. 102.
16 Ibid., p. 163.
17 Ibid., p. 164.
18 Ibid., pp. 178–9.
19 Ibid., p. 191.
20 Ibid., pp. 205–6.
21 Ibid., p. 206.

22 Ibid., p. 220.
23 Ibid., p. 266.
24 Jean Price-Mars, *So Spoke the Uncle: Ethnographic Essays*, trans. M. Shannon (Washington, DC, 1983), pp. 147–8. *Ainsi parla l'oncle* was first published in Port-au-Prince in 1928.
25 Melville Herskovits, *Life in a Haitian Valley* (New York, 1937), pp. vii, 246.
26 Louis P. Mars, 'The Story of Zombi in Haiti', *Man*, XLV (March–April 1945), pp. 38, 40.

6 After 1945: Zombie Massification

1 Susan Sontag, *On Photography* (Harmondsworth, 1977), pp. 19–20.
2 See Paul Boyer, *By the Bomb's Early Light: American Thought and Culture at the Dawn of the Atomic Age* (New York, 1985).
3 Norman Cousins, 'Modern Man is Obsolete', *Saturday Review of Literature* (14 August 1945), p. 5.
4 See Roger Luckhurst, *The Trauma Question* (London, 2008).
5 Robert Jay Lifton, *Death in Life: The Survivors of Hiroshima* (London, 1968), p. 21.
6 Ibid., p. 517.
7 Robert Jay Lifton, 'The Survivors of the Hiroshima Disaster and the Survivors of Nazi Persecution', in *Massive Psychic Trauma*, ed. H. Krystal (New York, 1968), p. 179.
8 Lifton, *Death in Life*, p. 540.
9 See Zdzisław Jan Ryn and Stanisław Kłodziński, 'Between Life and Death: Experiences of the Concentration Camp Musulmen', in *Auschwitz Survivors: Clinical-Psychiatric Studies*, trans. E. Jarosz and P. Mizia, ed. Z. J. Ryn (Krakow, 2005), p. 111.
10 Primo Levi, *If This is a Man* [1947], trans. S. Woolf (London, 1979), p. 96.
11 Giorgio Agamben, *Remnants of Auschwitz: The Witness and the Archive*, trans. D. Heller-Roazen (New York, 1999), p. 82.
12 Wolfgang Sofsky, *The Order of Terror: The Concentration Camp*, trans. W. Templer (Princeton, NJ, 1993), p. 199.
13 See Ryn and Kłodziński, 'Between Life and Death', pp. 116–19.
14 Sofsky, *Order of Terror*, p. 200.
15 Ibid., p. 204.
16 See Michael Rothberg, *Traumatic Realism: The Demands of Holocaust Representation* (Minneapolis, MN, 2000), or Robert Eaglestone, *The Holocaust and the Postmodern* (Oxford, 2004).

17 'The Living Dead', *Dark Mysteries* (October 1954), reprinted in *The Horror! The Horror! Comic Books the Government Didn't Want You to Read!*, ed. Jim Trombetta (New York, 2010), p. 182.

18 Ibid., p. 183.

19 Hannah Arendt, *The Origins of Totalitarianism*, new edn (New York, 1973), p. 316.

20 Aimé Césaire, *Discourse on Colonialism*, trans. J. Pinkham (New York, 2000), p. 41. For Rothberg's commentary, see Michael Rothberg, *Multidirectional Memory: Remembering the Holocaust in the Age of Decolonization* (Stanford, CA, 2009).

21 Arendt, *Origins of Totalitarianism*, pp. 171, xvii.

22 Césaire, *Discourse*, p. 49.

23 Albert Memmi, *Decolonization and the Decolonized*, trans. R. Bononno (Minneapolis, MN, 2006), p. 129.

24 Cited in Hugh Deane, *The Korean War, 1945–53* (San Francisco, CA, 1999), p. 114.

25 B.A.H. Parritt, *Chinese Hordes and Human Waves: A Personal Perspective of the Korean War* (Barnsley, 2011), p. 106.

26 Dan Gilbert, 'Why the Yellow Peril Has Turned Red!' [1951], excerpted in *Yellow Peril! An Archive of Anti-Asian Fear*, ed. John Kuo Wei Tchen and Dylan Yeats (London, 2014), pp. 299, 301.

27 Edward Hunter, cited in David Seed, *Brainwashing: The Fictions of Mind Control: A Study of Novels and Films since World War II* (Kent, OH, 2004), p. 29.

28 Joost Meerloo, 'The Crime of Menticide', *American Journal of Psychiatry*, CVII (1951), pp. 594–8.

29 Richard Condon, *The Manchurian Candidate* (London, 1960), p. 105.

30 Ibid., pp. 204, 230.

31 See Susan Carruthers, '*The Manchurian Candidate* (1962) and the Cold War Brainwashing Scare', *Historical Journal of Film, Radio and Television*, XVIII/1 (1998), pp. 75–94. 'The Paranoid Style in American Politics' was an essay by Richard Hofstadter, first published in *Harper's Magazine* in 1964.

32 Jack Finney, *Invasion of the Body Snatchers* (London, 1999), p. 179.

33 J. Edgar Hoover, *Masters of Deceit: The Story of Communism in America and How to Fight It* (New York, 1958), p. vi.

34 Ibid., p. 9.

35 Peter Biskind, *Seeing is Believing: How Hollywood Taught Us to Stop Worrying and Love the Fifties* (New York, 1983), p. 4.

36 David Riesman, *The Lonely Crowd: A Study of the Changing American Character* (New Haven, CT, 1950), p. 22.

37 Vance Packard, *The Hidden Persuaders* [1957] (Harmondsworth, 1977), p. 9.
38 Vance Packard, chapter Ten of *The Status Seekers* (1959), excerpted at www.writing.upenn.edu.
39 Susan Sontag, 'The Imagination of Disaster', in Sontag, *Against Interpretation and Other Essays* (London, 1987), p. 214.
40 Richard Hoggart, *Uses of Literacy: Aspects of Working-class Life, with Special Reference to Publications and Entertainments* (London, 1957), p. 204.
41 Bernard Rosenberg, 'Mass Culture in America', in *Mass Culture: The Popular Arts in America*, ed. B. Rosenberg and D. Manning White (Glencoe, IL, 1957), pp. 3, 5, 8, 9.
42 Dwight MacDonald, 'A Theory of Popular Culture', *Politics*, 1 (February 1944), p. 22. This essay was rewritten and retitled for the Rosenberg and Manning White collection as 'A Theory of Mass Culture'.
43 'Horror of Mixed Torsos', *Dark Mysteries* (August 1953), reprinted in *Zombies: The Chilling Archives of Horror Comics*, ed. C. Yoe and S. Barnes (San Diego, CA, 2012), pp. 50–55.
44 Trombetta, ed., *The Horror! The Horror!*, p. 167.
45 Last panel of 'Step into My Empty Shroud', *The Beyond* (January 1954), in *Zombies*, ed. Yoe and Banes, p. 30.
46 All quotes from 'CORPSES . . . COAST TO COAST', *Voodoo* (March 1954), reprinted in *The Horror!*, ed. Trombetta, pp. 193–9.
47 All quotes from 'Marching Zombies', *Black Cat* (May 1952), reprinted in *Zombies*, ed. Yoe and Banes, pp. 122–8.
48 Daniel F. Yezbick, 'Horror', *Comics through Time: A History of Icons, Idols and Ideas*, ed. M. Keith Booker, 4 vols (Westport, CT, 2014), vol. 1, pp. 1071–84.
49 Norbert Muhlen, 'Comic Books and Other Horrors', *Commentary* (January 1949), pp. 80–87, all citations from unpaginated online version at www.commentarymagazine.com.
50 Fredric Wertham, *Seduction of the Innocent* (London, 1955), p. 87.
51 Ibid., pp. 26, 34.
52 See Paul Hirsch, '"This is Our Enemy": The Writers' War Board and Representations of Race in Comic Books, 1942–45', *Pacific Historical Review*, LXXXIII/3 (2014), pp. 448–86.
53 Robert Warshow, 'Paul, the Horror Comics, and Dr Wertham', in *The Immediate Experience: Movies, Comics, Theatre and Other Aspects of Popular Culture* (Cambridge, MA, 2001), p. 73.
54 Testimony cited in Bart Beaty, *Fredric Wertham and the Critique of Mass Culture* (Jackson, FL, 2005), p. 159.

55 The 1954 Code is reprinted in full at www.comicartville.com/comicscode.htm, accessed 27 January 2015.

56 Markman Ellis, *The History of Gothic Fiction* (Edinburgh, 2000), pp. 205, 239.

57 Robert Kirkman, 'Introduction', *The Walking Dead*, vol. I: *Days Gone Bye* (Berkeley, CA, 2012), n.p.

58 Stephen King, *Danse Macabre* [1981] (London, 1988), p. 36.

7 The Zombie Apocalypse: Romero's Reboot and Italian Horrors

1 Cited in Elliott Stein, 'Night of the Living Dead', *Sight and Sound*, XXXIX (Spring 1970), p. 105.

2 Roger Ebert review, *Chicago Sun* (5 January 1969), cited in Kevin Heffernan, 'Inner-city Exhibition and the Genre Film: Distributing *The Night of the Living Dead* (1968)', *Cinema Journal*, XLI/3 (2002), p. 60.

3 See Leslie Fiedler's Zeitgeist essay 'Cross the Border – Close the Gap', in his *Collected Essays* (New York, 1971), vol. II. The convergence of low horror and high art is the subject of Joan Hawkins, *Cutting Edge: Art-horror and the Horrific Avant-garde* (Minneapolis, MN, 2000).

4 Eldridge Cleaver, 'The Death of Martin Luther King: Requiem for Nonviolence', *Post-prison Writings and Speeches* (London, 1971), pp. X, 75.

5 See Chris Marker, 'Sixties', *Critical Quarterly*, L/3 (2008), pp. 26–32, an essay that is a comment on his extraordinary documentary about the revolutionary years 1967–8, *The Grin Without a Cat*.

6 Ben Hervey, *Night of the Living Dead* (London, 2008), p. 88.

7 Stein, 'Night', p. 105.

8 Steven Shaviro, *The Cinematic Body* (Minneapolis, MN, 1993), p. 54.

9 Robin Wood, *Hollywood from Vietnam to Reagan* (New York, 1986), p. 93.

10 James Cameron, *The Time of Terror: A Survivor's Story*, cited in David Marriott, *On Black Men* (Edinburgh, 2000), p. 1.

11 See Tony Williams, *The Cinema of George A. Romero: Knight of the Living Dead* (London, 2003).

12 David McNally, *Monsters of the Market: Zombies, Vampires and Global Capitalism* (Chicago, IL, 2012), p. 1.

13 John Clarke, Stuart Hall, Tony Jefferson and Brian Roberts, 'The Rise of the Counter-cultures', in *Resistance through Rituals: Subcultures in Post-war Britain*, ed. Hall and Jefferson (London, 1976), p. 65.

14 Carol Bernick, quoted in John Hinshaw, *Steel and Steelworkers: Race and Class Struggle in Twentieth-century Pittsburgh* (New York, 2002). The role of Pittsburgh in *Martin* is discussed in Stacey Abbott, *Celluloid Vampires: Life after Death in the Modern World* (Austin, TX, 2007).

15 Margaret Morse, 'The Ontology of Everyday Distraction: The Freeway, the Mall, and Television', in *Logics of Television: Essays in Cultural Criticism*, ed. P. Mellencamp (Bloomington, IN, 1990), pp. 193–221.

16 This argument relies on the excellent account of the limits of this routine anti-capitalist reading of *Dawn of the Dead* by Evan Calder Williams in his *Combined and Uneven Apocalypse* (Winchester, 2011).

17 See Lee Karr, *The Making of George A. Romero's 'The Day of the Dead'* (London, 2014).

18 Jean and John Comaroff, 'Alien-nation: Zombies, Immigrants, and Millennial Capitalism', *South Atlantic Quarterly*, CI/4 (2002), p. 783.

19 Robin Wood, 'Fresh Meat', *Film Comment*, XLIV/I (2008), pp. 28–31.

20 Paul Boyer, *When Time Shall Be No More: Prophecy Belief in Modern American Culture* (Cambridge, 1992).

21 Kim Paffenroth, *Gospel of the Living Dead: George Romero's Visions of Hell on Earth* (Waco, TX, 2006), p. 23.

22 I have argued this at more length in my essay 'The Public Sphere, Popular Culture and the True Meaning of the Zombie Apocalypse', in *The Cambridge Companion to Popular Culture*, ed. D. Glover and S. McCracken (Cambridge, 2012), pp. 68–85.

23 See Jim Harper, 'The New Regime: Spanish Horror in the 1970s and the End of the Dictatorship', in *The End: An 'Electric Sheep' Anthology*, ed. V. Sélavy (London, 2011), pp. 63–70.

24 See Donato Totaro's explanation in 'A Genealogy of Italian Popular Cinema: The Filone', *Offscreen*, XV/11, www.offscreen.com (2011).

25 Lucio Fulci, quoted in Jay Slater, *Eaten Alive! Italian Cannibal and Horror Movies* (London, 2002), p. 176.

26 For a full but sceptical survey, see Kim Newman's 'Cannibal Zombie Gut-crunchers – Italian Style!', in his *Nightmare Movies: Horror on Screen since the 1960s*, 2nd edn (London, 2011), pp. 253–69.

27 Carolyn Korsmeyer, *Savoring Disgust: The Foul and the Fair in Aesthetics* (Oxford, 2011), p. 34.

28 Immanuel Kant, *Critique of Judgment*, cited ibid., p. 46.

29 Jeffrey Sconce, '"Trashing" the Academy: Taste, Excess, and an Emerging Politics of Cinematic Style', *Screen*, XXXVI/4 (1995), pp. 371–93.

30 See J. Hoberman, *Vulgar Modernism: Writing on Movies and Other Media* (Philadelphia, PA, 1991). The phrase 'trash vitality' comes from Newman, *Nightmare Movies*, p. 49.

31 Patricia MacCormack, 'Masochistic Cinesexuality: The Many Deaths of Giovanni Lombardo Radice', in *Alternative Europe: Eurotrash and Exploitation Cinema since 1945*, ed. E. Mathijs and X. Mendik (London, 2004), p. 107.

32 Ian Olney, *Euro Horror: Classic European Horror Cinema in Contemporary American Culture* (Bloomington, IN, 2013), p. 211.

33 John Clute, 'Vastation', *The Darkening Garden: A Short Lexicon of Horror* (Cauheegan, WI, 2006), pp. 147, 149.

34 Eugene Thacker, *Horror of Philosophy*, vol. I: *In the Dust of this Planet* (Winchester, 2011), pp. 8–9.

8 Going Global

1 Ulrich Beck, *The Risk Society: Towards a New Modernity*, trans. M. Ritter (London, 1992), p. 79.

2 Shinji Mikami, cited in Matthew Weise, 'The Rules of Horror: Procedural Adaptation in *Clock Tower*, *Resident Evil*, and *Dead Rising*', in *Horror Video Games: Essays on the Fusion of Fear and Play*, ed. B. Perron (Jefferson, NC, 2009), p. 252.

3 See, for instance, Leigh Alexander, 'Does Survival Horror Really Still Exist?', www.kotaku.com, September 2008.

4 Tanya Krzywinska, 'Hands-on Horror', in *Screenplay: Cinema/Videogames/Interfaces*, ed. G. King and T. Krzywinska (London, 2002), pp. 206–23.

5 See Colette Balmain, *Introduction to Japanese Horror Film* (Edinburgh, 2008).

6 For discussion of this case, see Wagner James Au, 'Playing Games with Free Speech', www.salon.com, 6 May 2002.

7 See Matthew J. Weise, 'How the Zombie Changed Videogames', in *Zombies Are Us: Essays on the Humanity of the Walking Dead*, ed. C. Moreman and C. Rushton (Jefferson, NC, 2011), pp. 151–68.

8 Report of the Ad Hoc Committee of the Harvard Medical School to Examine the Definition of Brain Death, 'A Definition

of Irreversible Coma', *Journal of the American Medical Association*, ccv/6 (5 August 1968), p. 337.

9 Many of the details in this paragraph derive from Dick Teresi, *The Undead: How Medicine is Blurring the Boundary between Life and Death* (New York, 2012).

10 Cited in Margaret Lock, 'On Making Up the Good-as-Dead in a Utilitarian World', in *Remaking Life and Death: Toward an Anthropology of the Biosciences*, ed. S. Franklin and M. Lock (Santa Fe, NM, 2001), p. 186.

11 Ibid., p. 189.

12 Susan Sontag, AIDS *and its Metaphors* (London, 1989), p. 87.

13 Heinrich Heine, *Conditions in France*, quoted in Marie-Hélène Huet, *The Culture of Disaster* (Chicago, IL, 2012), pp. 72–3.

14 Molly Caldwell Crosby, *Asleep: The Forgotten Epidemic that Remains one of Medicine's Great Mysteries* (New York, 2010), p. 25.

15 Wendell Stanley quoted in Priscilla Wald, *Contagious: Cultures, Carriers, and the Outbreak Narrative* (Durham, NC, 2008), p. 163.

16 Paul Farmer, AIDS *and Accusation: Haiti and the Geography of Blame* (Berkeley, CA, 1992), p. 2.

17 Wald, *Contagious*, p. 27.

18 Richard Preston, *The Hot Zone* (New York, 1994), p. 18.

19 Frank Kermode, *The Sense of an Ending: Studies in the Theory of Fiction* (Oxford, 1968), p. 8.

20 Achille Mbembe, 'Necropolitics', *Public Culture*, XV/1 (2003), pp. 11–40.

21 Mark Fisher, 'How to Kill a Zombie: Strategizing the End of Neoliberalism', www.opendemocracy.net, 18 July 2013.

22 John Clute, 'Fantastika in the World Storm', in *Pardon this Intrusion: Fantastika in the World Storm* (Harold Wood, Essex, 2011), p. 24.

23 Fred Botting and Justin D. Edwards, 'Theorizing Globalgothic', in *Globalgothic*, ed. Glennis Byron (Manchester, 2013), p. 15.

24 Max Brooks, *World War Z: An Oral History of the Zombie War* (London, 2006), p. 32.

25 See Sarah Juliet Lauro and Karen Embry, 'A Zombie Manifesto: The Nonhuman Condition in the Era of Advanced Capitalism', *boundary 2*, XXXV/1 (2008), pp. 85–108. The idea of the 'multitude' derives from Antonio Negri and Michael Hardt, *Multitude: War and Democracy in the Age of Empire* (London, 2009).

26 See Adam Lowenstein, *Shocking Representation: Historical Trauma, National Cinema, and the Modern Horror Film* (New York, 2005).

27 Sherryl Vint, 'Abject Posthumanism: Neoliberalism, Biopolitics, and Zombies', in *Monster Culture in the 21st Century: A Reader*, ed. M. Levina and D. Bui (London, 2013), pp. 143–4.

28 Tony Burgess, *Pontypool Changes Everything* [1995] (Toronto, 2009), p. 158.

29 Seth Grahame-Smith, *Pride and Prejudice and Zombies* (London, 2009), p. 1.

30 *Doctor Who*, 'The Unquiet Dead' (BBC One, 9 April 2005).

31 Stewart Home, *Mandy, Charlie and Mary-Jane* (Los Angeles, CA, 2013), p. 11.

32 See Lorna Jowett and Stacey Abbott, TV *Horror: Investigating the Dark Side of the Small Screen* (London, 2013).

33 Robert Kirkman, preface to *The Walking Dead*, vol. 1: *Days Gone Bye* (Berkeley, CA, 2012), n.p.

34 Judith Butler, *Precarious Life: The Power of Mourning and Violence* (London, 2006), p. 46.

35 Ulrich Beck, 'Zombie Categories: An Interview', in Ulrich Beck and Elisabeth Beck-Gernsheim, *Individualization: Institutionalized Individualism and its Social and Political Consequences* (London, 2002), pp. 202–13.

36 See Elizabeth Isichei, 'The Entrepreneur and the Zombie', in her *Voices of the Poor in Africa* (Rochester, NY, 2002).

37 See Luise White, *Speaking with Vampires: Rumor and History in Colonial Africa* (Berkeley, CA, 2000).

38 Jean Comaroff and John Comaroff, 'Occult Economies and the Violence of Abstraction: Notes from the South African Postcolony', *American Ethnologist*, XXVI/2 (1999), p. 289.

39 See Jean Comaroff and John Comaroff, 'Alien-nation: Zombies, Immigrants, and Millennial Capitalism', *South Atlantic Quarterly*, CI/4 (2002), pp. 779–805.

40 Isak Niehaus, *Witchcraft and a Life in the New South Africa* (Cambridge, 2013), p. 5.

Select Bibliography

Ackermann, Hans-W., and Jeanine Gauthier, 'The Ways and Nature of the Zombi', *Journal of American Folklore*, CIV (1991), pp. 466–91

Agamben, Giorgio, *Remnants of Auschwitz: The Witness and the Archive*, trans. D. Heller-Roazen (New York, 1999)

Blanchard, Pascal, et al., eds, *Human Zoos: Science and Spectacle in the Age of Colonial Empires* (Liverpool, 2008)

Boluk, S., and W. Lenz, eds, *Generation Zombie: Essays on the Living Dead in Modern Culture* (Jefferson, NC, 2011)

Bonsal, Stephen, *The American Mediterranean* (London, 1913)

Bourguignon, Erika, 'The Persistence of Folk Belief: Some Notes on Cannibalism and Zombis in Haiti', *Journal of American Folklore*, LXXII (1959), pp. 36–46

Boyer, Paul, *By the Bomb's Early Light: American Thought and Culture at the Dawn of the Atomic Age* (New York, 1985)

Césaire, Aimé, *Discourse on Colonialism*, trans. J. Pinkham (New York, 2000)

Comaroff, Jean, and John Comaroff, 'Alien-nation: Zombies, Immigrants, and Millennial Capitalism', *South Atlantic Quarterly*, CI/4 (2002), pp. 779–805

Consentino, D. J., ed., *Sacred Acts of Haitian Vodou* (Los Angeles, CA, 1995)

Dash, J. Michael, *Haiti and the United States: National Stereotypes and the Literary Imagination* (London, 1997)

Diederich, Bernard, and Al Burt, *Papa Doc: Haiti and its Dictator* (Harmondsworth, 1972)

Docherty, Thomas, *Pre-code Hollywood: Sex, Immorality, and Insurrection in American Cinema, 1930–1934* (New York, 1999)

Clute, John, *The Darkening Garden: A Short Lexicon of Horror* (Cauheegan, WI, 2006)

Craige, John Houston, *Cannibal Cousins* (London, 1935)

Emery, Amy Fass, 'The Zombie in/as the Text: Zora Neale Hurston's *Tell My Horse*', *African American Review*, XXXIX/3 (2005), pp. 327–36

Fanon, Frantz, *The Wretched of the Earth*, trans. Constance Farrington (Harmondsworth, 1985)

Farmer, Paul, AIDS *and Accusation: Haiti and the Geography of Blame* (Berkeley, CA, 1992)

Fujiwara, Chris, *Jacques Tourneur: The Cinema of Nightfall* (Jefferson, NC, 2011)

Gilroy, Paul, *The Black Atlantic: Modernity and Double Consciousness* (London, 1993)

Glissant, Édouard, *Caribbean Discourse: Selected Essays*, trans. J. M. Dash (Charlottesville, VA, 1989)

Haining, Peter, ed., *Zombie: Stories of the Walking Dead* (London, 1985)

Hearn, Lafcadio, *Inventing New Orleans: Writings of Lafcadio Hearn*, ed. S. Frederick Starr (New Orleans, LA, 2001)

—, *Martinique Sketches* [1938], in *American Writings* (New York, 2009)

Herskovits, Melville, *Life in a Haitian Valley* (New York, 1937)

Hervey, Ben, *Night of the Living Dead* (London, 2008)

Hesketh-Prichard, H., *Where Black Rules White: A Journey Across and About Hayti* (London, 1911)

Hulme, Peter, *Colonial Encounters: Europe and the Native Caribbean, 1492–1797* (London, 1986)

Hurston, Zora Neale, 'Hoodoo in America', *Journal of American Folklore*, XLIV (1931), pp. 317–417

—, *Tell My Horse* (New York, 1938)

Jones, Robert Kenneth, *The Shudder Pulps: A History of the Weird Menace Magazines of the 1930s* (West Linn, OR, 1975)

Karr, Lee, *The Making of George A. Romero's 'The Day of the Dead'* (London, 2014)

Korsmeyer, Carolyn, *Savoring Disgust: The Foul and the Fair in Aesthetics* (Oxford, 2011)

Loederer, Richard A., *Voodoo Fire in Haiti*, trans. D. Vesey (New York, 1935)

Lovecraft, H. P., *Supernatural Horror in Literature* (New York, 1973)

McNally, David, *Monsters of the Market: Zombies, Vampires and Global Capitalism* (Chicago, IL, 2012)

Mars, Louis P., 'The Story of Zombi in Haiti', *Man*, XLV (March–April 1945), pp. 38–40

Mathijs, E., and X. Mendik, eds, *Alternative Europe: Eurotrash and Exploitation Cinema since 1945* (London, 2004)

Mbembe, Achille, 'Necropolitics', *Public Culture*, xv/1 (2003),
    pp. 11–40
Memmi, Albert, *Decolonization and the Decolonized*, trans. R. Bononno
    (Minneapolis, MN, 2006)
Moreman, C., and C. Rushton, eds., *Zombies Are Us: Essays on the
    Humanity of the Walking Dead* (Jefferson, NC, 2011)
Newman, Kim, *Nightmare Movies: Horror on Screen since the 1960s*,
    2nd edn (London, 2011)
Obeyesekere, Gananath, '"British Cannibals": Contemplation of an
    Event in the Death and Resurrection of James Cook, Explorer',
    Critical Inquiry, XVIII (1992), pp. 630–54
Olney, Ian, *Euro Horror: Classic European Horror Cinema in
    Contemporary American Culture* (Bloomington, IN, 2013)
Parsons, Elsie Clews, *Folk-lore of the Antilles, French and English*, 3 vols
    (New York, 1933–43)
Patterson, Orlando, *Slavery and Social Death: A Comparative Study*
    (Cambridge, 1982)
Peirse, Alison, *After 'Dracula': The 1930s Horror Film* (London, 2013)
Penzler, Otto, ed., *Zombies! Zombies! Zombies!* (New York, 2011)
Perron, B, ed., *Horror Video Games: Essays on the Fusion of Fear and Play*
    (Jefferson, NC, 2009)
Possendorf, Hans, *Damballa Calls: A Love Story of Haiti*, trans.
    L. A. Hudson (London, 1936)
Price-Mars, Jean, *So Spoke the Uncle: Ethnographic Essays*, trans.
    M. Shannon (Washington, DC, 1983)
Ramsey, Kate, *The Spirits and the Law: Vodou and Power in Haiti*
    (Chicago, IL, 2011)
Renda, Mary, *Taking Haiti: Military Occupation and the Culture of U.S.
    Imperialism* (Chapel Hill, NC, 2001)
Rhodes, Gary, *White Zombie: Anatomy of a Horror Film* (London, 2001)
Roscoe, Theodore, *Z is for Zombie* (Mercer Island, WA, 1989)
Rosenberg, Bernard, and D. Manning White, eds, *Mass Culture:
    The Popular Arts in America* (Glencoe, IL, 1957)
Rutherford, Jennifer, *Zombies* (London, 2013)
Ryn, Zdzisław Jan and Stanisław Kłodziński, 'Between Life and Death:
    Experiences of the Concentration Camp Musulmen', in *Auschwitz
    Survivors: Clinical Psychiatric Studies*, trans. E. Jarosz and P. Mizia,
    ed. Z. J. Ryn (Krakow, 2005), pp. 111–24
St John, Spenser, *Hayti; or, The Black Republic* (London, 1884)
Schaefer, Eric, *Bold! Daring! Shocking! True! A History of the Exploitation
    Film, 1919–59* (Durham, NC, 1999)
Seabrook, William, *Jungle Ways* (London, 1931)

——, *No Place to Hide: An Autobiography* (Philadelphia, PA, 1942)

——, *The Voodoo Island* (London, 1966)

——, *Witchcraft: Its Power in the World Today* (London, 1941)

Seed, David, *Brainwashing: The Fictions of Mind Control: A Study of Novels and Films since World War II* (Kent, OH, 2004)

Shaviro, Steven, *The Cinematic Body* (Minneapolis, MN, 1993)

Siegel, Joel E., *Val Lewton: The Reality of Terror* (London, 1972)

Slater, Jay, ed., *Eaten Alive! Italian Cannibal and Horror Movies* (London, 2002)

Smith, Frederick, *Caribbean Rum: A Social and Economic History* (Gainesville, FL, 2005)

Stein, Elliott, 'Night of the Living Dead', *Sight and Sound*, XXXIX (Spring 1970), p. 105

Stephens, John Richard, ed., *The Book of the Living Dead* (New York, 2010).

Teresi, Dick, *The Undead: How Medicine is Blurring the Boundary between Life and Death* (New York, 2012)

Thacker, Eugene, *Horror of Philosophy*, vol 1: *In the Dust of this Planet* (Winchester, 2011)

Trombetta, Jim, ed., *The Horror! The Horror! Comic Books the Government Didn't Want You to Read!* (New York, 2010)

Turner, George E., and Michael H. Price, *Forgotten Horrors: The Definitive Edition* (Baltimore, MD, 1999)

Wald, Priscilla, *Contagious: Cultures, Carriers, and the Outbreak Narrative* (Durham, NC, 2008)

Wertham, Frederic, *Seduction of the Innocent* (London, 1955)

Whitehead, Henry S., *Voodoo Tales: The Ghost Stories of Henry S. Whitehead* (London, 2012)

Williams, Tony, *The Cinema of George A. Romero: Knight of the Living Dead* (London, 2003)

Wood, Robin, *Hollywood from Vietnam to Reagan* (New York, 1986)

Yoe, C., and S. Barnes, *Zombies: The Chilling Archives of Horror Comics* (San Diego, CA, 2012)

Zieger, Susan, 'The Case of William Seabrook: *Documents*, Haiti, and the Working Dead', *Modernism/Modernity*, XIX/4 (2013), pp. 737–54

Acknowledgements

For advice, help, clues and tips, book and DVD loans, invitations to speak and conversation, thanks are due to Andrew Abbott, Stacey Abbott (an extra big shout-out for reading the last draft and offering very useful suggestions), Simon Barraclough, James Bell, Mark Blacklock, M. Keith Booker, Mark Bould, Joe Brooker, Gerry Canavan, Julie Crofts, Barry Curtis, Robert Eaglestone, David Edgar, Justin Edwards, William Fowler, Paweł Frelik, Grace Halden, Stephen Hughes, Timothy Jarvis, Joe Kerr, James Kneale, John Kraniauskas, Mary Luckhurst, Tom McCarthy, James Machin, Dawn Mellor, William Mitchell-Reid, Glyn Morgan, Mpalive Msiska, Victoria Nelson, Kim Newman, Chris Pak, Adam Roberts, Laura Thomas, Tony Venezia, Sherryl Vint and Marina Warner. Thanks to my editor Ben Hayes and to Reaktion Books for commissioning this book.

This is for Julie, as always, even though she won't watch splatter horror and particularly not zombie films and so remains sadly unaware that the knitting needle is actually the ideal weapon for close fighting during the zombie apocalypse.

Photo Acknowledgements

The author and publishers wish to express their thanks to the below sources of illustrative material and/or permission to reproduce it:

Beinecke Rare Book and Manuscript Library, Yale University: pp. 42–3, 102; Library of Congress, Prints and Photographs Collection, Washington, DC: pp. 98, 107; image courtesy of HarperCollins: p. 105; Österreichische Nationalbibliothek, Vienna, Pf 25.322:B(1): p 27.

Eneas, the copyright holder of the image on p. 168, has published this online under conditions imposed by a Creative Commons Attribution 2.0 Generic license.

Readers are free:

to share – to copy, distribute and transmit these images alone
to remix – to adapt these images alone

Under the following conditions:

attribution – readers must attribute any image in the manner specified by the author or licensor (but not in any way that suggests that these parties endorse them or their use of the work).

Index

28 Days Later 12, 170, 182

Abbott and Costello 93–4
Adorno, Theodor 96, 129
Africa 10, 14, 194–6
Agamben, Giorgio 113
AIDS 55–6, 182, 195
Alderman, Naomi 192
Algeria 117
allegory 183
Allen, Grant 51
American Civil War 46
American empire 31, 32–6,
    69–70
'Andromeda strain' concept 182
anthropology 20, 99, 103, 108, 194
apocalypse 111, 121, 135, 140,
    148, 156, 167, 170, 179,
    182–3, 192
Arab hordes 185–6
Arendt, Hannah 116, 118
Argento, Dario 147, 158
Asian hordes 119–21, 135
atomic bomb 110, 119, 131
Auschwitz 110, 113

Baker, Josephine 24, 79
Bataille, Georges 24
Bava, Mario 158

Bellamy, Madge 84–5
Beyond, The (1981) 55, 160–61,
    165
biopolitics 180
Black Moon (1934) 79
Black Panthers 141
Blonde Venus 78
Boas, Franz 99
Bonsal, Stephen 49
Bourguignon, Erika 56
Boyle, Danny 12
brain death 175
brainwashing 121–4
British Empire 50–51, 117
Brodber, Erna 40
Browning, Tod 75
Buba, Tony 151
Buffy the Vampire Slayer
    (TV series) 10, 192
Burgess, Tony 190
burial alive 60
Butler, Judith 193
Butler, Smedley 69

Call of Duty 116
Cannibal Ferox 163
Cannibal Holocaust 159, 161–5
cannibalism 25, 47–53, 55, 56,
    143, 159, 194

Carey, M. R. 13, 182
Carmageddon 173
Carradine, John 89, 116
Cat People (1942) 90
Catholicism 34, 35, 44, 46, 54,
    70, 100, 156
Center for Disease Control and
    Prevention 9, 181
Césaire, Aimé 37, 118
Chagnon, Napoleon 165
Cleaver, Eldridge 141–2
Cockneys vs Zombies 188
Code Noir 44, 46
Columbus, Christopher 49–50
coma 176, 178
comics 115, 129–36
concentration camps 110, 118,
    153
    Auschwitz 110, 113
    and the living dead 113–15
contagion 179–80
Corman, Roger 138
Craige, John Houston 53
Crazies, The (1973) 147, 169
Creature with the Atom Brain 112
Crowley, Aleister 23
Cunard, Nancy 24–5

Dahomey 50
Davis, Wade 31, 56, 106
Dawn of the Dead (1978) 8, 128,
    138, 146, 147–52, 169
Dawn of the Dead (2004) 154,
    170
Day of the Dead 152–4
Dead, The (2010) 186
Dead 2, The (2013) 187
Dead Outside, The 188
Dead Snow 116
death, medical definition of 175
Deathdream 146
Debord, Guy 150

Deodato, Ruggero 161–5
Deren, Maya 100
Desert, The 189
Diary of the Dead 154–5
Dickens, Charles 51, 191
disgust 163–4
Douglas, Mary 163
Dracula 7, 75, 80, 159
Dunham, Katherine 100
Duvalier, François 54

Ebert, Roger 140
Ebola 179, 182
EC Comics 132, 135, 137, 143,
    144, 153

Fanon, Frantz 37–8, 46, 118
Felix-Mentor, Felicia 103–5, 187
Firbank, Ronald 74
Fisher, Mark 183
folklore 17, 18, 65, 71, 99
Foucault, Michel 180
French empire 33–4, 46
Fulci, Lucio 159–61, 192

Gaines, Bill (William) 132,
    133–4
genocide 110
Germany 69, 89–90, 115–17, 118
Ghost Breakers 88
ghoul 9, 137
Glissant, Édouard 39
globalization 167, 172, 183–6
Go Goa Gone 187
Gothic fiction 51–2, 60, 80,
    134–5, 184
Greene, Graham 54

Habermas, Jürgen 156–7
Haiti 10, 15, 22, 26, 30
    and American occupation
    32–6

in film 79–80
history and independence
   33–6, 44, 46–7
map of 42–3
as textual fantasy 53
Haitian American Sugar
   Company (HASCO) 32, 34–5,
   36, 69, 83
Halperin, Victor 75, 85, 86
Happiness of the Katakuris, The 188
Harlem Renaissance 96, 97, 99
Harman, Chris 184
Hearn, Lafcadio 17–22, 71, 188
Heine, Heinrich 180
Herskovits, Melville 107
Hervey, Ben 143
Hesketh-Prichard, Hesketh 52
Higson, Charlie 191
Hiroshima 111–12, 113
Hitchcock, Alfred 143
HIV 179, 181, 195
   see also AIDS
Home, Stewart 191–2
hoodoo 99–100
Hoover, J. Edgar 126
Hope, Bob 88
Horde, The 109, 188
Hughes, Langston 81
Hulme, Peter 50
Hurbon, Laënnec 56
hurricane Katrina 154
Hurston, Zora Neale 96, 97–108,
   186
Huxley, Francis 55

I Walked with a Zombie 90–93
Ingagi 76–7
Invasion of the Body Snatchers
   (1956) 124–8, 182
Ipcress File, The 124
Island of Lost Souls, The 78
Italian horror film cycle 158–66

Jackson, Michael, 'Thriller' 168
Jamaica 14
Jane Eyre 91
Japanese horror 172–3
Johnson, Noble 88
Jones, Darby 90
Jovovich, Milla 171
Juan of the Dead 188
jumbee 14, 71–2
juvenile delinquency 132, 133

Kant, Immanuel 164
Katrina (hurricane) 154
Kermode, Frank 183
King Kong (1933) 77, 88
King, Stephen 135
King of the Zombies 88
Kirby, Jack 130
Kirkman, Robert 134–5, 193
Korean War 119–24
Krzywinska, Tanya 172

Land of the Dead 154, 183
Last Man on Earth, The (1964)
   137, 143, 157
Left 4 Dead (computer game) 171
Leiris, Michel 24
leopard man cults 66
Levi, Primo 113
Lifton, Robert Jay 111
*Living Dead at Manchester
   Morgue, The* 157
Lock, Margaret 177
locked-in syndrome 177
Loederer, Richard 52–3
Lovecraft, H. P. 25, 60, 61, 63, 64,
   70, 73
Lugosi, Bela 75, 78, 80, *82*, 87, 94
lynch mob 145–6

McCarthyism 126
McCormack, Patricia 164

MacDonald, Dwight 129
McNally, David 11
Manchurian Candidate, The
     (1962) 123–4
Marker, Chris 142
Mars, Louis P. 108
Martinique 18, 21, 37–9, 118,
     188
Marvel Zombies 135
Marx, Karl 11, 195
mass culture 129, 134
Matheson, Richard 137
Mbembe, Achille 183
medical horror 170, 174–83
Memmi, Albert 118–19
mesmerism 44, 60, 63–4, 80–81
Messiah of Evil 146–7
métissage 15
Mikami, Shinji 169
miscegenation 78
modernism 23, 24, 27, 96, 97
Mondo Cane 161–2
Moreland, Mantan 88–9
mummies 7, 36, 84
Muse, Clarence 81
Muslim 113

Nazism 88, 89, 90, 110,
     112–13, 115–17, 118, 131,
     173
negrophilia 24
Nicotero, Gregory 192
Niehaus, Isak 196
Night of the Living Dead 7, 109,
     137–47, 156

Obeah 25, 37, 67, 101
Obeyesekere, Gananath 51
Olney, Ian 164–5
Only Lovers Left Alive 10
Osgood Mason, Charlotte 101
Ouanga 79–80

Packard, Vance 128, 151
Parsons, Jack 87
Patterson, Orlando 36
Pegg, Simon 12
persistent vegetative state 176
Phase 7 189
Picasso, Pablo 24
Pittsburgh 138–9, 151
Plan 9 from Outer Space 87
Plants vs Zombies 191
Poe, Edgar Allan 60, 138
Polanski, Roman 143
Pontypool 189–90
Porter, Cole 95
Possendorf, Hans 86
premature burial 60
Price-Mars, Jean 46, 106–7
public sphere 157
pulp fiction 58–74

Quinlan, Karen Ann 177
Quinn, Seabury 64

raft of the *Medusa* 51
Resident Evil (computer game
     series) 8, 169–70, 171, 172,
     173
Resident Evil (film series) 169,
     170, *171*, 174, 178–9, 182,
     187
Return of the Living Dead 153
Returned, The (*Les Revenants*,
     French series) 8, 188
Revenge of the Zombies 89
Revolt of the Zombies 85, 86–7,
     109, 120
Rhys, Jean 39–40, 91
Riesman, David 128
Ring (1998) 173
risk society 167, 179, 184
Roach, Joseph 14
Robeson, Paul 97

Rohmer, Sax 63
Romero, George 7, 12, 109,
    135–6, 137–57, 192
Roscoe, Theodore 66–70
Rothberg, Michael 118
rum 94, 95
Rutherford, Jennifer 9

Saint Croix 70–71
Saint-Domingue 33, 44–5
St John, Spenser 47–9, 51, 107
Saint-Méry, Louis-Élie Moreau
    de 44
SARS virus 179, 184
Sartre, Jean-Paul 37–8
Savini, Tom 146, 152
Sconce, Jeffrey 164
Seabrook, William 22–41, 49, 53,
    64, 73, 82, 85, 91, 108
Serpent and the Rainbow, The 31
setlotlwane 194–5
Shaun of the Dead 12, 188
Shaviro, Steven 144
slave rebellions 44–5
slavery 10, 14, 15, 32, 34, 36, 44,
    154, 183
Slaves (1969) 140, 146
Sofsky, Wolfgang 114
Sontag, Susan 110, 129, 179
Soulouque, Faustin 47
*Stacy: Attack of the Schoolgirl
    Zombies* 187
Stepford Wives, The (1972) 128
Suchodolski, January, *The Battle
    at San Domingo* 45
sugar 32, 33, 69, 94
superstition 20–21, 46, 48, 71,
    80
Survival of the Dead 155
survival horror 8, 11, 170,
    172–4
Svengali 81

Tales from the Crypt (comic) 130
Tales of Voodoo (comic) 68
Tales of the Zombie (comic) 134
Teenage Zombies 112, 128, 142
Thacker, Eugene 165
tiki bars 94–5
Tombs of the Blind Dead 157
Tourneur, Jacques 90–93
Transatlanticism 14
Trombetta, Jim 115
Turner, Victor 9
Tylor, Edward 21

vampire 29, 60, 66, 134, 137, 147,
    151, 192
Van Vechten, Carl 101
video nasty 158–9, 164
Vietnam War 146
Vint, Sherryl 189
virology 180–81
Vodou 17, 26, 35, 44–7, 51–4, 55,
    56, 66, 92, 93, 95, 99, 101–2,
    103, 131, 195
    origins of word 45
    in film 79–8
Voodo (Fautin Wirkus, 1933) 77
Voodoo *see* Vodou
Voodoo (comic) 131
Voodoo Devil Drums 59
Voodoo Man 87

Walking Dead, The (comic)
    134–5
Walking Dead, The (TV series) 8,
    55, 178, 182, 192–4
Wallace, Inez 91
war on terror 193
Warm Bodies 13
Warshow, Robert 133
Weird Tales 58, 60, 61, 62, 130
Wellcome Trust 9
Wertham, Fredric 132–4

White Zombie (1932) 7, 31, 65,
  75–6, 79, 80–85
Whitehead, Colson 191
Whitehead, Henry St Clair
  70–74
Wilson, Robert Anton 115
Wirkus, Faustin 32–3, 77
Wood, Robin 144, 149, 155
World War Z 8, 109, 119, 181,
  184–6

yellow peril 121
Yezbick, Daniel 132

Žižek, Slavoj 11
zombi 17–22
zombi astral 13, 84, 122
zombi cadavre 13, 84
zombie
  and apocalypse 36, 167
  and architecture 191
  arrival in English language
  22, 29
  and brainwashing 121–4
  and capitalism 11–12, 119,
  149–51, 183
  categories 8, 194
  and colonialism 15, 118
  and computer games 167,
  169–74
  and consciousness 13, 154
  as drug-induced state 30–31
  etymology of 14–15
  and legal codes 30
  as mass 10, 109, 114, 129,
  131, 134, 179
  and medicine 170, 174–83
  as metaphor 8–9, 40, 196
  and Nazism 115–17
  origins of word 14
  and psychiatry 55, 108
  in pulp fiction 58–74

and salt 14, 30, 65
shuffle 36
and slavery 32
and translation 14–15, 17–22
as viral outbreak 170, 179–83
walks 8, 167, 192
Zombie (Kenneth Webb, play) 85
Zombie (rum) 86, 94–6
Zombie Flesh Eaters (*Zombi 2*) 16,
  159–61
Zombie Lake 116
Zombieland 12
Zombies on Broadway 87, 93–4
Zombies of Mora Tau 112